SECRET OF THE ANKHS

ALSO BY NELLIE H. STEELE

<u>Maggie Edwards Adventures:</u>
Cleopatra's Tomb

<u>Cate Kensie Mysteries:</u>
The Secret of Dunhaven Castle
Murder at Dunhaven Castle
Holiday Heist at Dunhaven Castle

<u>Shadow Slayers Stories:</u>
Shadows of the Past
Stolen Portrait Stolen Soul
Gone

<u>Duchess of Blackmoore Mysteries:</u>
Death of a Duchess

SECRET OF THE ANKHS
A MAGGIE EDWARDS ADVENTURE

NELLIE H. STEELE

A Novel Idea Publishing

This is a work of fiction. Names, characters, places, and incidents either are the product of the author's imagination or are used fictitiously. Any resemblance to actual persons, living or dead, events, or locales is entirely coincidental.

Copyright © 2021 by Nellie H. Steele

All rights reserved.

No part of this book may be reproduced in any form or by any electronic or mechanical means, including information storage and retrieval systems, without written permission from the author, except for the use of brief quotations in a book review.

All rights reserved.

Cover design by Stephanie A. Sovak.

❦ Created with Vellum

In loving memory of my grandfather, Edward HuWalt

ACKNOWLEDGMENTS

A HUGE thank you to everyone who helped get this book published! Special shout outs to: Stephanie Sovak, Paul Sovak, Michelle Cheplic, Mark D'Angelo and Lori D'Angelo.

Finally, a HUGE thank you to you, the reader!

CHAPTER 1

Maggie bustled around her shop, *Maggie's Books and Baubles Boutique*. She adjusted items, dusted shelves and repositioned furniture.

"Hey, how does this display look?" Maggie called over her shoulder to her assistant, Piper. She received no response.

Maggie glanced back. Piper plopped on a stool behind the cashier's counter. The music from her earbuds blasted, reaching Maggie's ears across the shop. Piper scrolled on her phone, her head bobbing to the music. Maggie shook her head at the younger woman. She waved her arms in the air, failing to catch Piper's attention from whatever she stared at on her phone's display.

Maggie trudged across the shop, halting on the opposite side of the counter. She set her mouth in a firm line, her eyebrows raised. Maggie stood for several seconds waiting to be acknowledged, her impatience growing by the millisecond.

After a few breaths, Piper glanced up. She wrinkled her forehead and shrugged her shoulders at Maggie. "What?" she questioned after pulling an earbud from her right ear.

Maggie's jaw went slack for a moment. "Seriously?" she replied. "That's your response? I asked you a question, and you didn't even hear me with those things in! I have been standing here forever waiting for you to recall that you are at work!"

Piper rolled her eyes at Maggie. "Take it easy, boss lady, I was just checking out a song someone sent me. I'm not keeping them in!" Piper removed the other earbud and stowed them in her backpack under the counter.

Maggie pursed her lips. "You're lucky you're such a dependable worker overall, Piper."

"Aww, and here I thought you liked me," Piper retorted.

Maggie shook her head at Piper. "I do like you, Piper. Even though you're maddening at times."

"Except at those times when I can open the shop while you run around the world with your new boyfriend on vacation." Piper swiped the dust rag from Maggie's hands, stuck her tongue out and flitted around the shop to dust.

Maggie swung around, her mouth agape. "I was NOT on 'vacation,'" she retorted.

"What else do you call it when you travel the world?" Piper inquired.

"Saving my uncle's life is what I call it," Maggie said, crossing her arms and raising her eyebrows. "Oh, and finding Cleopatra's tomb, by the way."

"And the other time you disappeared after that?"

Maggie lowered her eyes to the floor and spun back to the counter, pretending to organize receipts. "I told you," she murmured. "That was a business trip."

"Riiiiiiiiiight," Piper said. "Three-week business trip with your new boyfriend. Uh-huh, sure."

Maggie preferred the subject to be closed without further discussion. "And my uncle, I remind you. Anyway, believe what you want."

"Any luck with hiring my assistant?" Piper questioned, referencing the "Help Wanted" sign hanging in the front widow.

Maggie rolled her eyes. "The position is for a shop clerk, not your assistant, Piper. And to answer your question, no."

"Shop clerk to assist the assistant manager. An assistant to the assistant manager. Like on *The Office*."

"I thought you were night manager."

"I upgraded my title when you took off and I worked days."

"Ohhhh, right," Maggie answered with a chuckle. "I forgot you upgraded your self-created, made-up title."

"Yes, I also had new business cards printed up to reflect the change in position," Piper said with a wink. "So, what was wrong with the last batch of candidates?"

Maggie sighed before answering. "Allison could only work every other Saturday from eleven in the morning until two in the afternoon." Piper knit her brows, raising one eyebrow. "And Tom," Maggie continued, "demanded a sixty-five-thousand-dollar salary with two weeks paid vacation and a four-day-per-week work schedule so he could 'pursue his dream to become a painter.'"

"Well, dang," Piper answered. "Guess you're learning how good you have it with me around, huh?"

"You are a good employee, Piper. I have always known how good I have it," Maggie assured her. Piper tossed her arms out to the side and spun in a circle before curtsying. "So…" Maggie said, changing the subject, "are you excited to go to the VIP exhibit opening party tonight at the museum?"

"Mmmm, thrilled!" Piper said. Despite always sounding unimpressed with life, Maggie detected a glimmer of excitement in Piper's voice. Maggie's enthusiasm was also building. Almost one year ago, Maggie, in search of her missing uncle, along with Henry Taylor, her uncle's associate, and several others, had found Cleopatra's tomb deep in the sands of the Egyptian desert. The museum exhibit planned to showcase a smattering of pieces found within the walls of the tomb. The prospect of seeing the pieces again thrilled Maggie.

"Are you taking what's-his-name with you?" Maggie asked, searching her mind for the name of Piper's latest beau. "Scratch, was it?"

Piper shot Maggie a look, her eyes narrowed, her mouth set in a line. "Sketch," she corrected. She returned her gaze to the shelf in front of her. "And no. We broke up," she murmured.

Maggie raised her eyebrows at this development. She loved relationship gossip. "Broke up?" she questioned.

"Yep," Piper answered, continuing her dusting, her work ethic suddenly multiplied.

"What happened? He acting too... sketchy?" Maggie asked with a chuckle.

"Wow," Piper answered, spinning to face her. "You should take that act on the road, you're hilarious."

Maggie gave her a wry glance. "I'll admit, I've been holding on to that one. I mean, what kind of name is Sketch, anyway? What parent looks at their newborn baby and names him Sketch?"

"Sketch is not his real name," Piper admitted.

"Oh, so it's one of those made-up names to make him sound cooler than he is, huh? What's his real name?"

"Heathcliff," Piper answered.

"HEATHCLIFF?!" Maggie responded. "Like the cat?"

"No, like his great-grandfather or something. I dunno. Anyway, we just didn't see eye to eye on stuff. No big deal, we just lacked the same goals."

Maggie raised her eyebrows, considering the statement. "Well, that's a shame," she answered. "But for the best if you didn't fit together. So, are you going stag tonight?"

"Nah, I found another date."

"Oh!" Maggie began to respond, about to ask who it was when the front door's bell jangled, indicating the arrival of a customer.

"Hi there!" Maggie greeted them. She and Piper spent the next two hours assisting customers as they browsed the shop. They were unable to return to the conversation. Maggie hoped to follow up on the new date discussion, but as the day waned and the hours ticked down to closing, the opportunity did not present itself.

Instead, she found Piper ducking out the door as 5 p.m. approached. "Gotta run, boss lady," Piper called. "Getting my hair did." She winked and pushed through the door, nearly bumping into the person entering.

Piper called an apology and kept going as Henry's tall, muscular form entered the shop. Henry's gaze followed Piper's retreating form. He turned to Maggie; his forehead creased. "Was that Piper?" he joked.

"Yes," she answered. "Why?"

"Did she just say she's going to get her hair done?" Henry questioned.

Maggie chuckled. "Yep, that's what she said."

Henry glanced side to side before shaking his head. "Never thought I'd hear those words from Piper."

"She seems pretty excited about the exhibit opening tonight," Maggie replied as Henry planted a kiss on her cheek.

"Yeah? That doesn't seem like Piper."

Maggie raised her eyebrow at Henry. "So, are you excited yet? We finally got Piper excited, are we two-for-two?"

Henry rolled his eyes. "I'd rather skip the monkey suit."

Maggie swatted at him with the dust rag Piper discarded on the front counter. "You'll look fantastic."

"In that dress you've got, no one'll be looking at me,

princess." Henry winked at her. "And speaking of getting hair done, don't you…"

"Oh, SHOOT!" Maggie interrupted. "My hair appointment! I'm going to be late!" Maggie raced behind the counter, grabbing her purse darting toward the door. "Can you lock up, babe?"

"Don't worry, I'll lock up," Henry called after her as Maggie disappeared through the door, the bell above it tinkling furiously as she flung the door open and shut.

* * *

Maggie slid on her black satin mermaid gown. She zipped up the back and adjusted her skirt. She glanced in the mirror as she slid into her peep-toe heels. A knock sounded at the door to her apartment. "Coming!" she shouted. She fiddled with her earring as she raced to the door.

Maggie flung it open and returned her attention to her second earring. "Good evening to you, too, princess," Henry said as he entered.

"Is it six-thirty already?" Maggie questioned.

"No, I came fifteen minutes early to make sure you weren't running late," Henry admitted.

Maggie rolled her eyes at him. "I'm not ALWAYS late," she retorted. Henry scrunched his eyebrows together. "Don't say anything." Maggie hurried from the room. "I just need to put on my necklace, my lipstick, perfume and grab my purse."

"Fifteen minutes, princess!" Henry called after her.

"Yeah, yeah, yeah," Maggie mumbled as she pulled her twisted pearl necklace from its box. She fastened it around her neck, letting it fall into position, framed by her sweetheart neckline. Maggie swiped the perfume bottle from her dressing table, spritzing it on her wrists and hair. She dug through her makeup collection, searching for the right shade of lipstick.

She pawed through tube after tube, a sigh escaping her lips after the tenth. A frown formed on her nude lips as she glanced in the drawer. "Tick tock, princess," Henry said. Maggie glanced up into her mirror, catching his reflection. He leaned against the doorjamb; his tuxedo jacket slung over his shoulder.

"I know, I know. I can't find my lipstick!" Maggie exclaimed.

Henry approached, staring at the growing pile of lipstick tubes on the dressing table. "Uhhhhh," he began. "Aren't all these lipsticks?"

"Yes," Maggie answered with a sigh, "but none of them are the right shade."

"Which is?"

"*Knock Me Dead Red*," Maggie replied, still digging in her drawer.

Henry combed through the discarded lipsticks on the table. "Here we are."

"You found it?!" Maggie exclaimed, spinning to face Henry, a smile forming on her bare lips.

"Yep," Henry said, triumph filling his voice. He handed the tube to Maggie.

"Oh," Maggie sighed, deflated, "this isn't it."

"Yes, it is," Henry countered. He snatched it back and opened the tube. He twisted the lipstick up until it showed from the top. "Red, just like you wanted."

"No, no, no," Maggie said with a shake of her head. "This is *Bombshell Red*, see?" She shoved the bottom of the tube toward Henry.

"What's the difference? It's red and we're going to be late."

"It's too orange. I want a true red."

"How about this? *Pucker Up Pink*," Henry suggested. He

opened it and stared at it. "It's, uh, pretty."

Maggie shot him a glance, answering without speaking a word. She returned to her search.

"Took us less time to find Cleopatra's tomb," Henry muttered.

"I heard that," Maggie warned as she reached her arm as far into the drawer's depths as she could.

"Every shade looks nice on you, princess, just pick one."

"Ah ha!" Maggie pulled a tube from the drawer. "*Knock Me Dead Red!*" Maggie grinned, uncapping the tube and gliding the red shade across her lips. She smacked her lips together, checked her reflection, shoved the lipstick into her evening bag and leapt from her chair. "Ready! Now wasn't this worth the wait?" She struck a pose.

"You, princess, are always worth the wait," Henry answered, slipping his jacket on and extending his arm to Maggie. "Shall we?"

Maggie accepted his arm, and they strolled out to the car. "We're not late," Maggie said as Henry slid in behind the wheel. "So, don't drive like a maniac."

"First, we are late, it's after six-thirty. And second, when have you ever known me to drive like a maniac," Henry contested, fastening his seat belt. Maggie's eyes went wide, and her eyebrows shot up. "Don't answer that," Henry retorted, cutting off any reply.

He fired the engine and pulled from Maggie's apartment building's parking lot. They arrived at the museum on the dot of seven.

"See, on time, just like I told you," Maggie said as they pulled up to the valet.

"Eh, listen, mate, I'll park it if you don't mind," Henry called out his open window.

"Just let them park it. I don't want to walk from the parking garage," Maggie groaned.

"This car has a sensitive suspension and requires a skilled touch," Henry argued.

"So, uh, do you want me to park it or not?" the attendant questioned through the window.

"Yes," Maggie answered as Henry answered, "No."

Maggie rolled her eyes at him, popping her door open and exiting the car.

"Just be careful with her, mate," Henry said as he slid out from behind the wheel.

Henry dashed around the rear of the car, catching up to Maggie who waited at the foot of the steps leading to the museum. A red carpet cascaded down the stone steps, greeting formalwear-clad VIPs. Flash bulbs burst every few seconds as press photographers captured pictures of event-goers.

"Are you sure you don't want to sneak in the back entrance?" Henry questioned, gazing longingly after his car as the attendant pulled away.

"Positive," Maggie answered. "I didn't search through twenty tubes of lipstick to sneak in the back door. Now come on, let's pose for a few pics!"

Maggie, who loved the spotlight, seized her moment to shine as she and Henry made their way toward the museum entrance. She stopped for several network photographers and spent a few minutes with various reporters answering questions about her part in finding Cleopatra's tomb and her excitement over seeing the artifacts from the tomb on display in her hometown.

Normally a museum the size of Rosemont's Natural History Museum would never host such rare and valuable artifacts, but since Maggie had been an integral part of the tomb's discovery, the museum got top billing to host the grand event first before the pieces were placed in their permanent location at the Cairo Museum.

They reached the top of the stairs. "At long last," Henry said, breathing a sigh of relief.

"Oh, stop," Maggie answered. "It wasn't THAT bad."

"I'd have preferred to skip it."

"You can't spend all your time on adventures with Uncle Ollie or in a dusty tomb, Henry," Maggie replied as they strolled through the massive entry doors.

"I can too," Henry retorted. "And I would have if I didn't have such a lovely girlfriend to escort to this party."

"Flatterer," Maggie answered with a smile. Their conversation ended as Maggie gasped as they entered the museum's lobby. "WOW!" she exclaimed. "The exhibit looks amazing!"

Maggie's uncle, Oliver Keene, approached from the docent's desk. He grinned from ear to ear. "Looks great, huh?" he asked Maggie as she leaned in for a hug.

"Hi, Uncle Ollie! Yeah!" Maggie agreed. "Wow, what a night for our little museum! I am so excited I could burst!"

Henry greeted Ollie with a firm handshake. "You clean up nicely," Ollie commented. "Can't believe Maggie got you into the monkey suit."

"That she did, mate," Henry answered, tugging at his collar. "Would have been tossed out on my ear if I showed up in my normal gear."

"We'll make a gentleman out of you yet," Ollie teased. "Well, as much as I am certain you would like to remain in the spotlight, Henry, I was hoping to steal Maggie to meet a few people."

"Don't let me hold you back," Henry quickly answered, holding his hands up in front of him. "I'll just be over here in the corner enjoying the artifacts."

Maggie blew him a kiss as Ollie guided her away to meet several of the museum's major donors. Maggie spent almost two hours chatting with various guests, describing her adventure, discussing her shop and making small talk. Henry skirted the edge of the room, smiling and nodding at her as she circulated from person to person.

After finishing her conversation with an avid artifact enthusiast and Fortune 500 business owner, Maggie scanned the room. She spotted Henry and Piper chatting together near a large bust of Cleopatra. Piper's multicolored hair was swept up into a large beehive style on her head. She wore a brightly colored jumpsuit consisting of gauzy palazzo pants topped off with a halter top.

Maggie sashayed over to them. "There you are!" she said, wrapping her arm around Henry's waist.

"Here I am, princess. Admiring the artifacts as promised."

Maggie turned her gaze to Piper. "Have you been enjoying the exhibit, Piper? I haven't seen you all night, though I'm surprised I missed you in that color!"

"Actually, it has been kind of interesting," Piper admitted. "It's pretty cool that you of all people found all this stuff when other people have been searching for it for centuries."

"Don't underestimate Maggie," Henry replied. "She's one smart cookie." Maggie glanced around the room. "Lost someone, princess?"

"No," Maggie answered. She turned to Piper. "Didn't you say you were coming with a date?"

"Uh..." Piper mumbled.

"Well?" Maggie inquired, her voice giddy with excitement. "Where is he?" She grinned, her eyes darting around for anyone she didn't recognize.

"You are the only person who can stand in a museum filled with priceless artifacts from the tomb of one of history's most influential figures... artifacts that YOU discovered in what some consider the greatest archeological find of history and be more concerned about my date than anything else," Piper retorted.

Maggie scrunched up her nose. "So, anyway, where is this

mystery man?" Piper crossed her arms, setting her mouth in a firm line. "Oh, come on, Piper! I just spent hours talking about this stuff with people. But we're friends! I'm interested in your life! If I didn't ask, you'd be complaining that I didn't care who you dated."

"We're not exactly dating..." Piper began.

"Semantics... you brought him with you to a major event, he must be special! Why are you being so coy about this? Come on! Who is he?"

"Listen, boss lady, I should probably explain a little backstory before I tell you..."

A new voice entered the conversation, interrupting Piper's explanation. "Stunning as always, Mags," Leo said. Henry rolled his eyes as Maggie's ex-boyfriend, Leo Hamilton, sidled up to their group. "Is that *Knock Me Dead Red*?"

"Good memory," Maggie replied.

"It was always your favorite lip color for an event. And we sure went to enough of them together over the years." Leo glanced around the room. "Whew, this really is something, huh? Can't believe I was a part of a discovery like this."

"Barely, mate," Henry reminded him.

"Just as much as you, Indiana Jones," Leo retorted.

"Henry's right, you were kind of just along for the ride and a constant objector during it, if I might add," Maggie said. She crossed her arms, her gaze falling on Leo as she cocked her head. "How did you get an invitation to this event, anyway? You're connected, but not this well."

Leo grinned at her, wrapping his arm around Piper. "I'm Piper's date."

Maggie's mouth dropped open, and she stared between Leo and Piper, stunned into silence. After a breath, Maggie raised her eyebrows, drawing in a deep breath. "Well..." she started.

"That's not an accurate representation of the situation," Piper said, cutting her off.

Maggie shook her head. "No, no, it's fine. There's no need to explain. You are both adults. I just didn't expect it, that's all."

"I had every intention of telling you and explaining..." Piper began again.

Maggie held up her hand, cutting her off. "No explanation needed. Like I said, we're all adults here. You don't need to explain your choices to me." Maggie swallowed hard. "Well, we'll leave you two to enjoy the exhibit. Come on, Henry, there's a few people I want to introduce you to."

Maggie grasped his hand in hers, dragging him away. "Slow down, princess," Henry objected as Maggie stormed across the room. He tugged her to a stop in front of a display of ornate jewelry.

"I don't want to miss Sir Livingston. He'd love to meet you. He's a charming old Brit. You'll just love him," Maggie rambled.

"Maggie," Henry interrupted. "Are you okay?"

Maggie stared at him, wide-eyed with a smile plastered on her face. "I'm fine!" she insisted. "Why wouldn't I be fine?"

Henry's eyes slowly drifted back and forth as though the answer was obvious. Before he could respond, Piper rushed up to them. "Listen, Maggie... I can explain."

"Oh my gosh! Will everyone stop treating me with kid gloves? I am fine. I'm not upset. There are no explanations needed. I am perfectly fine. I ended things with Leo, remember? There's nothing between us. I've moved on, he's moved on. I was just surprised. You hardly seem each other's type, but it's not my business. So, let's just drop this!"

"No one would blame you for being upset, princess. Not even me. Although, you clearly got the better end of the deal here," Henry chimed in with a wink.

"We aren't dating!" Piper shouted. Conversation near them ground to a halt, heads turned their way, music stopped. Piper rolled her eyes, crossing her arms and staring at the floor.

Maggie smiled graciously at the crowd and gave a nervous chuckle. "Classic Cleopatra love triangle," she joked.

A few chuckles erupted before people returned to their conversations and the music resumed. "Nice going," Maggie breathed. "All right, all right, if it's so important to explain, come on." Maggie grabbed Piper's arm, then turned to Henry. "You wait here for me. I was serious about meeting Sir Livingston."

Maggie pulled Piper along, threading through the crowd toward the ladies' room. Maggie pushed through the door and into the restroom. She made her way to one of the mirrors, opening her purse and pulling out her compact. "Good time to touch up my makeup," she noted. "So, how did you end up with Leo as a date?"

Piper shifted her weight from side to side as she launched into her story. "I was totally going to come with Sketch, but then he flaked on me, like I said. I was super mad at him, fuming actually. I went to the pastry shop for a chai latte and a cool off and I ran into Leo. He asked me about the shop and whatever and then about the party. I was so mad I told him about Sketch. And then he offered to be my date. And at first, I was like, no way, dude, whatever. But then I was like that would really stick it to Sketch. But still, I was like nah. But then he said he'd pay me fifty bucks, so I figured what the heck, right? I can make some jingle and shove it in Sketch's face at the same time, win-win! I fully meant to tell you, but then I just didn't know how so I didn't. I totally did NOT mean to spring this on you though, boss lady."

Maggie reapplied her lipstick, shoved it in her purse and spun to face Piper. She pursed her lips and raised her eyebrows. "Honestly, Piper," Maggie said with a shake of her head. She sighed.

Piper grimaced. "Yeah?" she questioned.

"I'm not mad at you. I was just shocked, that's all. I mean, who would have EVER thought you'd be here with Leo?!"

"Really? You're not mad?" Piper inquired.

"Really, I'm not," Maggie said, squeezing Piper's arm. "Why would I be mad? Leo and I are not together anymore. I'm happy with Henry." She glanced around then added, "Although, I'm impressed you care so much, Piper. I didn't realize how much I meant to you." Maggie pressed her hand over her heart, pretending to tear up.

Piper returned to her usual flippant self. She shrugged her shoulders, taking a nonchalant stance. "I mean, I don't. Like if you were mad, okay, so what? I just figured, you know, I didn't want to get fired or whatever."

Maggie gave her a knowing glance. "Uh-huh," she murmured. Maggie stole another glance in the mirror. Satisfied, she turned back to Piper. "Well, with that over with, I guess we should get back out there. I wouldn't want you to miss another second with your enchanting date."

"OMG, I am never going to hear the end of this, am I?" Piper complained.

Maggie gave her a wry smile. "Nope," she answered. "Now, come on, I've missed enough of this party discussing this. Let's get back out there!"

"You are waaaaaay too excited about this," Piper moaned.

"Come on, I want to show you a few of the pieces I like. It's really too bad they didn't send the boat from the first chamber we visited. That was amazing!" Maggie grasped Piper by the arm and dragged her toward the door.

They took one step before they were plunged into darkness.

CHAPTER 2

Blackness settled around them. Maggie stopped short with a gasp. Several shouts and surprised exclamations reached her ears from partygoers outside of the bathroom.

"Uh," Piper muttered, "what happened to the lights?"

"No idea, the backups should come on soon though." They waited a moment, still surrounded by darkness. As her eyes adjusted, Maggie dug through her purse. She snatched her cell phone and toggled on the flashlight.

"So much for the so-called backups," Piper groaned.

"Yeah," Maggie answered. "Something is weird here."

"Somebody didn't do their job," Piper said in a sing-song manner.

Maggie glanced around the empty ladies' room. She shined her light under the stall doors, confirming they were alone.

"What are you doing?" Piper inquired.

"Something seems off," Maggie answered. "Come on." She grabbed Piper by the hand. "Let's go find Henry."

"And Leo," Piper reminded her.

"Yeah," Maggie said with a groan. "Because he's always useful in a crisis." With a roll of her eyes, she pushed through the bathroom door. The lobby outside remained dark, as did all other spaces in the museum. Only the starry night sky, peeking in through the sky-lit rotunda overhead and a few cell phone flashlights illuminated the space. Soft murmurs arose around the room as other guests conjectured about the power failure.

Maggie scanned the room, searching for Henry's familiar form. Fingers brushed her arm, causing her to jump. She spun to face her adversary, finding Henry. Her flashlight shined brightly in his eyes and he held a hand up to block its light. "Maggie, are you all right?" Henry questioned.

"Sorry, yes," Maggie responded, lowering her flashlight. "We're fine. We were still in the ladies' room when the lights went out. What's going on?"

Henry grasped her elbow, guiding her to a corner. "No idea, but I don't like it." Maggie grabbed Piper's hand, pulling her along with them.

"Neither do I," Maggie agreed. "Something is wrong."

"I'd put money on that, yeah," Henry answered.

Cast in moving shadows as Maggie's cell phone flashlight bobbed around, Piper screwed up her face. "What are you two yammering on about? The lights went out, big deal!"

"Nah, something's off," Henry disagreed as Ollie joined their group.

"Uncle Ollie!" Maggie exclaimed. "Are you okay? What's going on? Have you heard anything?"

"The guards rushed past me a few moments after the blackout," Ollie responded. "They did not seem optimistic about the outage."

"What did they say?" Maggie questioned.

"I didn't overhear much, but from the sounds of their conversation, they suspected the power had been tampered with. Both the primary and secondary emergency lighting," Ollie answered.

"Hmm," Maggie murmured.

A figure rushed toward them. As he approached, Maggie made out Leo's face. "There you are. Thank God you're all right," Leo said, staring at Maggie.

"Uh, yeah, and I'm fine too," Piper chimed in. "You jerk," she added under her breath.

"Uh, yeah, I mean, that's what I meant," Leo said as Henry raised his eyebrows at him.

"We're all fine," Maggie assured him in an attempt to break the tension. "But something is very off here."

"Yeah, you've said that like a hundred times," Piper groaned. "We get it, something is weird. But, like, why would someone cut the power and tamper with the backup lights? It makes no sense."

"It makes complete sense," Maggie countered. "Some of the most priceless artifacts in the world are in this room."

"So, what?" Piper questioned. "This is a robbery? I don't see anyone stealing anything. Everyone is just hanging out until the power comes back on."

"I doubt you'd see them, Piper," Henry retorted. "If they are worth their salt as a thief, they're long gone by now."

"Oh, right, because you know so much about thievery, huh? I think you're all making more out of this than it is. The power went out, and the generators didn't kick the backup lights on. Someone probably forgot to maintenance the generators or something."

"We'll see," Maggie declared.

An outburst sounded across the room. "Sounds like trouble," Henry noted.

"Wow, thank you for that astute observation," Leo retorted. "Still on top of your game there, I see."

"Give it a rest, Leo," Maggie chided. Voices floated across

the room, allowing them to make out the conversation. An argument ensued between a contingent of guests and museum security guards. The guests demanded to leave the event but the guards refused their request.

"No one is leaving until we've got this figured out," one guard contended.

After a few additional moments of bickering, the small party surrendered, returning to the bar area for a complimentary drink, as suggested by the guard. Within another moment, lights shined at one of the room's many entryways. Several museum guards, flashlights glowing, entered the space. Maggie recognized the museum's director, Stan Gibson, among them.

"Folks!" Stan shouted. "Folks, if I could have your attention, please?" After several shushes, the din in the room quieted. "Ah, thanks. First off, I'd like to apologize for the inconvenience. And second, I'd like to let you know that we're working on solving the problem and hope to have the lights on very soon. At this time, we ask that everyone remain here. For everyone's safety, we don't want people wandering around the museum or outside the museum. Again, we're very sorry for the inconvenience and please have a complimentary beverage on us and try to enjoy yourselves. Hope to have the lights on soon!"

Murmurs rose through the room as groups of party guests discussed the new information or headed for a drink.

The man and his contingent of guards crossed the room, passing Maggie and her group along the way. Maggie caught part of their conversation as they hurried past her.

"... close are we with the damage?" Stan asked.

"Cut clean through," one of the guards answered. "Electrician's almost got it wired..."

The rest of their conversation was lost in the din of the room.

"Cut wire," Henry murmured.

"Yeah," Maggie answered. "That's got to be on purpose." Ollie glanced around the room. "What is it, Uncle Ollie?"

"Oh, ah, nothing, nothing," Ollie responded.

Maggie crinkled her brow and was about to follow up when bright lights burst on overhead. The room filled with fluorescent light from the emergency lighting as people squinted and glanced up at the source. Applause and cheers broke out as the room illuminated.

"There!" Piper exclaimed. "See!"

Maggie rolled her eyes at Piper as the museum director appeared at the entryway again. "Folks, if I could have your attention once again. As you can see, we have the backup lighting working and we're continuing to work on restoring the main lighting. I know several of you have asked about leaving. Unfortunately, at this time, we cannot allow anyone to leave the building. I'm sure you understand the value of the objects we house within these walls. We need to do a quick inventory before we can allow anyone to leave."

Groans rose from a crowd and the director held his hands up. "I know, I know. We're working as quickly as we can. And again, in the meantime, we've got plenty of refreshments and exhibits to keep you entertained." A few chuckles emerged from the crowd, and the director offered a weak laugh at his own joke. "Even with the limited lighting!"

Maggie narrowed her eyes as he disappeared again from the room. "Twenty bucks says they find something missing," she said.

"I'll take that bet," Leo answered.

"I'm with Maggie," Henry said.

"Shocker," Leo retorted. "I hope you're happy losing twenty dollars!"

"You can't possibly think the lights just happened to go out," Maggie responded.

"Yes, Mags, I do. This is a museum. They have priceless artifacts here all the time. Even in this small museum, they have security. It's not the local dollar store where someone's going to pocket a lipstick." Leo glanced around as he polished off the drink in his hand. "I mean, look," he motioned toward a display case near the center of the room. "The jewels of Cleopatra are still here. If anyone was going to steal something, don't you think they'd steal that! It's got to be worth millions! It can easily be slipped into something to be carried out and you can cut it up and sell it piece by piece, making it completely unidentifiable. If the motive was theft, that's where the money is."

"Certainly know a lot about pulling off a jewelry heist, mate," Henry countered. "Down to how to divvy up the pieces to sell them."

Leo rolled his eyes. "Oh, come on," he groaned. "Everyone knows that! Haven't you seen *Ocean's 8?*"

"Was that the one with the girls?" Piper asked.

"Yeah, the girl one. They steal the jewelry and cut it up and make new jewelry and wear it out of the event to get away. Anyway, clearly that didn't happen here," Leo answered.

"The jewelry isn't the only valuable thing here," Ollie added.

"No, I realize that," Leo answered. "I'm just pointing out that everything else is harder to steal and sell off without being caught."

"The black market is not THAT hard to sell on, mate," Henry responded.

"Let's quit arguing about it. We should know soon enough if anything is missing," Maggie said, ending the argument.

"How about a drink? Ladies, can I bring you anything?" Leo inquired.

"Sure, I'll have a beer," Piper responded.

"Nothing for me, thanks," Maggie answered.

Leo crossed the room, heading to the bar to retrieve Piper's requested beverage.

Henry closed his eyes for a moment. "I really hate that guy," he lamented. "Why did you bring him?" he questioned Piper.

"Never mind that," Maggie hushed him. "Look!" she breathed, tossing her head toward the main entrance. "The police are here."

A smirk crossed Henry's face. "Looks like you may be twenty dollars richer, princess."

* * *

Another forty-five minutes passed before the director addressed the crowd again. He ran a shaky hand through his hair before beginning. "Hi, folks, ah, thanks again for bearing with us. This is not the evening any of us expected. At this time, we're going to begin to disperse the party. Uh, we're asking everyone to form an orderly line. Each of you will be asked to speak with one of the detectives before you leave. And, I am very sorry, but we'll be doing a sweep with our wands and checking your purses." Murmurs shot through the crowd.

"Is something missing?" someone shouted, interrupting the director's speech.

"Ah," Stan hesitated. He glanced toward the detective to his right and swallowed hard. Stan raked his hand through his hair again. "We are, uh, still completing our inventory, but to be safe, we'd like to take a look. I am more than sorry for the inconvenience. We'll be sending out free museum passes to each of you for the trouble."

The detective nodded as the director side-eyed him again after his less-than-eloquent explanation. "Ah, now if everyone could please form an orderly line. We'll be as quick as we can. Just form a line. That's right. Thank you." The director continued shouting instructions to the crowd as the line began to form.

"Well, I guess that's our cue," Maggie said. Before they could step toward the rapidly forming line, two men stepped toward them, blocking their way.

"Dr. Keene?" the taller of the two queried.

"Yes, that's me," Ollie answered, raising his hand.

"Would you mind coming with us? And if you, Miss Edwards, and you, Mr. Taylor, wouldn't mind joining us as well, thanks."

"Ooooooooh," Piper murmured. "Somebody's in trouble!"

Maggie shot Piper a glance as Piper giggled. "Lead the way," Maggie answered.

"Don't call me to bail you out, boss lady!" Piper called as they departed.

The two men, museum guards, led the trio through the museum to a door marked PRIVATE: EMPLOYEES ONLY. They pushed through the door and wound through the hallways to a large office. Furnished in dark woods with bookshelves on two walls, the office belonged to the museum's director. Two men in less-than-expensive suits stood in the center of the room.

Maggie gazed at the two men, awaiting an explanation. Before they spoke, the door opened, and the museum director strode in along with another security guard. "Oh, Bryan, you found them, good, yes," the middle-aged director said, stumbling through his words. He ran a shaky hand through his medium-brown hair again. "Thank you, you, Tim and Gary may go." The two men who escorted them departed along with the third guard who pulled the door shut behind them.

"What's going on, Stan?" Ollie questioned.

"Oh, it's terrible, Ollie, just terrible." The man sank into the chair behind his desk, staring at the floor as though in disbelief. "Well, not too terrible at least. Awful, but not horrible. I may yet save my job." The man rambled.

"I'm sorry, Mr. Gibson," Maggie interrupted. "Can you tell us what 'it' is that's awful but not horrible?"

"Something was stolen from the museum tonight," one of the detectives answered in Stan's place.

"Yes, yes, quite right," Stan agreed.

"Something from the Cleopatra collection?" Maggie inquired.

Stan nodded. "Yes, though thankfully, a smaller, less valuable item compared to some of the others. Still, every piece is invaluable in its own way…"

"It was the ankh, wasn't it?" Ollie asked, interrupting Stan's musings.

Stan's brows furrowed, and he glanced at Ollie. "Yes, but how did…" he began to question before his voice dropped off.

"Same thing I'd like to know," the tall detective stated.

"Just a hunch," Ollie stated with a shrug of his shoulders.

"That's some hunch, professor," the older detective countered. "Out of all the priceless artifacts in that room, some of them worth hundreds of thousands, even millions, you guessed a small, nondescript stone cross was the missing item?"

"Not a cross, an ankh," Ollie corrected. "And not stone, it's faience."

The detective offered a less-than-impressed stare Ollie's way. "Listen, doc," the second detective chimed in, his accent sounding distinctly like someone from the Bronx, "maybe you can explain to us dummies here why you guessed that. Like my partner said, it's not the most valuable item. Not even the flashiest! If you're going to go through the trouble to rob a museum, cut the power, cut the gennies, you'd think it would be over something a little more... valuable."

"So, the power was cut to facilitate the theft?" Maggie questioned.

The Bronx detective glanced at Maggie. A smile crossed his face. "Well, hello Miss... ah, I don't believe we were introduced."

"Maggie Edwards," Maggie said, extending her hand. "Ollie's niece."

"Nice to meet you, Miss Edwards. Detective Giovanni Russo. You can just call me Gio." He winked as he squeezed her hand.

Maggie offered a demure smile. "Maggie, please."

"Maggie," Henry said, wrapping his arm around her shoulders, "is also one of our team. In addition to being Ollie's niece. And my girlfriend."

"Oh, ah, thank you, Maggie's boyfriend," Gio retorted.

"Henry Taylor's the name," Henry said, extending his hand for a handshake.

"Anyway," Maggie continued after shooting a confused glance Henry's way, "you said the power was cut. So, this suggests the theft was planned."

"Yes, the power was cut," the older detective, who introduced himself as Detective Sharpe, answered. "Obviously the theft was planned." He sighed in annoyance at the question.

"What I meant," Maggie corrected, "was this wasn't a crime of convenience. No one grabbed this..."

"Ankh," Ollie filled in.

"Ankh, right. No one grabbed the ankh in the heat of the

moment. Cutting the power AND the generators took some doing."

"Which brings me back to my original question," Gio said. "Why go through all this trouble for a piece of carved... uh, what did you say it was again, doc?"

"Faience," Ollie repeated. "One of the oldest known forms of glazed ceramic in the world. It's a non-clay-based ceramic. It wasn't carved, but rather, formed. It normally carries a blue-green luster. Though this has lost some of that glazing, making it appear stone-like. Likely the years of..."

"Thanks for the history lesson, professor," Detective Sharpe snapped, interrupting Ollie. "But we've got more important things to consider. Such as why someone took this rather worthless artifact and why you immediately guessed it was the one missing."

"Well..." Ollie began, rubbing his chin. "Its value depends on who you talk to."

"So, it's worth some money?" Gio inquired. "How much do you estimate?"

"Oh, no, no, I doubt it would fetch much in general. Only the most informed would know its value."

"You're talking in circles, doc," Gio said.

"What he is referring to," Stan chimed in, "is an old wives' tale about the object." The director waved his hand in the air dismissively. "Ollie, you can't possibly think..." His voice trailed off as though he could not finish the statement because it was so fantastic.

"Old wives' tale?" Maggie questioned. "Now I'm the one who'd like some explanations."

"Yes," Ollie answered. "Well, no, not a wives' tale."

"More of a legend," Henry added.

"Right," Ollie confirmed. "A legend."

"And this legend suggests the ankh holds some value? Is it

because it belonged to Cleopatra, or is there some other reason?" Maggie inquired.

"Another reason," Ollie responded. "The ankh in and of itself is worthless. Just a hunk of ceramic, pieces like that were a dime a dozen in that era. No, it's not the ankh, it's what the ankh points to."

"Points to?" Maggie queried. She shook her head, not understanding.

Ollie nodded, a tight-lipped grin on his face. "It gives the location of the Library of Alexandria."

"What?!" Maggie exclaimed. "Like the famous one?"

"The very same."

Stan snorted in response. He rolled his eyes, waving his hands in the air again. "A bunch of hooey!"

"And this library… it's important?" Gio questioned.

"Infinitely," Ollie answered. "The materials held in that library would advance knowledge of the ancient world by leaps and bounds."

Maggie's brow furrowed. "I thought the Library of Alexandria was destroyed. Burnt down in one of those wars they were always having back then."

"It was," Stan said with a sigh.

Ollie wagged his finger in the air. "Most scholars believe it was, yet the remains have never been identified. A library the size of the one that stood in Alexandria should be identifiable."

Ollie's statement was met with another eye roll from the museum's director. "While not finding the remains is not beyond the realm of possible events, the leading theory is the library, at least in the form we imagine it existed in, did not, in fact, exist at all."

"Too much is written about it for it not to exist," Ollie countered.

"I didn't say it didn't exist, I said it didn't exist as we

imagine it. As a large library that dominated the landscape of Alexandria. Perhaps the library was much smaller and contained far less."

"Not likely. The library was legend, even in ancient times. It is implausible that it was referenced so much throughout history if it were, in fact, a small library."

"Uh, gentlemen?" Gio interrupted. "Could we perhaps debate the finer details another time?"

"My partner's right. The matter at hand is the missing object and retrieving it. The reason we pulled your team in, Dr. Keene, is because our FBI contact, who should be arriving any moment, told us you may have some insight about the missing object."

"I do," Ollie said. "And I have shared it. The reason the object was stolen, the reason I knew immediately, was because of its connection to the Library of Alexandria."

A disgusted sigh rose from Stan. "All right," Gio said, "let's assume this theory of yours is correct. Then, someone stole it so they could find the Library of Alexandria and what, get rich from that?"

"The contents of that library are invaluable."

"And worth money?"

"Yes, probably worth millions on the black market," Ollie admitted.

"Uncle Ollie," Maggie interjected, "if this ankh gives the location, why didn't you examine it and find the library already? You oversaw the dig site. This must have crossed your desk."

"There were thousands of items," Ollie nodded. "I didn't examine each one of them myself before they were catalogued and sent out for cleaning and exhibits. When I saw the description on the inventory, I made certain to view it more closely this evening. It's consistent with what I expected. But it does not contain a complete map, only a partial one."

"Okay, I'm going to need you to back up a step, doc, and explain this again," Gio said. "Call it Intro to the Library of Alexandria for dummies, okay?"

"Yeah, I'd be interested in hearing this, too," Maggie agreed.

Ollie launched into his lecture. "The Library of Alexandria was one of the largest libraries of the ancient world. So much so that Alexandria was regarded as the capital of learning, much of that due to the library. Most people believe the library was destroyed. But this is not exactly true."

"If I remember your story correctly," Henry chimed in, "it actually declined over time."

"Correct. Scholars believe it declined due to waning support by the rulers. Lack of money and support, all that. And many believe Julius Caesar himself accidentally burned part of it during one of his wars."

"Julius Caesar DID burn part of it during one of his wars," Stan countered.

"Or Caesar moved the contents in secret and pretended it had burned."

"Again, we can debate who did what later," Detective Sharpe chimed in. "The FBI seems to put some stock in Dr. Keene's theory, or they wouldn't have pointed us in his direction. So, please, doctor, continue."

Ollie nodded at him and Stan shook his head, tossing his hand in the air. "Where was I?" Ollie questioned.

"Most people believe the library was destroyed, but that's not the whole truth," Maggie reminded him.

"Ah, yes," Ollie answered, pacing the floor, his arms clasped behind his back. "Most scholars believe the library was destroyed after being in significant decline for many years. But that's not what others believe, myself included."

"And what do you believe?" Detective Sharpe questioned.

"That the library's contents were moved, hidden somewhere else for safekeeping," Henry answered.

"Yes," Ollie agreed. "Despite the library's membership continuing in the 200s A.D., I believe most of its contents were moved. The new location, a secret location, was not discussed openly."

"Who moved everything?"

"Julius Caesar," Ollie answered. "His ruse was the fire, though I believe he moved items in actuality."

Maggie shook her head. "How does this relate to a worthless ceramic ankh in Cleopatra's tomb?"

"After Caesar moved the library, he coded its location on three ankhs. One he kept, one he gave to his good friend Marc Antony, and the third…"

"He gave to Cleopatra," Maggie answered.

Ollie ceased his pacing and nodded, touching his finger to his nose and pointing the other to Maggie.

"So, you believe the stolen ankh is a piece of the map pointing to the lost Library of Alexandria?" Maggie asked.

Ollie nodded while Stan shook his head. "He's wrong," the director said.

Ollie shrugged. "I may be, but the odds I am correct have gone up since the robbery this evening."

"He wasn't wrong about the golden scarab of Cleopatra," Maggie replied. "I believe you, Uncle Ollie."

"As do I," Henry added.

"Doc's explanation seems legit," Gio said. "And unless anyone else has any other idea why this specific item was stolen, it'll be our working hypothesis. Now, who would want access to this coded map?"

Ollie shrugged again and shook his head. "The list is long and varied. It's a major archeological find. Beyond that, anything found there not only lends itself to the world's knowledge of ancient people but is worth a mint to collectors."

"Like on the black market?" Gio questioned.

"Right. Antiquities are sold constantly on the black market, some of them going for millions. Owning a piece of history like this in one's private collection gives some a thrill and great bragging rights. Among certain circles of the super-rich, it's a popular pastime."

"Okay," Gio said, "so, this ankh is a piece of the puzzle leading to this famed library in your estimation, doc. Where are the other two pieces?"

"Antony's would likely have been buried somewhere in or near Cleopatra's tomb. They committed suicide together and were buried together. We haven't found any of his remains at the tomb site though," Ollie admitted.

"Okay, so one of them is still missing," Gio replied. "And the other?"

"Probably in storage somewhere at an Italian museum," Ollie guessed. "Or in a private collection. I'd have to do some digging in my research to determine the most likely place."

A knock sounded at the door, interrupting any further conversation. A uniformed officer appeared as the door swung open. "We're almost finished, detective. Nothing's turned up yet. And we've got a pair out there who refuse to leave. Say they know a Miss Edwards who is still in the museum and aren't leaving without her."

"Oh," Maggie replied. "That'd be Leo and Piper, I'd bet. I'll go tell them it's fine to go."

Maggie excused herself from the room and followed the winding hallway back to the museum's exhibit galleries. She traversed through the exhibit rooms leading back to the main lobby. As she plodded along, she glanced to the many cases holding objects from Cleopatra's tomb. Who else knew the legend her uncle relayed to them? Who else believed it with enough conviction to rob the exhibit while two pieces remained at large?

With no answers, Maggie arrived in the lobby, spotting Leo and Piper arguing with another uniformed officer. She crossed the room, approaching the trio.

"THERE you are!" Leo exclaimed. "I was just telling officer whoever here that you vanished with a detective and we haven't seen you since." Maggie held back from rolling her eyes.

"And I was explaining to you and Miss Brooks that you've got to leave. We're clearing the museum," the officer grumbled back.

"We're not leaving until she does," Leo threatened.

"Now, look here, mister…"

Maggie held up her hands. "Just a minute, just a minute," she interrupted. She turned to the officer. "Could you give us a moment alone? Thanks."

The officer withdrew with a shake of his head and an admonishing glance at Leo and Piper.

"What a total jerk that guy was," Piper complained.

"He's just doing his job," Maggie said.

"Where were you?" Leo questioned.

"Talking to the detectives. And we're not finished. I just came out to tell you both I'm fine and you can go."

"I'm not leaving without you, Mags."

This time, Maggie could not hold back the eye roll. She crossed her arms. "I'm fine, Leo. Just go. There's no need for you or Piper to be here."

"Are you in some kind of trouble?" Leo inquired. "If you need an attorney…"

"I do NOT need an attorney. I'm not in trouble!"

"Then why did the detectives want to question you?" Leo pressed.

"Question me?" Maggie retorted. "They're not questioning me. They asked to speak with me about the theft, not question me. Oh, by the way, you owe me twenty bucks."

"Why would the cops want to discuss the robbery with you?" Leo questioned, his brows wrinkling with confusion.

Maggie's expression changed from unimpressed to annoyed. She set her jaw, her lips closing to form a thin line. "They have their reasons," Maggie grumbled. "Which are none of your business, now go. I'm busy, I don't have time to babysit you, Leo."

Maggie spun on her heel, stalking away from the couple. "Oh, yeah? Well, don't call me if you need bailed out!" Leo called after her.

Maggie stormed back to the employee's door. She fumed at Leo's statements. "Why would the police want to talk to YOU?" she mimicked. "Is he kidding?"

Maggie reached the door and tugged on it. It didn't budge. She glanced at the card reader next to the door. "Seriously?" She banged against the door. Her action garnered no response. With a huff, she crossed her arms. Her foot tapped on the penny tiles adorning the floor.

Maggie's eyes bore an imaginary hole through the windowed door. At last, she spotted Henry turn the corner and hurry down the hall. Maggie flung her arms out. "Finally!" she exclaimed as Henry pushed the door open.

"Sorry to keep you waiting, princess. What did the idiot want?"

Maggie waved her hand in the air. "Just Leo being Leo. Believing he was the only one who could help the situation because I was somehow in trouble. Never mind, what's the latest? Any leads?"

Henry smirked at her. "What?" Maggie questioned as they traversed the halls back to the director's office.

"Nothing. Just you being excited to pursue a lead."

"I enjoy a good adventure," Maggie answered.

"I'll remind you of that if we have to ride another camel into the desert and sleep in a tent," Henry said with a wink as he pulled the director's door open for her.

"Oh, please," Maggie groaned with an eye roll. "Let's hope this library is within the city limits."

The couple entered into a heated argument between Ollie and Stan. The two debated the working theory that the ankh's value stemmed from its ability to lead to the famed Library of Alexandra's final resting place. The two detectives watched the scene unfold, unable to interject any pertinent comments.

Maggie raised her eyebrows at the scene. She stuck her fingers in her mouth and gave a loud whistle. All faces spun to face her. "THAT is ENOUGH!" she declared. "It's pointless to debate the reason the ankh was stolen. It's gone. Period. The fact that it's gone lends some credence to Uncle Ollie's theory. But that argument aside, the thing is gone. Where are we on identifying who took it?"

Maggie placed her hands on her hips, facing the detectives. When they failed to respond, she raised her eyebrows. "Well?" she demanded.

"Oh, ah..." Gio began. He flipped his notebook open and relayed his notes to the group. "Okay, power cut at nine thirty-seven, generators' power already cut or cut at the same time, no video surveillance, nothing found on any departing guests. That's where we are. We got bubkas."

"No video surveillance?" Henry inquired. "Is there no coverage on the ankh or is the footage missing?"

"The camera covering it was malfunctioning. There's no footage," Gio answered.

"Malfunctioning... right," Maggie said, her eyes narrowing. She shot a glance to Henry who raised his eyebrows at her.

"Did any of the guests see or hear anything? You questioned them, right?"

"We…" Gio hesitated. "Searched them all and…"

"You didn't ask anyone if they saw or heard anything?" Henry questioned.

"Well… no," Gio answered. "Look, we're not broadcasting the theft here, okay?"

Henry guffawed. "Crikey," he groaned.

"All right, all right," Maggie said. "Given the lack of information, the best place to start is the guest list. Anyone have a criminal record? Anyone known for collecting this type of stuff?"

"Whoa, whoa, whoa," Gio responded, holding up a hand to stop Maggie's questions. "As much as I'd love to partner with you, Miss Edwards, this is a job for the police."

Maggie shot him an unimpressed stare. She crossed her arms, narrowed her eyes and pursed her lips. Gio opened his mouth to continue when a knock sounded at the door. Without receiving an invitation, the door swung open. A man in a dark suit entered, his dress shoes clicking across the bare floor. His chiseled features appeared even more sculpted thanks to his closely cropped haircut.

"Who the hell are you?" Gio questioned.

The man reached into his pocket, withdrawing a small black wallet. He flipped it open, flashing a badge. "Agent Thomas, FBI," he said, pocketing the badge again.

"FBI?" Gio queried.

"Yes, you must be Detectives Sharpe and Russo, I presume?" the man asked.

"Yeah, that's us," Gio replied.

"Perfect. Can you fill me in on the specifics of the case so far?"

"Fill you in?" Gio questioned. "I thought you were advising not boots on the ground."

"There isn't much," Maggie answered for him. "Power was cut, generators were tampered with and video surveillance is missing. No one left with the object that we are aware of and no one was questioned. That's about as far as we've gotten."

Gio shot Maggie a confused and annoyed glance.

"Thanks," Agent Thomas answered. "All right, gentlemen, unless you have anything else to add to Ms. Edwards' summary, you can go."

"Go? What do you mean go?" Gio exclaimed. "We're in the middle of an investigation here!"

"Not anymore you're not," Agent Thomas answered. "This investigation now falls under the purview of the Federal Bureau of Investigation."

CHAPTER 3

A moment of silence fell between them after Agent Thomas announced his role with the FBI. Gio recovered first.

"Says who? This is our jurisdiction, bub," Gio spat. "And I ain't rolling over for nobody."

"Says the Director of National Intelligence. This investigation is now a matter of national security. We thank you for your time, gentlemen. Now, if you wouldn't mind." Agent Thomas motioned to the door.

Gio glanced to Detective Sharpe, who shrugged. He shook his head in disgust. "Unbelievable! Since when did some stupid ceramic cross become a matter of national security." He snatched his blazer from the nearby chair with a huff before he stormed from the room. Detective Sharpe followed him, plainly less frustrated than his younger partner.

The door slammed shut behind the two men, cutting off Maggie's view of Gio's glare.

"Nice to see you again, Frank," Henry said.

"Henry, Maggie, Ollie. Good to see you all. Got yourselves in the thick of it again, I see."

"I warned you," Ollie said.

Stan eyed the exchange curiously, his forehead wrinkled as he listened. "Director Stan Gibson?" Frank questioned.

"Yes," Stan answered.

"Agent Frank Thomas, FBI," Frank said, extending his hand.

Stan shook it slowly. "Yes, I got that part. What I don't understand is why the FBI is involved. Does this have to do with the pieces being on loan?"

"No, it has to do with the stolen piece pointing to the Library of Alexandria," Ollie corrected.

"Correct," Frank confirmed. "We would like to ensure the piece is found as quickly as possible. Despite at least one other piece still being unaccounted for, it's vital this doesn't end up in the wrong hands."

Stan's face was incredulous. "Are you saying the FBI really believes Ollie's conjecture about the ankh containing a clue to the location of the Library of Alexandria?"

"We do," Frank answered. "And we'd like you to cooperate fully with Agents Keene, Taylor and Edwards to ensure the piece is found."

"Agents?" Stan gasped.

"Yes," Ollie confirmed.

"Of what? The FBI?"

"No, DARPA," Henry chimed in.

"The Defense Advanced Research Projects Agency?" Stan repeated, spelling out the acronym.

"One and the same," Ollie answered. "We work on special projects related to ancient civilizations that could prove beneficial to the government. Obviously, the Library of Alexandria falls into this category. The knowledge gained there would be extensive."

Silence filled the room as Stan digested the information. "Well... I..." he began. "Ah... how can I help?" he finally managed.

"We need a copy of the guest list," Maggie answered. "And I'd like to speak with your security guards about the security camera footage. We know the camera covering the ankh didn't catch anything, but maybe one of the other cameras did."

Stan glanced around the room at everyone. After a breath, Frank raised his eyebrows. "Is there a problem, Director Gibson?"

"Ah, no," he answered. "No. Let me just make a copy of the list and then I'll show you to the security surveillance room."

Stan dashed from the office to retrieve copies of the guest list. "Good job, princess," Henry said, beaming at Maggie.

"Thanks!" she said with a demure smile.

"Yes," Ollie agreed, a smile on his face, "your training proved most successful!"

Maggie reflected on the three-week crash training course with DARPA. She had learned so much. This time around, she would control the investigation, unlike the search for her uncle and Cleopatra's tomb. The smile on her face broadened. She was ready for another adventure.

* * *

MAGGIE SCANNED the guest list while lounging on the couch. Nothing jumped out at her. They still waited on the background checks for each name on the list, but neither Ollie nor Henry flagged any suspects. Maggie recognized some of the names on the list. They were prominent citizens of the area. She doubted any of them would be involved, but with no leads, everyone was a suspect.

"Put it down and relax, princess," Henry prodded. He sat on the opposite end of the couch.

Maggie lowered the page, glancing over it at Henry. "There has to be SOME clue here!" Maggie exclaimed.

"We don't have to find it tonight, though. Patience, princess, patience."

Maggie tossed the paper onto the coffee table and let her head fall onto the cushion behind her. "You're sure you didn't recognize any of these names?" she asked after a moment.

"Positive," Henry responded. "Though it's more than likely they're using an assumed name that no one would recognize."

Maggie continued with her questions. "No one looked familiar at the party?"

"Nope."

"Is that because you were hiding in a corner most of the time or because you actually didn't recognize anyone?" Maggie queried.

"I didn't recognize anyone. I had a pretty good vantage point from that corner, I'll have you know." Henry cocked his head and raised one eyebrow at her.

"Too bad you weren't in your perfect vantage corner when they stole the ankh," Maggie said with a sigh.

"No, we were distracted by the antics of that bloody ex of yours."

Maggie rolled her eyes at the reference to Leo. "He has never been good at losing," she commented. She crossed her arms, staring into space. "I can't believe none of the cameras picked up anything related to the theft."

After hours of combing through footage, Maggie and Henry had found nothing suspicious. Outside of the guests, no one entered or exited the museum through any doorways in the time leading up to or following the theft.

"Did they climb out a window? Did they loop the video footage? What are we missing?" Maggie pondered aloud.

"There was no evidence the footage was looped. We could see movement on the cameras before the power was cut."

"Maybe they sneaked out while the cameras were down," Maggie suggested.

"When and how did they get in?" Henry queried, testing Maggie's theory.

Maggie lifted her head, her brow crinkling as she worked out the details in her mind. "They came in as guests, cut the power, stole the ankh and slipped out before the cameras were restored."

Henry shook his head. "All the guests were accounted for. Everyone in attendance was searched before they left. No one was missing from the guest list."

Maggie threw her arms up in disgust. "And none of them had the ankh on them."

"Nope," Henry agreed. "It's small, but not small enough to hide for a pat down. And all the ladies' purses were searched."

"So, we're at a dead end."

"Seems so," Henry agreed.

Maggie sunk down, plopping her head against the cushion behind her. Henry gave her leg a quick pat before standing. "Well, we aren't going to work it out tonight, princess. So, I'll leave you to get some rest."

"Rest? Are you kidding me? This will play through my mind all night!"

"You? Maggie Edwards? Overthinking a situation."

Maggie rolled her eyes at him. "Yeah, I know. A novel concept, but I can't help it. Ever since I met you, I've turned into an overthinker."

"Oh, so this is my fault, huh?"

"Yep. I take no blame in this," she joked.

Henry approached her, leaning forward to kiss her forehead. "Put it out of your mind, princess. You won't solve it tonight. We'll start fresh in the morning. Things have a way of looking differently after some sleep."

"Yeah, right," Maggie said, her arms still snug against her chest. She sighed as he sauntered away, still pouting. Before he reached the door, Maggie popped up, glancing over the back of the couch. "Hey, Henry!"

"Yeah?" Henry asked, pivoting to face her.

"Good night, babe," she said with a wink.

"Good night, princess."

Maggie spent a few more moments lounging on the couch before she dragged herself to her bedroom. As she readied for bed, her mind poured over the mystery. Maggie had never been an overthinker before, but she certainly was turning into one. She searched the information for the clue they were missing.

With a shake of her head and no new conclusions, she climbed into bed. After snuggling into the covers, she stared at the ceiling. Perhaps there was a clue they were missing in the video feeds. Some telltale sign that an expert could glean. Maggie reached to her night table, grabbing her phone.

Her thumbs flew across the tiny electronic keyboard on her smartphone. She fired a message to Henry: *Possible to get Charlie here to look at that video footage? Maybe he'll see something we missed.*

Henry answered within a minute: *You're supposed to be sleeping*

Maggie sighed and sent a reply text: *Can you call him or not?*

She smiled as she received the response: *Your wish is my command, princess*

Thanks she replied. *Let me know when you hear from him and how soon he can get here... see you tomorrow.*

Maggie toggled off her phone. Satisfied with the miniscule plan in place, she closed her eyes to sleep.

* * *

Bright sunshine greeted Maggie the next morning as she strode from her favorite coffee shop to her boutique. Charlie Rivers, tech extraordinaire, was en route from London and due to arrive in the early afternoon. Perhaps his expertise in all things high-tech would detect something their untrained eyes had missed.

For now, all they could do was sit and wait. Maggie pulled open the door to the shop with a sigh, propping it open. "Wait, wait, wait. Wait for the background checks on the guest list. Wait for Charlie to study the footage. Wait for something to break. I HATE waiting," she fumed aloud as she flicked on the lights in the shop. She stomped over to the register and slammed her keys and coffee on the counter.

"Careful, you'll break the counter," Henry said as he leaned in the open doorway. In his customary t-shirt, cargo pants and his favorite hat, he was limned from behind in the morning sun. He looked like a figure out of an adventure movie.

"Don't worry, it's reinforced."

"Ah, to compensate for the weight of the register?" Henry guessed.

"No, I cracked it once already during an argument with Leo. Slammed my phone down and put a big splintering crack right in the middle," Maggie admitted.

"Oh, temper, temper, princess."

Maggie smirked at him. "Those days are behind me," she said with a wink. She leaned across the counter, brushing Henry's lips lightly with hers.

"Yeah, because now you've got the world's perfect man," Henry said, stealing another kiss.

"That's right," Maggie said, staring into Henry's eyes before a third kiss.

"Ugh!" Piper exclaimed, emerging from the doorway leading to the backroom. "Get a room."

Maggie pulled back from Henry, rolling her eyes. "Oh, stop, it was one kiss."

"Don't you have a job or something to go to?" Piper queried Henry.

"Not at the moment," Henry responded. "Which gives me all day to spend here with you girls in the shop."

"Fabulous," Piper said with an exasperated sigh. "If you're going to hang out here all day, why don't you at least fill in as my assistant?" Piper flung a rag toward Henry. "You can start by dusting the shelves over there." She pointed to the far wall before disappearing into the storeroom.

Henry shot Maggie a confused glance. "Is she serious? Her assistant?"

"That's what she's been calling the new hire we're searching for," Maggie explained, pointing to the HELP WANTED sign in the window.

Henry glanced at the rag, tossing it from one hand to the other. "What should I do with this?"

Maggie shrugged. "Sounds like you better get dusting."

Henry frowned at the rag but made his way across the room, rubbing the cloth across each shelf. Maggie slumped onto the stool behind the counter. "I can't believe there's no information yet from anyone. No hits on anyone on the guest list? And what time is Charlie arriving?"

"I'll text Frank again, maybe there's something new on the guest list," Henry answered, setting the dustrag on the shelf and pulling his phone from his pocket. "Charlie should be here around one or two. He's coming here to meet us before going to the museum."

Maggie glanced at her watch. She flung her head back in frustration, impatience building. Henry witnessed her irritation. "Only a few more hours, princess."

"Too many hours," Maggie lamented. She stalked across the shop, snatching the discarded rag from the shelf and continuing the dusting.

"Whew," Henry said. "Thanks. I needed a break!" He collapsed into a leather armchair nearby, wiping his brow in an overstated show of exhaustion.

"You're getting soft," Maggie said with a chuckle.

"Must be small-town life creeping up on me," Henry mentioned as his phone chimed an alert.

"Well?" Maggie inquired. "Is that Frank?"

"Yeah, just as I suspected."

"What?"

"No hits on the guest list."

"Not one?"

"Nope. Maggie, if someone was about to rob a museum, they wouldn't use their real name. So, I doubted we'd find anything of any consequence."

"So, short of Charlie catching something, we're stuck," Maggie complained.

"Appears so," Henry agreed.

With a sigh, Maggie returned to her duties. The hours crept by. She busied herself with anything she could find to distract her from the waiting.

"If you keep staring at that watch, it'll never move," Henry warned her over lunch.

"Hot date?" Piper teased.

"Something like that," Maggie mused, staring out the window.

Piper shifted her glance between Henry and Maggie. "We're waiting to see an old friend," Henry explained.

"Well, I'm off to continue organizing the storeroom," Piper responded, tossing the remainder of her lunch into the trash.

Henry's gaze followed Piper to the backroom. "Wow, organizing the entire storeroom herself? You're a tough boss, princess." He winked at Maggie.

"I didn't ask her to do it. She decided to do that herself," Maggie said. "The idea came to her when she had to get something from back there while we were 'on vacation.'"

"We didn't take a vacation," Henry said in a questioning tone.

"I know. But Piper insists we took a lavish vacation. It doesn't help that I was vague in my explanation of where we were during those three weeks."

Henry nodded, giving Maggie a knowing glance and a half-smirk. "Well, I suppose it keeps her busy."

"Yep," Maggie agreed as the door's bell tinkled, indicating a new customer entering the store.

Frank strode into the shop with another man trailing behind him. His disheveled blond hair and lanky form slogged through the door. He carried a backpack, his hands thrust in his pockets, earbuds shoved in both ears. Maggie recognized Charlie Rivers immediately.

A smile crossed her face. Perhaps now they would get somewhere on this investigation, she mused.

Henry stood, greeting the two men. Charlie pulled the earbuds from his ears, letting them dangle around his neck. He noted Maggie's grin. "I knew you'd be happy to see me again, chicky," he teased.

"For once, you are correct!" Maggie exclaimed.

"Heard you asked for me special!" He leaned over the counter and whispered, "Knew it would only be a matter of time before Mr. Macho got on your nerves and you came searching for me."

Maggie offered a wry glance and a shake of her head. "You haven't changed a bit, Charlie," she said.

He smirked at her, wiggling his eyebrows up and down in his usual manner. "We need your help, mate," Henry interjected.

"Yeah, Frank filled me in on the way over. Got nothing, huh?"

"Nothing, mate, nothing. Unless the guest list turned up something interesting?" Henry questioned Frank.

"Not a thing," Frank admitted.

"Is that normal?" Maggie inquired.

"Yes," Frank responded. "If someone is planning a heist like this, they aren't going to hang a sign out that says 'I'm a criminal with a record.'"

Maggie nodded, frustrated but not surprised by the answer.

"Never fear," Charlie said. "Charlie to the rescue."

"We'll head to the museum now and let you examine that footage," Frank said.

"Oh, just a minute, let me get Piper out here to tend the shop," Maggie said. "Piper! PIPER!" Maggie called into the back room.

Charlie shoved his earbuds into his ears and wandered around the shop.

They waited a moment. Maggie drummed her fingers on the glass counter. She offered a nervous smile to Frank, who scrolled through the emails on his phone.

"Piper!" Maggie called again. "Come on! I need to get going!"

The door to the storeroom swung open. "Yeah, yeah, yeah, okay, boss lady! I'm coming already!" Piper stepped into the main shop, colliding with Charlie, who rounded a bookcase at an inopportune moment. Piper stumbled backward, toppling onto her backside. Her pink earbuds slipped from her ears, one becoming tangled in her multi-colored hair.

"Ow! What the hell, dude?!" she exclaimed as she landed hard.

She searched the air above her for the cause of her fall. Charlie hovered over her. He pulled the earbuds from his ears, leaving them dangling around his neck again.

"Oh, ah…" he stuttered. "Sorry there, miss. I didn't see you."

Piper stared up at him. Maggie waited for the impending berating she assumed Piper would lash out with. Instead, Piper remained silent. The reaction puzzled Maggie. She wondered if Piper may be seriously hurt, though she didn't see how.

Maggie was about to inquire when Piper spoke up. "Oh, no problem," Piper said in a voice Maggie had never heard before.

"Here," Charlie said, extending a hand, "let me help you up."

"Thanks," Piper responded, accepting it with a half-smile. Charlie pulled Piper to her feet, the two still clinging to each other's hands even after she had regained her footing. Piper stared up at Charlie, a sweet expression on her face.

"Name's Charlie, Charlie Rivers," Charlie said, swaying her hand up and down to simulate a shake.

Piper's smile broadened. "Piper Brooks, Assistant Manager," Piper breathed.

"Nice to meet you Piper Brooks, Assistant Manager," Charlie said with a grin. "In the future, I shall try to not knock you down, fair maiden."

"In the future, I shall appreciate that, good sir," Piper answered. Their fingers remained entwined for another moment before Piper, her cheeks pink and dewy, pulled her hand away and strode to the cashier's counter.

Maggie's brow furrowed at the exchange. She glanced at Piper; her jaw open with a questioning glance. Piper met her expression with an equally confused one. "What?" she whispered.

"Are we ready?" Frank questioned before Maggie could respond.

"Sure are, mate," Henry said with a nod. He glanced at Maggie.

"Uh, y-yeah," Maggie answered, recovering from her stupor. She retrieved her purse and, with one final puzzled glance at Piper, followed the men out of the shop's front door.

CHAPTER 4

Maggie paced the floor of the museum's small security office. Henry sat in a chair; his feet propped up on the desk as Charlie worked at the monitor in front of them.

After another few trips across the room, Maggie exclaimed, "Oh, come on! You've been at that for over an hour!"

"Patience, chicky, patience," Charlie said, his eyes never moving from the screen. "Delicate work."

Maggie sighed, setting her mouth in a line. She stared at Henry; her eyes narrowed. Henry held his arms up in surrender. "Don't shoot those daggers at me, princess, I'm just the support staff."

Maggie made another trek across the room before Charlie pushed back from the monitor. Maggie spun to face him. "Well?!" she demanded.

"Nothing," Charlie responded.

Maggie scowled as Henry inquired, "What do you mean nothing?"

"I mean, there's nothing, mate. Footage is clean, no

tampering, no cameras shifted, nothing."

"Nothing that you can see," Maggie grumbled.

"No, nothing period, chicky. Tampering with footage is no easy business. I would have detected it."

Maggie shot Charlie an incredulous glance. "What do you mean it's not easy? You did it! Twice that I know of, in fact!"

"Yeah, but I'm an expert. And any expert they called in after I did it would have picked up on it. It's not as clean as you'd think. There'd be artifacts left."

Maggie dropped her head between her shoulder blades with a sigh. "So, we're at another dead end."

"Appears that way," Henry noted, climbing to his feet.

"Now what?" Maggie whined.

"We look for another angle," Henry informed her. "Don't sweat it, princess. We'll catch a break. For now, what do you say we get something to eat?"

"Good call, mate. I've been dying for some American pizza or something. A nice New York slice."

Maggie pouted. This was not how she hoped her first case would begin. "Come on, princess," Henry encouraged, "you'll feel better after you eat."

"All right, fine," she acquiesced. She shot a glance at Charlie. "But you can't get a New York slice here. This is Illinois. We eat deep dish here."

Charlie shrugged. "Sounds good to me. Hey, do you think your Assistant Manager, Piper, would want some deep-dish pizza."

The comment elicited a half-smile from Maggie. "Yeah, I bet she would," Maggie responded, giving Henry a knowing glance.

They collected their belongings, making their way to the museum's lobby. "Oh, just a sec, I want to use the ladies' room," Maggie said. She crossed past the docent's kiosk and disappeared through the ladies' room door.

This is where she had been when the lights went out and the theft occurred, Maggie reflected. She glanced around the starkly lit room for a moment before ducking into one of the stalls.

The ladies' room door creaked on its hinges as it swung open. The din of the crowd outside floated in before tapering off as the door swung shut. Maggie glanced under the stall's door, spotting a pair of flat, black Mary Jane-style shoes peeking out from a paisley maxi skirt.

What a hideous choice of footwear, Maggie reflected. The ill-fashioned feet approached Maggie's stall, and the door shook as the woman attempted to push into the stall.

"Occupied!" Maggie called out, shaking her head at the person. Of all the stalls to pick, she brooded! Five empty stalls surrounded them! Was this woman kidding, Maggie fumed?

Maggie held in a sigh as the feet shuffled away but did not enter another stall. Instead, they approached the sink and Maggie heard the water run. With a roll of her eyes, she grabbed her purse from the hook and unlocked the stall door.

She exited the stall, glancing in the direction of the bathroom's other occupant. The woman bent over the sink, her brunette hair obscuring most of her face. The water tap shut off, and the women stood. She wore large black sunglasses, which hid most of her face. She turned away from Maggie, crossing the distance between the sink and the stalls, and entered the stall Maggie just exited.

Maggie shook her head as she washed her hands. Strange, she reflected, as she pulled a paper towel from the dispenser and dried her hands. The other occupant had not dried her hands after washing them, Maggie contemplated. And she had been insistent on getting into one specific stall.

The oddities triggered Maggie's radar. Something felt off.

SECRET OF THE ANKHS

Maggie stared at the stall door. As a shop owner, she encountered shoplifters before. Similarities between this situation and a shoplifter ricocheted through her mind. On instinct, Maggie took a step toward the stall.

She lowered her eyes toward the floor, glancing under the stall door. The woman stood facing the toilet rather than facing the door. Maggie's brow crinkled; her suspicions further confirmed.

"Excuse me, miss?" Maggie voiced. "Are you all right?" Maggie kept her gaze trained on the feet on the opposite side of the stall. It appeared the woman stiffened at Maggie's voice.

Maggie inched closer to the door. "Miss?" Maggie inquired again.

The door swung open. A racing figure blindsided Maggie, knocking into her as she sprinted from the stall and toward the ladies' room door. Startled, Maggie lost her balance, tumbling onto her backside. She sprawled across the floor, the contents of her purse spilling as it toppled with her.

Various items clattered across the tiles as Maggie struggled to recover. "Hey!" she shouted. "Hey! Stop!"

Maggie scrambled to her feet as the woman darted through the restroom door. With her purse still wrapped around her forearm, devoid of its contents, Maggie rushed to follow her. She flung the slowly closing restroom door open, scanning the lobby outside. Across the room, she spotted the woman's lumbering form.

"Hey!" Maggie yelled. "Hey, stop that woman!"

Maggie raced after her. Henry spotted the commotion, diving in front of the fleeing form. The woman skirted by him. He reached out, grabbing hold of her sleeve. The woman shook him off, ripping her coat sleeve from his grasp as she spun away from him.

A guard near the door attempted to block her escape, but

the woman barreled into him, knocking him to the floor. She pushed through the revolving door as Maggie reached Henry. Breathless, Maggie puffed with exertion after her unsuccessful sprint. In a desperate attempt to catch the woman, she continued through the revolving door. She scanned the parking lot in search of the fleeing female.

Maggie hurried down the front steps, stepping into the parking lot flanking the building. She spun in circles, searching. As she circled, the sound of squealing tires reached her ears. She twisted toward the noise, finding a car racing toward her. Maggie's eyes grew wide as the car barreled in her direction. Its engine roared as the car lurched forward, increasing its speed.

"Maggie!" Henry shouted as he tackled her to the ground, knocking her out of the speeding car's path.

"Oof," Maggie exclaimed as she hit the ground, tangled with Henry. The air pushed out of her lungs as she landed hard.

"Are you all right, princess?" Henry asked, his breath ragged from the effort. "Maggie?!" he questioned again when she didn't answer immediately.

"Yeah," Maggie answered when she recovered her breath.

Henry breathed a sigh of relief, climbing off Maggie and pulling her to standing. "You sure you're all right?"

"Well…" Maggie paused.

"Yeah, what is it? Where does it hurt?"

"Nowhere. I just wanted to say you still have the power to knock me off my feet." She giggled and winked at him.

Henry's jaw dropped. "Wow, you should take that act on the road, princess," he mustered.

"I just did," Maggie said with a giggle.

"Correction: I did," Henry said with a shake of his head. "All jokes aside, why were you chasing that woman?"

Charlie hurried down the stairs toward them, trailed by

two security guards. "Oi, what was all that about? Are you all right?"

"Yeah, yeah, I'm fine." Maggie sighed, brushing the dirt from her clothes. She shrugged. "I don't know. She was in the restroom. Something just wasn't right about her. I was the only other person in there and she came right for my stall and then when she couldn't get in, she waited to use it. It just seemed strange. So, I asked if she was okay and the next thing I knew I was sprawled on the floor. She ran out of the stall, knocked me over and kept running."

Henry's eyes narrowed and Maggie continued. "Stupid, probably. I guess she was pretty angry at me for disturbing her."

Henry shook his head. "Yeah, I'd agree she was angry, but not because you were stupid. You don't try to run someone down because they interrupted your trip to the loo."

"Perhaps she didn't see me," Maggie conjectured.

"Maggie, she gunned the car right at you. She saw you. Nah, I don't buy it. Your instincts were correct, something was off."

Maggie shook her head, her brow furrowing. "But what?"

"A day after a theft at the museum, I'd venture to say it's related to that," Charlie conjectured.

Maggie raised her eyebrows, considering it. "Really? I mean, it's a possibility, but..." She paused. "Maybe she just shoplifted something from the gift shop."

Henry mulled it over. "Eh, maybe, though I doubt it. You don't try to run someone over because you nabbed a souvenir from the gift shop."

Maggie crossed her arms, the crease in her forehead deepening. "So, if it's related to the theft... perhaps we can make some connection between that woman and someone from the party."

"Maybe we can identify her from the security footage,"

Charlie suggested. "Use facial recognition to match her to one of the guests."

"Yes!" Maggie exclaimed. "Yes, maybe this is the break we need! Come on!"

Maggie grasped Charlie's shirt, pulling him along behind her. "Careful, chicky, careful. I bruise easily." He winked at her.

"We should check the stall, too!" Henry called after them.

"Good idea," Maggie replied as they entered the museum. "You check the stall. I've got to get my stuff." The trio crossed the lobby to the restroom. Maggie opened the door. A woman washed her hands at the sink. A quick check of the rest of the ladies' room showed no one. They waited for the woman to leave before Maggie and Henry entered.

"Which stall?"

Maggie pointed to the second from the right. She retrieved all the items that spilled from her purse as Henry pushed the stall door open and studied the space. He sunk to his knees, checking around the toilet. He reached his hands around it, feeling blindly near the back. He rose to standing, pulling the lid from the tank.

"Anything?" Maggie called in.

Henry replaced the lid. "Nope, nothing. Whatever she was after, she got it."

Maggie sighed, and they retreated from the ladies' room. She dragged the pair back to the security office. Several guards were already discussing the strange incident. Maggie burst through the doors. "We need to review your security footage of the main lobby from the last thirty minutes," she demanded.

The stunned guard manning the CCTV cameras glanced around the room before turning his attention to the monitor in front of him to retrieve the requested files. Henry shot Maggie a glance. "What?" she questioned.

"Nothing, just… you sure you weren't a cop before?"

Maggie chuckled. "No, just a fast learner."

"All right, here we go," the guard said as the footage on his screen sped backward. It slowed to a stop, reversing course and playing at a normal speed. They waited for a few moments as visitors strolled through the lobby.

Maggie spotted Henry, Charlie and herself appear on the top of the screen. "There we are," Maggie pointed out. "Oh, hmm."

"What is it, Maggie? Do you see something?" Henry questioned. He squinted at the screen for a breath, then glanced to Maggie.

"I'm not loving the way this dress looks on me from this angle," Maggie noted.

Henry clicked his tongue at her. "Go forward a minute or two," Henry instructed the guard.

The guard accelerated the video. People sped across the lobby. Maggie's form raced toward the restroom. "Okay, okay, slow down," Maggie instructed. "The woman came in the bathroom not long after I went in." She leaned closer to the screen and studied it.

Maggie's past self disappeared into the ladies' room. She stared at the restroom door. Within two minutes, another woman pushed through the door. "There!" Maggie exclaimed. "There she is!"

The brunette appeared outside the ladies' room. She wore sunglasses, her long hair obscuring her face as it had when Maggie encountered her.

"So bizarre!" Maggie exclaimed.

"Yes," Henry agreed. "Her behavior is bizarre. I'm surprised I didn't pick up on it when she passed us."

"Oh," Maggie corrected. "I meant her outfit. It's just… no one wears those shoes with…" She glanced at her male colleagues. "Never mind. Go forward a minute or so."

The guard pushed the video forward. When it returned to normal speed, the restroom door burst open. Maggie viewed the replay of events on the screen. The guard switched the view to the camera covering the parking lot. Maggie gasped in horror as she witnessed the car speed toward her before Henry knocked her out of its path.

"Go back," Charlie instructed after they viewed the entire episode. The guard rewound the footage. "Freeze there!" Charlie commanded. The camera froze as the woman turned to face it before entering the ladies' room. "All right, let's cross reference that with all the guests from the footage before the power outage and see if we've got a match."

"Huh?" the guard questioned, spinning in his chair to offer Charlie a confused stare.

Charlie rolled his eyes. "Move," he directed. He shooed the man from his chair and collapsed into it. He clacked around on the keyboard before pulling his laptop from his backpack.

"What are you doing?" the guard questioned.

"Sending the footage to my laptop so I can analyze it."

"I'm not sure I can let you do that," the guard interjected.

Charlie waved at him as though his opinion was inconsequential.

"Don't worry, mate. We've got the authority. If you have any questions, you can talk to Agent Frank Thomas of the FBI." Henry handed him the card.

"Okay, done," Charlie said, slamming his laptop closed.

"And?" Maggie asked.

"My program is working its magic. Checking every woman at that party against this one. It'll take a few hours to run. In the meantime, I believe you promised me some pizza, chicky!"

CHAPTER 5

Maggie tossed her napkin onto her empty plate and took another sip of her soda. She gathered the empty dishes from the table, delivering them over the kitchen bar and into her sink. "So, how did you like the deep dish?" Maggie inquired of Charlie.

"That is one hearty pizza, chicky," Charlie admitted, patting his belly.

"It's too bad Piper couldn't join us," Maggie answered.

"Yeah," Charlie agreed. "I mean because of the free pizza."

"Sure you did," Maggie replied with a chuckle as she plopped back down in her chair. She sunk her head into her palm with a sigh. "Isn't that program of yours finished yet?"

"Nope, not yet. It'll alert us when it's finished." Charlie glanced around the apartment. He rose from his chair, stalking around the room as he stretched. "Nice place you got here, chicky." He patted the couch. "Nice couch. Very firm. You know, if you're unnerved by what happened today, I'd be happy to sleep on the couch in case you need me." He wiggled his eyebrows at her.

Maggie shook her head at him. Same old Charlie, she

reflected. Before she responded, a loud rap beat filled the air. Maggie glanced around.

"What is that?" Henry questioned.

"Not sure," Maggie answered, glancing under the table.

Charlie raced back to the table. He slid his laptop from his backpack. The music grew louder as he plopped it on the table and pulled it open. "Program's complete," he announced. He clacked around on the keyboard. The music ceased.

"And?" Maggie inquired. She leapt from her chair and hurried around the table, peering over Charlie's shoulder. Henry joined her, squinting at the screen over Charlie's other shoulder.

A large text box stared back at them with bold white letters announcing the result of the program's search. NO RESULTS FOUND, the screen read.

"No results found! Ugh, are you kidding me?" Maggie groaned. She returned to her chair and collapsed into it. "Stuck AGAIN!"

Henry crossed to his chair and sunk into it. Charlie frowned at his screen while he typed furiously.

"Could your program have made a mistake?" Maggie questioned.

Charlie shot her a glance over the laptop's screen. "Okay, sorry!" Maggie said, holding her hands up in defeat. "Just asking!"

"Would the sunglasses prevent an ID?" Henry asked Charlie.

"Maybe in some programs, but not mine. My program compares over five hundred different variables. While the sunglasses didn't help, they would not prevent a match from showing up. This woman was not at the VIP party."

Maggie sighed, her lips forming into a pout. She leapt from her chair, pacing the floor. After a moment, she flung her arms out. "Maybe the woman had nothing to do with the theft," she suggested.

Henry mulled it over for a moment. He drew in a deep breath, raising his eyebrows. "Perhaps you're right," he admitted.

"No, I'm not right," Maggie countered.

A puzzled expression crossed Henry's face. "No, right, you're right about being wrong."

"It fits, right?" Maggie asked, then continued speaking, answering her own question. "She steals the ankh, she ditches it in the ladies' room and comes back for it the next day. The ankh was not found on anyone leaving the party because she hid it until she could retrieve it when there was less heat on her."

"It seems reasonable," Henry agreed.

"There's only one problem with that theory," Charlie argued. He spun the laptop around to face them, pointing at the screen. "The woman was not at the VIP party."

"Ugh!" Maggie shrieked. "We've got nothing! Uncle Ollie texted me earlier. He's found nothing about the other two pieces! No suspicious characters on the guest list. No matches on the suspicious lady from today."

"Got to find a new angle to work," Henry stated.

"WHAT angle?" Maggie huffed.

Henry took a deep breath. "That's the million-dollar question, princess."

Silence filled the room. Maggie dropped into her chair, a frown on her face. "I have a headache," she moaned.

"Don't sweat it, princess. We'll figure something out. For now, I think we all need some rest." Henry rose and kissed the top of Maggie's head. "See you in the morning."

Maggie grabbed his hand, squeezing it before she smiled up at him. "Good night," she responded.

Henry glanced at Charlie. "Well?" he asked.

"Oh!" Charlie exclaimed, stiffening in his chair. He closed his laptop, stowing it in his backpack. "Sorry, mate, I wasn't sure if the lady preferred me to stay. She never answered earlier."

Maggie rolled her eyes at him. "The lady is just fine on her own, thanks."

"If you insist," Charlie responded. He stood, shrugging his backpack onto both shoulders. "But should you need me in the middle of the night…"

"Good night, Charlie," Maggie interrupted him.

Maggie saw them out, closing and locking the door behind them. She slumped against it, heaving a sigh. Maggie shuffled to the couch and threw herself on it. She flung her arm across her eyes, shutting the world out.

She could have died today. The words rattled through her brain. Tears filled her eyes as she realized the enormity of what happened. She blinked them away. Perhaps she had made a mistake in joining her uncle's team. It sounded like an adventurous challenge when he proposed it. Fresh off the Cleopatra's tomb triumph, Maggie agreed. She had survived that escapade. She could handle anything. Now self-doubt filled her. Who was she kidding? She didn't have the skills for this. Her first mission was proving that with each passing moment.

Maggie uncovered her eyes and glanced around the room for her phone. She found it on her end table. With her text app toggled open, Maggie began and erased a text to Henry five times before she switched off her phone's display. She shook her head. No, she resolved, she wouldn't panic. Henry's last statement was correct. She needed sleep. She dragged herself to her bedroom for what she hoped would be a clarifying rest.

* * *

Maggie bolted upright in her bed. In the dark, she flailed wildly as she reached to turn her light on. Items spilled from her night table, clattering to the floor as she searched for her phone or the lamp, whichever she found first. Her hand struck the cold metal of her bedside light. She followed the lamp's body to the switch, flicking it on and filling the room with light.

Maggie squinted as the bright glow offended her eyes. With her eyes open a slit, she hunted for her phone. In her frantic blind search, she had knocked it onto the floor. She leaned over the side of the bed and snatched it.

Her hands shook as she scrolled through her contact list. She located Henry's number and tapped the phone icon to dial. The line rang as Maggie pressed the phone to her ear. "Come on, come on!" she urged under her breath.

On the third ring, Henry's voice greeted her. "Maggie? Are you all right? What happened?"

"Henry! Nothing, I'm fine. But I had an idea."

"What?" Henry mumbled. "What time is it?"

"Uh…" Maggie glanced at her clock. "Two forty-one."

Henry yawned. "Okay, let's get some sleep and talk about it in the morning."

"No!" Maggie exclaimed, jumping from her bed to stalk around her bedroom.

"Maggie, it's not even three in the morning. It can wait a few hours."

"Shh," Maggie shushed him. "Just listen."

Henry yawned again, then sighed. "All right, go ahead, princess."

"Okay. I was asleep. And I was dreaming. I was wandering around the museum, except it wasn't the museum it was like a museum mixed with a mall. I stopped outside a shoe store. They had this killer pair of heels in the window. They were fuchsia with a cute ankle strap, a rhinestone buckle and..."

Henry cut her off. "Maggie, I love you, but you can tell me about the shoes in the morning. What idea prompted a 3 a.m. call?"

Maggie sighed. "Right. Okay, anyway, in the dream, I remember recalling the woman that ran into me today. The one who nearly ran me over. Her shoes were so horrible. And with that skirt! I started to think about who would wear that kind of outfit. I mean, no one at the VIP party was THAT un-chic! I caught a reflection in the store's window. When I spun around, the woman was there, and she had a knife! She charged me, but I woke up and that's when it hit me!"

"What hit you?" Henry inquired.

"No woman from the VIP party would dress like that."

"O-okay?" Henry questioned. "And this warranted a middle of the night call?"

"Yes, because that person WAS at the VIP party! And I wanted to have Charlie start the facial recognition software so we have an answer in the morning."

"But you said..." Henry began.

"I said no WOMAN would dress like that. But it hit me when I woke up. That was no woman! That was a man!"

"A man?!" Henry responded, the pieces beginning to fall into place.

"Yes! A man! The outfit, the sunglasses, the hair obscuring the face, the way the person ran, how hard he knocked into me when he came out of the stall. It was a man. Charlie ran his software on the women's faces at the party. He excluded the men to expedite the search. He needs to run it on the men!"

"Ohhhhh," Henry answered. Maggie overheard the rustling of his covers. "Maggie, you are a genius!"

Maggie smiled to herself as she waited on the phone. "Hey, mate, wake up, wake up," Henry murmured on the other end of the line.

Maggie overheard Charlie. "Huh, what? What's going on? Did something happen?"

"Maggie's had a brilliant idea. You need to run your facial recognition program again."

"Ugh, go to sleep, mate. I ran it. My program is perfect. There was no match."

"Hey, hey, get up. You ran it on women only, right?"

"Yeah, so?"

"So… the idea came to Maggie that it wasn't a woman but a man. She wants you to run the program against the MEN at the party."

There was a momentary lapse in the conversation. "All right," Charlie agreed. "That her on the phone?"

"Yeah," Henry responded.

"Coulda called yourself, chicky, if you wanted to talk to me that bad," Charlie shouted.

Maggie rolled her eyes. "Just tell him to run it," Maggie told Henry.

"She's not impressed, mate," Henry replied.

"No?" Charlie responded. "She will be if this works," he promised. "It'll take a few hours though."

"Yeah, hence the three-in-the-morning call. She wants it done when she wakes up."

Maggie overheard the keyboard clacking, then Charlie said, "Done. Running."

"He's got it running, princess."

Maggie smiled again. "Good."

"Now get some sleep. I'll call you as soon as the search finishes."

"Okay," Maggie agreed. "I'll keep my fingers crossed we get a hit."

After saying their good nights, Maggie disconnected the call and climbed into bed. She switched off the light, relaxing back into her pillows. Maggie stared at the moonlit ceiling. She sighed, wondering if her idea would pay off.

* * *

Maggie checked her phone's display. No new messages awaited her. With a sigh, she set the phone down on the shop's counter. She tapped her foot on the floor. What was taking so long, she wondered? Charlie began the program in the wee hours of the morning. When Maggie arose at seven, she immediately checked her phone. It showed no missed calls, no messages. She called Henry over her morning coffee. No results yet, he told her.

Perhaps this was a fool's errand. Maybe there was nothing to her idea. Maggie paced the floor of her shop. The bell sounded as the front door opened. "Good morning!" Maggie called, spinning to greet her customer. "Oh."

Piper traipsed through the door. Her rainbow hair pulled into pigtails, she sported retro sunglasses, a contrast to her modern earbuds dangling from her ears. Something seemed different about her, Maggie contemplated.

Piper spotted Maggie and waved a to-go coffee cup at her.

"Thanks," Maggie said, meeting Piper at the counter. She popped the lid off, inhaling the strong scent of the coffee. Maggie enjoyed a sip as Piper stowed her stuff and took a sip of her own coffee.

Maggie stared at Piper over the rim of her cup as she took another sip. She lifted an eyebrow. Piper's makeup! Yes, she reflected. Still heavy and leaning toward goth, Piper's makeup was toned down. Her normally thick eyeliner was slimmed down to a thin line. She had replaced her black lipstick with a nude shade. What prompted this change, Maggie wondered?

A chime from her cell phone interrupted her thoughts. She snatched it from the counter and toggled on the display. She let out an annoyed sigh at the notification, announcing an email regarding a sale at a department store.

Piper glanced at Maggie. "Jumpy, huh? What's the matter? Have a fight with Henry?"

"No, I didn't have a fight with Henry," Maggie informed her. "I'm waiting on some information."

"Oh," Piper replied. She pulled a tray of jewelry out of the display case and began rearranging it. "So... how did your little pizza thing go last night?"

Piper avoided any eye contact with her. Maggie smirked at her. "It was fine. Too bad you couldn't come over."

"Yeah, well, I mean I was, like, busy," Piper responded, still avoiding Maggie's eyes.

"I'm surprised you're interested. Don't you hate my social life in general?"

Piper shrugged. "Just conversation."

"Uh-huh," Maggie answered. "Sure."

"What?" Piper questioned, finally raising her eyes to meet Maggie's.

Maggie leaned across the counter, a grin on her face. "Are you sure your interest isn't in a certain lanky, light-haired Brit?"

"What?!" Piper exclaimed. She guffawed. "Ah, what are you even saying? You're losing it, boss lady."

Piper grabbed a dust rag and raced to the nearest bookcase. Maggie spun to follow her. "Oh, come on! It's so obvious! The way you were staring at him yesterday. All that weird but flirty talk. The new make-up today, the interest in my pizza party. You like him! You like Charlie!"

"Uh, no!" Piper insisted, flitting away to another bookshelf.

Maggie followed. She crossed her arms, leaning against the shelf as Piper dusted. "Oh, really? Explain then."

"Explain what? There was no flirting. I slept in and ran out of time this morning. And I was just making conversation. Excuse me for being nice!"

"Uh-huh," Maggie said, grinning. "Not buying it. You like him!" She tapped Piper on the arm with the back of her hand. "You know, I could put in a good word for you."

Piper rolled her eyes. "Whatever."

Maggie's phone chimed from across the shop. As much as she wanted to continue the conversation with Piper, she raced to grab her phone. A message from Henry waited: *Got something!*

With shaky hands, Maggie pressed the phone icon to call Henry. He answered on the first ring. "Maggie, we got something," he announced.

"Yes!" Maggie exclaimed. "Got a match?"

"Yep, got a match on a male from the VIP party, just like you said. One James Michael Dean."

"James Michael Dean," Maggie repeated. "I don't know the name. Nor do I recall meeting him at the party."

"I'm trying to get more information on him now," Henry replied. "I sent his information over to Frank. Let's see what we can get on him."

"Okay, let me know as soon as you hear anything." Maggie disconnected the call after Henry promised to keep her informed.

"Who's James Michael Dean?" Piper questioned, popping up behind Maggie.

"Ugh, lurk much?" she answered. "Someone from the party, that's all."

"Is this connected to the robbery thing?"

"Yeah," Maggie answered, typing on her phone.

"I still don't get why the police asked to talk to you about it."

Maggie shrugged as she scrolled through her phone. "Figured we knew something about the missing item since we found it, I guess, I dunno." Maggie frowned at her phone. A quick internet search of the name James Michael Dean returned nothing of interest.

"Really? They seem pretty persistent."

"They only asked once!" Maggie responded.

"Uh," Piper disagreed. "No."

"Huh?" Maggie glanced to Piper, her focus finally leaving her phone's display. Piper pursed her lips, pointing behind Maggie. Maggie spun around, finding Detective Russo standing behind her. She had been so preoccupied with her phone, the door's ringing bell had not even registered in her brain when the door opened. "Oh! Detective Russo! I didn't even hear you come in."

"Gio, please," he said with a smile. "Do you have a minute to discuss something privately?"

"Sure," Maggie answered. "We could take a walk. I was just about to head out to pick up some lunch!"

After confirming Piper's lunch preference, Maggie grabbed her purse and departed with the detective through the front door.

"So, what brought you by?" Maggie inquired as they strolled down the sidewalk.

"Following up on a few loose ends on that robbery," Gio admitted.

"Correct me if I'm wrong, but isn't the case no longer under your jurisdiction?"

Gio shrugged. "Jurisdiction is always a subjective matter. I find it's best to continue investigating in the event the case comes back across our desks."

"Ah, I see," Maggie noted. "So, what can I help with?"

"Well, perhaps you can tell me if you came across anything since the party. You seemed pretty tight with the fed. I'm just curious."

Maggie considered her response. "Not really," she hedged.

"Not really? That's a surprise."

"Is it?" Maggie questioned as they approached the café she planned to order from.

"Yeah. Well, I mean, I heard about the incident at the museum yesterday. Heard you nearly got run down by some crazed patron."

"That's a bit of an exaggeration."

"That's not what the cameras said," Gio answered.

Maggie shrugged. "It was unrelated. Some woman took exception to me asking if she was okay in the ladies' room. She knocked me down, and I ran after her. I very stupidly stood in the road while scanning the area for her. There's really nothing to it."

Gio guffawed. "Nothing to it, huh?"

"Nope," Maggie answered.

He smiled at her. "What is that pretty face hiding, Ms. Edwards?"

"Hunger," Maggie answered. "Listen, sorry, I can't help you much more, but I don't have any information. Now, if that's all, I'd like to grab my salads and get back to the shop."

"Yeah, yeah, that's all… for now. You take care, Ms. Edwards. Watch out for those crazy museum visitors." He flashed another smile before backing away.

"Will do," Maggie assured him. She turned back to the café's entrance with a sigh. She shook her head at the strange conversation and made her way inside to order.

With her order in hand, Maggie juggled all the items. She bought lunch for four, planning on Henry and Charlie stopping at the shop to discuss the results of the ID match. The large drinks overwhelmed the flimsy drink carrier, making it hard for Maggie to manage along with her purse and the bag containing their food.

Maggie struggled to steady the container as she stepped outside. She set them on one of the café's outside tables and slipped her sunglasses on, shielding out the bright sunlight. Grasping the drink carrier with both hands, Maggie spun to begin her journey to the shop. As she whirled, she failed to spot someone next to her. The passerby clipped the edge of the drink carrier, toppling it into Maggie. Cold iced tea sloshed backward, drenching Maggie's dress and filling her sandals. The drinks spilled across the sidewalk, leaving a trail of ice and amber liquid.

"Ugh!" Maggie exclaimed. Her face incredulous, she stared after the man who ran into her. "Hey!" she called after him. He ignored her, continuing down the sidewalk. "Yeah, just keep walking, you jerk!"

This elicited a slight response. The man glanced back at her. His chiseled features remained expressionless as he continued moving away from her. Light-brown stubble covered the bottom half of his face, making his piercing blue eyes even more blue. Maggie threw her hands in the air at him as he turned away.

She grabbed a few napkins from her bag, trying her best to clean her dress and shoes. She glared in the direction of the stranger who caused her trouble. Her eyes narrowed. Her lips set in a pout. She continued drying her dress as she watched him climb into an ostentatious red sports car. Typical, Maggie speculated, must be making up for some deficiency.

Maggie balled up the wet napkins, tossing them on what

remained of the drink carrier. She gathered the half-empty drinks and discarded everything in the nearby trash can. She didn't bother refilling them. They could do without. Instead, she returned to her shop before any other tragedies befell her.

* * *

Maggie pushed through the door into the shop. "Lunch!" she called. "And listen, there're no drinks because some jerk ran into me and spilled them all over me, so I had to ditch them."

Henry greeted her with a kiss on the cheek and relieved her of the bag containing their food. "Ah, thank you!" Maggie said. "My arm is almost numb! Where's Piper? And Charlie?"

"Back room," Henry answered as he pulled food containers from the bag. "Discussing some inventory system."

"What?" Maggie questioned, finally taking stock of her damp dress.

"Yeah, I dunno, something about Piper rearranging the stock room and Charlie said he could help her with a program to keep inventory straight. They disappeared back there about ten minutes ago to discuss it."

"Ohhhhh," Maggie answered with a wink.

"Oh, what?" Henry inquired.

Maggie leaned across the counter and whispered, "I think she's sweet on him."

Henry raised his eyebrows. "I think he's sweet on her," he whispered back.

Maggie and Henry giggled together, sorting through the food as Charlie and Piper emerged from the stock room. "What are you two laughing about?" Piper asked.

"Nothing," Maggie answered. "Here's your salad."

"No drink?" Piper questioned.

Maggie shot her a glance. "I'm wearing what's left of your drink," Maggie said, flashing her a shot of her wet front.

Piper made a disgusted face, opting for water. "I guess your drink is gone, too," she said to Charlie. "Can I make you a coffee or something?"

"Uh," Charlie hesitated. "I can pop 'round to a shop if there's one close. Grab a soda and whatever you'd like?" He directed the question toward Piper.

"Oh, why thank you, kind sir!" Piper answered. Maggie wrinkled her eyebrows. "Why don't I come with you? The directions to the nearest convenience store are tricky. Wouldn't want you getting lost!"

"Lead the way, Piper Brooks, Assistant to the Stars!" Charlie answered with a grin.

The two disappeared through the shop's front door. "Isn't the nearest convenience store on the corner?" Henry queried. He thumbed in the direction of the nearest corner.

"Yep," Maggie answered. "Four doors down and across the street. Tricky, tricky." Maggie chuckled as she popped open her salad container, drizzling ranch dressing over it. "So, Charlie got a match, huh?"

"He did!" Henry answered. "Great call on checking the men, princess."

"So, what's this guy look like? I didn't remember his name, but maybe I met him and don't remember."

Henry glanced around. "Damn! Charlie took the laptop with him. We've got a photo of him from the party. We'll have to wait until they get back."

"Anything from Frank?"

"Nothing yet, though I'm sure that name's an alias."

"Maybe facial recognition will give us his real name," Maggie suggested. "Or at least some information on him."

Piper and Charlie returned with drinks in hand. "Got you

an iced tea, boss lady," Piper said, shoving a bottle toward Maggie.

"Thanks!" Maggie answered. "Gosh, it's a good thing you were here to show Charlie the way. He'd never had made it on his own."

Piper shot Maggie a glance as Charlie answered. "It certainly was faster finding and navigating to it, thanks to the awesome Piper." He grinned at her. Color rose in Piper's pale cheeks and she grinned back.

Maggie raised her eyebrow at them before glancing at Henry who shrugged. "Umm, hey, Piper, while you were rooting around in the storeroom, did you happen to see any straws?"

Piper still smiled at Charlie. "Piper?" Maggie questioned. Piper seemed oblivious. "Piper!" Maggie shouted.

"Huh?" Piper answered.

"I said did you see any straws in the back?"

"Oh, umm, yeah, I think so," Piper replied.

"Would you mind getting one?"

"Are your legs broken?"

Maggie frowned at her. "No, but I have no idea where they are. You 'rearranged' everything, remember?"

"Oh, right. Yeah, okay, fine, I'll get one."

"Thank you." Maggie followed Piper's departure across the room with her eyes. Once she disappeared into the storage area, Maggie spun to face Charlie. "I didn't want to ask in front of Piper, but can I see the man your program IDed?"

"Sure, chicky," Charlie answered. "Though why all the secrecy?" He lifted his laptop from his backpack.

"I didn't want Piper asking questions. She doesn't exactly know the role we all play with our employer."

Charlie popped the laptop open on the counter. "Sure, sure," he answered.

"What?"

Charlie shrugged as he banged on the keys. "Just seems like you wanted my attention all to yourself." He wiggled his eyebrows at her.

Maggie pursed her lips at him. "Just show me the guy."

"Sure thing, chicky." Charlie pulled up his program and tapped around on the keyboard. The picture of the "woman" who attacked Maggie in the ladies' room appeared. Next to it, the picture of a man in a tuxedo. "Here he is. I give you James Michael Dean."

Charlie turned the laptop to face Maggie. Her jaw fell open as she stared at the picture. "Any hits on that face through the database you were searching?" Henry queried.

"Ah…" Charlie pulled the laptop back toward him, clacking on the keyboard. "Nope, nothing yet."

Henry sighed. "So, we've still got nothing. James Michael Dean is probably long gone, and we've got no leads."

Maggie recovered her voice. "He's not long gone."

"What?" Henry asked.

"It's likely he is, chicky. If it was me, I'd be long gone."

"He's not gone," Maggie insisted. "I just saw that man not an hour ago! He's the one who spilled the drinks all over me!"

CHAPTER 6

Henry leapt from his chair at Maggie's admission. "Maggie, are you sure?"

"Here you go, boss lady!" Piper called, waving a straw in the air. Charlie slammed his laptop shut. Piper glanced around at them. "Why is everyone acting so strange?"

"Strange?" Maggie said with a nervous chuckle. "What do you mean?"

Piper frowned at them. "Uh, yeah... strange. What's the big secret? Everyone stopped talking when I walked in."

"Oh," Maggie fibbed. "We were just talking about you, no big deal." She shrugged it off with a chuckle. She reached out to snatch the straw from Piper when Henry knocked it from Piper's hand.

"Oops," he said.

"Seriously, dude? What the hell?"

"Can't use that one, Maggie. It's been on the floor, it's all dirty. Come on, let's go find another." He started toward the backroom. Maggie followed him.

Piper gawked at them. "I can't even with you two."

Henry pulled Maggie through the door into her storeroom. "Are you sure, Maggie?"

"Yes, I'm positive. I wouldn't forget that face." Henry wrinkled his nose at her. "Not like that. He looks like a Class A jerk! Total narcissist! Even had the tricked-out sports car to prove it."

"Oh, right," Henry replied. "You spotted his car?"

"Yep! He is definitely still in town."

Henry frowned, placing his hands on his hips. He remained silent for a moment.

"Why the long face?" Maggie inquired. "This is just the break we need!"

"Why is he hanging around? Like Charlie said, if it were anyone else, they'd be long gone."

"Perhaps he's waiting for his buyer or contact or whoever he stole the ankh for to give him his next steps."

"Hmm. Doesn't add up," Henry contemplated aloud as the door to the storeroom popped open.

Charlie pushed open the door, peeking inside. "Was it him?" he inquired.

"Yes," Maggie and Henry answered together.

Charlie slipped inside and closed the door behind her. "According to Maggie, he's definitely still here," Henry confirmed. "But why?"

Charlie shrugged. "No idea, must be some reason though."

"It doesn't matter why he's here. This gives us a chance to find him!" Maggie exclaimed in a hushed tone.

"Don't get too excited, princess. We realize he's here, but it doesn't help us find him."

"Well," Maggie countered, her brow furrowed in thought, "I've seen his car, so we could check the local hotels for it." Maggie raised her eyebrows. "Oh! We could check city CCTV! Charlie, can you hack into the town's system?"

A sly grin crossed Charlie's face. "Chicky," he responded, "is the sky blue?"

"Good, get on that," Maggie ordered. She glanced at the storeroom door. "What'd you tell Piper about coming back here?"

"Told her I wanted to interrupt any romantic liaisons that might be occurring. She was fully supportive of the move."

"I'll bet," Maggie groaned. "We better get back out there."

"All right," Henry agreed. "Get on that search for this character as soon as we get back to my place."

"Will do, boss man," Charlie answered as he pulled the door open to the shop. "I found them!" he called to Piper. "Hanky-panky plans have been subverted!"

Maggie rolled her eyes, following him into the shop.

* * *

"Hey, Piper! I'm heading out!" Maggie called across the shop.

"Is it five already?" Piper questioned, glancing at her phone.

"Just after! I'm actually running late," Maggie informed her.

"So, what else is new?" Piper murmured.

Maggie shot her a look with narrowed eyes and pursed lips. "If you need anything, just call or text. Hey, don't forget to re-shelve those books on the cart. Have a good night!"

"Yeah, yeah, yeah. I'm all over it, boss lady."

Maggie grinned at her as she slung her purse over her shoulder and darted out the front door. The warm evening air greeted her. She glanced up at the clear, dusky sky. Despite running late, Maggie savored her walk to her apartment building, enjoying the evening.

When she reached her building, she headed for her car

instead of the building's front door. Maggie tossed her purse into the passenger's seat as she slid in behind the wheel. She fired the engine and sent a quick text to Ollie before pulling from her spot: *Running late, sorry! Be there soon!*

Maggie eased out of her parking space and onto the road. She aimed her car for the neighboring town of Aberdeen. She navigated to the outskirts of town, finding her uncle's Craftsman style home with its perfect lawn. She pulled into the driveway, hopped from the car and hurried up the walk.

Ollie waited for her on his porch. "Sorry!" Maggie called, "I lost track of the time."

"No problem, Maggie," Ollie answered as he stood from his porch swing. "I started dinner fifteen minutes late to accommodate for the inevitable."

"I'm not ALWAYS late," Maggie countered as she approached him. Ollie shot her a questioning glance. "What? There has been a time or two when I've been on time!"

Ollie chuckled as he held the door open for her. Once they were settled on the back patio, Ollie poured two glasses of wine and handed one to Maggie. She sipped it as he tossed the salad with dressing. "So, any luck on the search for the other two ankhs?"

"Possibly, yes," Ollie answered.

"That sounds intriguing," Maggie responded.

Ollie shook his head as he flipped the steaks on the grill. "It's not much of a lead, but at least I've made some progress. Though I have no idea if it will pan out." He sighed. "Too much is uncertain."

"Run it by me. We'll poke it full of holes and learn from it," Maggie said, using a quote she'd heard from Ollie on multiple occasions throughout her life.

Ollie smiled over the grill at Maggie. "You learn well, grasshopper," he said with a chuckle.

"I had the best teacher," Maggie quipped.

Ollie plated the steaks and grilled vegetables and delivered them to the patio table. "I'm starting to wonder about that," Ollie said.

"Come on, Uncle Ollie! What kind of attitude is that?"

"An honest one. This one's got me beat! There's so little information."

"There wasn't much information on the Golden Scarab of Cleopatra either, but you found that!"

"After a lifetime of searching, Maggie," Ollie reminded her.

"Well, now you have my help. So, let's hear it. Where are these two other ankhs?"

Ollie shrugged as he cut into his steak. "Well, we have Cleopatra's accounted for, which means the other two belonged to Julius Caesar and Marc Antony."

"Right," Maggie interjected.

"It's widely believed Marc Antony was buried with Cleopatra. The two did commit suicide, you recall," Ollie mentioned, raising his eyebrows at Maggie.

"Yes, I did my research. He stabbed himself with a sword, believing Cleopatra was already dead. Though she wasn't. It was too late. His friends took him to Cleopatra, and he died in her arms. She poisoned herself days later," Maggie noted.

"Correct," Ollie said with a smile.

"It's kind of a romantic story," Maggie admitted.

Ollie rolled her eyes at Maggie. "Oh, please. It's no Romeo and Juliet."

"I know, I know. There was a lot more going on," Maggie said, waving her hand at him. "Anyway, continue."

"Okay, so Antony is buried with Cleopatra. Meaning there should have been TWO ankhs in that tomb."

"But you found no evidence of Antony in the tomb. No belongings, no sarcophagus, nothing."

Ollie nodded. "Right, the ankh should be there. So should

Antony's remains, but... nada! The first dead end." Maggie chuckled. "What?"

"Dead end... it's just funny."

Ollie pursed his lips at her. "No pun intended."

"Okay, okay, so Antony's ankh is probably buried with him. And we believe he was buried with Cleopatra, but we didn't find anything. So, we missed something at the tomb, perhaps?"

Ollie considered it. "It's the best place to begin searching. We have no other information about the whereabouts. We've got to go over that tomb with a fine-tooth comb. We must have missed something! Perhaps in my excitement to catalog the tomb's contents, I overlooked a clue."

"Sounds like a plan. Now what about the other ankh? Caesar's?"

"That's where things go from bad to worse, I'm afraid," Ollie lamented. "Julius Caesar's burial site is well known. Of course, it's no longer intact, but there is no secret or mystery about his final resting place."

"Great! How is this bad news?" Maggie questioned.

"I've scoured every resource I could find. None mention the ankh amongst his belongings."

"It's not listed anywhere?"

"Not that I could find," Ollie admitted with a frustrated sigh.

Maggie narrowed her eyes at him. "You said you had a lead. Small, but a lead. So, let's hear it."

"I can never slip anything by you, Maggie," Ollie said with a wag of his finger. Maggie grinned at him. "All right. I tracked down every resource about any displays of Caesar's belongings."

"And?"

"I found an obscure reference to a stone cross, currently being housed in storage at the Natural History Museum in

London." Ollie produced a folded piece of paper from his journal on the table. He pointed to a specific line on an item list from the museum.

"Stone Cross—Tan," Maggie read aloud. "That does sound promising!"

"I wish I shared your enthusiasm," Ollie replied. "Even if that obscure reference is to the ankh, not a stone cross, we'd need a plan to gain access to it."

"Can't you just ask nicely? You are the world-renowned Dr. Oliver Keene," Maggie said with a giggle.

"Also, the infamous Dr. Oliver Keene, associated with disappearing artifacts," Ollie joked.

"Good point. We don't have the best track record, do we?"

"That's putting it mildly," Ollie retorted with a chuckle.

"Well, at least we've got a start. Oh! I was so interested in your news, I didn't tell you ours!"

"You found Cleopatra's ankh?" Ollie asked, a hopeful tone in his voice.

"Well, close!" Maggie answered. "Charlie ran a search on the 'woman' from the ladies' room against all the VIP guests at the party."

"Yeah, I heard. No matches."

Maggie gave him a wry glance. "No matches when compared to the ladies at the party." She raised an eyebrow.

Ollie's eyes shot from side-to-side. "Okay?"

"Remember I mentioned how terribly the lady was dressed?"

"I do. Her taste in clothing seemed inconsequential, though I wasn't surprised you mentioned it. You always were quite the fashionista."

"That's where you're wrong. Her fashion choices were NOT inconsequential. I don't know why I didn't consider it before. But no respectable woman would have dressed in that get-up. Then it hit me in the middle of the night. That was no woman!

"I had Charlie re-run his software. This time matching the 'woman's' face to men at the VIP party."

"And?" Ollie asked, his voice filling with hope.

"And we got a match!"

"Any info available on the guy?"

"Doesn't seem to be. Guest list identified him as James Michael Dean. Who basically doesn't exist."

"Aw, shucks," Ollie lamented.

"But there's more!" Maggie exclaimed. Ollie raised his eyebrows, prompting her to continue. "I ran into this guy today. The jerk spilled a few iced teas all over me. So, he's still in town! We can still find him!"

Ollie screwed up his face. "Strange he's still in town."

"Henry said the same. You two are stick in the muds. I consider it a lucky break!"

* * *

MAGGIE CHECKED her phone as she slid under the covers. No messages awaited her. She sent a text to Henry as she pulled the comforter higher around her: *Anything yet?*

Henry answered within seconds: *Nothing yet, princess. Heading to bed?*

Maggie responded: *Yep. Tell Charlie to hurry up with his magic. I expect results in the morning!*

Maggie's phone chirped, indicating Henry's response: *He promises you will not be disappointed*

Maggie smiled at the screen as she read the message before powering off her display. She set the phone on her night table and switched off the light.

* * *

Maggie grabbed the book Piper retrieved from the storeroom. "Here's the book you were looking for," Maggie said to her customer.

"Ah!" the woman responded. "Yes, that's it! Thank you so much! My daughter will be so pleased I found a copy!"

"If that's everything, Piper can ring you out right over there." Maggie pointed at the cash register.

"Yes, that's all, thank you!"

"You're very welcome and thanks for stopping into *Maggie's Books and Baubles!*"

Maggie stalked a few steps away, pulling her phone from the waistband of her skirt. She checked her messages for the umpteenth time. Her display showed no new information. Maggie sighed, her shoulders sagging with disappointment.

She had eagerly awaited a message this morning from Henry, some news about locating the man they sought. So far, no luck. After Maggie checked in with Henry, she learned they had found nothing thus far. No clues led them to his location.

A steady stream of customers kept her from checking her messages for most of the morning. As the lunch hour approached, she expected to have something waiting. Instead, no messages met her when she checked.

This coupled with Ollie's lack of leads put Maggie in a sour mood. She slogged through her shop, tidying books. She shoved them back on each shelf, taking her frustration out with each book she slammed into place.

The front door's bell chimed as the latest customer departed from the shop.

"Whew!" Piper called. "What a morning!"

"Yeah," Maggie shouted.

"You got all those books taken care of, or do I need to head back?"

"Got 'em!" Maggie hollered.

"Cool. Ugh," Piper exclaimed as Maggie heard her plop onto the stool behind the counter. "Whatever you're doing to drive traffic to the store, please stop. I enjoyed this place when it was quieter."

"It's probably the museum story in the papers. Curiosity seekers," Maggie yelled.

"Yeah, speaking of, why are the cops so interested in you with that?"

"No particular reason," Maggie called, retreating further into the bookshelves. "I think Gio just likes a pretty face."

"Wow, humble, aren't we?" Piper shot back. "And Gio? On a first name basis with the cop, huh?"

Maggie rolled her eyes. "Hey, I saw that," Piper said, appearing at the end of the aisle and grabbing a stack of books from Maggie.

"You put way too much time into dissecting my personal life," Maggie commented. "You should spend more time analyzing your own. You might find a witty Brit at the heart of it then."

"Will you quit with that already? There's absolutely nothing going on between me and Charlie."

"Oh, isn't there? Miss 'I had to walk him to the shop that's just down the street?'"

"He's British, I was afraid he'd get lost. Walk on the wrong side of the street or something."

"Uh-huh, right. Come on, admit it. You think he's cute."

Piper attempted to side-step around Maggie and avoid the question. Maggie blocked her, staring her right in the eyes. She raised an eyebrow at her, her lips curling into a smile at the corners. Piper stared at her a moment.

The front door's bell rang. "Gotta go!" Piper sang, spinning and dashing toward the front.

"Saved by the bell," Maggie noted as she finished the shelving. Maggie heard a man's voice conversing with Piper.

She started toward the front of the shop when her phone rang. She checked the display. It showed Henry's name. Maggie swiped to answer it.

"Well?" she demanded.

"Hello to you, too, princess," Henry answered. "And how is your day going?"

Maggie chuckled. "Hi. It's going just fine. It would be going better if you told me we had a lead. So, are you going to make my day or what?"

"It's a good thing I specialize in making your dreams come true." A smile crossed Maggie's face. She heard a shout in the background. "Was that Charlie? What's he saying?"

"Yep. He's telling me HE made your dreams come true, not me."

"I'll consider it a joint effort. So, what do you have?"

"Charlie's sleuthing caught our man in the area of North Street. A quick perusal of a map shows about five hotels scattered around the area. We're heading there now to take a peek. If we're lucky, we'll find that ostentatious sports car parked outside one of them."

"That sounds promising. Tell Charlie I owe him a big kiss."

"Hey!" Henry objected.

Maggie chuckled. "Just kidding. But tell him great work! Good luck with the search. Keep me informed! I'd come with you, but Piper and I are slammed at the shop."

"No problem, princess. I've got it covered. I'll keep you updated."

They said their goodbyes and Maggie ended the call. The smile remained on her face as she stalked toward the shopfront. She no longer heard voices. Piper must have handled the customer.

Maggie rounded the corner of one of the shelves, stepping into the open area near the shop's front. Piper stood in the middle of the space. Worry creased her face, and she wrung her hands.

"What's wrong?" Maggie inquired, finding Piper's reaction odd. Piper didn't respond. "Piper, what is it?"

Piper's eyes shifted, focusing just over Maggie's shoulder. Maggie began to swivel her head when her blood went cold. She swallowed hard as she felt the barrel of a pistol push against her spine. Instinctively, she raised her hands in the air. Her heart pounded in her chest and her pulse quickened.

"That's right, nice and slow. And I'll take that phone," a man's voice informed her as he tugged the cell phone from her hand.

"Money's in the register," Maggie choked out. "And let my assistant go, she doesn't need to be involved."

"I'm not here for the money, Ms. Edwards," the voice answered.

Maggie's brow furrowed. The man shoved her roughly toward the cashier's counter. "I want to know what you know about the location of the other two ankhs."

"What?" Maggie questioned as she stumbled to the counter. She spun to face him, grasping the counter behind her. She recognized James Michael Dean. Before he could speak again, she grasped Piper's arm, pulling her back and shoving Piper behind her.

"The ankhs, Ms. Edwards. I want the locations of the other two."

"I don't... I don't have the locations!" Maggie cried.

The man shoved his hand forward, leveling the gun at Maggie. "I don't buy that story," he growled.

"I don't!" Maggie insisted.

The man cocked the gun. "I'm going to ask you one more time."

Maggie breathed raggedly as her mind raced for a solution. She swallowed hard again, holding her hand out in front of her. "Okay, okay, wait," she breathed. "I don't know the locations of the ankhs, but I may have a lead for you. My uncle may have learned something about their location. M-Maybe he can help."

"The renowned Dr. Keene? Yes, Ms. Edwards, I expect he can. In fact, I expect he already did!"

"All right," Maggie stalled. "So, let's call him and…"

"Tell me what he told you!" the man insisted.

"He didn't tell me anything!" Maggie shouted.

The man raised his eyebrows at her. "You had dinner with him last night. He didn't tell you then? Come on, Ms. Edwards, I find that hard to fathom."

Maggie shook her head. Her mind spotted a temporary solution, and she took it. "No. No, I didn't have dinner with him last night," she lied.

"You're lying!"

"I'm not! I'm not. I can prove it." The man narrowed his eyes at her. "Check my phone," Maggie exclaimed, pointing with a shaky hand. "Check it. The code is 1753. Check the texts. You'll see, I told him I was running late. And then check the call log. I called him and we rescheduled. For tonight, actually! So, I haven't spoken with my uncle about anything."

The man squinted at Maggie before swiping through her phone. He fiddled on it for a few moments before he toggled off the display. He narrowed his eyes further at her. "See?" Maggie questioned. "I could call…"

"No!" the man roared. "No calls." His lips twisted into a gruesome smirk. "Let's pay dear Uncle Ollie a visit, Ms. Edwards."

CHAPTER 7

Maggie swallowed hard, fighting back tears as she flipped the shop's sign to closed and pushed the door shut. She turned the deadbolt, locking the door. Maggie crossed to the cashier's counter to retrieve her purse. "Uh-uh-uhhh," the man said.

"I need my purse. It has my keys! Unless you're proposing we walk to Aberdeen? Or maybe you're planning on taking that swanky sports car?"

The man smirked at her. "No, we'll take your car. But I'll handle the bag. I don't want any surprises." The man shooed Maggie and Piper from the counter, grabbing hold of Maggie's purse from the cabinet underneath it. "Where are the keys?"

"Middle pocket," Maggie directed. The man reached inside the purse. "No, no, the other middle. On the left. No…" Maggie sighed. "It would be easier if you let me get them."

The man grumbled but waved Maggie over with his gun. He pulled the purse away from her as she approached. "Don't do anything stupid," he warned.

Maggie nodded in response and reached into her purse. She withdrew her keys, dangling them in front of the man. The man's mouth curled into a smile. Palming them, Maggie pressed a button on her key chain, exposing a small but sharp blade. She swung it at the man, slicing his shoulder. He cried out in pain but managed to block her second swing.

He caught her arm mid-swing and twisted it behind her. Pain shot through her wrist. "Drop 'em," the man growled in her ear.

With a defeated cry, Maggie dropped the keys. The man snatched them from the floor, ripping off the key chain and tossing it to the ground. It clattered across the floor and out of Maggie's reach. Maggie choked back a sob. The man shoved the keys toward her. "The next time I won't be as generous. Now, let's try this again."

Maggie grimaced at him, plucking the keys from his hand. She wiped at a rogue tear that had fallen onto her cheek during the struggle. "My car's out back," she choked out.

The man shimmied the gun in the direction of the shop's rear. Maggie stalked across the shop. "You too, Rainbow Brite," he growled, signaling for Piper to follow Maggie.

Piper sniffled; her arms crossed tightly over her chest. Maggie put her arm around Piper's shoulders, drawing her close as they proceeded to the shop's rear entrance. "Stick close to me," she whispered. "We'll be okay."

Piper nodded without responding verbally. Maggie felt her tremble as they reached the back door. Bright sunlight streamed in as Maggie swung the door open. They descended the stairs and Maggie slid into the driver's seat of her sedan. Piper crossed to the passenger side, but the man waved her back. "No, you're in the back seat with me."

He shoved Piper into the rear of the car and climbed in behind her. He wrapped his arm around her shoulders and pressed the gun into her ribs. "There we are, nice and cozy. Any funny business and Rainbow Brite gets a bullet to the lungs, got it?"

Maggie nodded as she fumbled with her keys, dropping them once before successfully shoving them into the ignition and firing the engine. She glanced in the rearview mirror as she shifted into reverse. Tears streaked Piper's face. Maggie eased the car from her parking space, shifted into drive and pulled onto the road.

As Maggie aimed the car toward neighboring Aberdeen, she glanced in the rearview mirror again. "Could you at least take the gun out of her ribs?"

"Worry about yourself, Ms. Edwards."

"Unlike jerks like you, I don't just worry about myself," Maggie shot back.

The man lunged forward and clutched her throat. "I wouldn't tick me off any further, Maggie," he hissed in her ear.

Maggie shrieked as his hand grasped her throat. She choked down a swallow as he released her. He sunk back next to Piper, pointing the gun at her again. This time he kept it a small distance away.

Maggie navigated the short distance to Aberdeen, winding through the streets toward the outskirts. She turned the car onto a tree-lined street. Houses dotted the sides, each of them with generous yards. Maggie swung the car into a driveway a quarter of the way up the road.

Ollie's neatly trimmed lawn fronted his Craftsman-style porch. Maggie killed the engine. "Now what?"

"Now we pay Uncle Ollie a visit."

The man popped his door open, dragging Piper out of the car with him. Maggie emerged from behind the wheel. With legs that felt like jelly, Maggie forced herself up the walk to

Ollie's porch. She rang the bell and waited outside the door. Within a few moments, the door swung open.

"Maggie?" Ollie questioned, glancing around her at the other two people. His brow furrowed.

Maggie's lip trembled, and she pouted her lower lip as she tried to force a smile. "Hi, Uncle Ollie," she said in a shaky voice. "Can we come in?"

Ollie stood to the side, silent as he motioned them inside. "I'm sorry," Maggie whispered as they crossed the threshold.

The man shoved Piper through the door and stepped inside. He pushed the door shut behind them. "Let's all sit down, shall we?" he said, using his gun to wave them into Ollie's living room.

"What's going on?" Ollie whispered to Maggie as they made their way to the couch.

"Hey!" the man objected. "No talking!"

Maggie sunk onto the edge of the couch with Piper as Ollie eased into an armchair. "This… person," Maggie spat out, "wants to know the location of the other two ankhs. I told him you may have some idea but… since I missed dinner last night, I didn't know anything." Maggie stared at Ollie, giving him a slight nod and praying he picked up on her lie.

Ollie nodded back. "No, you wouldn't have any idea. I planned to share my research with you tonight… assuming you were on time," Ollie noted, playing along.

The man waved the gun in front of him as he spoke. "I don't care about your missed dinner date, doc. I want to know where the other two ankhs are located. And I want to know now."

Ollie nudged his glasses further up on his face. "All right," he said calmly. "But first, let my niece and her friend go. There is no reason to involve them."

"I'm not going to play your games, Dr. Keene. Tell me the locations."

"Not until Maggie and Piper are safe!" Ollie argued.

The man leapt from his chair. He grasped Maggie's wrist, jerking her to standing. His arm wrapped around her, his hand clutching her throat. He pressed his gun to her cheek. Maggie whimpered and tugged on his hand but could not escape. A tear rolled down her cheek as her knees threatened to buckle underneath her. Ollie rocketed from his chair.

"I'm not playing games, old man," the man growled. "Tell me what you know, or your pretty little niece gets a bullet in her brain."

"Okay, okay, please," Ollie begged, "let her go."

The man shoved Maggie toward Ollie. She stumbled a few steps and Ollie caught her. "Don't tell him," Maggie insisted.

"It's okay, Maggie," Ollie answered, squeezing her shoulders. "It's okay. It's not worth your life."

Maggie sniffled but nodded. She sunk onto the couch next to Piper. Maggie's hand found Piper's. She grasped it and squeezed it hard.

"Now," Ollie began, "I don't have any clear answers…"

"The location, professor, NOW!"

"Germany," Ollie responded.

"Germany? I'm going to require more information than that, Dr. Keene."

Ollie swallowed hard. "The Ruhr Museum. In Essen. One of the ankhs is on display there."

The man's brow furrowed as he considered the information. "Here," Ollie said, "let me show you." The man rose cautiously from his chair again. Ollie held his hands up. "I'd just like to retrieve my laptop and show you proof."

The man waved him on with his gun and Ollie snatched his laptop and notebook from the desk against the far wall. He popped the display open and typed a few words before spinning it to face their attacker. "Here," he said, pointing to the screen, "the museum contains artifacts from the Roman occupation. It houses Julius Caesar's ankh."

The man squinted at the screen and rubbed his chin. "How certain are you of this?" he questioned.

"Very," Ollie answered as he pushed the laptop closed.

The man directed his gun toward the two women on the couch. "Enough to bet their lives on it?"

Ollie nodded. "Yes," he stated.

"All right then, professor. That's one. Now what about the second?" He pointed the gun back at Ollie.

"Well," Ollie croaked. "That's where things get hazy."

"You'd better not be stalling!" the man warned.

"I'm not, I'm not. I'm just mentioning that this one I am less certain of." Ollie paused a moment, then continued. "After extensive research, and not very many leads, I've narrowed it down to one of two places. Either the Louvre or the Cairo Museum."

"Those are pretty distinct places, doc. Sure you can't be more specific?"

"Not with one hundred percent accuracy, no. But I can say my bet would be on the Louvre. I found an obscure reference to a stone cross in storage there." Ollie paged through his notebook with a shaky hand.

"Come on, come on, doc, I don't have all day!" the man yelled.

"All right, all right, just let me find it. I'm sorry, I'm nervous, I'm not thinking." Ollie paged backward and forward a few times before settling on a page. "Here, here it is. See?" Ollie turned the book toward him. Maggie spied the page from her position on the couch. In typical Oliver Keene fashion, messy, nonsensical notes filled the pages.

The man shook his head. "What am I looking at?"

"Right here!" Ollie insisted, pointing to a note dead center on the page.

"Small stone cross," the man read aloud. "So?"

"So, this is the reference I found. I'd bet it's the third ankh. It's listed as being in storage at the Louvre along with several other pieces. The other pieces in the collection all have some tie to Marc Antony. My educated guess tells me this 'stone cross' is Marc Antony's ankh."

The man paced the floor for a moment while he rubbed his chin. "All right," he said. "Now it's time to play a little game. Let's all move to the dining room."

"Why?" Maggie demanded.

"I'd tell you, but I'd hate to spoil the surprise. NOW MOVE!"

They filed across the room and entered Ollie's dining room area. "Everyone pick a seat except Ms. Edwards." The man sneered at them as Ollie and Piper sat at the dining room table. "Now," he said to Maggie, "tie them up. Zip ties around their wrists and ankles." He produced a fistful of black cable ties from his pocket. They landed at Maggie's feet as he tossed them to her.

Maggie retrieved them, a tear escaping her eye. She wiped it away hastily with the back of her hand. Maggie approached Ollie. "Why don't you just go…" Maggie began.

"The zip ties, Ms. Edwards," the man encouraged.

"We'll promise to give you a head start," Maggie argued.

"Wrists and ankles or I'll give myself a head start in the form of a bullet in each of you."

Maggie's lower lip trembled as she nodded. "Sorry," she whispered to Ollie as she knelt behind him.

"Nice and tight," the man instructed.

Maggie pulled the cable ties tight around Ollie's wrists, binding them together. She then secured each of his ankles to the chair legs. The man eyed her work. Satisfied, he turned his attention to Piper as Maggie secured her to the chair.

Maggie stood when she completed her work. She glared

at the man, her jaw set, her eyes narrowed. "Good work, now it's your turn. Take a seat," he directed.

Maggie sunk into a chair next to Piper. The man zip tied her wrists together behind the chair's back before securing her legs to the chair. "Ow!" Maggie objected, twitching as he secured her left leg.

The man stood and crossed the room to retrieve Maggie's keys from the coffee table. "And now, I bid you…" The man's voice cut off sharply as a new sound rung through the house.

Chimes echoed throughout the space. The man whipped his head toward the front door. Someone stood on the opposite side. He crept to the front window, inching the curtain back a tad to peer outside. He swore under his breath. His eyes scanned the room, his fist tightening on the grip of his gun.

The chimes rang through the house again. He grimaced, his jaw tightening. The man shoved the gun in his waistband. He crossed the room and grasped the poker from the fire tools near the fireplace.

A knock sounded at the door. "Ollie?" a voice called.

Maggie's heart leapt at the sound of Henry's voice. She craned her neck around to view the door. The man swung the door open, using the bulk of it for cover.

"Henry!" Maggie called from across the room. "Don't!"

Her warning came too late. The man leapt from behind the door as Henry entered the foyer. He swung the poker, striking Henry in the gut. Henry doubled over, choking as the air left his lungs. The man used his temporary shock to continue his assault. He raised the poker high overhead, then swung it downward, pummeling Henry across the back. Henry swung blindly at him with his fist.

The man attempted a third swing, but hands grabbed the poker, stopping him from finishing the attack. Charlie grasped hold of the poker from behind the man. As Henry stood, the man elbowed Charlie in the gut, then the face. The attack sent Charlie stumbling back several steps as blood poured from his nose.

Henry swung at the man again, this time his fist connected with his target's ribs. The man swung the poker but missed Henry. Henry leapt back a step, and the two circled each other. Henry lunged forward at him, but the swinging poker drove him back. They danced around each other a second time.

With a shout, Henry lunged at him again. The two locked together as Henry pelted his fists into the man's gut. In response, the man trounced him with the poker, earning a yelp from Henry. He landed a second blow, driving Henry back.

The man retreated several steps, throwing the poker down and pulling the gun from his waistband. "Uh-uh-uh, I wouldn't do that if I were you, Taylor," the man warned.

Henry heaved a sigh as he raised his arms. Charlie followed Henry's lead. The man waved them over to the dining room. "Why don't you have a seat and join our little party?" the man instructed.

Henry took a seat across from Ollie next to Maggie. Charlie, blood covering his face, sunk into one of the remaining chairs. The man pulled a pocketknife from his pocket and swung it open. He approached Maggie. With his gun trained on Henry, he cut Maggie's bonds.

She grasped her wrists and rubbed them. He nodded to the zip ties on the dining room table. "You know the drill, Ms. Edwards. Nice and tight, especially on your boyfriend."

Maggie rose from the table and grasped the cable ties. She made her way to Henry, securing him to the chair, then she moved to Charlie. As she pulled the last zip tie around Charlie's second ankle, the man yanked her to standing. She stumbled along as he dragged her around the table and shoved her into her seat. He secured her wrists behind her, then her ankles to each chair leg.

He scanned the table, a smile forming on his lips. "Today must be my lucky day," he said. "To take you all out in one fell swoop. And without a mess or risk of being caught!"

"Why don't you let me loose and we'll fight this out like men?" Henry suggested.

The man's smile dissolved into a grimace. "That'll be quite enough from you," the man stated. He swung the butt of his gun and cracked Henry on the skull. Blood streamed down Henry's face as a split formed on the side of his forehead. Henry's eyes rolled back, and his chin dropped to his chest.

"Now," the man continued, "it has been fun, but I must leave you. Enjoy the rest of your short lives." The man snickered. He pulled a small bottle of lighter fluid from his pocket. A steady stream of the flammable liquid sprayed over the couch and curtains in the living room. He emptied the bottle across the carpet in a line leading toward the dining room.

"That should do," he said, admiring his handiwork. He flung open a lighter and snapped it. The flame danced on the wick. Maggie followed its path as the man lobbed it across the room and onto the couch.

CHAPTER 8

The sofa burst into flames. The man smirked and offered them a final snicker before he disappeared through the front door. Maggie heard her car's engine spring to life. She glanced around the table. Henry's head still lolled near his chest. Charlie struggled against his restraints, but to no avail. Tears streamed down Piper's face.

"What are we going to do?" Piper cried, her voice shrill with panic.

"Can anyone get free?" Ollie questioned.

Maggie scanned the room behind her. The flames on the couch shot higher. They climbed the curtains inch by inch with each passing moment. The fire crept closer toward them. The building smoke reached the smoke detector. It screamed its shrill alarm through the house. Maggie struggled against her bonds. "I may be able to," she choked out as she struggled against her bonds. She wiggled her left leg up and down as she grunted with effort.

Maggie squealed as she contorted her foot and pulled her leg upward, freeing her foot from her shoe. After a moment, her left leg was freed. Ollie raised his eyebrows at her. "Good going, Maggie! Can you free your other leg?"

"Mmm," Maggie murmured as she struggled. "I'm not sure. He caught the buckle of my left shoe with the zip tie, so it wasn't tight. I was able to wiggle out. I'm not sure I can get my right foot out."

She battled against the zip tie for a few moments but was unsuccessful. She heaved a sigh. "It's no use. This ankle's stuck." She breathed heavily with effort.

Maggie hung her head in frustration for a moment. "Can you make it to the kitchen on your free leg?" Ollie inquired.

Maggie tried to stand but found it impossible to balance with her hands behind her and one leg still attached to the chair. She sunk down with a sigh, hanging her head.

"It's okay, Maggie. It's okay," Ollie assured her.

Her head shot back up. She stared at the table in front of her. "I have an idea!" she exclaimed.

Maggie pushed back in her chair. She drew her leg up to her chest. She raised it above the table and extended it toward the table's center. Her brow pinched as she stretched to reach the vase that graced the dining table. Her toes grazed the blue glass. She strained her leg to extend to its limit. Muscles pulled and stretched as she attempted to reach the vase.

Maggie shrieked as she lengthened her leg until it connected with the vase. The glass vase fell on its side, thudding against the wooden table below it. It rocked back and forth before settling. "Come on!" Maggie groaned through clenched teeth.

She rolled the vase toward her. It oscillated to and fro as she inched it closer to the table's edge. In another moment, the vase teetered before it crashed down to the floor. The glass object shattered as it hit the hardwood.

Piper stared at the fragmented glass. "Why did you do that?" she questioned.

"We need something sharp to cut the zip ties," Maggie informed her.

"But it's just all over the floor! We can't use that!" she shouted.

Charlie gave Maggie a half-smile, understanding her plan. "Smart, chicky," he commented. "If you wouldn't mind speeding it up, though," he said, jutting his chin toward the living room behind Maggie. Smoke began to fill the room as the flames crawled across the ceiling. Ollie coughed as the smoke thickened in the room.

"Sure thing," Maggie promised. She hopped on her chair until her back faced the mess on the floor. Once it did, she pushed with her left leg. Her chair toppled backward. Maggie landed hard against the chair's back. The force knocked the air from her lungs. She groaned as she regained her breath. Her hands searched the floor under her. Her fingers grazed the glass. Blindly, she worked to wrap her fingers around a glass shard. Tiny pebbles of shattered glass cut her fingertips, but she managed to grab hold of a thick piece.

Maggie spun the shard in her hand and pushed it against her zip tie. As she sawed at the cable tie, she eyed the flames. They crept closer to them. Her eyes stung from the smoke, though the air on the floor was clearer and easier to breathe. Piper began to cough along with Charlie.

Maggie yelped as the glass cut into her palm as she continued to slice through the bond. Finally, the zip tie severed, freeing Maggie's hands. She rolled to her side, slicing through her final bond.

Maggie stood on shaky legs. She coughed as the smoke burned her eyes, nose and throat. After steadying herself, she raced to the kitchen and grabbed two knives. Maggie ripped a kitchen towel from the oven door, wrapping it around her sliced and bleeding hand.

She raced back to the dining room. Henry's head still lolled; he hadn't regained consciousness yet. She hurried to Charlie and began to saw at the zip ties binding his wrists. "Hurry, chicky," Charlie urged, "your friend isn't doing so good."

"I know, I know. I can't believe Henry hasn't regained consciousness yet," Maggie admitted.

"No," Charlie corrected. "Piper."

Maggie glanced up and across the table. Piper's head hung limply. Maggie returned her attention to Charlie's bonds. In seconds, his hands were freed. He grabbed the second knife and used it to slice the zip tie binding his left ankle while Maggie freed his right.

"Cut Piper loose and take her out," Maggie shouted. "I'll get Ollie and Henry."

Charlie raced around the table and began to slice at Piper's cable ties. Maggie severed the ties binding Ollie's wrists, then cut his legs free. Charlie had Piper freed. She fell forward into his arms and he tossed her over his shoulder. He raced to the patio door, flinging it open and stepping outside.

The influx of fresh oxygen intensified the flames. Ollie grabbed Charlie's discarded knife and he and Maggie crossed to Henry. Ollie freed his wrists while Maggie cut the ties around his ankles. "Henry," Maggie prodded. "Henry! Come on, babe, wake up!" She patted his cheeks in an attempt to rouse him.

"I must get my notes!" Ollie shouted to Maggie as she continued her attempts to rouse Henry.

Maggie coughed, choking on the smoke-filled air. "Uncle Ollie, you can't! It's too dangerous!"

"I can make it!" Ollie insisted, eyeing the notes on the coffee table.

Maggie growled as he raced toward the flames. She returned her attention to Henry. "Henry!" she called again. It made no impact. She would be forced to drag him from the room. She prayed she had the strength. As she stood to begin her rescue operation, she spotted a watering can next to a potted plant near the patio door.

Maggie hurried to it. She breathed a sigh of relief as she lifted it, feeling the water slosh inside. She sprinted back to Henry and dumped the cold water on his head.

Henry's head shot up. He blinked several times before glancing around. "Maggie!" he shouted as he scanned the room.

"I'm here! Come on, we have to go!" Maggie shouted as flames licked the chair she had occupied. She grabbed his hand and pulled him out of the chair. "Uncle Ollie!"

"Here," Ollie answered, skirting the burning couch and rejoining them. "I got it! Now let's go!" Ollie held up a worn leather journal. Maggie nodded in agreement. They rushed across the room to the open patio door.

Everyone gasped for breath as they emerged into the warm, clear air. Sirens screamed in the distance, sounding closer with each passing moment.

Maggie rushed into the grass where Piper lay sprawled on her back. Her eyes remained closed. "Piper!" Maggie shouted. She grasped Piper's wrist and felt for a pulse.

"Pulse is okay, she just inhaled a lot of smoke," Charlie answered. "She needs oxygen."

"We need to move the smoke from her lungs," Maggie responded. "And get her oxygen."

"I hear sirens. They should have oxygen," Charlie answered.

"No, we can't wait," Maggie countered. She blew air into

her mouth. She waited a few seconds and blew again. After the third try, Piper began to cough. Maggie sat back on her haunches and breathed a sigh of relief. Henry squeezed her shoulder. She grasped his hand as Piper's eyes fluttered open.

"You're okay, Piper, you're safe," Maggie assured her.

"How…" Piper began, her voice hoarse from the smoke. She pushed herself up to sitting.

"Charlie dragged you out after you passed out," Maggie informed her.

Piper's eyes flitted to Charlie, who gave her an awkward wave and a half-smile. Piper flung her arms around Charlie's neck. "My hero!" she exclaimed.

Charlie, surprised at her unexpected display of affection, uttered a flabbergasted, "Oh!" as the color rushed to his cheeks. Maggie smiled at the touching scene.

She turned her attention to Ollie and Henry. "Are you all right?" she asked Ollie.

"I'm fine, Maggie, I'm fine. Thanks to your smart thinking!"

"Hey, you had some pretty smart thinking there, too! Good going giving him completely wrong answers about the location of the other two ankhs!"

"It won't take them long to find out I lied," Ollie admitted, "but at least it bought us some time."

Maggie eyed the cut on Henry's forehead. "How's your head? This cut looks nasty," she said.

"I'm fine, Maggie. How are you?"

"I'm okay," Maggie answered. Henry eyed her. "Really, I am."

A bevy of emergency responders interrupted their conversation. In short order, firefighters doused the flames consuming the interior of Ollie's house with water while paramedics checked the group.

After everyone's health was attended to, they gathered on the front lawn.

"We need a place to hole up, regroup," Henry suggested.

"I agree," Ollie answered. "We should put some distance between us and Aberdeen though."

"Agreed," Henry responded.

"We can't leave Piper here," Maggie chimed in. "That maniac nearly killed her. I'm not risking her life."

"Fine," Henry answered. "She comes with us for now."

"Whoa, whoa, whoa," Piper challenged. "Would someone mind filling me in on what the hell is going on here? Some crazy gun-wielding dude just kidnapped Maggie and me, insisting she knew the location of some ankh and then almost killed us. Now everyone's all like 'let's hole up and regroup.' What the hell is going on here?"

Maggie sighed. "It's a long story," she answered. "Come on, I'll explain in the car."

"I'm not going anywhere until I get some answers." Piper crossed her arms and set her jaw.

"Piper, we don't have time for this! Once they realize we're not dead, they're going …"

"WHO ARE THEY?!" Piper shouted.

Charlie stepped between Maggie and Piper. "Fair maiden, if I may entreat upon you to forgive the lack of explanation. Everything will be explained, but for now, the most important thing is your safety. And I trust these people with my life. If you could see fit to trust my judgement, I am certain you will not regret it."

"What the hell is he talking about?" Henry whispered to Maggie.

Piper's face softened. "Okay," she agreed. "Okay, I trust your judgement. I feel safe with you. After all, I owe you my life, good sir."

"Who cares," Maggie responded in a low voice. "It worked."

"All right," Ollie said. "With that settled, let's head out, then."

They piled into Henry's car. Maggie shared the backseat with Piper and Charlie. She smiled as she spotted Charlie's hand wrapped around Piper's. Henry drove for an hour, adding as much distance as possible between the group and Aberdeen.

Henry veered off the highway at an exit signifying various hotel options. He wound around the roads as he followed signs leading to a hotel hidden from the main highway.

As Henry eased the car into a parking space, he asked, "Up to your standards, princess?"

Maggie scoped the building. "You're getting better at picking hotels," she admitted. Piper eyed the hotel, then Maggie, a slack expression on her face. "First place he ever took me to was a real dump."

"Wait here, Maggie and I will check in alone. They'll be searching for a group of us, not a couple," Henry said.

He and Maggie exited the car and entered the hotel, checking in under assumed names. They retrieved the keys and gathered the rest of their group before proceeding through a side entrance to their room.

"Anybody else hungry?" Maggie asked as they settled into the room. She perused the nearby delivery options. "We could grab a couple of pizzas. Pepperoni? Mushroom? Any special requests?"

"Hungry?" Piper questioned. "Dude, are you serious? We almost just died, and you're worried about pizza toppings?"

"Yeah," Maggie answered. "It's BECAUSE we didn't die that I'm worried about eating. It wouldn't be a concern otherwise." Maggie offered her a wry smile.

Piper stared at her, crossing her arms in an unimpressed display. "Would someone mind explaining to me what is going on here? Against my better judgement, I came with you. AFTER WE ALMOST DIED. After you told me 'they' would try to kill us again once they realized we were alive. Who 'they' are, I'm still not sure. So, my topping of choice would be answers."

"Would you settle for mushroom?" Maggie inquired, wrinkling her nose.

"Not funny," Piper responded.

"It's okay, Piper," Ollie chimed in. "We'll explain everything. But Maggie's correct. We should eat and rest while we can."

Piper's eyes grew wide. "While we can?"

Charlie put his arm around her shoulders and guided her to sit on one of the beds. "Food's the best thing. You'll feel much better once you eat something."

Henry placed their order. "Forty-five minutes," he announced as he replaced the receiver on the cradle.

"Perfect," Maggie answered with a sigh. "Just enough time for us to make a plan on moving forward."

"Agreed," Henry responded. "We need to find the other two ankhs. Any leads on those?"

"I have a few," Ollie answered as he waved his notebook in the air. "Not great but…"

"Okay, stop!" Piper exclaimed. She leapt to her feet, glancing between the other four in the room. "Stop! No more plans, no more 'moving forward.' I want some answers and I want them now!"

Maggie glanced at Henry. He raised his eyebrows at her. She shrugged. "She deserves the truth. That madman nearly killed her," Maggie said.

Ollie nodded at her, as did Henry. Maggie began her

explanation. "It relates to the theft at the museum," Maggie admitted.

"I KNEW it!" Piper exclaimed. "You DID have something to do with it! You're in trouble!"

Maggie scoffed, her jaw slack. "No," she corrected. "We're trying to SOLVE it! We didn't do it!"

Piper eyed them all. "You're trying to solve it? You?" Piper inquired. Her lips curled into an amused smile.

"Yes, us, Piper. Why are you laughing?"

Piper shrugged, a chuckle escaping her. "Well, I mean Dr. Keene, I understand maybe as a consultant. And perhaps even your rough-and-tumble boyfriend, although he looks more like he's on the opposite side of the law than the right side of it. But you, boss lady? Why would the police ask a boutique owner for help to solve a crime?" She issued another chuckle as the last question came out of her mouth.

Maggie set her jaw and crossed her arms. "I resent that," she responded. "I am smart and capable and..."

"It's not the police. We work for the government," Henry interrupted.

"The government? You all work for the government?" Piper questioned.

"Yes," Ollie confirmed. "Yes, Maggie, Henry and I work for the government. Charlie is a contractor who often works with us providing tech support."

Charlie saluted as Piper glanced at him.

"So, you're all secret agents or something?"

"Well, no. There's not really anything secret about it. Even though we don't broadcast it. We work on special projects," Ollie explained.

"Special projects?" Piper repeated, suspicion creeping into her voice.

"Yes, like hunting down Cleopatra's tomb or retrieving this artifact," Ollie answered.

"Why is it so important? Why would the government have any interest in retrieving a worthless artifact from the Cleopatra exhibit?" Piper inquired.

"It's not worthless," Maggie countered. "It's…"

Piper held up her hands. "Okay, not like totally worthless. Obviously, it is worth something because it came from Cleopatra's tomb but it's not worth as much as something like the jewels or the twenty-four-carat gold cat statue or something."

Ollie raised his eyebrows and cocked his head. "Some may argue its worth far more than either of those."

"The stone cross thingy is worth more than a massive solid gold cat? On what planet?" Piper inquired sarcastically.

"Yeah, Piper, it is," Henry answered.

"Why?" Piper queried.

"Because it leads to the lost Library of Alexandria," Maggie responded.

CHAPTER 9

"What? Didn't we learn in history class that it burned down or something?" Piper questioned.

"A cover story," Ollie answered. "Another theory is that the library was moved piece by piece to a new, secret location."

"And this ankh points to it? Why was it on display then? Why didn't you use it to find the library?"

"As I explained to most of the group earlier, this minor item didn't cross my desk before it was sent out for cleaning."

"So, you missed it and now someone else has it and can find the library."

"It only contains a partial map," Maggie explained. "There are two other pieces. Two other ankhs. Which is where our focus should be. The first ankh is lost to us, but Uncle Ollie's quick thinking may have bought us some time to find the second and third."

Henry glanced to Charlie, who smirked. The exchange intrigued Maggie. "What? What's that look between you two?"

Henry shrugged. "I wouldn't say 'lost,' princess," Henry replied. He raised an eyebrow, offering a devilish grin. He reached into his cargo pants and retrieved an object wrapped in a white cloth.

Maggie's jaw dropped. Then her brow furrowed. "Is that… How?"

"Indeed, it is, princess," Henry assured her, unwrapping the object. "Cleopatra's ankh. The first piece of the map leading to the Library of Alexandria."

Maggie raced to Henry and relieved him of the object. She studied it, sharing it with Ollie. "Great job, Henry! How did you get it?" Maggie repeated.

"That'd be thanks to me, chicky," Charlie answered as he rose from the bed. He wiggled his eyebrows at her.

"He's not wrong," Henry agreed. "As I mentioned when I called you his program found our friend in the area of North Street. We checked out five lodgings before we found a sports car matching the description you gave us."

"Completely out of place," Charlie chimed in. "Swanky sports car at some dive motel."

Henry nodded. "Parked outside of room 6. We…" Henry hesitated. "Let ourselves in. And after some finagling on Charlie's part, we opened the room safe. Found the ankh inside."

"I can't believe he left it there!" Maggie exclaimed. "But I am so glad he did! We should snap some pictures of this and make a plan to find the next two."

"You said you had a lead on that?" Henry questioned.

"Not much of a lead, I'm afraid, but an idea." Ollie recapped the clue he found to the second ankh in London and the theory the third ankh still lay hidden in Cleopatra's tomb. "As I said, it's not much, but it's a start."

"We need to move on this," Henry noted. "Especially with the opposition on the move for the other ankhs."

Maggie photographed the ankh with Henry's phone before re-wrapping it and returning it to Henry for safekeeping. She shook her head. "We have some time."

"Maggie, they may have people closer than we are to that London museum. At least the tomb site is secure."

"They aren't going to London," Ollie replied.

Henry's brow furrowed. Maggie explained, "Uncle Ollie told him the second ankh was in a mid-size German museum and the third piece was in the Louvre."

"Did he buy it?"

"Yes, I think so," Ollie commented. "I showed him 'proof.'" Ollie waved the notebook in the air.

"Uncle Ollie's notes are so scattered. I doubt he made heads or tails out of them, but it sure lent some credence to Ollie's 'theory.' He bought it. They'll be on the move in both France and Germany. Leaving us to explore London!"

Henry smiled at them. "Great job, you two! All right, I'll make arrangements for us to head to London tomorrow."

"Uh," Piper murmured. "I hate to be a super-huge pain here but... I'm not exactly prepared to travel out of the country."

"You don't need to be," Henry answered as he tapped around on his phone. "You're staying here."

A ruckus erupted at Henry's comment. Both Maggie and Charlie objected along with Piper. "We can't leave her," Maggie objected.

"Yeah, mate," Charlie added. "I'm not comfortable with that."

"Neither am I!" Piper continued. "I almost got killed! And now you're just going to ditch me and run off to London? Dude, no way."

"Their focus should be off Rosemont at this point. Piper was just in the wrong place at the wrong time earlier. You should be fine if you just lie low for a few days," Henry contended.

"Oh yeah, I trust that! Right! No way, dude!" Piper shouted.

"I agree with Piper, Henry. We have no guarantee they won't try to use her again. She could still be in danger here!" Maggie argued.

"I feel responsible for her safety," Charlie stated.

"She's safer with us," Ollie commented.

"All right, all right," Henry answered, holding his hands up in defeat. "Travel for five." He held the phone up to his ear and stepped into the bathroom for the call.

Piper paced the floor as a knock sounded on the door. Maggie answered it and delivered three piping hot pizzas and soda into the room.

"Nice, I am starving," Charlie cheered. He popped open a box and filled his plate with two slices, biting into one before he sat down.

"Me, too!" Maggie agreed. She grabbed a slice of pepperoni and poured herself a soda. "What kind do you want, Piper?"

Piper continued to pace. "Piper?" Maggie tried again. "Mushroom? Pepperoni? Either? Both?"

"Am I the only one concerned that I have no passport, clothes or anything I need to travel? I have zero desire to be left behind but… I can't go traipsing across the globe with no ID!"

"We'll handle it," Maggie assured her. "Now, pepperoni or mushroom? If you don't answer, I'm going to pick it for you!"

Piper stared at Maggie as though she spoke in a foreign language. "It's okay, fair maiden. We have it handled," Charlie added. "Relax and enjoy your pizza."

Piper stared at Charlie for a moment. "Mushroom," she

replied as she sunk onto the bed next to Charlie. "Thanks. You make me feel so much better."

Maggie screwed up her face as she loaded a plate with two mushroom pizza slices. "I literally just said the same thing!" She handed the pizza off to Piper as Henry emerged from the bathroom. "All set?"

"All set," he answered. "On our way to London out of Chicago tomorrow morning."

"Chicago?" Maggie questioned. "Like on a real plane? Please tell me it's not a cargo plane."

"Cargo plane?!" Piper exclaimed.

"Not a cargo plane," Henry confirmed.

"Thank heavens!" Maggie exclaimed.

"We're not actually ever going to fly in a cargo plane, right? That was a joke, right?" Piper pressed.

"It's not, don't ask," Maggie answered.

"Just get some rest," Henry counseled. "We leave tomorrow morning at three to make our flight."

* * *

Piper fidgeted as she stood next to Maggie, Charlie and Ollie in the airport terminal. She raked her hands through her rainbow-colored hair a dozen times as they waited for Henry to retrieve their tickets from the ticket counter.

"Will you stop that?" Maggie scolded.

"Sorry!" Piper whispered. "I'm nervous! I still don't see how we're going to get to London with no passports!"

"Henry has it covered, just trust me."

"Sure, right, dude. I'll just trust you. The last time I did that, I almost got killed!"

"But you didn't. You could stay here and take your chances on your own!" Maggie countered.

Piper sighed. "Fine, fine. Okay." She inhaled deeply,

blowing the air from her lungs in a slow and controlled manner. "I'm fine. Calm. Composed."

"I wouldn't put you in any danger, fair lady," Charlie assured her.

Henry approached the group, tickets in hand. "All set," he said. He directed them to an unmarked door in a corner of the terminal. The door opened and a security guard waved them inside. They traversed the halls, following the guard who led them to a plane waiting on the tarmac.

"We have a short layover in New York," Henry informed Maggie as they settled into their seats.

Maggie glanced behind her. Piper and Charlie sat a few rows behind them. Piper stared out the window. She bit her lower lip, a nervous habit. Charlie showed her something on his phone, drawing her attention from the window. She smiled at him and he offered her an earbud.

Uncle Ollie sat across the aisle and two rows back. The plane rolled back, then lurched forward as it taxied to the runway. Within moments, they were in the air.

"Another trip to London," Maggie said. "I'm so glad this one isn't starting with a cargo plane."

Henry smiled at her and kissed her forehead as she laid her head on his shoulder. "We need a plan when we get there. Ollie'd be the best to go. He could identify the ankh easily."

"Uncle Ollie said he can't go."

"Can't go?" Henry questioned.

"He said he'd be too easily recognized."

"All right, so one of us has to go," Henry concluded.

"Or both of us."

"Perhaps Charlie and I," Henry countered. "We may need technical backup."

"Uncle Ollie said it's not on display. If it's in the Natural History Museum, it's in storage. That should make 'borrowing' it much easier. There probably aren't as many security cameras in the storage areas."

"Fair point."

"And someone needs to stay with Piper," Maggie added. "She's most comfortable with Charlie."

Henry smirked. "Yes, she seems quite attached to him."

"All right, well, we may still need some of Charlie's expertise. We need to get into that museum first and see what we're working with. What time do we land?"

"Not until ten tonight," Henry answered with a sigh. "Anything we attempt will have to be tomorrow."

Maggie sighed. "At least we're one step ahead of the bad guys."

"Thank goodness for small mercies," Henry agreed.

WHEN THEY LANDED IN LONDON, Piper's nervousness resumed. "Please tell me there's a guard to sweep us through the back halls here like there was in Chicago," Piper whispered to Maggie as they traversed the terminal.

"We'll be fine," Maggie responded. She glanced at Piper, who bit her lower lip until it was colorless. "Let's hop into the ladies' room before the customs queue."

Maggie guided Piper into the ladies' room, leaving the men to wait for them outside. When they emerged, Henry winked at Maggie. "I assume you pulled your magic trick?" Maggie inquired.

"I did," Henry assured her. "Let's find a quiet corner."

The group followed Henry to a secluded area. The bustle of the crowd passed them by as Henry passed two passports to Charlie and one to Ollie. Ollie opened his and glanced inside. With a nod, he stepped back. "See you on the other side," he stated, then disappeared into the throng of people making their way toward the exit.

Piper followed his departure, her brow furrowed. "All right," Henry said. "You two go next."

"Next?" Piper questioned.

"Yes, you and me, fair maiden," Charlie answered with a grin. "The fair and happy couple! Mr. and Mrs. Anderson!"

"What?!" Piper exclaimed.

"Just let me do all the talking and we'll be fine," Charlie assured her.

"Fake names, fake passports," Maggie explained in a lowered voice. "We don't want to be tracked. Now you and your new husband, Ben, should head to the immigration and customs agents."

Piper swallowed hard and nodded. She glanced at the passport she held in her shaky hands. With a lick of her lips, she glanced up to Charlie, who grinned at her. "Come on, missus!" he encouraged. "Best cover I've ever used."

The remark brought a nervous smile to Piper's face, and she took his hand as they departed from Maggie and Henry.

The two stood for a few more moments before Henry said, "Well, Mrs. Harvey, ready?" He offered his arm.

"I am ready, Mr. Harvey," Maggie answered, recalling the fake names they used the last time they came to London.

They made their way to the customs queue. Maggie searched the crowd, not finding Ollie but spotting Charlie and Piper twenty people ahead of them in another line. The couple was next. Maggie eyed Piper, recalling her first visit here with Henry. The second visit evoked memories of her taut nerves, her beating heart, her pounding pulse. Piper likely experienced something similar at this moment. With any luck, within less than thirty minutes they would be together in a taxi.

Maggie stepped forward as the line moved up. Piper and

Charlie advanced to the agent. Charlie slid the passports across to the stone-faced man. He grinned and put his arm around Piper. Piper forced a smile as the man glanced up from their passports at them. He slid them back to Charlie and uttered a few words before Piper and Charlie stepped away from the desk.

Maggie breathed a sigh of relief, realizing she had been holding her breath. Henry's hand pressed against her back as he prompted her to move forward. They waited as the line progressed, finally making it to the agent.

Within a few moments, they were walking into the damp London air. Ollie waved them over to a cab. "Come on, slow pokes!" he called jovially. "I want to get a good night's sleep before sight-seeing tomorrow."

"Sorry!" Maggie called as she slid into the cab. Everyone piled in and Ollie imparted an address to the cab driver.

They wound through the streets of London. Lights glittered across the city as the buildings closed in on them. The cab pulled alongside a nondescript high-rise. Maggie recognized the building. Ollie kept an apartment here. She and Henry traveled here on their last adventure in London.

They all climbed from the cab and Ollie paid the driver in cash.

"Only one night here," Henry cautioned as they entered the building.

Ollie pressed the elevator button and doors whooshed open. "I figured this was easier, at least for tonight. No one realizes we're here. Apartment isn't registered in my name," Ollie answered. The elevator pulled them upward.

"Everything okay?" Maggie questioned.

Henry nodded. "Yeah, but even with no one aware of our presence here, I'd rather be safe than sorry."

"We can get some rest, gather supplies and come up with

a plan," Ollie said as they stepped off the elevator and into a long hallway.

Ollie navigated to an apartment halfway down the hall. He reached into his pants' pocket. A frown formed on his face. He tried the other pocket. He patted his shirt and jacket pockets.

Henry dug into his pocket and produced a key. "You're terrible with keys, mate," he said with a chuckle as he unlocked the door for them.

They entered the apartment and Ollie flicked on a few lights. Piper collapsed onto the couch. "Running from the law takes a lot out of you," she said.

"We're not running from the law," Maggie answered, plopping onto the couch next to Piper.

"We may as well be! We just used fake passports to enter another country illegally!"

"Wishing you didn't come?" Henry inquired as he twisted the knob of a safe.

Piper shook her head and sighed. She held her hands out, toggling them up and down. "Stay behind and commit no crime, but possibly be killed. Commit an international crime and stay alive. Hmm. This is a tough one."

Maggie chuckled at her horrible joke. At least Piper kept her sense of humor in the intense situation. "I, for one, am glad you came, fair maiden," Charlie said.

"You should try to get some rest, Piper," Maggie advised.

"Right," Piper answered. "Yeah, I'm totally sure I can sleep."

"Don't worry, you're perfectly safe," Henry assured her. He pulled a pistol from the safe and checked the clip before replacing it and loading a bullet into the chamber.

"Wow, that makes me feel so much better," Piper responded.

"Here," Charlie responded. He clacked on his keyboard.

"I've hacked into the CCTV around the building. If anyone's coming, we'll know!"

"Happy?" Maggie inquired. "Get some rest, Piper."

"There's a bedroom just through that door," Ollie informed Piper.

"Okay, okay, I'll take the hint." Piper groaned as she climbed to her feet and slogged to the bedroom.

Maggie yawned as Piper disappeared into the bedroom. "She has the right idea. I'm exhausted, too!"

"We need a plan," Henry countered as Maggie let her head fall back onto the couch cushion.

"I plan to lie low," Ollie replied. "But we need to access the storage area. Perhaps the best idea is to visit the museum tomorrow and gather some intel."

Maggie yawned again. "That sounds like a plan. Recon," she said as her eyes closed. Henry sunk onto the couch next to her, wrapping his arm around her. Maggie leaned into him, letting her head rest on his shoulder. She fell asleep in minutes.

CHAPTER 10

Maggie awoke the next morning to the scent and sound of crackling bacon. Her head rested against a pillow as she sprawled on the couch. A blanket covered her body. She inhaled deeply as she stretched and pushed herself up to sitting. "Mmmm," she said, "is that bacon?"

"Indeed, it is, princess," Henry announced from the kitchen. He stood over the stove tending the bacon and scrambled eggs.

"Oh, perfect!" Maggie exclaimed, climbing to her feet. Henry poured her a cup of coffee, adding cream and two sugars before passing it to her. She sat down on a stool at the counter next to Charlie.

"Mmm, thank you!" she murmured as she sipped it.

"I bought you a burner phone. It's charging now," Henry said. He spooned eggs onto a plate along with toast and bacon before handing it to Maggie.

"Hey, mate," Charlie objected, "I was here first!"

"But you're not as pretty as she is, mate," Henry answered.

"That's debatable," Charlie answered as Henry slid a dish to Charlie.

"Mmm, that's true," Maggie responded. "Charlie is very pretty."

"You know it, chicky," Charlie answered with a chuckle as he dove into the eggs. He wiggled his eyebrows at her.

"Where's Uncle Ollie?" Maggie questioned.

"Shower," Henry answered. "Wanted to get in there before you used all the hot water in the building."

Maggie gave him a wry glance. "Haha, hilarious."

Piper wandered from the bedroom. "Coffee," Piper mumbled. Her hair stuck out at every angle and her clothes were rumpled.

"Hey, good morning to you, too," Maggie said with a laugh. "Looks like you slept at least."

Piper plopped down on a stool next to Maggie. "I did. Is that… bacon?"

Henry set a plate of food in front of Piper. "It is," Henry answered. "Eat up!"

Piper scooped up a forkful of eggs and bit off a piece of bacon. "Mmm, no wonder you're dating him, boss lady."

Ollie emerged from the bathroom. "Any breakfast left?"

"I saved you some," Henry answered.

Maggie shoved the last piece of her breakfast into her mouth and swallowed another few sips of coffee. "I call next!" She raced to the bathroom.

Maggie emerged forty-five minutes later. "It's about time!" Piper complained.

"Sorry!" Maggie said. "After that flight, I needed some extra time with the steam! So did my clothes!"

Piper rolled her eyes at Maggie as she darted into the bathroom. "So, what's our plan?" Maggie asked as she poured herself another cup of coffee.

"Recon. Charlie, Piper and Ollie will stay in a van near the museum. We'll check out what we're working with on the inside."

"The old tourist act, huh?" Maggie inquired.

"That's it, princess."

"Worked last time," she admitted.

"We'll head out as soon as Piper's ready."

"So, if this thing's in storage, we'll need access to the storage areas," Maggie added. That's easier said than done."

"We'll soon find out," Ollie answered.

"Are you sure you can't just ask to see the storage areas, Uncle Ollie? As a favor to the world-renowned archeologist? It might work!"

Ollie chuckled. "It's best we don't let anyone know we're here. And I'm not certain it would work, anyway."

"Okay, so we do it the hard way," Maggie said with a shrug. "Do you have the list from the museum? Perhaps it will help us locate the ankh if we are able to gain access."

Ollie retrieved the paper from his journal on the counter. He handed it to Maggie. She unfolded it and glanced at it. "A vase, coins, a dagger, the cross," Maggie read. She shrugged. "Oh well, it can't hurt!" She refolded the page and slipped it into her blazer pocket. "We probably should get a change of clothes while we're out, too. While I love this outfit and these shoes, they aren't going to work well if we need to do more than reconnaissance."

"Good idea, princess. We'll do your favorite activity after the museum trip: shop."

"It's not my favorite when it's with you. Shopping with you is the worst. I can only buy black, no heels, shall I continue?"

"No," Henry replied, "I already realize how much you hate my shopping trips."

Piper emerged from the bathroom. Her wet hair was pulled into two French braids. The shower's steam managed to remove some of the wrinkles from her clothes. "Ready?" Maggie questioned.

"For what?" Piper asked.

"We're going to the museum for some recon," Maggie answered. "Don't worry, you can stay in the van with Charlie and Uncle Ollie."

"Wait, what? No way! If we're in London, I'm at least going to see something."

Maggie raised her eyebrows at Piper. "Seriously?"

"Yes, seriously. No one's going to kill us in the middle of a museum, right?"

"Don't tempt fate," Maggie answered as she grabbed the burner phone from the charger and shoved it into the pocket of her dress. "We will want to grab some clothes before we come back here."

The group exited the apartment building and walked to a nearby parking structure. Maggie recognized the nondescript white van as they approached it. Henry climbed behind the wheel and Maggie slid into the passenger's seat. Ollie, Charlie and Piper entered the back. Charlie began setting up his laptop as soon as they were on the road.

Henry eased the car along the curb a street away from the museum.

"All set, mate," Charlie announced from the back. "In their system. I'll be your eyes in the sky."

Henry and Maggie climbed from the van. Henry slid the van's door open. Piper climbed out as Charlie handed an earpiece to Henry. "Thanks, mate. Test, test. You read me?"

"Loud and clear, mate," Charlie answered.

"I'll note the entrances and exits, security measures, employee doors," Henry noted.

Charlie held out another earpiece. "Want one, chicky? I'd love to be in your ear."

Maggie snatched it from him. "Sure, I'll take one."

Maggie placed the small device in her ear. "Have any more of those?" Piper inquired.

"For you, I have anything and everything, fair maiden," Charlie answered, handing an earpiece to her.

She shoved it in her ear as Henry slid the door shut. The trio made their way down the street toward the museum. As they approached the Gothic Romanesque-style building, Piper stared up at the structure. "Wow," she murmured. "That's one heck of a building."

"Yeah, looks like a palace or a castle," Maggie commented.

Charlie's voice crackled in their ears. "I'd love to take you on a proper tour of it some time, fair maiden."

Piper smiled. "I'd really like that. This place looks lit!"

"Lit, indeed, fair maiden, totally Gucci."

They climbed the stone steps leading to the main entrance and entered the museum. Maggie's eyes were drawn upward immediately. "Wow! This place is amazing! I wish we were here to just enjoy it!"

"All right, let's take a peek around," Henry said. His eyes darted around, taking in the details of the enormous space. Unlike Maggie and Piper, Henry's eyes searched for security measures and their potential weaknesses.

"You're no fun," Maggie lamented as they began their "tour."

They climbed the stairs overlooking the massive exhibit space. Maggie leaned against the stone banister overlooking the room below. She admired the expansive room, its tall columns supporting the rounded ceiling and the skylights flooding the room with light from outside.

"Got you on the cameras here. How's it look from there, mate?" Charlie asked.

"Not great," Henry admitted. "We've no idea where this thing could be behind these walls and no solid plan to enter the museum."

"Come through a skylight, maybe?" Charlie suggested.

"I wouldn't rule it out," Henry answered. He stared up at the skylight before returning his gaze to the floor below. "Still have to make our way into the storage area and find the ankh. That'll take time."

"Time we're not going to have," Charlie said. "I'll map the employee doors and run a time sequence. Can you walk around and stop in front of them so I can mark them?"

"Sure," Henry glanced to Maggie and Piper. "You girls all right here? It might be less obvious if I go alone."

"We're fine," Maggie assured him. "We'll just enjoy the museum while you boys play."

Henry nodded and disappeared down the stairs. The conversation between Henry and Charlie continued in each of their ears as Henry traversed the large museum.

"Dude, this does NOT sound good," Piper admitted after about ten minutes.

Maggie sighed. "No, it doesn't. Though we've been through some tight spots before. You should have seen what we pulled at The British Museum last time we were here!"

"Maybe we need to think outside the box," Piper suggested.

"Huh?"

Piper rolled her eyes as the men continued discussing options for a less-than-legal way to enter the museum. "Come on," Piper said as she grabbed Maggie's hand and pulled her down the stairs.

They navigated to the gift shop. Piper wandered around the store, selecting a few items. Maggie's brow furrowed as she followed her around the store. When she collected an odd assortment of items, she approached the check out. Piper dug into her pants pocket and pulled her phone from it. She flipped open her wallet case and purchased the items.

With her new purchases in hand, she dragged Maggie out of the store and to the ladies' room nearest the shop.

"What in the world are you doing?" Maggie asked her.

"Making a plan," Piper answered.

Maggie wrinkled her brow. "With a few notebooks, a pair of reading glasses, two toy ID badges and a pen?"

"Yep," Piper said as she removed the badges from their packaging. She hung one around Maggie's neck and the other around hers, ensuring both were turned backwards. She handed Maggie a hair tie. "Here, pull your hair into a low ponytail or a bun or something."

"What? Why? Would you mind explaining what you expect to achieve here?" Maggie glanced at the badge before holding it up to Piper. "How exactly is Officer Cute E. Kidd going to help us?"

Piper pulled the power sticker from the reading glasses and shoved them into Maggie's hands. She bent the notebooks various ways to appear used and placed the pen in the middle of one. "You are going to pose as a curator from another museum. Tell them you had an appointment with the museum director here. I'll look up his name in a second. Hopefully I'll find it before my phone dies. Tell them you made arrangements to review the stuff in storage."

"Are you crazy? This isn't going to work."

"This plan is NOT going to work," Henry chimed in through the earpiece.

"It might, and it's better than breaking in. What's the worst that can happen? They tell us no and we leave. But come on, you totally look the part. Just pull your hair back and look a little… brainier… like a history geek."

Maggie faced the mirror and pulled her hair into a low bun with Piper's hair tie. She slid on the glasses and adjusted her skirt and jacket. She grabbed the notebooks and practiced holding them tight to her chest. "This is insane," she breathed. "Okay, fine, let's go."

"No, Maggie, don't," Henry warned.

"We have to try. It can't hurt," Maggie answered.

Henry sighed as Charlie added, "Director's name is Stephen Thompson. Good luck, chicky."

"Just... use a fake name and be insistent," Piper whispered as they exited the bathroom. "Flash the badge, act like you're important. You know, your normal attitude."

Maggie shot her a glance. Before they approached the docent's desk, Maggie recalled the inventory list in her pocket. She pulled the folded sheet from her pocket and shoved it into the notebook.

Maggie's pulse pounded and her heart thudded as she approached the semi-circle wooden desk. She hoped she could hear the woman behind the desk speaking over the blood that rushed through her ears. Her throat went dry, and she swallowed hard.

She gave one final glance to Piper before she stalked to the desk. She cleared her throat and raised her eyebrow at the brunette behind the desk. "Hello," the brunette answered in a crisp British accent, "how may I help you."

"Dr. Ingrid von Bergenstein of Ruhr Museum to see Director Thompson," Maggie said in an exaggerated German accent. She flashed the badge before turning it to face away from the woman. "I am here to study the items in the private collection."

"Do you have an appointment?" the woman asked.

Maggie paused a moment. She raised both her eyebrows and stared at the girl. "Yes, of course!"

The girl smiled and nodded as she picked up a receiver behind the desk. She pressed a few buttons, then waited. After a moment, she spoke into the phone. "Yes, I have a Dr. von Bergenstein for Director Thompson." She paused.

Her brow furrowed. "Oh, yes, I will let her know. Thank you."

"I'm sorry, Dr. von Bergenstein, but they do not have you on the schedule."

"There must be some mistake!" Maggie continued.

"I am terribly sorry but…"

"Sorry?! You're sorry?" Piper interjected. "You're going to have to be a lot more than sorry. I cleared this appointment with Director Thompson TWO MONTHS ago. I specifically recall speaking with Kelly."

The girl glanced between Maggie and Piper. "Kelly? I'm sorry, I don't know of a Kelly."

"Buy me two more moments and I'll have a message in your inbox from the museum director confirming this appointment," Charlie assured them over the earpiece.

"Ah, well, I'm not surprised. She was probably fired for her incompetence," Piper said. "I made an appointment with Director Thompson for June 15 at 12:20 p.m. I specifically remember it because it was on my sister's birthday and the time was so odd. Who schedules an appointment at twelve twenty?" Piper tapped around on her phone as she continued. "Someone who takes a twenty-minute lunch, perhaps, is what I figured. But who does that? Anyway, I wouldn't forget a detail like that."

"I am so very sorry about that, but it appears the director is out of the office."

"Here," Piper said as she shoved her phone into the docent's face. "Here is the confirmation email from the director himself."

"You're welcome, ladies," Charlie said over the earpiece. "One email from Director Stephen Thompson himself confirming the appointment and blabbering on about how much he is looking forward to meeting you."

Maggie held back a smile at Charlie's adept tech skills.

The girl perused the email and offered Maggie and Piper a nervous smile. "I... I... the director is not here..." she stuttered.

"Then perhaps someone else can assist me! I must have access to the private collection! It is imperative that I study it for my work on the Roman period!"

The docent forced a smile, unsure of what to answer. "Uh," she hesitated.

Maggie frowned at her. "Here," she said, pulling the list from the notebook. "It is these items I am interested in! I was emailed this list from the director and told I could view the pieces today! This is most unacceptable! I demand to speak to someone!"

The woman glanced at the list, noting the museum letterhead at the top. She nodded again and picked up the phone. "Uh, what did you say your name was again?" she asked Piper.

"This is my assistant..." Maggie began. "Urkel Grue."

She dialed another number. She turned her back and spoke a few words into the receiver. She paused and glanced at Maggie and Piper over her shoulder. She held up a finger, requesting their patience with the gesture.

Maggie tapped her foot on the floor. The girl turned away and nodded. She spoke a few more words, then spun to replace the receiver. She smiled at Maggie and Piper. "I have great news! One of our curators is able to assist you. I am so sorry for the misunderstanding, but Ms. Sheffield can handle your request with ease. She is on her way now." The girl smiled broadly as though she had settled a major ordeal.

"Thank you," Maggie said, continuing her unimpressed and annoyed act.

Within a few moments, a short brunette scurried toward the docent's desk. "Dr. von Bergenstein?" she inquired as she approached Maggie.

"Yes," Maggie answered. "I am the doctor. I am here to view the private collection."

"Hello, I'm Emily Sheffield. I'm a curator here at the museum." She extended her hand to shake Maggie's and Piper's. "May I see the list of items you hoped to peruse?"

"Of course," Maggie answered. She snatched the list from the desk's top and shoved it toward the woman. "I am most unimpressed with this delay."

The woman glanced over the list. "I apologize, Dr. von Bergenstein, if you'll follow me, I can set you up in an examination room with the items."

Maggie nodded to her in response and motioned for her to lead the way.

"How was your trip to London? Are you enjoying your stay so far?"

"I am finding it most tedious," Maggie answered. "The weather is always damp, and the city is too large and overcrowded."

Emily offered a nervous smile. "And then the debacle with the appointment has gotten on the last nerve!"

"My last nerve, doctor, MY last nerve," Piper corrected.

Emily licked her lips and glanced between the two women as she led them through a door marked STAFF ONLY. "Yes, I am so very sorry about that. Director Thompson was called away. Quite unexpectedly, from what I understand. I am certain it was an unfortunate oversight that you were not notified. But I am so pleased that I can assist you."

"As am I that this was not a wasted trip!"

The woman wound through the corridors and arrived at a door. She pulled it open and ushered Maggie and Piper inside. "If you'll wait here, I will have the items brought to you. You'll find everything you need to examine them here."

She motioned to the table, which contained gloves and a table-mounted magnifier.

Maggie nodded to her. "I shall return!" Emily joked.

"I should hope so," Maggie answered, pretending not to understand the joke.

Emily gave a nervous chuckle as she pulled the door closed.

Maggie breathed out a sigh of relief once they were alone.

"I can't believe that worked!" Piper exclaimed.

"Me either," Henry chimed in.

"Hey! My acting skills are Oscar-worthy," Maggie teased. "And good job, Urkel Grue!"

"Oh, dude, next time, how about don't call me Urkel Grue? That was the worst name ever."

"Sorry, it was all I could think of!"

"Seriously?" Piper questioned, her face a mask of disbelief. "You couldn't think of any other name but Urkel Grue?"

"Well..." Maggie began when the door popped open. Two men wheeled two crates into the room. "Here we are," Emily announced. She used a crowbar to pop open the lids of both boxes. "I assume you'd like some time to peruse the objects."

"Yes, thank you." No one moved. Maggie widened her eyes. "Eh, thank you, that is all."

"Oh!" Emily exclaimed. "Of course. I'll step out to finish some work. If you need anything, simply ask Tyler," Emily said, motioning to one of the men, "and he can assist you or call me."

Maggie nodded, already peering into the bins as though only they could hold her interest. "Yes, thank you," she mumbled.

"We will, thank you," Piper followed up.

Emily nodded to her before exiting. Tyler remained in the room.

Maggie adjusted her glasses and cleared her throat.

"Would you mind? I need solitude to find the clarity for my research. I cannot have distractions."

"Uh..." Tyler mumbled.

"Dr. von Bergenstein requires isolation to maximize her concentration. Only I can remain in the room," Piper informed him.

"Exactly right," Maggie agreed, still feigning her German accent. "My concentration must be razor sharp. You are a distraction. Now, if you please." Maggie made a shooing motion with her hand before sliding on a pair of gloves.

"I'll be just outside, doctor," Tyler said.

Maggie nodded, waving him away. The door closed and Maggie breathed a sigh of relief. "Okay, we're alone," she reported.

"Good," Henry answered. "Where are you?"

"In an examination room with the artifacts!" Maggie exclaimed with a squeal. "There's two bins. The ankh must be in one of them. We're starting to dig through the bins now. I'll let you know as soon as we have it! I don't know how we'll get out with it but... we'll cross that bridge when we come to it." Maggie removed her glasses. "I can't see a thing with these on!"

"I'm staying in the museum in case you need something," Henry answered.

Maggie and Piper dug through the packing materials in the first bin. They carefully removed the items inside. They laid each on the exam table. "First bin is emptied, no ankh," Maggie reported.

"So, it must be in this one," Piper surmised.

They dove into the second crate and pulled out the items in a similar fashion. They reached the bottom of the crate. Maggie frowned. She pushed the packing material from one side to the other. Maggie returned to the first bin and shoved the packing material around.

She glanced at Piper and shrugged her shoulders. "It's not here!" she exclaimed.

Piper did another check of both bins. "Are you kidding?" Henry asked.

"Nope," Maggie answered. "It's not here." She grabbed the inventory list from the table and scanned it. "Okay, wait, there are a few items missing. A dagger, a shield, a helmet and the ankh."

"Maybe they forget to pull a bin," Piper suggested.

Maggie nodded in agreement. "Let's hope," Maggie said as she crossed to the door.

"Looks like you're on again, Dr. von Bergenstein," Piper said. "Oh, wait! Your glasses!"

"Right!" Maggie grabbed the glasses from the table and shoved them on her face. She flung the door open. "Timmy?!" she called in her faux German accent.

"Ah, Tyler, doctor," the man answered, stepping into the room.

"Ah, whatever, whatever," Maggie answered, waving her hand at him. "There are several items missing."

"Missing?" Tyler questioned.

"Yes!" Maggie exclaimed. "Missing! Gone! Vamoose!" She stared at Piper, flinging her arms out.

Piper explained. "There are several items on this inventory list," she said as she passed the list to Tyler, "that are not in the bins." Piper pointed out the missing items.

"Let me call Ms. Sheffield," Tyler offered as he picked up the phone on the wall. He spoke a few words into the receiver before replacing it. "Ms. Sheffield is on her way."

Maggie crossed her arms and tapped her designer shoe on the floor. Emily appeared in the doorway. "Hello again," she greeted them. "Tyler says there are a few missing items?"

"Yes," Piper explained again. "These four items, in particular." She pointed them out.

"Hmm," Emily murmured. "Just a moment." Emily approached a computer station in the corner. She input her username and password before clicking through several screens. She typed into a dialogue box and scanned the output on the screen. "Ah, yes, I see."

"Is there a missing box?" Piper inquired.

"No. The items you pointed out are no longer with us."

Maggie's heart sank. She kept up her tough exterior as she asked, "What?!"

Emily pointed to the screen. "They were sent to the Natural History Museum in Venice two months ago."

"What?!" Maggie exclaimed again. "Why was I not informed? These pieces are vital to my research!"

"I am so sorry, Dr. von Bergenstein," Emily answered. "Though the remaining pieces from your list are quite intriguing. Did you notice the…"

Maggie waved her hand in the air to stop the woman's words. She pressed a hand to her head, then drew in a deep breath. "No. This is quite unacceptable. I must have the other pieces to complete my research. I shall make arrangements at once to travel to Italy!"

Maggie stepped toward the door.

"Oh, just a moment, Dr. von Bergenstein," Emily said, stopping her. "We must inventory the items here before you leave. I'm sure you understand the protocol."

Maggie huffed at her, folding her arms across her chest. Emily offered another nervous smile as she pulled the inventory list from the side of each crate. She checked each item on the list before spinning to face Maggie. "Okay! All set!"

"Satisfied?" Maggie inquired without waiting for an answer. She gathered her materials from the table. "Come, Urkel, let us depart from this useless, overcrowded and noisy city!" Maggie spun on her heel and stormed from the room. Piper raced to follow her.

"I can't believe this," Maggie breathed as Piper caught up to her. She pulled off her glasses. "Did you catch all that?"

"Yeah," Henry answered. "Meet me at the entrance and we'll get out of here."

"Looks like we're headed to Venice," Ollie chimed in.

"Oh good! Another country I can illegally enter," Piper complained.

"I'll take you on a gondola ride, fair maiden," Charlie offered.

"Ah, there you go!" Maggie said to Piper as they wound through the halls. "That's totally worth committing a crime for!"

They reached the door leading to the museum. "I want a bonus for this," Piper joked as Maggie pulled the door open.

They stepped into the crowded museum beyond the door. Maggie's eyes scanned the exhibit room as she got her bearings. As she searched for the way to the front entrance, a man caught her attention. His clothes did not fit with a standard tourist or even a Londoner on a day trip. His behavior drew Maggie's attention. He milled around the hallway, paying no attention to any exhibits. His eyes darted around the space.

Maggie stared at him a moment as her instincts warned her something was amiss. Before she could mention this to Piper, the man turned to face her fully. He stopped in his tracks. The wrinkle between his brows deepened. They locked eyes for a moment as Maggie's heart thudded in her chest. Something was not right, she surmised. She grasped Piper's wrist with the intention of making a beeline to Henry at the front entrance. Then darkness consumed the room.

CHAPTER 11

The room plunged into darkness as the lights overhead went black. Shouts echoed in the large space.

"Ugh, again?" Piper groaned. "What is it with museums and the lights going out?"

"I'm not sure, but something is very wrong here," Maggie answered.

"Maggie?!" Henry's voice called through the earpiece.

"Yeah, yeah, I'm here. We're coming. Something isn't..." Maggie's voice cut off. As her eyes adjusted to the minimal light streaming from the skylights above, she spied the man moving toward her. "We need to go."

Maggie grabbed Piper's wrist and pulled her along. She moved away from the man, pressing against the wall behind them and sliding along it.

"What are you doing? The entrance is that way," Piper objected. She yanked against Maggie's arm.

Maggie shook her head. "No," she said. "Something's not right. Trust me." She continued away from the front entrance, moving toward a lit EXIT sign.

"What?" Piper questioned as she followed Maggie.

"Maggie, what's wrong?" Henry's voice asked.

"There was a man. Something was off about him. He didn't fit. His clothes, his behavior. He was waiting for something. Or someone. If we go toward the entrance, we're going to run right into him, and I'd rather not do that. We're following exit signs. Meet us outside."

"Copy that," Henry responded.

"We've got the van on the move, heading to the front entrance," Charlie chimed in.

Maggie hurried toward the sign. People scurried everywhere, some shouting, others on their phones. Maggie hoped the chaos further separated her and Piper from the man following them. She glanced back, unable to spot him in the dim light and crowded space.

As they rounded the corner, following the arrow on the exit sign, Maggie risked another glance over her shoulder. She spotted the man behind them. He threaded through the crowd and pushed toward them.

"Come on," Maggie urged. She fought through a throng of school children grouped together as their chaperones called out their names. Maggie's breath quickened as they neared a door leading outside.

Light streamed in from the cloudy sky. She pushed past a few people and into the outdoor air. Piper emerged behind her, still clutching Maggie's forearm. Maggie searched the outside. Several museum-goers milled around in the area, likely waiting for the lights to come back on and resume their tour.

She took a few more steps away from the museum. The man emerged behind her, spying Maggie. "Let's go," Maggie breathed. She shoved Piper in front of her toward the main entrance. "We're on our way to you," Maggie informed Henry.

"I'm outside the main entrance. Which way are you? I'll come to you."

"No," Maggie answered. "We're being followed, we can't wait here. We're coming to you." As she pushed Piper forward on the path toward the front entrance, she checked behind her. The man was weaving through the cluster of people toward them. She pushed Piper to walk faster. As they approached the building's corner, another man, similarly dressed, emerged in their path. He locked eyes with Maggie, a smirk forming on his face.

Maggie's eyes widened and her breath caught in her throat. The second assailant blocked their path to Henry. With the first man closing the gap behind them, they had no choice but to veer off away from both men. The new direction would take them further from the entrance and the van.

Maggie cursed under her breath. "This way," she said, redirecting Piper on their new course. She increased their pace. Piper puffed with exertion as Maggie hurried away from the museum. "We can't get to you. There's two of them," Maggie informed Henry via earpiece. "Heading north away from you."

"Keep moving, keep me informed. I'm coming for you," Henry responded. Labored breathing resounded in the earpiece, then the sound of a door slamming. "Go," Henry called.

Maggie dragged Piper across the street, dodging cars in an attempt to put as much distance between them and their assailants as possible. The men were closing the gap. She raced up the sidewalk and darted down a small alley surrounded by buildings.

"Maggie, where are you?" Henry's voice crackled through the earpiece.

"Queen's Gate," Maggie reported.

Maggie traveled further down the alley, ducking into a smaller side street. "Turning off on first right."

They made their way further down the building-lined street. As they continued, they realized the street ended. A dead-end faced them. They had nowhere to go. Maggie spun around to find the two men approaching. They were trapped.

Maggie's heart raced and her pulse pounded as her fight-or-flight instincts kicked in. As the men approached, Maggie spotted a van turn onto the road. It raced toward them. Relief coursed through her as she recognized the nondescript white van even at a distance. The engine roared as the van lurched toward them.

The noise drew the attention of their assailants. They whipped their heads in the direction of the vehicle, which threatened to run them down. The two men dodged out of the way, each flinging themselves in the opposite direction. The van sped past them and screeched to a halt near Maggie and Piper. Ollie flung the side door open. "Get in!" he shouted.

Maggie shoved Piper ahead of her and raced toward the van. Piper climbed in, followed by Maggie. The men, already recovering from their mishap, climbed to their feet in the hopes of catching one of the women. Before Maggie could shut the van door, Ollie shouted, "GO!" and the vehicle lurched forward. Behind the wheel, Charlie gunned it as he turned sharply. The van's wheels squealed as it fought to gain traction on the pavement while making the sharp turn.

Maggie struggled to cling to the door without toppling out. Piper clutched at Maggie's jacket as Maggie nearly pitched to the pavement. Ollie reached out and grabbed hold of Maggie's arm. As the van swung around, one of the men sprinted toward them. He reached out and grabbed Maggie's flailing limb. Maggie screamed as she attempted to cling to the van. The man ran alongside as he attempted to wrench her from the moving vehicle. Ollie grasped Maggie with both hands and pulled her toward him. Piper still grasped Maggie's jacket and kicked the man's stomach. He lost his grip for a moment, allowing Ollie and Piper to haul Maggie back into the van as she slid the door shut.

They collapsed to the floor; their breathing labored. "Is everyone all right?" Henry called from the passenger seat.

"Yeah," Maggie gasped. "Yeah, we're good."

Maggie let her head fall back against the van's side wall. "Ugh," she moaned. "That so did not go the way I hoped."

"Dude," Piper choked out between gasps of breath, "remind me never to travel with you again."

Maggie shot her a glance but offered a weak laugh in response. Maggie crawled across the van floor and poked her head between the two front seats. "What's our plan?"

"Well, we can't go back to Ollie's, that's for certain," Henry answered.

"How'd they find us?" Charlie questioned.

"Must have followed us," Ollie surmised. "In case I was lying."

"I thought they were going to Germany, whoever 'they' is. I'm still not clear on that," Piper said.

"People you don't want to know about," Henry assured her.

Maggie sighed. "They most likely have someone in Germany checking out that lead. They probably discovered pretty quickly the fire didn't kill us. Somehow they tracked us here."

"We've got to get to Italy," Ollie replied. "Before they figure that out."

"Yes," Maggie responded. "We need to get moving as quickly as possible. Please tell me we brought everyone's fake passports."

"In the duffle, chicky," Charlie responded, tossing his head toward the bag in the back.

"Great," Maggie answered as she collapsed against the van's side again. "What's our best way to get there as fast as possible."

"Air is fastest," Henry responded, "but the last-minute arrangements may be tricky."

"Could do the train, mate," Charlie suggested. "Eurostar goes to Paris early tomorrow morning. Then we can head into Italy from there. Takes about a day."

"That may be our best option," Ollie chimed in. "We've got some down time, though."

"I'd like to buy a change of clothes," Maggie suggested.

"Yeah, we should pick up a few things," Henry agreed. "Then lie low until the train tomorrow."

Everyone agreed. They parked the van in a parking garage, wiped it down and left it behind. They spent the afternoon hours shopping for various necessities before settling into a hotel suite with takeout.

Shortly after ten, Maggie rose from the bed she shared with Piper. She stalked toward the living room area. Henry slept on the pull-out sofa. Maggie stared down at him. His presence comforted her. She stretched and rolled her neck around, working out the kinks. Her left arm ached from where the assailant grabbed her.

Maggie paced the living room. Impatience and frustration filled her. She raked her hands through her hair, wincing as her left arm offered a complaint.

"What are you doing, princess? You're supposed to be sleeping," Henry murmured.

Maggie's heart skipped a beat. "You startled me," she answered.

"Try waking up to you pacing around the room," Henry replied.

"I can't sleep," Maggie admitted. "My mind is spinning. I'll feel better once we're on our way to Venice. I HATE waiting."

"You don't say," Henry noted. He patted the sofa bed next to him. Maggie sat on the edge, then relaxed into his embrace. "You need to get some rest."

"I'll have a day to rest on the stupid train," Maggie complained.

"We'll need to vet a plan while we're on the train," Henry countered. "Preferably one that doesn't involve you risking yourself and Piper to gain access to the ankh."

"Well, it was better than your usual plans, which always involve less-than-legal methods like rappelling from one dangerous location to another."

"I quite like my plans, princess," Henry said with a chuckle.

"Your plan wouldn't have gotten us the information about the current location of the ankh. We'd be at a dead-end right now if not for Piper's brilliant idea."

"True. All right, I admit defeat. Piper's plan was better. But next time, let me play the rude researcher, huh?"

"Hey," Maggie objected, "I thought I fit the role quite well."

"Mmm-hmm, I especially loved that German accent," Henry teased.

"Watch yourself, Mr. Taylor," Maggie said in her fake German accent, "I am not to be trifled with."

"Not to be trifled with, huh?" Henry asked. "We'll see about that."

Maggie giggled as she closed her eyes. The simple conversation lulled her mind into a relaxed state. She drifted off to sleep next to Henry within moments.

* * *

HENRY WOKE Maggie a few hours later. "Huh? What?" she groaned without moving or opening her eyes.

"Time to get up, princess."

"Ugh, you're kidding. Are you kidding?" Maggie questioned.

"Nope. We're moving out in ninety minutes. Figured you'd want to hop in the shower before we go."

Maggie whined for a moment. "I DETEST mornings, especially early ones," she moaned.

"What happened to the 'I can't wait to be on the train' attitude?"

Maggie's eyes popped open, and she glared at Henry. He raised his eyebrow at her. "I hate you sometimes," she said as she climbed from the sofa bed. She stalked two steps toward the bathroom before she returned and kissed Henry on the cheek. "But that sensation usually doesn't last long." She winked and disappeared through the door into the bathroom.

Maggie emerged from the bathroom forty-five minutes later. "What the hell takes you so long?" Piper questioned. "I got up like ten minutes earlier than I needed to figuring you'd be finished."

Maggie opened her mouth to respond. She closed it, pursing her lips before she answered. "Not before my coffee," she said.

"Which I have for you," Henry said as he handed her a to-go cup of the dark aromatic liquid.

"Oh, yay!" Maggie exclaimed. She removed the lid and took a deep inhale of the coffee before she sipped it.

"Do you still hate me?"

"Nope," Maggie answered. "The coffee's redeemed you."

They packed their gear and readied for the train trip to Italy. Departing on the train before 6 a.m., they would be in France before eleven and in Italy just before four-thirty, arriving in Turin. After another three-hour train ride, they would arrive in Venice. It would be mid-evening, far too late to begin any investigation at the museum. That would need to wait until tomorrow.

With everything and everyone ready, they traveled to the train station and boarded the Paris-bound Eurostar. Once they were settled for the hours-long journey, Maggie prodded everyone for a plan. "So, what's our plan for tomorrow?"

"Check out the museum, see what we're working with," Henry said.

"Dude, are your plans always this vague?" Piper inquired.

"No," Maggie answered, "they usually involve a lot more questionable details."

"We're likely going to need some of those questionable details to get our hands on that ankh," Charlie postulated.

"I agree," Maggie said.

"Why?" Piper questioned.

"It's more than likely the Natural History Museum in Venice didn't borrow it to take up shelf space in their storeroom," Maggie responded.

"She's correct," Ollie chimed in. "It's most probable it is on display there."

Henry nodded in agreement. "Which means we'll need my questionable methods to 'borrow' it before someone else does."

Maggie nodded. "More than likely. Uncle Ollie, can I take a peek at the ankh we have? I want to remind myself exactly what we're searching for tomorrow at the museum."

Ollie pulled the ankh from his cargo pants' pocket. He unwrapped the ceramic item and passed it to Maggie. Maggie studied it. Intricate protrusions covered the top surface while the bottom remained smooth. "What are these ridges?" Maggie asked. She traced her finger over them.

Ollie shrugged and shook his head. "That I'm not certain of," he answered. "No one knows for certain. I assume once we have all three ankhs, perhaps they will provide us with instructions to locate the library. Perhaps they form one or more hieroglyphs or give coordinates of some kind."

Maggie shook her head. "These don't remind me of anything specific," she said. "It doesn't appear that they are forming anything intelligible. It's just random lines and squiggles."

"It'll be interesting once we have all three to determine what they say or how they inform us of the tomb's location."

Maggie held the object toward Ollie to return it. "Wait!" Piper exclaimed. "Do you mind if I take a peek?"

"Not at all," Ollie answered.

Maggie handed the object to Piper, who studied it. "It's… kind of… sick that Cleopatra held this and now I am."

"Totally, fair maiden," Charlie answered. "Two Gucci chicks separate by centuries holding that ankh."

Piper smiled and offered him a demure glance before she handed the ankh back to Ollie.

The remaining hours of their trip dragged by. Exhausted from the day-long journey, they arrived in Venice after the sun set. Henry guided them to a hotel for the night. No one experienced any trouble sleeping after the long but boring trip.

* * *

THE ALARM WOKE everyone at seven the following morning. They prepared for the trip to the museum. Charlie would enter and setup his laptop to monitor security protocols. Henry, Maggie, Ollie and Piper would peruse the museum in pairs and note the location of the ankh along with all visible security issues.

They hoped not to run into any trouble with anyone else that may be searching for the ankh. Maggie postulated they had a head start, arguing that only they knew the location of the ankh from the museum curator. Henry pointed out they had no guarantee the other group lacked the same knowledge or confirmation they had not been followed. The discussion resulted in the conclusion they needed to work fast to collect the second ankh and move on.

They arrived at the museum, fronted by the Grand Canal. As they climbed from their private water taxi, Maggie stared up at the building. Its many columns with rounded windows fit into the surrounding Italian landscape perfectly. They paid the fee and began their tour. Charlie found a quiet spot and pulled his laptop open. He clacked on the keyboard. Maggie and Henry wandered through the museum in one direction as Ollie and Piper took another.

While impressive, none of the exhibits on the first floor contained the ankh. The group proceeded to the second floor to explore the exhibition rooms.

"How's it looking?" Henry asked Charlie through the earpiece connecting them.

"Not bad, mate. This is like a cake walk for me. Give me something hard to try."

"I'll work on making the next assignment more challenging," Henry commented.

"How's it looking on your end? Any sign of the item?"

"Not one," Henry answered. "Ollie? You got anything?"

"Nothing," Ollie admitted.

"I really hope this wasn't a wasted trip," Maggie said with a sigh.

"I hate to sound like the ugly American here," Piper chimed in, "but everything's in Italian. I can't read any of this. I hope I recognize the ankh because I certainly won't recognize a description of it."

Henry tugged Maggie's arm toward another display room. "Come on, let's keep going. We've got a good amount to see yet."

They wandered through another exhibition room but found nothing. A variety of mounted or skinned animals covered the walls. "Ugh," Maggie groaned.

"What? You have animal mounts at your shop!" Henry answered.

"Yeah, but I don't have an ostrich climbing my wall," Maggie responded, motioning to the ostrich mounted near the ceiling. "Or a skinned gorilla who looks like he's grimacing in pain!"

"Don't be a hypocrite, chicky. I saw that stuffed squirrel in your window. He looked upset."

"I'm taking him out when we get home," Maggie promised. "The ankh is not in this room, that's for sure. Let's move on."

They exited the room, moving to another gallery. Frustration built in Maggie. She huffed as they entered a corridor-like gallery. Windows overlooking the Grand Canal made up one side of the space. Display cases sat in front of them. Floor-to-ceiling display cases lined the opposite wall.

Maggie glanced at the shelves far above her head. "I hope it's not up there," she mumbled. She stood on her tiptoes and peered into one of the cases.

Henry stared into the case at eye-level. "Nothing here."

"Nothing up here either," Maggie said. "At least not that I can spot." Henry scanned the case above and confirmed Maggie's verdict.

They shuffled to the next case. "This time you take the top shelf," Maggie suggested.

"Fair enough," Henry agreed.

Maggie browsed the middle shelves. She squatted down

SECRET OF THE ANKHS

to peruse the bottom few shelves. With a sigh, she rose to standing. "Nothing."

"Me either."

They moved on and inspected three additional display cases with no results. "Five down," Maggie said with a sigh, "nine to go."

They moved to the next case. Maggie scoured the interior of the lower display case. She fought to keep her focus. With only five cases completed, Maggie's hopes waned with each passing moment. She stooped over and inspected the bottom shelf.

Maggie's brow pinched together. No cross lay on the bottom shelf, but the items triggered something in her memory. "A sword and a shield," she mumbled to herself. She glanced at the information near the items. Written in Italian, Maggie understood none of it. She scanned the text. One word stuck out to her: London. London, Maggie mulled, yes! These were two of the items sent here from the Natural History Museum in London!

A renewed energy buzzed through Maggie. She searched the bottom shelf for signs of the ankh. She found none. She re-checked the shelves above. Maggie searched them over and over, twisting and turning to see behind objects in the case.

"What is it? Do you see something?" Henry inquired.

"Not the ankh, but these," Maggie responded, pointing to the sword and shield. "These two items came from London. It mentions it on the write-up. They were on the inventory sheet with the ankh. It must be here somewhere!"

Henry scanned the shelves of the display case. "Not in this case."

"No, but hopefully not far from this case!" Maggie exclaimed. She sidestepped to the next case, her eyes skimming the contents. She shook her head when she came up empty and moved on.

Two cases later, Maggie's hopes began to dwindle. Perhaps her assumption was incorrect. Perhaps the items weren't here. Maggie ran her fingers through her hair and puckered her lips. She stomped to the next case.

Maggie browsed the middle two shelves. Devoid of the ankh, she shifted her gaze lower. The third shelf held nothing of interest. She crouched to examine the case's second to last shelf. Her heart skipped a beat. On the shelf, offset by a green velvet pad, the ankh lay propped in a holder.

Maggie grasped Henry's hand. "It's here!" she whispered excitedly.

Henry followed her pointing finger. His eyebrows raised as he spotted the object. "So it is," Henry answered. He squatted to examine the object.

Maggie slid her phone from her pocket and snapped a few pictures.

"We got it," Henry mentioned into the earpiece.

"Got your location, mate," Charlie responded. "Got you on... two cameras."

"Can you loop those?"

"Is the sky blue, mate?"

"What gallery are you in?" Ollie asked.

Maggie gave him directions to their location. Within moments, Ollie and Piper joined Maggie and Henry. Henry's eyes darted around the exhibit room, noting every detail he could.

"Let's grab a few pictures," he suggested.

The group spent twenty minutes posing for pictures, appearing like typical tourists. Henry took care to capture as much of the room and its security measures as possible, using Ollie, Piper and Maggie as his cover.

The group spent another hour wandering the museum. They paid careful attention to points of entry and exit, security at these points, and overall. As the afternoon wore on, the group departed from the museum and returned to their hotel to plan.

CHAPTER 12

Maggie lounged on the sofa, reading the area's takeout menus. Discussions regarding the retrieval of the ankh had stalled. While Charlie assured the group the electronic security measures would not be an issue, entry into the museum proved another matter.

"Maybe we should go for pizza," Maggie suggested. "I mean we are in Italy."

"You know pizza wasn't as popular here as…" Ollie began.

"It was in the US, I remember," Maggie finished for him. "But still."

Piper snatched the menus from Maggie's grasp. "Pizza it is," she said. "Thank God I dated that Italian guy whose family owned a pizza shop. I know enough Italian to order a pizza." She shuffled through the menus and called one eatery, placing an order. "Thirty minutes," she reported as she replaced the phone's receiver.

Maggie slumped further into the couch. Her head fell back onto its arm. Henry lifted her legs off the couch and slid under them. He stared at a few of the photos he'd taken of the museum.

"So, we need a boat," Maggie noted.

"Yep," Henry retorted.

"And a way in," she continued.

"Yep."

"And then it's easy. Because there's literally no major security on that case," Maggie said.

"Right," Henry agreed. "I just need a glass cutter and we've got it. So, in other words, we're nowhere."

Maggie scrunched up her face. "Let's work backwards," she suggested.

"Good idea," Piper added in. "Starting at the end, we're in a boat, sailing happily away from the museum with the ankh and we're not in jail or anything."

"Right," Maggie answered. "Just before that, we're sneaking out of the museum with the ankh. We're coming out the same way we went in, which is… what?"

"Through the window. We climb up from the boat," Henry answered.

"Already established that won't work," Charlie answered.

"Wait, why doesn't that work again?" Piper questioned.

"Alarm trigger," Charlie answered.

"Can't you just turn off the alarm?" Maggie asked.

"Sorry, chicky. I'd love to, but that's entirely different from looping a video and feeding it into their system."

"Why?" Maggie queried.

"Looping a video on their closed circuit is simple. I snatch a few seconds of clean video and feed it back to them. It's called closed circuit for a reason. It's closed. No one else involved in the equation. Just me and them."

"Okay, that makes sense. It's a closed loop." Maggie sat up as she continued to formulate ideas.

"Right," Charlie answered. "Alarm is different. It's connected to an alarm company who also monitors it right along with the on-site security."

"So, bypass it at both levels," Maggie proposed.

"I'd have to hack both the inside security AND their monitoring system. That would take time and information I don't have."

"It's not an option," Henry agreed. "It would take time we don't have."

"Okay," Maggie said, taking a deep breath before continuing, "can you disable the alarm?"

Charlie shook his head. "I monitored those security systems the entire time we were at the museum. The alarm systems on those windows were never off. Disabling them is going to draw a red flag somewhere. Disabling the doors after hours, same thing."

"Can we do what you did in London when we 'borrowed' the staff piece?" Maggie asked.

"No electronic security badges to open a door."

"UGH!" Maggie exclaimed, throwing herself back on the couch.

"We're stuck," Piper groaned.

"Any chance you can borrow it because of your fame, Uncle Ollie?"

Ollie, who had remained silent for much of the conversation, chuckled. "As terrible a plan as that is, sadly, it may be the option with the highest probability of success."

A knock sounded at the door. "Oh, please be the pizza," Maggie whimpered.

Henry crossed the room and checked the peep hole before pulling the door open. He passed a few bills to the delivery man and returned with two pizza boxes.

Maggie leapt from the couch and hurried to the boxes. She grabbed a plate and laid two slices on it. On a second plate, she places two more slices. She delivered one plate to Ollie before settling on the couch and taking a bite of the cheesy delight. Henry joined Maggie on the couch while

Piper elected to eat her pizza sitting cross-legged on the floor. Charlie returned with his slices and plopped into the armchair next to Ollie.

"Mmm, real Italian pizza!" Piper exclaimed.

Maggie was about to agree when Ollie issued a hoarse shout. He tossed his plate on the table and gulped his water. "Hot!" he gasped after a moment.

Maggie frowned and stared at her pizza slice. "It's not that hot," she answered. "Seems like it's been out of the oven a while."

Ollie shook his head, breathing through his mouth as he attempted to cool it. "Spicy hot," he choked out.

"Ohhhh," Maggie answered. "The peppers."

Ollie nodded. "Oh, sorry," Piper apologized. "I got hot peppers. I didn't think anyone would mind."

Ollie sipped at his water. "Whew," he said. "I didn't expect them to be that hot! That's like a five-alarm fire!" He retrieved his discarded plate and removed a few of the peppers.

Maggie snapped her head in his direction. She narrowed her eyes. "What did you just say?" she questioned.

"I said I didn't expect these to be that hot!"

"No," Maggie contended, "no, there was something else."

Ollie glanced at the ceiling in thought. "It's like a five-alarm fire?" Ollie phrased it as a question.

Maggie's eyes widened. She dropped her pizza slice on her plate and tossed the plate onto the coffee table. "That's it!"

"That's what?" Ollie inquired.

"That's how we're going to sneak into the museum!" Maggie exclaimed.

"With hot peppers?" Piper questioned.

"No," Maggie answered with a shake of her head. "With a five-alarm fire!"

"Huh?" Piper asked.

"You were monitoring the alarm system today, right?" Maggie asked Charlie.

"Yeah?" Charlie answered.

"And you said you couldn't intercept the alarm signal before it got to the alarm company, nor could you disable the alarm without it going unnoticed, right?"

"Right," Charlie agreed.

"But could you trigger the alarms?"

Charlie furrowed his brow. "Trigger them? Why would I want to trigger them?"

"We'll trigger the one on the window when we go in there," Maggie explained. "Which is a dead giveaway that something is wrong."

"Obviously," Henry said. "I'm not sure what you're getting at, princess."

"If Charlie can trigger multiple alarms at the same time, it'll appear that the alarm system may be malfunctioning. On both ends! The alarm system will see multiple triggers, as will the guards. They may investigate, but after a few go off with no issues, they'll assume there's some malfunction with the alarm. We can go in and out with the video looped without them even bothering most likely."

Everyone sat for a moment, pondering Maggie's plan. "Could this actually work?" Piper asked after a moment.

"Uh," Charlie murmured, "in theory, yeah. Yeah, I think it could."

"You can trigger the alarms?" Henry queried.

Charlie nodded. "Yeah, I could set them off."

"We need to make sure they don't come searching the gallery while we're in it."

"There'll be no reason for them to," Charlie answered. "They'll see nothing on the cameras, and we can keep them plenty busy searching all over."

"The last place they'll check is the second floor. Set alarms off all over the museum, but make sure a bunch of them are on the ground floor. They'll search there first," Maggie said.

"Good idea," Charlie agreed. "I can do that."

"This could work, Maggie," Ollie agreed.

"We don't have many other options," Henry said. "We'll make it work."

"All right, we have our plan!" Piper exclaimed. "When do we leave?"

"It might be best for you to stay here with Ollie and Maggie," Henry suggested.

"Wait a minute! No!" Maggie exclaimed.

Piper chimed in at almost the same time. "What? No way! I'm not getting sidelined with the prof! Besides, we're sitting ducks alone here!"

"We need to get in and get out with no complications," Henry countered. "Just Charlie and I will go."

"You never know what could happen," Maggie argued. "Or if you'll need backup. And Piper's correct! We're sitting ducks here. We're better off sticking together."

Henry weighed the argument. He sighed. "All right," he admitted, "you make a decent point. We shouldn't split up given what happened in London."

"They couldn't have followed us, could they?" Piper queried.

No one answered. "Okay, it's really bothering me that no one is answering right now," she continued.

Maggie shrugged. "They followed us to London," Maggie answered. "It's just better safe than sorry."

Piper's eyes widened. "So, you suppose they followed us."

"I didn't say that," Maggie began.

"Maggie's right," Henry interrupted. "Better safe than sorry. And the sooner we have our hands on that ankh and are moving out of here and on to the next place, the better. Once we have the ankh, we go on to Cairo and from there to the tomb. We'll head out around eleven tonight."

Maggie checked the time on her phone. "A few hours to go."

"We'll pack our stuff in the meantime and be ready to move out," Henry said. "Be prepared not to return here."

"Okay," Maggie answered. "That's probably best. I don't want to be here any longer than we have to after London."

"I agree a million percent," Piper said. "Although I don't think I like the sound of 'on to Cairo and the tomb,'" Piper confessed.

"Oh, you'll love it there!" Maggie answered. "We'll be perfectly safe! Right, Uncle Ollie?"

"That's right. The tomb site is secured by the military," Ollie confirmed.

"Still secure, no issues?"

"None so far," Ollie answered.

"That's good," Henry answered.

"See, Piper? Nothing to worry about!" Maggie exclaimed. "Once we're done here, it's smooth sailing!"

* * *

MAGGIE SHRUGGED her hoodie tighter around her as the boat zipped down the canal. The cooler night air chilled her along with the prospect of the task that lay ahead. Despite her confidence earlier, doubts raced across her mind. What if they were unable to pull this off? They needed the ankh. The people chasing them wouldn't stop until they recovered all the puzzle pieces. They had proven that.

The night's lights waltzed past them in a dizzying display as Henry aimed their rented boat toward the museum. Next to Maggie, Piper's leg bounced up and down. Despite not wanting to be left behind, Piper's nerves were getting the better of her. Maggie attempted to calm her own nerves. If things went to plan, they would soon have the second ankh in their possession, and they'd be on to Cairo.

The prospect excited Maggie. She missed the beauty and solitude of the desert. The chance to explore the tomb while not being held at gunpoint enthused her. Soon, she mused, soon. By the wee hours of the morning, they'd be moving on from Venice.

Maggie inhaled deeply and squared her shoulders. She convinced herself everything would work out.

The boat's motor quieted as they approached the museum. Henry swung the watercraft into the canal alongside the museum. They'd hide in the boat there while Henry entered the museum to retrieve the ankh.

Charlie pulled his laptop from his bag and popped it open.

"Let me know when you're in and I'll get in place," Henry said.

"Will do," Charlie answered as his fingers flew across the keys.

After a moment, he stopped. He stared at the screen. He cracked his knuckles and began furiously typing again. He stopped again, growling at the screen.

"What is it?" Henry questioned.

"Something's wrong," Charlie answered.

"What do you mean 'wrong?'" Maggie inquired.

Charlie clacked across the keys again. "Something's blocking me from the system," Charlie groaned.

"What? Blocking you how?" Henry asked.

"Yeah, I thought you were in this afternoon. You said it was child's play!" Maggie followed up.

"I was! It was!" a frustrated Charlie exclaimed.

"New system?" Ollie inquired.

"Nah, they couldn't have changed it this fast," Charlie countered. "It's something else."

Maggie glanced up at the museum beside them. "But what?" she murmured.

The boat rocked in the canal as Charlie battled with the security system. "Huh?" Charlie murmured as he glared at the screen.

"What is it?" Maggie asked.

Piper peered at the screen from her seat next to Charlie. Maggie repositioned herself to stare at Charlie's screen over his shoulder. "Something's weird," Charlie answered.

"Can you fix it?" Henry asked.

"I'm trying, mate," Charlie answered, "but it's like something has me locked out."

"Didn't you say this was a breeze earlier today?" Maggie questioned.

"It was, but…" Charlie answered, his voice trailing off as he pounded the keys on the laptop.

"But?" Maggie pressed.

Charlie stopped typing and narrowed his eyes. He cocked his head to the side and slammed the keyboard wildly. A smile spread across his face. "There you are."

"Who?" Maggie queried further.

Charlie shrugged. "No idea," he answered, "but whoever it is got into their system before me and put up a block."

Maggie screwed up her face. "Why would someone else be hacking into the museum's security system?" Maggie inquired. Henry's eyes darted around after he learned about the development.

"Good question," Charlie mumbled as he continued to type. "If I can get around their block, I can take a peek at what's going on in there." He paused a few moments. "Almost… there… and…"

Charlie ceased speaking; his eyes wide as he stared at the

screen. A frown formed across his face and he balled his hands into fists. With her jaw hanging open, Maggie gaped at the screen. "What is that?"

A skull appeared on the display. The open windows melted behind it. A deep, robotic laugh emanated from the laptop.

"NO!" Charlie exclaimed. "No, no, no, no, no, no!" He typed hurriedly.

"What is going on?!" Maggie exclaimed.

"Let him work," Henry cautioned.

Charlie continued to clack across the keyboard. Within a few seconds, the skull disappeared. In a flash, Charlie reopened several windows. They flew around the screen as he used keyboard shortcuts to open, close and toggle between windows.

Maggie gawked at the screen with little idea about what, if anything, Charlie was achieving. Charlie's frown began to turn into a sly smile. "Almost," he said. "And… got you!"

"Got who?!" Maggie cried in frustration.

"The hacker who thought he could run all over Charlie Rivers like a treadmill. Black Death, as he calls himself. Didn't realize who he was toying with."

"Black Death?"

"Yep. The laughing skull is his signature trademark. I've got him on the run now. And within a few seconds, I should be in the museum's security system." Charlie paused for a moment. "And… cameras coming up now."

"Why would someone named Black Death be hacking into the museum's security system?"

Interior cameras from the museum flashed on across the screen. They showed an empty lobby and several empty galleries. A small square in the top right corner blipped on last. It showed the gallery containing the ankh. Maggie gasped. Piper's jaw went slack. Charlie pointed to the screen. "There's your answer."

"What is it?" Ollie asked. He and Henry grouped around Charlie, both of them peering over his shoulder.

"They're robbing the museum, that's what!" Maggie exclaimed.

The group stared at the screen as two masked men pulled the ankh from the display cabinet. One dropped it into a small backpack-style bag before the other slung the bag over his back. They crossed the room to a window and began to crawl out.

Henry cursed under his breath as he raced to return to the boat's motor. Another boat's engine whirred to life further down the small canal. Their boat rocked as a second boat sped past them. Maggie collapsed onto a seat as the boat swayed violently.

The second boat fishtailed around the corner before it halted in front of the museum. Henry fired the boat's engine. It roared to life, and he started the boat moving toward the other watercraft.

As they rounded the corner, Maggie spied two men slide down two ropes. They landed in the waiting boat below them. Henry raced toward the craft. He aimed for center of the boat. Maggie winced and braced herself for the impact.

CHAPTER 13

"Hang on," Henry shouted over the din of the engine. Maggie clutched the seat. She glanced across the boat. Piper clung to the side; her knuckles white. Ollie grasped the side of the boat, his eyes fixed on the other boat ahead of them.

The other craft throttled its engine. The front end of the boat lifted from the water before the boat shot forward. The sudden movement propelled the craft diagonally. Instead of a full collision, they only glanced the side of the other boat. The motion shoved their boat to the side, spinning it to face the museum entrance.

The driver of the other boat took advantage of the temporary setback. As Henry swung their boat around, the other watercraft increased speed. The gap between the two crafts widened. It whizzed away from them and veered into a side canal.

Henry revved the boat's engine. The craft shot forward in pursuit.

"TO THE RIGHT!" Ollie called. He clasped the boat's side as he peered into the darkness, attempting to follow the other boat's course. The boat's engine issued a high-pitched whine as Henry urged it faster. They shot across the Grand Canal as Henry aimed for the smaller canal on the right.

Henry swung the boat into the narrower waterway. Maggie tumbled to her side as their craft slid sideways before Henry righted it. They picked up speed, flying through the water and down the canal.

The other boat came into sight ahead. "THERE!" Ollie shouted as he pointed to the dark craft.

Henry nodded. Their boat maintained its high-speed. They closed the gap. An object whizzed past Maggie. "GET DOWN!" Ollie shouted over the engine's roar.

Maggie ducked and focused her attention on the boat ahead. Muzzle flashes signaled gun fire from the fleeing boat. Despite the danger, Henry showed no signs of yielding. He crouched at the rear of the boat, still aiming the rudder for the other craft.

Buildings and parked watercrafts flew past them as they continued their chase. The distance between them shortened. "Maggie!" Henry called. "Come handle the engine!"

Maggie crawled across the boat's bottom and traded spots with Henry. "Keep the speed up and aim just to the side of the boat."

Maggie nodded as Henry crept forward to the middle of their boat. Within seconds, the boats were only feet away. Maggie urged more speed from the engine. She swung to the right. Their boat pulled alongside the other.

Henry leapt from their boat to the other craft. His jump caused the craft to swerve. Maggie failed to correct for his movement and struggled to maintain their course. The boat grazed another parked on the side of the canal.

Maggie grimaced. "Oops!" she called as she winced.

"KEEP GOING!" Ollie urged. Maggie swung the boat back toward the other. In tandem, they sped down the canal.

Maggie struggled to focus on navigating the craft as she witnessed the chaos ensuing on the other boat.

Henry wrestled with one of the boat's passengers. Their hands clutched a gun. Henry struggled to aim it away from their boat. A second man jumped on Henry's back and attempted to pull him from his associate.

Ollie picked up an oar from under one seat. He swung it toward the other boat. After two missed swings, he connected with one of the boat's passengers. The oar struck the man square in the back. He yelped in pain before he recovered. He grabbed Henry by the shoulders and readied to slam his head into the boat's bottom.

Ollie swung again, this time connecting with the man's head. The man stumbled two steps before he pitched over the side of the craft. Maggie glanced behind them for a moment, spotting the man flailing in the water.

Three men remained on the other boat. One manned the boat's engine. The other clung to the boat's side with white knuckles. The third still engaged in a battle with Henry.

Maggie called to Piper. "PIPER!" she screamed over the roar of the engine. "PIPER!"

Piper whipped her head in Maggie's direction. Maggie motioned for Piper to approach. Piper crawled to Maggie at the boat's rear. "Take the engine."

"WHAT?!" Piper exclaimed.

"Handle the engine. Keep us alongside that boat!" Maggie placed Piper's hand on the tiller. She nodded to Piper, then crept forward.

"I can't get a good crack at this one!" Ollie shouted, referencing his inability to strike the man with the oar without striking Henry at the same time.

"I know!" Maggie shouted. "I'm going over."

"WHAT?!" Ollie exclaimed.

Maggie put a foot on the boat's side. Her hair whipped

around her face and the wind whistled through her ears. She swallowed hard as she judged the distance between the two boats. Piper kept them close, a fact Maggie appreciated. With another gulp, she steadied her nerves.

Maggie flung herself from her boat to the other craft. Her top half landed on the starboard side of the other boat. Her legs trailed in the chilly water. She clung to the boat's side as she attempted to climb aboard.

Across the boat, the man who clung to the side spotted her. He glanced at her, then to the other two men. The man at the stern focused on navigating the tight canal. The other's attention remained on Henry. He punched Henry in the jaw before Henry struck back.

Maggie pulled herself higher and attempted to swing her leg into the craft. The white-knuckled passenger pulled himself away from the boat's side. He crawled on his hands and knees across the boat, approaching Maggie.

Maggie hooked her foot on the side and tried to roll into the boat. The man pushed her foot back over the side. Maggie moaned as her lower half toppled out of the boat, but she managed to maintain her grip.

The man picked up an oar. He swung at Maggie's arms. Maggie released her grip on the boat, clinging to it with only one hand as the oar cracked against the boat's side. Maggie swung her right arm back down as the man attempted to smack her left arm.

A quick zigzag motion from the boat's helmsman to increase the distance between the boats sent the man sprawling. He pitched over and dropped the oar as he attempted to stay aboard. Maggie used the interruption in his attack to finish climbing aboard. She rolled into the boat, gasping for air from exertion.

The man regained his footing and retrieved the oar. He straddled Maggie and raised the oar overhead. He aimed for

Maggie's head. Maggie pulled her legs to her chest and kicked them both out. She struck him square in the chest with all the energy she could muster.

The force was enough to drive him backward two steps. The oar flew from his hands as he again flailed his arms to steady himself. Maggie heard it crack off their boat before being pulled under the water.

As the man struggled to regain his balance, Maggie reeled back again. She thrust her legs out a second time. She struck the man again. In this instance, he failed to maintain his footing. He toppled over and pitched into the water.

Maggie sat up, spying the man bobbing in the boat's wake. She stood and retrieved the second oar. She lumbered across the boat, finding it hard to maintain her balance. The boat waggled as the helmsman attempted to toss Maggie from it.

Maggie planted her feet and swung the oar. She hit nothing. Henry landed another punch, and the man stumbled backward a step. "Now, Maggie!" Henry shouted.

Maggie swung again. The oar connected with her mark. She smacked him across the back. He doubled over. Maggie swung the oar again and landed another hit. The man curled forward further. Henry gave him an uppercut. His body reeled backward. Maggie swung again and cracked him in the legs. He dropped to his knees. A final punch sent him overboard into the water.

Maggie dropped the oar and raced to Henry. Henry grasped her arms. "We have to find the ankh!" he shouted. Maggie nodded.

Three black bags were visible in the craft. Two sat together, the third toward the boat's rear. "You get those two, I'll go for that one!" Maggie yelled.

"Okay!" Henry nodded. "Toss them to our boat!"

Maggie nodded and hurried toward the bag. She picked it

up and hastened toward their boat. She flung it over. It glanced off the boat's side, but Ollie caught it and dragged it into the boat. Henry tossed one of the bags over. It landed inside the boat. He tossed the second bag over.

"Time to go back!" he said.

Maggie nodded in agreement. They neared the canals' end. Before they could return to their watercraft, both boats shot into the open water beyond. Without the tight confines of the canal, the boats drifted apart.

Piper fought to regain a close enough proximity to allow Henry and Maggie to return to their craft. The man piloting the boat veered sharply away. The boat pivoted ninety degrees and raced for open water.

"Stay here!" Henry ordered. He took one step toward the boat's stern. He halted, his eyes widening. He swung back toward Maggie and wrapped her in a bear hug. Maggie felt her feet leave the boat's bottom as they flew through the air. They smacked into the water head-first.

Maggie surfaced inches from Henry. An explosion sounded behind them. Maggie whipped her head in the direction of the noise. The boat they had been on flipped over in a fiery ball. Maggie spun back toward their boat. Charlie stood with the flare gun still pointed toward the flaming boat.

"You okay?" Henry questioned.

Maggie nodded as she treaded water. "Yeah. You?"

"I'm fine, princess. And thanks for the save."

"You're welcome. You needing saved is really becoming a habit," she answered as their boat approached.

"Very funny, princess, very funny."

Piper killed the engine as the boat glided next to them. Ollie and Charlie hung over the side and grasped Maggie's arms. They hauled her into the boat, followed by Henry.

Maggie pulled her wet jacket off and wrung it out. She

sunk into a seat. Piper removed her hoodie and put it around Maggie's shoulders.

"Thanks," Maggie said as she squeezed water from her hair.

"Sure," Piper answered. "Although that was kind of stupid to jump to the other boat." Maggie rolled her eyes at Piper as she pulled the hoodie on. "But also, pretty brave." Maggie offered her a half-smile.

"Quick thinking with the flare gun, mate," Henry said, clapping Charlie on the back.

"I spied the gun in his hands," Charlie explained. "I'm glad you spotted my signal before I fired."

Ollie slumped into a seat. "Remind me never to come to Venice with you guys again."

Henry dug through the bags they had tossed before leaping from the boat. "Never again, huh?"

Ollie shook his head. "I'll stay on dry land, thanks."

"Dry land or not," Henry answered as he held an object up. "We have the second ankh."

Maggie leapt from her seat. "We got it!" she exclaimed.

* * *

MAGGIE EYED the second ankh as she sat wrapped in a blanket. The group holed up in a hotel room across town as Henry made arrangements to travel to Egypt. Maggie and Henry's clothes tumbled around in the dryer a few feet from their first-floor room.

With few shops open in the middle of the night and their clothes soaked after their dunk in the frosty waters, they needed a place to dry off. Both of them had stripped down and sent their clothes to the laundry room with Piper and Charlie. Maggie waited impatiently to retrieve her warm clothes from the dryer. Despite no longer being chilled,

Maggie longed to wrap up in her hoodie rather than the clunky blanket.

While she waited, Maggie picked up the ankh. She studied it. Similar to the first, ridges covered the top. She compared it to the other. The patterns didn't match. She laid the two ankhs side by side. Maggie examined them, leaning back to view the pattern from afar as well as close up. Nothing jumped out at her. She switched the order and inspected them again.

She cocked her head from side to side as she willed the two pieces to give her some information.

"Have you had a chance to examine these, Uncle Ollie?" Maggie inquired.

"Yes. Expert craftsmanship!" Ollie commented.

"Beyond that, did anything jump out at you?"

"If you mean, did I notice any messages giving us a clue to the location of the library, no."

Maggie sighed. "That's exactly what I meant."

Ollie shook his head. "Sorry, Maggie. I hoped when we retrieved the second ankh, something might jump out. Perhaps I could identify writing or hieroglyphs or coordinates of some kind, but..." Ollie's voice trailed off, and he shrugged his shoulders. "Nothing."

"And there's no information on this at all? Nothing you've run across in your research?"

"No," Ollie answered. "I'll admit I've not completed much research in this area, but what I've done has offered nothing definitive."

"So, all we've learned is there is a legend that suggests the three ankhs give the location to the library, but nothing you've found suggests how they do that. Is that right?"

Ollie nodded. "That's correct. I wish I knew more. I hoped it would be obvious once we had more than one ankh. Unfortunately, it isn't."

"Maybe when we get the third it'll be obvious," Maggie replied.

"If we get the third," Ollie responded.

"That sounds like you're beaten before you try," Maggie said.

Henry pulled his lips into a thin line. "We've been over every inch of that tomb. There's no sign of the ankh or another burial chamber that could contain it."

"So, you missed it!" Maggie suggested.

Ollie shot her a glance. "Months studying the structure, every detail, every hieroglyph, every object. How could we miss it?"

Maggie shrugged. "It's plausible. You had no idea what to search for."

"No, but we did realize we should search for something. The story is they were buried together. We DID attempt to find Antony's burial chamber. We couldn't find it."

"Just because you didn't find it, doesn't mean it's not there," Maggie countered.

Ollie opened his mouth to reply when the door opened. Charlie and Piper strolled through, bundles of clothes in their arms.

"Here we go. We dried them on the hottest setting. I hope they didn't shrink," Piper said.

"You and me both," Maggie answered as she accepted the clothes from Piper.

Charlie tossed Henry's clothes through the small opening in the bathroom door. "All dry, mate," Charlie shouted.

"Thanks!" Henry yelled.

Maggie clutched her blanket as she stood outside the door. "Come on, hurry up, I want to get dressed!" she complained.

"Yes, princess, give me a minute!" As he tugged his shirt over his chest, Henry emerged from the bathroom.

"About time!" Maggie teased him.

He gave her a half smile and a kiss on the forehead. "Go get dressed, princess, while your clothes are still nice and warm from the dryer."

"Did you get our travel arrangements set?" Maggie called through the door as she slid her pants on.

"Yep. We leave at six," Henry answered.

"Great! I can't wait to get going!" Maggie pulled her t-shirt on and slipped into her hoodie. She zipped it tightly around her before she pulled her hair into a ponytail.

Maggie emerged from the bathroom. "Can't believe you're excited to go back into the desert," Henry replied.

"I'm excited to see the tomb again!" Maggie exclaimed. "Piper, you're going to love it!"

Piper made a face at her. "I'm not convinced."

"It's AMAZING!" Maggie assured her.

"Isn't it laden with deadly traps?"

"No," Ollie answered, "we've disabled them. Don't worry, there is no danger there now!"

"I was there BEFORE the traps were disabled," Charlie explained to Piper. "Dangerous stuff. I survived, though. Thanks to my quick wits and cunning."

"Also, thanks to me who came back for you before that tomb raider killed you," Maggie reminded him.

"Well, also that," Charlie admitted.

"I'm still shocked you're looking forward to this, princess," Henry chimed in. "I thought you hated camel rides."

Maggie's jaw went slack, and her eyes widened. She whipped her head to face Henry. "Wait, what? I... I thought we were flying to the site?"

Henry lowered his eyes, unable to keep a straight face. Maggie shook her head at him, realizing he was joking. "Very funny, Henry."

"Wait, no camels?" Piper questioned.

"No," Henry admitted. "No camels. Chopper flight straight to the dig site."

"Aww," Piper lamented. "I wanted to ride a camel!"

Henry raised his eyebrows. "We could always…"

"No," Maggie interrupted. "No, no. You do NOT want a camel ride. There will be no camel rides. Tell you what, Piper, when this is all over, I will pay for you to have a ride around town on a camel, okay?"

Piper giggled at Maggie's reluctance to ride a camel, joining Henry, who already chuckled.

Maggie continued. "This is not funny. You'll see. I'm going to make you ride a camel and then you'll see."

The group continued to giggle at Maggie. Maggie kept on, "Sure! Laugh it up! I am very much looking forward to flying straight to the safety of the tomb."

"Safety of the tomb? That just doesn't sound right," Piper contended.

Ollie chimed in and assured the group. "That tomb isn't open to the public yet and is guarded twenty-four seven by a military presence, especially after the theft of the ankh in Rosemont. We couldn't be in a safer place once we arrive there!"

CHAPTER 14

Maggie stood on the tarmac staring up at the plane in front of her. She crossed her arms and shot a glance at Henry. Her jaw was taut, her eyes narrowed, and her mouth set in a firm line.

Henry avoided her glance. "You can't avoid me forever," Maggie said.

"Huh?" Henry said, pretending he hadn't heard her.

"A cargo plane, Henry? AGAIN?!"

Henry shrugged. "It's not that long of a flight."

Maggie sighed. "At least there're no camels," she said as the group climbed aboard.

Maggie nestled next to Henry and leaned on the cargo behind her. Piper sat across from them. Her gaze wandered around the cargo hold. She focused on Maggie. "Is this normal?" she mouthed.

"Yes," Maggie answered with a sigh. "Yes, it is... unfortunately."

"It's the easiest way into the country. No red tape," Charlie mentioned.

"You mean we're not on a packing list?" Piper joked.

"Nope. Completely incognito, fair maiden," Charlie assured her.

Ollie slid down to the floor next to Maggie. "Oof," he groaned. "This never gets any easier. Be glad you're still young."

"It's not that easy when you're young. Can't we get the government to upgrade us at some point?" Maggie inquired.

"I'll put the request in," Ollie said with a laugh.

The group spent the next several hours on the bumpy flight before touching down in Cairo. The afternoon summer sun rose high overhead by the time they landed, scorching the air.

"Whew!" Maggie exclaimed. "I forgot how hot it is here!"

"Just wait 'til we're in the middle of the desert," Piper groused. "I'm still not thrilled about heading into the desert to this dusty tomb." She crossed her arms in a pout as she stalked across the tarmac.

"The tomb's underground," Maggie explained. "It'll be nice and cool in there."

The group crossed to the parking lot where a familiar face greeted them. "TARIK!" Maggie exclaimed. She jogged ahead of everyone and tossed her arms around his neck.

"Maggie!" he greeted her, returning her embrace. "It's good to see you again!"

"It's good to see you, too!" Maggie answered.

"Are you excited to be back in Egypt?"

"I am! I'm really excited to see the tomb again. This time not at gunpoint!"

"And with no deadly traps!"

Maggie nodded in agreement. "Next time, you'll have to come to visit us, though," Maggie said. "We have to stop meeting under these circumstances."

Tarik gave a loud laugh. "I agree. After this, we will plan a trip to your hometown!"

"Hey, careful, mate," Henry warned. "That's my girlfriend you've not stopped hugging!"

Tarik chuckled at Henry as he released Maggie and grasped Henry's hand in a firm handshake. He pulled him into a hug, too. "Good to see you, my friend, good to see you."

Tarik shook Ollie's hand, then Charlie's. Maggie introduced him to Piper, who offered a curt "hello."

"I have brought a van," Tarik said as he motioned to the vehicle next to him.

"Great, let's head straight to the other airfield," Henry suggested. "I'd like to get a look at that tomb."

"Do you expect it's there?" Tarik inquired.

"I hope so, mate," Henry answered.

"I cannot imagine where else it could be," Ollie offered as he slid into the passenger seat. Charlie and Piper climbed into the far back of the van while Maggie and Henry took the captain's chairs in the middle.

"You've been over that tomb thoroughly already, no?" Tarik questioned.

"We have," Ollie admitted. He sighed before continuing. "Perhaps we missed something. At least, that is my sincere hope."

"I've never known you to miss anything, Dr. Keene."

"Let's hope there's a first time for everything, Tarik," Ollie answered.

"Had some trouble in Venice, I hear," Tarik said as he glanced at Henry in the rearview mirror.

"Nothing we couldn't handle, mate," Henry assured him.

"And you have both ankhs?"

"We do!" Maggie exclaimed.

"Any clues on how they lead to the library?"

"Not even a hint!" Ollie responded.

They drove in silence for a few moments before Ollie spoke again. "Tomb's secure?"

"Yes," Tarik confirmed. "Well guarded and completely secure. I checked again this morning."

"Perfect," Henry replied. "It'll be nice not to be chased by the bad guys while we search for the last ankh."

Tarik turned into a parking lot. He eased the van into a parking spot next to a truck with a large trailer attached. "Here we are," he said as he threw the shifter into park.

They climbed from the van. Henry approached the trailer. "Can't believe you got the camels arranged on such short notice," Henry commented.

"You know me, my friend, I can work miracles!" Tarik answered.

Maggie shuffled around the van and joined the two men. Her brow crinkled, and she stared at the trailer. "C-Camels?" she stuttered. "I thought… I thought we were taking a chopper?"

"No, camels, princess. Say, did Sefu have the same camel Maggie had last time?"

A grimace settled on Maggie's face. "O-oh," she mumbled. She swallowed hard as she stared at the trailer. "Was there no chance of the helicopter?"

Henry squeezed his lips together. Tarik pursed his, avoiding Maggie's gaze. Within a few moments, the two broke out into a fit of laughter.

"What's so funny?" Piper inquired.

"Yeah, I'd like to know the same thing!" Maggie demanded.

"Oh, princess. There're no camels, we're taking a chopper."

Maggie breathed a sigh of relief. "You're lucky I'm too relieved to be mad at you."

"I thought you grew to like your camel!" Tarik said as they walked to the waiting helicopter.

"Not enough to want to repeat the performance," Maggie said. "Especially if we can make it there in a fraction of the time!"

"Fair enough," Tarik answered as they climbed aboard.

Piper eyed the helicopter before entering. "Are we sure the camels aren't the better idea?" she inquired.

Maggie screwed up her face. "What? Come on, this is WAY better!"

"I dunno," Piper answered. She eyed the bird warily.

"What's the matter with you?" Maggie asked.

"Dude," Piper whispered, then lowered her eyes to the ground. "I'm afraid."

"Oh!" Maggie answered. "There's nothing to it." She grabbed Piper's hand. "It's just like flying. Only slower! And lower. And bumpier. And louder. And..."

"You're not making it better," Piper interrupted.

"Trust me, it's better than a camel," Maggie said.

Charlie sidled to them. He slid his backpack down his arm. "What's this?" Charlie inquired. "Afraid of the metal birdie, fair maiden?"

"Well..." Piper hesitated, color rising in her cheeks.

"Let me tell you about the first time Henry got me on a chopper," Charlie said.

Henry glanced back as he climbed into the helicopter. "Ugh," he groaned. "Don't remind me of that."

Piper shifted her gaze between the two of them. "What happened?" she inquired.

"I'll only tell if you're brave enough to fly with me," Charlie bargained.

"Come on, Piper!" Maggie entreated. "I want to hear this story!" Maggie grabbed Piper's hand, pulling her along. With some reluctance and a helping hand from Henry, Piper climbed aboard. Sandwiched between Henry and Charlie, she snugged her seatbelt across her waist. Maggie selected a seat between Ollie and Tarik, across from Piper.

Piper clutched at Charlie's hand as the copter commenced its clumsy climb into the sky. As they bobbled to reach flying altitude, Piper choked out, "S-so, what's your whirlybird story, good sir?"

Charlie leaned his head back on the wall behind him. A grin crossed his face, and he gave his head a slight shake. "We were on the run from some bad guys," Charlie began. "Serious stuff, machine guns, trained killers, you get the picture."

Henry held back a chuckle as Charlie laid out the situation. "Where were we, Taylor? Iraq? Turkey?"

"The Sudan, mate," Henry filled in.

"Right, the Sudan." Charlie nodded in agreement. He slid his eyes sideways toward Piper. "Real dangerous. Worse than the trouble we had in Iraq." Charlie lowered his voice to a gravely pitch, his gaze staring ahead as though disturbed. "But that's a story for another time."

Henry rolled his eyes at Maggie; offering an amused smile her way. Charlie turned his attention back to Piper. "So we're in the Sudan. On the run from some dangerous, dangerous guys. Taylor says he can get us out... if we can stay alive long enough to get to the rendezvous point.

"He gets on his sat phone, calls for a pickup at a pre-arranged LZ. You know what an LZ is, don't you, fair maiden?"

"Landing zone?" Piper answered.

Charlie raised his eyebrows at her. "One hundred points to the smart AND pretty maiden!"

Piper grinned at him. "Please, continue!" she said, engrossed in the story.

"Okay. Taylor calls for an extraction at the LZ. They

refuse. Say it's too dangerous to come in. They're surprised we're still alive!"

Piper raised her eyebrows. "OMG! They were just going to leave you? What did you do?!"

"We're in a Jeep. The bad guys are following in three SUVs behind us. I'm driving at breakneck speed while Henry's arguing for the extraction. Bullets are whizzing past our heads. Henry's clutching the handhold because I'm taking the bends on two wheels, fair maiden, no joke, two wheels."

Henry blinked his widened eyes at Maggie, who held in a chuckle.

"I can't look back, there's no time, it's too dangerous. But I blindly point my gun back and fire off two rounds. One takes out the driver, the other his passenger. One pursuit vehicle goes straight into a ditch and a second crashes into it. There's only one vehicle left between us and escape.

"Taylor screams into the phone 'Charlie's just leveled the playing field! Bring the chopper!' Finally, they agree. They'll send the helicopter into the LZ. We just need to get there in time. Chopper's on its way but they don't plan to wait."

"This is not really the way I recall it," Henry interjected.

"Probably the fear," Charlie answered. "Fear can really scramble the memories."

"You don't say," Henry answered.

"Shh," Piper scolded. She turned to Charlie. "Please, continue, good sir."

Charlie smiled at her, the smile vanishing as he mulled over the memory and continued. "I tromp on the accelerator, racing to get to the LZ in time. We're going over one hundred-sixty kilometers per hour and I'm urging more speed from that little Jeep's engine." He stared into Piper's eyes. "Our lives depended on it."

Piper's jaw dropped, and she nodded slowly, her

eyes wide with dismay. "The road's rocky, potholes everywhere. I'm dodging them right and left. 'HARD LEFT' Taylor shouts to me, pointing to the location of the LZ. I swerve to the left, the Jeep skids across the dirt road, fishtailing. Taylor almost falls right out, but I've got him. One hand's still fighting to keep the Jeep on the road, with the other I grab him by the shirt and haul him back into the Jeep with me."

Henry's eyes went wide as he turned to stare at Charlie. He furrowed his brow as he glanced back to Maggie and Tarik. He gave a slight shake of his head. Maggie bit her lip to avoid giggling.

"Wow, you're so brave," Piper mumbled.

"I can see the chopper coming. If we don't get there in time, they'll leave us to die. And I can't let Henry die. I can't! So, I hit the accelerator hard again. It's on the floor, I can't give it anymore. The Jeep shoots forward. In seconds, the chopper's hovering right in front of us. I slam on the brakes and skid the Jeep sideways. I leap out and race around the side, pulling Taylor out and dragging him with me.

"I'm waving my free arm at the copter and racing as fast as I can, but I'm almost carrying Henry, so I'm slowed down. The third pursuit vehicle's coming up fast. The chopper starts to pull up. They're going to leave, they're too afraid."

Piper's eyes shot wider.

"I have no choice. I'm screaming for them to wait. I fling my arm behind me and fire. I've only got two bullets left…"

"Wait, you've only used two bullets, mate," Henry interrupted.

Charlie raised his eyebrows at Henry. "I used a bunch before that, mate. You probably don't remember. You were nearly out of it."

"Ah…"

"Anyway," Charlie spoke over him. "I've only got two bullets left. And there's three bad guys."

Piper shook her head at the admission. "So, I fire them both."

"And?" Piper inquired.

"First one hits the driver. Second one hits the passenger. Square between the eyes." Charlie pointed his fingers between his eyes.

"And the third guy?"

"Driver slumps over the steering wheel. The vehicle veers to the left. It crashes directly into our Jeep in a fiery explosion!" Charlie mimicked the sound of a large blast, his fingers extending outward to create a visual.

"Wow," Piper whispered.

"The chopper lowers down. I toss Henry in before I climb aboard. I view the black smoke rising into the sky as we leave the hellscape behind."

The group fell silent as Charlie finished his story. Maggie's eyes shifted around as she wrinkled her brows. "So, what happened on the chopper?" she questioned.

"Huh?" Charlie answered.

"You said you'd tell Piper about what happened on your first helicopter ride. What happened?"

"Oh, ah…" Charlie hesitated, shifting his gaze to his hands.

"I don't recall the events leading up to that helicopter flight quite the same as Charlie," Henry said, "but AFTER we got on board, Charlie was a little green around the gills."

Charlie nodded. "It wasn't my best flight."

"Nor mine," Henry admitted. "I liked those trousers."

"That bad, huh?" Maggie inquired.

"That bad, princess," Henry assured her.

Piper shook her head. "No wonder. After everything you went through to save Henry, it's no wonder you threw up!"

Charlie brightened at her statement. "Yeah, that's it. After all that, I was so relieved, I couldn't hold it in."

The group went silent again. "Well," Maggie said, breaking the silence, "I, for one, am very grateful you saved Henry."

"Anytime, chicky, anytime," Charlie answered, wiggling his eyebrows at her.

Maggie chuckled as the helicopter began its descent toward the tomb.

"Are we here?" Piper inquired. "That wasn't so bad."

"I knew you could do it, fair maiden," Charlie told her.

Maggie leaned over Tarik to stare outside at the tomb's site. "Gosh, it'll be like being here the first time. You said you sent the staff home, right?"

"Yes," Ollie answered. "For safety. We didn't want to chance any hostage situations. Only the guards are here. And... one employee."

"Oh? Who drew that unlucky straw?" Maggie asked as they landed.

CHAPTER 15

Maggie stared at the tent's sole occupant. She narrowed her eyes. Her face set in a scowl, she crossed her arms and raised her eyebrows. Tarik, Henry and Ollie stood in a row behind her.

"I can't believe you didn't tell her," Tarik whispered to Henry and Ollie.

"If looks could kill…" Ollie breathed.

"That girl would be dead," Henry finished.

"Hello, Emma," Maggie said, ice in her voice.

Emma matched her stance. "Maggie," she responded, her tone as icy as Maggie's.

"Still here, huh?"

"Yep."

"I thought you said the tomb was secure," Maggie called over her shoulder.

"It is," Ollie assured her.

"Not with a traitor in our midst. They won't have to storm the place; Emma will just hand it over!"

Emma rolled her eyes. "Oh, give it a rest, Maggie."

"Me? I'll give it a rest when you…"

"LADIES, PLEASE!" Ollie shouted. "We're all on the same side here..."

"That's questionable," Maggie murmured. Ollie shot her a glance. She tightened her lips, lowering her eyes.

"As I was saying, we're all on the same side here. We must work together to find that third ankh."

"About that," Emma began. She pushed several objects on a nearby table to the edges, revealing a schematic of the tomb. "I've been over this and over it. I've searched this schematic. I've explored the tomb. Scrutinized every inch of ANYTHING that could lead to a chamber."

"And what did you find?" Ollie inquired as he studied the schematic.

Emma shrugged her shoulders and held up empty hands. "Absolutely nothing."

"Or she found the ankh and gave it to her friends," Maggie mumbled.

Emma spun her head to face Maggie. "That's a cheap thing to say," Emma spat back at her.

Maggie shrugged her shoulder nonchalantly. "If the tacky shoe fits..."

"Oh, sorry, I wasn't born with a silver spoon so I can wear my designer kicks around the dig site. Some of us have to WORK to get anywhere, we're not just handed things."

"And some of us have to be honest and not sell out our friends!" Maggie stamped her foot on the ground at Emma.

"I didn't sell out my friends, I..."

"Yes, you did!" Maggie interrupted. "You were ready to leave us to die..."

"ENOUGH!" Ollie roared. "That is enough out of both of you. If you can't learn to get along, one of you is going to have to leave."

Maggie set her jaw and stood her ground. She crossed her arms and glowered at Emma. "I'm not going anywhere."

"Neither am I," Emma replied as she raised her eyebrows at Maggie. The two glared at each other.

"Then you'd better learn to get along."

"Fine," Maggie replied.

"Fine," Emma repeated. "Now, as I was saying, since I am the one who works here and has the BEST knowledge of the tomb, I haven't found any clues about where we could have missed anything."

Ollie stared at the tomb's map spread on the table. Henry and Tarik joined them. Maggie approached the table, positioning herself opposite Emma.

"Find anything yet?" Charlie asked as he entered the tent with Piper.

Ollie sighed. "No. We were just going over the map, but we've found nothing new."

"We've spent most of the time arguing," Emma admitted.

Ollie shot her a glance. "Let's leave that in the past, please, Emma."

"Sure, Dr. Keene," Emma said after shooting a scowl Maggie's way.

Maggie narrowed her eyes at Emma and pursed her lips. "Best thing to do," she suggested, "is roll up our sleeves and start searching."

"Oh, what a brilliant suggestion," Emma retorted. "Why didn't I think of that?"

"Unfortunately, Maggie has a point," Ollie responded.

"Of course," Emma murmured. "Doesn't she always?"

"The tomb is the most likely place to search. We MUST have missed something."

"I can't see what, but…" Emma sighed. "Fine. We'll give it another inspection."

"Can we identify the most likely areas to search?" Henry asked as he studied the layout.

Ollie considered the map. "It's most likely not off the

entrance passage nor the main antechamber that passage leads to."

"What about the ship's chamber?" Charlie inquired.

"Possible, but not the most likely place," Ollie answered.

"Where is the most likely place?" Henry inquired.

"Off Cleopatra's chamber," Ollie said. He tapped the map with his fingers, revealing the location.

"That makes sense," Henry replied.

"Anywhere else?" Tarik queried. "What about this chamber?" He motioned to the chamber across from the ship's chamber.

Ollie shook his head. "It's not probable Antony would be buried off a chamber containing the servants' remains."

Tarik nodded in understanding. "I see."

"That's not to say we shouldn't check there," Ollie said.

Emma nodded. "We've had no luck anywhere else, so it can't hurt."

"Perhaps we should split up and check the less likely chambers before we reconvene in the larger chambers we've identified as Cleopatra's. If that's the most likely spot, we should concentrate our manpower there," Henry suggested.

"Good plan, Henry," Ollie agreed. "We'll begin tomorrow morning."

"Maggie and I will take the ship's chamber," Henry said. "Tarik and Emma can inspect the servants' area. Charlie and Piper can scour the entry passage…"

"Whoa, whoa," Piper interrupted. "Piper isn't scouring anything in that tomb!"

Maggie scrunched her nose at Piper. "Why?"

"I am not going into any dusty old tomb filled with deadly traps and poking around trying to find a new secret passage where my head gets chopped off or the floor falls out from under me and I end up in a pit of vipers or a giant rock crushes me."

"A giant rock crushes you?" Maggie asked with a chuckle.

"Yes, a giant rock that rolls down from behind me and crushes me."

Maggie laughed harder. "Like on Indiana Jones? This isn't the movies, Piper."

"Yes, like on Indiana Jones. And you spent MONTHS telling me how DANGEROUS that tomb was when you went in. That combined with Leo constantly calling him Indiana Jones, it's just… left a bad taste in my mouth." She thrust her thumb in Henry's direction.

"That bloke is really a pain in the arse," Henry muttered. "I look nothing like Indiana Jones."

"It's the hat," Maggie explained.

Piper nodded. "Yep."

Henry pulled his hat off his head and stared at it. Maggie winked at him and nodded. Henry shrugged and replaced his hat.

"The traps in that chamber have been disabled," Ollie assured her. "Though if you are uncomfortable, no one's going to force you."

"Come on, Piper! It's really something to see! And like Uncle Ollie said, the traps are disabled. If you find anything, come and get someone!"

Piper sighed and pursed her lips into a pout. She stared at the floor.

"Come on, fair maiden," Charlie entreated. "It is something to see! I'd love to show it to you."

"Well…" Piper hedged.

"The intricate carvings, the detail, the vastness of what they built all while hidden under the sands," he continued.

His words impressed Maggie. The tomb had a profound effect on everyone who came in contact with it. "I can show you where I nearly died, yet my wits saved me." Maggie ceased being impressed, rolling her eyes.

Piper raised her eyes to meet Charlie's. "Okay," she agreed. "If you can return here after your experience, I guess I can brave having a peek around."

"That's the spirit, fair maiden!"

"All right, there's our plan," Henry said.

Everyone nodded in agreement. "For now, it's getting late. We'll get going first thing in the morning."

"Perfect," Ollie answered. "Let me show you where your tents are."

They filed out of the tent and Ollie led them to the housing area. "We'll stay in side-by-side tents, just in case," Ollie said. "Don't worry, the guards will ensure nothing happens. It's just easier to keep everyone in the same area."

Maggie nodded. "Tarik, Charlie, Henry and I will be in this tent here," Ollie stated as he pointed to the tent on the right. He paused. "And… ah…" Ollie hesitated again. "You ladies will stay in this one."

"Wait, ALL of us?"

Ollie swallowed hard. "Yep," he said, his voice cracking a bit. He cleared his throat. "Yep."

Maggie scrunched her face and nodded.

"Come on, princess," Henry said, rubbing her shoulders. "Let's go watch the sunset."

"Good idea," Maggie agreed.

Maggie allowed herself to be led away from the tents and further into the desert sands. Two armed guards stood at the fringes of the encampment. As Henry and Maggie passed them, one of the guards stepped to follow them.

"We'll be all right, mate," Henry assured him.

The guard stepped back and allowed them to pass. Henry led Maggie west toward the setting sun. They climbed a sand dune and collapsed at the top. The setting sun streaked the summer sky with deep oranges and reds.

Maggie admired the sky, allowing the quiet moment to

relax her nerves. She let her head rest on Henry's shoulder, and he wrapped his arm around her. "It's so beautiful here," Maggie said as she admired the scenery.

Henry kissed the top of her head. "Mmm-hmm," Henry agreed.

Maggie gazed up at him. "It's nice being back here when my life isn't in turmoil and my uncle and friends aren't missing."

"You really like the desert, don't you?" Henry questioned.

"I do! There's nowhere else on earth quite like it!" She paused for a moment and admired the untouched beauty of the desert. "What about you?"

"I love the desert. It's one of my favorite places!"

"Because of the solitude?" Maggie inquired.

"Because it's where we shared our first kiss," Henry admitted.

Maggie smiled up at him and leaned up for a kiss. They sat together in silence for another few breaths before Maggie spoke again. "So, do you expect us to find anything tomorrow?"

Henry breathed deeply, weighing his answer. "I hope so."

"Hope so? That's it? No encouraging words? No glimmer of certainty?"

"Your uncle's a smart man. If he expects it's here, it's here."

"That's more like it."

"Still, being so smart, it's surprising he hasn't found it yet."

"Perhaps he just... missed it! That tomb was packed full of great finds! They spent most of their time cataloging that! It's easy to have overlooked."

"Easy to have overlooked another burial chamber?"

Maggie shrugged. "If it's hidden, sure."

Henry raised his eyebrows. "We'll see." He paused. "I'm not sure where. They haven't found any clues."

"Oh, right," Maggie tossed her hands in the air before falling backward to lie in the sand. "EMMA, the supreme authority on the tomb, can't find it, so it must not be there!"

The sun dipped below the horizon as Henry lay back next to her. They stared at the night sky, awaiting the first star to appear. Henry remained silent.

"You know, I'll remind you she struggled to read the staff when we were searching for the tomb, so she's not got a great track record on this stuff."

Henry studied the darkening sky.

"Why aren't you answering me," Maggie inquired. She rolled over to stare at him.

"Huh?" he said.

Maggie shot him a glance. "You heard what I said."

"Oh, right, yes, I heard you, princess."

"Then why didn't you answer?"

"Ah, well…"

"It bothers me you're not answering. It usually means you don't agree."

"Now, princess, you know when I don't agree, I just tell you."

"Oh, really? Like the time you didn't agree about that lasagna I made? I said it tasted okay and asked if you agreed and you pretended not to hear me?"

"Well, that was different."

"How?"

"Just was," Henry hedged.

Maggie sat up and crossed her arms. She stared at Henry.

"Look!" Henry pointed to the sky. "The first star, princess!"

Maggie raised her eyebrows at him, her mouth forming into a pout. Henry grimaced. "Okay, okay," Henry said. "I just… don't see why she gets to you."

"She's a traitor!" Maggie exclaimed.

"She had a reason, Maggie. She was backed into a corner."

Maggie scowled and flung herself back down onto the sand.

"Don't be mad at me, princess. I just hate to see you upset."

Maggie sighed. "I'm not mad at you," she admitted. "She just bugs me."

"I thought you understood. Plus, part of the reason she was backed into a corner was because we put her there," Henry reminded her.

"I know. And I did understand! At least I thought I did. When we went back to Cairo after we found the tomb, I realized what the situation was. But then I just went over and over it and got madder and madder." Maggie rolled over to stare at Henry, propped up on her elbows. "I mean, she literally was ready to leave you, Charlie, Tarik AND Uncle Ollie behind to die! She just wanted to walk away! How are you okay with this?"

Henry shrugged. "People make snap decisions when they're under duress. Everyone reacts to a stressful, life-and-death situation differently."

"Oh, so you're okay with excusing her poor choices and potentially costing four people their lives because she was stressed?" Maggie argued.

"Don't put words in my mouth, princess, I didn't say that at all."

Maggie's shoulders sagged. "I'm just saying she's got a poor character! How can you not agree?"

"Leo was ready to leave us behind, too," Henry countered.

"Yes, and I dumped him," Maggie contended. "Plus, you DO think he has poor character! And stop deflecting! We're talking about Emma NOT Leo."

"Emma's not my favorite person either," Henry admitted. "But she's not worth this much upset. And the decision she made is understandable. She was frightened. They probably threatened her."

"Oh, so are you ready to let Leo off the hook?"

"I thought we were leaving Leo out of this?"

"You brought him up!"

"I don't want to argue," Henry began.

"Neither do I, but it's too late for that!"

"Why do we always end up arguing about that bloke every time we're in the desert?"

MAGGIE SHOOK her head without answering.

"All right, all right. I guess…" Henry paused, grimacing. "I guess Leo's decision is understandable. And yes, I think it shows poor character on his part. And Emma's. But she's not a terrible person." Henry lowered his voice to a mumble. "And neither is Leo."

"Wait, what? Neither is Leo? Henry Taylor! Are you admitting he's not an ass?"

"Oh, no," Henry countered. "He's definitely an arse. He's just not a terrible person."

Maggie giggled at his admission.

"Your turn," Henry said.

"My turn for what?"

"Admitting Emma is not a terrible person."

Maggie rolled over to stare at the sky, now full of stars. She bit her lower lip. After a breath, she answered. "Fine, okay, she's NOT a terrible person."

"And you're not going to let her bother you?"

Maggie groaned. "And I'm not going to let her bother me."

"Promise?"

Maggie rolled her eyes. "Fine, I promise."

Henry put his arm around her, pulling her close to him.

He kissed the top of her head. "You do NOT have poor character. That's why I love you, Maggie Edwards."

Maggie giggled. "And that's why I love you."

"Because I also have great character?"

"No, because you realize how great I am," she joked. They settled back into the sand to watch the stars for another hour before heading to bed for the night.

Maggie tiptoed into the large tent. Blackness surrounded her. Unfamiliar with the layout, Maggie bumped into a small table, scattering its contents onto the tent's floor. "Shoot!" she hissed as she hopped on one foot to stop the pain from panging through her big toe.

She placed her foot on the floor only to raise it after stumbling on an unidentified object. With a sigh, she staggered a few more steps as she pulled her phone from her pocket. Maggie toggled on the flashlight.

"Hey!" Emma shouted from her cot. She held her hand up in front of her face to block the light. "Turn that thing off, we're trying to sleep!"

"Yeah, boss lady," Piper chimed in, "we're trying to sleep."

"Sorry!" Maggie exclaimed. "I'm just trying to get to bed without hurting myself!"

"If you would have gone to bed when everyone else did instead of slinking off to make eyes at Henry, you could have without disturbing the rest of us," Emma complained.

Maggie bit her tongue as she recalled her promise to Henry. "I'll just be a minute," she promised.

"Turn off the light," Emma entreated.

"Just turn over," Maggie suggested.

"I'll still see the light shining even if I turn over."

Maggie rolled her eyes. "What happened to Emma 'I can sleep through anything' Fielding?" Maggie muttered.

"Huh?" Piper responded.

"Nothing, go to sleep, Maggie," Emma snarked as she rolled over on her cot.

"In college, Emma could sleep through ANYTHING," Maggie explained. She chuckled to herself. "One time, the guys from Kappa Kappa Sigma raided our sorority house and…" Maggie giggled. "Emma slept RIGHT through it. I mean, not even a peep."

"Really?" Piper inquired.

"Yeah, really. Oh, those boys were blowing those little party horns. You know, the kind you get on New Year's Eve. And running through the house. Girls were screaming and Emma never budged."

"This does not need to be discussed," Emma complained.

"Oh, come on, Emma," Maggie replied, "it's funny!"

"It's not funny," Emma countered. "You only find it funny because it makes me look bad."

"How does it make you look bad?" Maggie asked. "Stop being a spoil sport."

"Just get in bed and turn that light off."

"Fine, whatever," Maggie answered. She climbed under the thin blanket on her cot. With her flashlight toggled off, she plugged her cell phone into the generator-powered charger and settled back into the pillow.

Maggie tossed and turned on the cot. She spent a few minutes laying on her back before she flipped onto her side with a sigh. Her cot creaked with every movement.

"Will you quit jumping around?" Emma grumbled into the darkness.

"I can't get comfortable!" Maggie answered.

"Bed not cushy enough for you?" Emma retorted.

"First of all, this isn't a bed, it's a cot. Second, no, it's not cushy enough for my tastes. And third, I'm not going to lie here uncomfortable because my squeaky cot is annoying you."

"Well, there are two other people in here trying to sleep, but you're right. Don't trouble yourself with being considerate."

Maggie rolled her eyes at Emma in the dark. She flopped from her side to her back. Her cot protested under her movement. She heard a sigh from Emma. Maggie tossed the thin covering off her. She fumbled around on the small table next to her. Items rattled around as Maggie searched for an object to fan herself.

Light shattered the darkness. Maggie squinted against it. "What are you doing?" she asked Emma.

"What are YOU doing?" Emma inquired. She held a large flashlight in her hands, aimed directly at Maggie.

"Trying to find something to fan myself with. It's hot in here."

"It's the desert. It's hot. Get over it. If you lay still, you won't be so hot."

Piper pulled her pillow from under her head and squashed it over her face.

"Fine, fine," Maggie acquiesced. "Just turn that off and let's try to go to sleep."

Maggie laid awake for over an hour contemplating their situation. If they found nothing in the tomb, then what? They would have no leads. They had risked their lives to gather the first two pieces of the puzzle. Would they find the third? Emma did not expect they would. What if she turned out to be right? As much as Maggie hated to admit it, Emma may be correct. Despite the issues between them, Emma was knowledgeable, especially about the tomb.

Maggie shook her head and rolled onto her side. There had to be something here. They weren't beaten yet. She had to hold on to that hope.

CHAPTER 16

The bright sun beat down on the desert sands. Despite the early hour, temperatures already soared. Maggie stood over the schematic of the tomb, fanning herself with a stack of folders.

"Still hot, huh?" Emma snarked.

"Yes, it's the desert, remember? And unlike some people, I don't have ice water coursing through my veins."

Henry pinched Maggie's arm, sliding his eyes sideways and his eyebrows up in a silent warning. Maggie held her arms up in defeat.

"Are we all ready?" Ollie inquired, steering the conversation back to the task at hand.

Everyone nodded. Ollie continued. "Search every inch of your area. If you find ANYTHING, report it to me. I'll stay in the antechamber for this portion of the search."

"And if we find nothing…" Maggie began.

Ollie nodded. "If we find nothing, we move on to the larger treasure and burial chamber area this afternoon. All right, everyone have their flashlights?"

Everyone nodded. "Okay, let's move out!" Ollie commanded.

They filed from the tent and hurried through the heat across the short distance to the tomb's entrance. Maggie took a deep breath as they faced the large gaping entrance to the tomb. A flicker of memories from her last encounter here flitted through her mind. She swallowed hard and shook the memories from her brain. There was no danger here this time. She could enjoy perusing the tomb. The craftsmanship and intricate details enthralled her even when she was held at gunpoint. She would enjoy the exploration this time.

Excitement built as she stared into the lit entrance. A smile spread across Maggie's face. "Wait until you see this place!" Maggie said to Piper. "It's AMAZING!"

They entered the passageway leading to the tomb's antechamber. Maggie's eyes took in the space. She lowered them to the stone floor. Her foot rubbed one of the stone tiles. She explained to Piper about the poison-dipped arrows triggered by them.

"They've been disabled," Ollie assured them. To prove his point, he trod on several of the tiles. "All right, Piper and Charlie, you two start here."

Maggie, Ollie, Tarik, Emma and Henry continued down the passage and to the massive antechamber at the end. Here they split into two teams, with Maggie and Henry stepping into the left chamber where a massive ship to serve Cleopatra in the afterlife had sat. Emma and Tarik entered the servants' burial chamber across the antechamber. Large temporary lighting lit the area.

"Gosh," Maggie said, her voice echoing in the colossal space, "this room is so empty without the ship."

"Yep," Henry answered.

"That ship was amazing," Maggie added. "Too bad it wasn't still here. I'd have loved to show it to Piper."

"She doesn't seem too keen on this whole thing."

"No," Maggie admitted. "I didn't realize she was such a 'fraidy cat! She seems so carefree."

"When she's in her comfort zone," Henry noted.

Maggie nodded in agreement. "Well, I guess we better start our inspection!"

"Pick a corner, princess, any corner."

Maggie spun in a circle. "That one!" she declared, pointing across the room.

Maggie strode to their starting point. Hieroglyphs covered the walls even in this room. She studied them. In the middle, a depiction of Cleopatra sailing in a dark river adorned the wall.

They worked their way around the room, studying the pictures. Maggie hoped to find a clue suggesting a hidden passage, though she didn't expect much. People with far more knowledge of hieroglyphs and tomb structure likely already poured over these. They had found nothing.

Maggie rounded to the final wall. "I wonder what all of this says," she pondered aloud.

"I can't help you there, princess. I don't have much knowledge of Egyptian hieroglyphics."

"Do you think they translated all of this already?"

"Good question. Let's get the answer." Henry wandered to the entrance as Maggie continued her circuit around the room. He called Ollie into the chamber.

"Did you find something?" Ollie asked breathlessly as he hurried inside.

"Sorry to get your hopes up," Maggie answered. "No. We were wondering if all this has been translated yet."

Ollie shook his head. "Not yet," Ollie admitted. "We've photographed all of it and sent it out to be analyzed, but we don't have full translations back."

"I wondered if anything on these walls suggested another passage."

Ollie shrugged his shoulders. "Nothing was obvious to me, but I'll admit I didn't translate the entire thing. It seems mainly to discuss the ship, to detail the building of it, who was involved, how it would be used by Cleopatra in the afterlife and a little about her use of ships during her lifetime."

Maggie returned her gaze to the walls. "Got it. Well, we'll make a thorough inspection of the room, anyway."

"Good luck! I'll check on the other teams." Ollie strolled from the room.

"Okay!" Maggie said. "Let's get to it!"

They examined every inch of the wall with their hands. Henry climbed the scaffolding, working his way around the top of the room as Maggie worked on the bottom half. They felt for any triggers, abnormalities, or hidden mechanisms. Maggie's enthusiastic attitude waned with each passing moment.

They reached the end of the first of the four walls. Maggie's fingers ached from meticulously testing the stone walls. She collapsed on the floor. "I need a break," she said with a sigh.

Henry descended from the scaffolding, sliding down to sit next to her. "Tired already?"

"Frustrated," Maggie admitted.

Henry put his arm around Maggie and pulled her close to him. "You can't win 'em all, princess."

"My fingers are sore."

"Let's take a break."

Maggie sighed and rubbed her fingers against her leggings. "No," she said with a shake of her head. She climbed to their feet. "No, let's keep going. Let's at least get halfway done before I pitch a fit."

Henry chuckled at her as he stood. "If you insist! We'll take a break for your pity party after this wall."

Maggie pursed her lips at him. "It's not a pity party. It's an 'I'm frustrated' party."

She began her inspection of the wall's lower half. "Don't let it get you down, princess," Henry said as he climbed the scaffolding for his probe.

"You realize if we find nothing here, we have no leads on what to do next."

"Let's keep our fingers crossed we find something then."

"Which is why I'm frustrated with each hieroglyph that passes with no breakthroughs!"

Maggie reached the corner after over forty minutes of careful work. Maggie pounded against the final few inches of the wall. "Found something?" Henry questioned as he joined her on the floor.

"Yeah," Maggie answered. "I found just how frustrated I can become in under an hour."

"Come on, let's take a break before we tackle the other half of the room."

"Good idea. I need a break from this place."

Maggie stomped from the room into the antechamber beyond. "Maggie!" Ollie called from the room's center. "Great timing! I just brought drinks and sandwiches for everyone."

Emma, Piper, Charlie and Tarik already sat on the floor nibbling on sandwiches. Maggie collapsed next to Piper. She grabbed one of the sandwiches, unwrapped it and took a bite.

"Anyone find anything?" she inquired.

"No," Piper answered, "but you were right. This place is awesome!"

Maggie grinned at her. "I told you!"

"How about you?"

"Nothing but sore fingers, a sore back and sore feet," Maggie admitted.

"How about you two?" Maggie inquired of Tarik and Emma.

"Nothing," Tarik replied. "We have several more locations to inspect."

"I told you I didn't think we'd find anything," Emma responded in her know-it-all voice.

Maggie sighed, her irritation mounting despite the break from the tedious work. "If we don't find anything, we're at a dead-end," Maggie lamented. "We HAVE to find something!"

"Dead-end or not, the tomb isn't going to just do what you want because it's easier for you," Emma retorted.

"I didn't say it was going to do what I want. I'm just pointing out if we find nothing here, we may never find the third ankh because we have no leads on it!"

"That doesn't mean we WILL find it here because it's inconvenient for you if we don't and all signs point to not finding it," Emma argued.

Maggie scowled and opened her mouth to counter, but Ollie beat her to it. "Let's think positive and hope we catch a break somewhere."

Maggie nodded. The group finished their lunch in silence for the most part before returning to their afternoon work. Maggie and Henry returned to the ship's chamber and elected to begin on the side wall, saving the wall with the doorway for last.

As they neared the center of the wall, Maggie detected an acute change in the stone. She rubbed her fingers over the area. Unlike the rough stone of the other portions, this part was smooth, almost silky to the touch.

Maggie's heart skipped a beat. She stooped to examine it closer. She detected the slightest difference in shade from the surrounding stone wall. Her pulse quickened as she slid her hand across the portion of the wall different from the rest. A clear outline existed. Maggie's fingers traced the shape, a square stone placed in the middle of the wall. She blew around the edges. Her breath revealed a dark line delineating the stones.

A smile spread across Maggie's face and she straightened her posture. "I think I found something!" she exclaimed.

"Really?" Henry inquired. He hurried down the scaffolding, skipping the last few rungs and leaping to the floor. "Where?"

Maggie pointed to her discovery. "Here. The stone feels different from the other portions of the wall. And look, there's a clear outline. This stone has been placed here. The wall isn't solid!"

Henry crouched to examine the area. "Yeah, I see it," Henry murmured as he studied the wall.

Maggie scurried to the doorway. "Uncle Ollie!" she shouted into the antechamber. "Uncle Ollie! Come in here! We found something!"

Maggie returned to Henry's side, breathless with excitement. Ollie hastened through the doorway and to the couple. "Where?" he asked, his breathlessness matching Maggie's.

"Here!" Maggie exclaimed. "See the outline of the stone set in the wall? This stone is different from the surrounding material."

Ollie adjusted his glasses and leaned closer to the wall. He reached out and traced the dark edge of the stone. "Yes! Yes!" he exclaimed. "I see it!"

Maggie clapped her hands and bounced on her toes. "This HAS to be it!"

"I must grab a few tools," Ollie responded. "Henry, will you help me?"

"Sure thing, Ollie," Henry answered. The two disappeared from the chamber.

Maggie focused her attention on the discovery. She bit her lower lip as her smile broadened. They'd soon have the third ankh in their possession, she mused. Her mind spun in a million directions. How did the pieces of the puzzle fit together? Would it become obvious once they had all three pieces?

Maggie's mind shot forward beyond the problems to the solution. The Egyptian sands shimmered around a beautiful building. White columns held the roof at bay. They met large stone steps leading to the entrance. Inside, the structure held ancient secrets, hidden from the world's view for millennia.

Soon, Maggie mused, soon those secrets would be exposed. She relished in the building excitement. Henry and Ollie returned with the remaining four group members in tow.

"You found something?" Tarik questioned.

"Yes!" Maggie exclaimed.

"Unbelievable," Emma murmured under her breath. Despite Emma's best attempt, Maggie overhead the comment. She ignored it. Maggie's excitement allowed her to overlook the mumbled remark.

"Great work, chicky," Charlie said.

Maggie beamed at him. Ollie and Henry set their tools out in an array on the floor. Ollie began revealing the stone's edge with a brush. Sediment and dust spilled to a drop cloth placed on the floor as he carefully swiped the edges with the tool.

The form of the stone took more shape with each passing moment. Satisfied, Ollie dropped the brush on the floor.

"Pry 'er loose?" Henry inquired.

Ollie nodded. "Let's give it a try. Gently," he cautioned as Henry picked up a pry bar. "Don't force it too much. Let's see what we're working with."

Henry nodded in response and began to pry the edges.

Maggie held her breath as she waited to spot some movement from the stone. Nothing happened.

Henry tried another spot and a different angle. His muscles flexed as he put pressure on the stone. It did not budge. Henry tried a third time. The results remained the same.

Maggie sighed as Ollie waved for Henry to halt. "She's stuck good," Henry noted.

"Perhaps sediment is still holding it," Tarik suggested.

"That well may be the case," Ollie agreed.

He selected several tools from his array. For the next hour, Ollie worked to separate the stone from the surrounding wall. Emma joined in with him after retrieving another set of tools from the antechamber. Maggie paced the floor as she watched them work.

Ollie set his brush down. "All right, let's give this another try."

Emma stood and backed away, rubbing her dusty hands against her blouse. Henry retrieved his pry bar and inserted it in the groove between the stone and the wall. He jiggled it back and forth gently.

"Anything?" Ollie queried.

Henry nudged the bar a few inches further into the crevice. He pivoted and pushed against the tool. A scraping sound emerged.

"It's moving!" Maggie exclaimed.

"Yes!" Ollie concurred. "Carefully now, rock it loose."

"Right," Henry agreed. He yanked the bar from the crevice and moved it to the stone's opposite side. He tapped it into the slit with a hammer before wresting the pry bar to inch the stone further from its spot.

Henry continued working side to side until the stone hung halfway out of its spot. He paused for a moment to wipe the sweat from his brow. "This isn't getting any easier. In fact, it's getting harder."

"I'll take over, my friend," Tarik offered.

"Thanks," Henry answered and handed the tools to Tarik.

"If you get it a bit further out, we may be able to remove it by hand," Ollie suggested.

"I'll do my best," Tarik promised.

He thrust the tool into the space between the wall and the stone. Tarik tugged on the bar, groaning with effort. He pulled the crowbar out and wedged it in the opposite crevice. The stone refused to budge despite the effort Tarik used.

Ollie studied the large stone. "Perhaps it's hanging up because it's falling as it moves out."

"Catching against the top?" Henry inquired.

"It's possible," Ollie conjectured.

Henry grabbed a second crowbar. "I'll wedge it from the bottom, you wiggle it loose."

Tarik nodded in agreement. "Okay."

"You ready?" Henry asked.

Tarik nodded again. Henry shoved the pry bar under the stone and pushed it toward the floor. Tarik jounced his lever. The stone shifted forward.

"Switch sides!" Ollie called. "It's almost there!"

Tarik raced to the opposite side and drove the crowbar into the gap. One yank on the bar drove the stone forward several inches.

"Stop!" Ollie instructed. "We'll have to work the rest by hand!"

"Let's strap it to the hoist so it's manageable," Henry suggested.

"Good idea," Ollie responded.

Henry retrieved the hoist from the antechamber. Tarik tossed the crowbar on the floor and assisted Henry in setting up the lift. They secured the strap around the stone.

"You take one side, Henry, I will take the other," Tarik said when they finished.

"I'll grab this corner if the ladies can manage the other," Charlie offered.

"Got it," Maggie replied. She positioned herself at the corner. Emma grabbed the middle of the stone's side. Piper and Ollie gripped the stone's front.

"Now, slide the stone. We may need to jiggle it a bit," Ollie advised.

They all heaved together, but the stone did not budge.

"Pull your way, mate," Henry told Tarik.

"Right," Tarik said with a nod.

Henry pushed as Tarik pulled. "Now back my way," Henry groaned.

The group shimmied the stone side to side. It inched from its hole. Even on the hoist, its weight stretched everyone's muscles to the limit. After a painstaking twenty minutes of work, the stone gave way.

"Let's lower it to the floor," Ollie grunted as they tried to keep it steady. Henry lowered the stone down to the floor.

Maggie wiped a bead of sweat from her brow. "Whew!" Maggie exclaimed. "Glad that's over. Now it's time to find the ankh!" Maggie grinned, her hands on her hips. "Who's got a flashlight?"

Ollie grabbed a large flashlight from the array of tools spread on the floor. He toggled it on, shining it into the gaping hole in the wall.

"Well?" Maggie inquired. She peeked over Ollie's shoulder.

"Nothing," Ollie stated. He continued panning the flashlight into the hole.

"What?!" Maggie said. "What do you mean nothing? Let me see." Maggie pushed in front of Ollie. He handed her the flashlight.

She swept the beam around the empty space. The pocket in the wall held nothing but dust. The two-foot-thick space ended with a stone back. Maggie checked the sides, top, bottom and back. She stepped back, irked. "There's nothing there!"

Tarik and Henry glanced into the space. "Maybe we're missing something," Maggie conjectured. "It can't be just a stone stuck against the back wall!"

"It can be," Emma retorted. "There's no reason to think there would be a hidden chamber off THIS room."

"Then why would they bother putting a fake stone in the middle of this wall if it led to nowhere?" Maggie argued.

Emma shrugged. "Maybe the original stone broke or cracked during construction. Perhaps a mistake was made carving the hieroglyphs, or a change to the script was made. There could be any number of reasons why that stone didn't match the surrounding ones."

"Or it could be a clue leading us to the ankh," Maggie insisted.

"Either way, Maggie's right. It does require further investigation to ensure we've missed nothing," Ollie chimed in.

Emma rolled her eyes. "I'm heading back to finish the other chamber while you investigate this."

"Good," Ollie said. "Yes, we should all finish our tasks."

The group disbanded after a few moments, each pair heading back to their respective chamber to finish their investigation. Henry returned to his inspection of the remaining portions of the walls.

Maggie stayed with Ollie. "I just can't believe this is meaningless," she murmured to him.

"It's okay, Maggie. Even if it is, you did a wonderful job of detecting it! I told you you'd be a wonderful addition to the team!"

Maggie smiled at him. "Thanks for the vote of confidence,

Uncle Ollie. But I wasn't looking for a pat on the back. I was hoping for some encouragement that this wasn't an exercise in futility."

"Let's find out for sure," Ollie said, squeezing her arm.

Maggie nodded, deflated but determined. Together, she and Ollie spent the next hour inspecting every inch of the opening. They searched the back, sides, top and bottom surfaces as well as the area around the stone for any trace of a compartment or trigger to open another chamber. They found nothing.

"Ugh!" Maggie said as she collapsed onto the floor. "I can't believe this."

"Don't let it get you down, Maggie," Ollie responded.

Maggie sighed and shook her head. "Should we try drilling into the back wall to see if there's another chamber beyond that? Maybe we just haven't found the trigger."

Ollie smiled at her. "If we find nothing else, we'll consider it. For now, I'd rather not destroy any portion of the tomb unless it's absolutely necessary."

Maggie sighed but otherwise remained silent. "Maggie..." Ollie began.

"No, it's okay," Maggie interrupted. "I understand." She paused a moment as Henry joined them.

"Nothing on my end," Henry said. He pulled Maggie to her feet.

"Looks like we're back at it tomorrow in the main burial chamber," Maggie said, dusting herself off.

"There's the spirit," Ollie said with a grin. "Yes, it's too late to begin now."

"Let's see if anyone else had better luck," Maggie suggested.

"Don't get your hopes up, princess," Henry answered.

"I know, I know. If they had, we'd have already heard about it, but a girl can hope!"

The trio crossed the antechamber and checked with Tarik and Emma. "Nothing," Tarik announced. "We have just finished."

"I suppose you found nothing?" Emma questioned.

"No, nothing," Ollie confirmed.

"I suspected as much," Emma responded.

"Thanks for the vote of confidence," Maggie retorted.

"Well…" Emma began before Ollie cut her off.

"Perhaps we'll have better luck tomorrow. Let's collect Charlie and Piper on our way out. We could all use a break, some dinner and some rest."

"I agree," Maggie answered. "I'm starved and sore!"

They collected Piper and Charlie, who had no luck unearthing anything of interest. The group exited the tomb. They spent the remainder of the day resting and discussing a plan for tackling the remaining chambers in the tomb. Ollie advocated if any discoveries led to hidden chambers, they were most likely to find them in the burial chambers.

CHAPTER 17

Maggie sat on the edge of her cot. Her eyes remained bleary. Despite sleeping soundly, fatigue still hung over her.

"What's the matter, boss lady? You sick?" Piper inquired.

"She is NOT a morning person," Emma disclosed as she pulled her blonde hair into a low ponytail.

"Ugh. For once, she's right," Maggie groaned. "I am NOT a morning person. I hate mornings. I hate everything about mornings. I need coffee."

Maggie rose from the cot and pulled a t-shirt over her camisole. She pulled her hair into a high ponytail before she shoved her feet into her shoes. She slogged from the tent with Piper and Emma. The group headed to the dining tent.

As Maggie stepped into the space, Henry waved a cup of coffee at her from a nearby table. "Oh, thank heavens!" Maggie raced toward him and grabbed the cup. She collapsed into the chair next to him and sipped the coffee.

"Breakfast, princess?"

"Yes, please," she answered, taking another sip of coffee. She moved to stand, but Henry waved her down.

"I'll get it." He kissed her cheek and headed toward the food to retrieve a plate for Maggie.

The coffee and breakfast improved Maggie's mood. When they finished, Maggie felt ready to tackle the task ahead. "Let's go!" she said as she jumped to her feet.

"How strong did you make that coffee?" Piper asked Henry.

"Apparently strong enough," Henry answered.

"If we're all ready," Ollie said, "let's head to the tomb and begin. We have a lot of ground to cover today."

The group crossed the hot sands and descended into the coolness of the tomb. They made their way through the antechamber. Across from the entrance, they accessed the corridor leading to Cleopatra's burial chambers.

Maggie admired the walls as they entered the passageway. Beautiful painted images and carved hieroglyphics decorated the walls.

"Perhaps there's some clue here about where the other burial chamber may be," Maggie suggested. "We found the instructions for entering Cleopatra's chamber here. Maybe the directions for locating or opening Antony's tomb are here, too!"

"There's no indication of any concealed openings in this area," Emma said. "Nor any guidance for locating other burial chambers."

"Oh, has this all been translated?" Maggie inquired.

"Not all of it," Ollie answered. "Though the clue to Cleopatra's chamber was apparent. There is nothing so apparent here that would refer to another burial chamber. But we should confirm that through a careful investigation."

"Let's get started," Henry suggested.

"Everyone spread out and take a section of wall," Ollie instructed.

The group dispersed throughout the chamber. With all

seven people concentrating on the passage, they finished their inspection in under an hour. Not only did they find no hidden chambers, but they also found no hint of one either.

After a brief refreshment break, Ollie led the way into the main burial chambers. Maggie's eyes slid upward as they entered the gargantuan space.

"WOW!" she exclaimed, her voice echoing off the walls.

"Just as impressive empty as it was filled, isn't it?" Ollie answered with a smile.

"It is!" Maggie agreed. "The last time we were here, this place overflowed with treasure! But even without all its bounty, it's just as impressive!

"You never saw the actual burial chamber," Ollie said to her. "It's something too!"

"I can't wait to see it! The pictures of it looked amazing!"

"There's your motivation to finish checking this chamber, princess," Henry said to her.

Maggie smiled at him. "Let's get started! I'm feeling lucky today! I KNOW we're going to find something!"

Emma rolled her eyes, stalking to the opposite side of the chamber to begin her search as far from Maggie as possible.

The morning hours wore into afternoon. The group broke for a late lunch. Minimal conversation took place over their meager meal. Maggie ruminated over their lack of progress. With each inch of wall that revealed nothing, they came one step closer to arriving at a dead end.

Maggie stared at her sandwich with a pout on her face.

"You okay, princess?" Henry questioned.

Maggie paused for a moment before she sighed. "Yeah. Just lost in thought." She took another bite of her sandwich, forcing herself back to reality.

"Don't get too dejected, princess. There's still another whole room to investigate!" Henry encouraged her.

Maggie offered a slight smile and a nod.

"I thought you were feeling lucky?" Emma taunted.

Maggie glared at her. "Like Henry said, there's still another room to go." She finished her sandwich and climbed to her feet. After a quick drink from her water bottle, she turned to Henry. "Ready?"

Henry shoved his final bite of food into his mouth and stood. "Yep," he answered.

"Let's go find that ankh!"

Already finished with his lunch, Ollie joined Maggie and Henry, allowing the others to finish their meal before joining them. Ollie led them into the next chamber. The second chamber served as Cleopatra's final resting place. While her mummy had been removed, Maggie was certain the place still held some reverence.

They crossed the threshold into the second space. Maggie's jaw dropped. "Wow!" she whispered. She scanned the opulent space.

"Amazing, isn't it?" Ollie inquired.

"I'm not sure 'amazing' quite captures it," Maggie replied as she continued to take in the space. Despite most of its treasures already being removed, murals and hieroglyphics decorated gilded walls. Ornate lanterns hung in the space. Two towering golden statues of Anubis stood on either side of a golden slab positioned in the center of the room.

"Such opulence," Maggie stated as she ambled around the room.

"Befitting of a great pharaoh," Ollie said.

Maggie halted in the center of the room near the slab. "Is this where she was?"

Ollie nodded, approaching the slab. "In a beautifully painted golden sarcophagus. The sight stopped my heart for a moment. I'll never forget that occasion."

"I'll bet!" Maggie raised her eyebrows and smiled at Ollie.

For an archaeologist, the experience must have been staggering.

The rest of the group joined them in the chamber. "Well, I guess that's enough gawking around," Maggie said at the sight of them. "We better get to work."

"WOW!" Piper exclaimed as she entered.

"It's really something, huh?" Maggie said.

"Dude, this is incredible! I'm so glad Charlie talked me into exploring the tomb."

"Any time, fair maiden," Charlie answered.

"I guess we'll all start in our separate corners?" Maggie suggested, phrasing it like a question.

"Let's get this finished," Emma answered.

Maggie rolled her eyes as she stalked to the corner furthest from Emma and Tarik. Henry followed after her. They began their investigation of the space. Maggie ran her hands over the golden walls.

She attempted to focus on the task at hand rather than the splendor of her surroundings. After twenty minutes, though, her gaze flitted around the room. She continued to rub her hands against the wall as she peered over her shoulder.

Henry glanced at her, doing a double take. "Something wrong?"

Maggie pursed her lips, continuing to stare behind her at the golden pedestal in the middle of the room.

"Maggie?" Henry questioned again.

"Huh?" she asked, whipping around the face him.

"Something wrong?"

"No," Maggie answered. "I guess I'm just losing focus."

Henry smiled at her. "Almost done, princess. Then we can have a nice rest."

"Yeah, almost done, and nothing to show for it." Maggie

searched the area in front of her for any signs of a hidden passageway or trigger for one.

Her eyes slid sideways again and within moments, she found her attention focused on the sarcophagus' base. Maggie gave up on her investigation of the wall. She spun around and leaned against the wall behind her.

"Giving up, princess?"

Maggie crossed her arms and narrowed her eyes. "No," she said, her eyes never leaving the pedestal. "Just... thinking."

"About?"

"That platform."

"What about it?"

Maggie shrugged. "I don't know. I just..." She paused. "It's REALLY something."

"She was a queen," Henry responded.

Maggie raised an eyebrow at him. "What a life," Maggie answered. "To be buried in this much opulence. If they surrounded her in this much lavishness in death, can you imagine how luxurious her life was?"

"I'm sure she had only the best," Henry replied as he concentrated on his task.

"Yeah," Maggie answered. After a moment, she stalked to the plinth.

Maggie stared down at it. The gold gleamed back, reflecting the bright lights placed around the chamber. Maggie rubbed her hand across the slab's top. Her palm glided over its smooth, cool surface.

She traced her fingers along the edge and down the sides. The top overhung the pedestal beneath it. Carved hieroglyphs decorated the pedestal on every side. They surrounded murals. Maggie knelt down, studying the writing. She traced the carvings with her fingers. The sight mesmerized her.

"What do these say?" she called to Ollie.

Ollie twisted to face her. "Stunning, aren't they? They describe her life. From birth to death."

Maggie cocked her head as she stared at the painted scene and its surrounding hieroglyphics. She shimmied around to study the front. Maggie continued her circle of the sarcophagus' base.

As she approached the final side, she stared at the final depiction. Her brow wrinkled as she stared at the picture. In the picture, a woman knelt in front of a pedestal. She reached toward the underside of its slab.

Maggie paused as she considered the mural. She expected to see the death of Cleopatra depicted in the final artwork. Instead, the painting depicted a live woman reaching for an empty pedestal.

"Why is this last one not depicting her death?" Maggie questioned.

"It is," Emma snapped.

"It's not," Maggie answered, still confused. "The woman in the picture is alive. And there's no body on the slab."

"No, there wouldn't be. They put the body in a sarcophagus," Emma lectured.

"There's no sarcophagus either."

Ollie interjected, "It's likely indicative of someone paying homage to the fallen queen."

Maggie frowned. "Then why isn't her body on the slab?"

"There wouldn't be a BODY," Emma repeated.

Maggie rolled her eyes. "Fine, fine. Why isn't her SARCOPHAGUS on the slab?"

Ollie shook his head. "That's the only puzzling feature of that illustration. Though I believe its symbolic of honoring her in death."

Maggie continued to stare at the depiction on the podium base. The explanation regarding its meaning did little to satisfy her. Something struck her about the picture. Her instincts compelled her to investigate further. Maggie reached out and traced the picture with her finger.

In the illustration, the woman's hand reached toward the platform. Though she did not reach to the top of the slab. Her hand fell short. It appeared to reach under the slab. Was it a poor drawing? Perhaps the artist lacked the talent to appropriately represent the woman.

Maggie shook her head at her ponderings. They would not have employed a substandard artist to decorate Cleopatra's final resting place. So why the disproportionate representation, Maggie ruminated?

She sat back on her haunches, considering the artwork. Maggie pursed her lips and narrowed her eyes. After a moment, she reached toward the pedestal. Maggie placed her arm in the same position as the picture, reaching to the bottom of the slab.

She turned her palm to face upward, matching the woman's posture in the picture. Maggie stretched her arm until her fingers touched the underside of the slab. Cool metal caressed her fingertips. She slid her hand toward the middle of the slab.

Her hand touched a new texture. The new sensation startled Maggie. She snapped her arm back. Her heart skipped a beat and her pulse quickened. With hard, beveled edges, it offered an acute change to the pedestal's cool gold. She crinkled her brow, concerned about what she had touched.

Maggie swallowed hard as her imagination ran wild with the number of living desert creatures her fingers may have brushed. She steeled her nerves, determined to find the source. Maggie leaned forward and cocked her head to find the texture's source.

A glint of red caught her eye. Maggie squinted as she tipped further forward to identify the object. Hidden in the shadow of the pedestal's underside, a red stone was inlaid. She toggled her cell phone's flashlight on and pointed it at the stone.

Maggie reached out to touch the stone. She traced the outline of what appeared to be a large heart-shaped ruby.

"What's caught your attention, princess?" Henry called over.

"There's something under here," Maggie answered.

"What?" Ollie inquired. He spun to face Maggie.

"There's a stone under here," Maggie repeated.

"Stone? Like a rock?" Piper queried.

"No, like a giant ruby!" Maggie responded. "It's huge! It's the biggest gem I've ever seen! And it's shaped like a heart!" Maggie's fingertips caressed the red gem.

"Don't…" Emma began as Maggie reached out toward the stone.

Maggie pushed against it. A loud clank reverberated throughout the room. The chamber shuddered. Maggie fell back onto her rear. A deafening bang resounded as a whirring noise reached Maggie's ears. Dust fell from the ceiling as the room trembled again. Those standing in the group lost their footing as the shock wave rocked the room.

The pedestal slid away from Maggie. The grinding sound of stone scraping against stone filled the air. A cloud of dust billowed as the slab continued on its path toward the wall.

The sarcophagus base ceased moving after a full minute.

"… touch that," Emma finished as silence fell over the room.

Dust still obscured the atmosphere. Maggie choked on the particles floating in the air. She waved the cloud away from her face as she coughed. The dust began to settle as everyone recovered from their fall.

"Dude! What the hell just happened?" Piper questioned. She pushed herself up to sitting.

"Maggie!" Henry called. "Are you all right?"

"Yes," Maggie answered as Henry rushed to her. "I'm fine."

"My God!" Ollie exclaimed.

"What is it, Ollie? Are you hurt?" Henry inquired.

"No, no, I'm not hurt," Ollie answered. "But look!" Everyone focused their attention on Ollie. He extended his arm, stretching it toward the center of the room. Maggie followed the trajectory of his pointed finger. Her eyes grew wide when she spotted the object of his attention. She blinked, wondering if she may be imagining the sight.

Maggie glanced to Henry, then back to the room's center. A gaping hole stared back at her from where the sarcophagus base sat only moments ago. She crawled toward it.

"Careful, Maggie!" Ollie cautioned as he approached the cavity.

Maggie stared into the void. Stone steps led into blackness.

"What's down there, chicky?" Charlie called as he pulled Piper to standing.

"I'm not sure. It's pitch black. I can only see the first few steps. It seems to be a passageway."

"Quick, bring a flashlight!" Ollie requested.

Henry dashed to the outer chamber, returning with two large flashlights. He toggled one on and aimed it into the passage. Maggie grabbed the other and trained it into the darkness.

The group gathered around them. Everyone peered into the hole. The two flashlights did little to beat back the darkness. The lights revealed a few more steps, however, the bottom remained hidden, still shrouded by blackness.

Maggie clicked her tongue, sinking back on her haunches. "I can't see a thing!"

"No, those steps must lead quite a long way down," Henry assessed.

"One way to find out," Maggie answered. She climbed to her feet and started toward the opening.

"No!" Ollie exclaimed. "We must check it for traps first!"

Emma circled around the hole and pushed in front of Maggie. "Let me," she stated. "YOU'VE done enough already." She shot a glance at Maggie.

Ollie and Emma bent over the orifice. They each scanned the edge and underside of the opening. Ollie moved the flashlight as they searched for any hidden triggers or mechanisms. With none visible, they moved on to check the first step.

"I'm not seeing anything," Emma said after a quick sweep of the top step.

"Henry, Tarik, grab a few of the floor jacks from the outer chamber. Let's see if there are any pressure triggers," Ollie requested.

After Tarik and Henry retrieved the jacks, Ollie instructed them to place them on the first stair. They positioned the jacks on the step and applied pressure. Nothing happened.

"Okay, let's proceed step by step. We'll start by checking for any triggers, then try the floor jacks to test the pressure," Ollie advised. "Everyone else sit tight until we're sure the chamber is safe."

Maggie slumped to the floor to wait. She drummed her fingers against her forearm.

After over an hour, Ollie poked his head up through the opening.

"Well?" Maggie asked.

"All clear!" Ollie called.

"Yay!" Maggie climbed to her feet. "Any sign of the ankh?"

Ollie shook his head. "We haven't done a thorough search of the items down there."

"Well, let's start our search! This MUST be where it is!"

Maggie insisted. She followed Ollie down the stairs. "Aren't you coming?" she asked Piper and Charlie.

Piper shook her head. "Nah, I'll wait up here, thanks. I'm not one hundred percent sure I want to go any deeper into a part of this place that hasn't been thoroughly vetted."

"Suit yourself!" Maggie said as she continued to descend the steps.

"Don't get your hopes up, Maggie," Ollie warned. "There's no sign that this chamber is the burial chamber of Marc Antony."

"No mummy?"

"No. No sign of his body."

Maggie heaved a sigh as they arrived in the chamber below. Cool air caressed Maggie's skin. Her eyes adjusted to the darker light. Only two flashlight beams lit the space. One sat on the floor, pointing upward to cast light throughout the space. Emma held the second, using it to study a few items scattered on the floor.

"We need more light here," Ollie said.

"We'll grab some of the temporary lighting from one of the other chambers," Henry offered. He and Tarik disappeared up the steps.

Ollie picked up one of the flashlights and used it to scan the room. His brow furrowed.

"What is it, Uncle Ollie?"

"Did they take the floor jacks with them?"

"Yes, they did," Maggie confirmed.

Ollie pursed his lips. "We should probably keep them down here, just in case."

"I can run back up..." Maggie began.

Ollie handed her the flashlight. "I'll go. Take a peek around! I've already had a chance."

"If you're sure!" Maggie accepted the flashlight as Ollie disappeared up the stone steps.

Maggie swung the beam around the space. A few scattered items sat on the floor. The walls in this chamber were noticeably devoid of any carvings.

Maggie wandered around the cavernous space. She sidled to Emma, who bent over a small box on the floor. "Find anything?"

"I haven't found the ankh if that's what you're asking," Emma answered.

"Yet. It could be anywhere down here."

"I've had a good look around while we checked for booby traps. I haven't found it."

Maggie rolled her eyes and moved past Emma to the back of the chamber. A stone wall stared back at Maggie. Maggie frowned at it.

"Seems strange that they put this chamber down here for nothing."

"Not really," Emma mumbled.

Maggie swung her beam around the unadorned wall. She sighed. Why put an illustration showing how to open this chamber if there was nothing to be found here? Surely the chamber hidden by Cleopatra's own body held some significance. Why was it here if it meant nothing? If it contained nothing?

Maggie reached out and touched the stone wall. She closed her eyes as thoughts tumbled through her mind. Her hand slid across the cool, smooth stone. As she reached toward the corner, Maggie's fingers felt something rough.

She popped her eyes open and trained her flashlight on the ridged area. From this angle, the stone appeared dimpled. Maggie moved toward the abnormality. Her breath caught in her throat as she identified the irregularity. Carved in the stone was a heart.

The symbol matched the gem on the underside of the pedestal. Maggie reached out and touched the carving.

"Hey, I found something!" Maggie shouted over her shoulder.

"Whatever you do…" Emma started.

Maggie rubbed the heart carving. The stone retracted under the pressure of her hand. A boom sounded from the ceiling. A whirring sound filled the room.

Maggie swung around to face the center of the space. Light glowed from the chamber above. The rectangle of light narrowed with each passing second.

"No!" Emma shouted. She raced toward the steps. Shouts sounded from overhead. Emma reached the second step when the last sliver of light disappeared. Emma groaned and slapped her hands against her sides. She spun to face Maggie. "You just HAD to touch it, didn't you?"

CHAPTER 18

"Sorry," Maggie squeaked.

Emma stalked down the steps and over to her discarded flashlight. "Next time don't touch anything!" she snapped. She snatched her flashlight from the floor.

"Sorry, Emma! But I thought it would lead to another chamber or something. Not lock us in!"

"Well, thanks to your brilliance, we ARE locked in!"

Maggie shrugged a shoulder. "For a few minutes. All they have to do is press the button up there and we're out!"

"Oh, really?" Emma inquired.

"Yeah. Quit freaking out. We're fine."

"If it's so easy, why haven't they pressed it already?"

Maggie considered the statement for a moment. "Probably just Piper and Charlie were in the room. She's probably too afraid to push it herself. Uncle Ollie will do it as soon as he's back."

"I hope our air lasts that long."

"Oh, quit being a pessimist. Let's just keep looking around. Maybe we'll find the ankh."

Silence fell between them. Maggie stalked across the

chamber and scanned the floor with her flashlight. After a moment, a muffled sound reached Maggie's ears. She stopped, listening hard.

"Did you hear that?"

"What? The sound of our air slowly running out?"

"Shh! No! That sound. Sounds like…" Maggie paused, listening again.

"Voices!" Emma said.

Both women raced to the steps and clamored up them. "Henry?" Maggie called.

"Ollie?" Emma shouted.

"Maggie!" Henry's voice sounded miles away.

"Henry! Henry, I pushed something down here and it closed the opening. Push the gemstone so we can get out!"

A garbled answer came through the slab. Maggie glanced at Emma. The flashlight's beam cast an eerie glow across her face. Emma shook her head.

"Henry! We can't hear you. You'll have to yell!" Maggie shouted back.

A disjointed response came back. "… stuck… your end!"

Maggie turned her ear toward the ceiling, her brow wrinkling in concentration. "Try again, we still can't hear!"

Both Emma and Maggie pressed as close to the ceiling as they could. Henry's muted voice answered them in a slow, forceful manner. "The gemstone is stuck. Is there a trigger on your end?"

Maggie's heart skipped a beat. She glanced wide-eyed at Emma. "Did he say stuck?"

Emma shouted at the ceiling. "Repeat! Did you say stuck?"

"Yes!" Henry shouted back. "Stuck. We cannot open on our end!"

Emma shook her head and shouted back, "Get Ollie."

"Ollie's here!" Henry's voice returned. "Sit tight while we work on this."

Maggie slumped to sit on the step. Emma settled next to her and sunk her head into her hands.

Maggie glanced sideways at her. "They'll get it unstuck," she assured Emma.

"Why did you have to touch that?"

"I didn't realize it would shut the door from all the way over there! I figured it would open another passage or a little hiding spot for the ankh!"

"Figures the one time things don't go your way, I'm the one who pays the price!"

"Hey! We're both stuck down here!" Maggie paused. "And like I said, I'm sure they'll have us out in no time."

Maggie checked her phone and noted the time. She clicked off the display and toggled off her flashlight. "No sense wasting batteries."

Emma switched hers off as well. The chamber plunged into darkness. "Wow," Maggie murmured. "It's darker in here than I expected."

"We're in a sealed underground chamber, what did you expect?"

"I expected it to be less creepy than this."

Emma sighed at Maggie's response.

"Oh, stop being so gloomy."

"Gee, maybe your special sunshine can light the darkened chamber, Maggie!"

"Will you get off my case?"

"Just stop talking, Maggie." Emma sighed. "Ollie's wrong. Rosemont isn't big enough for the both of us," she murmured.

"What?" Maggie questioned.

"Nothing."

"No, it's not nothing." Maggie toggled the flashlight on and shined it toward Emma. "You said something about Rosemont. Did you say it wasn't big enough for the both of us?"

Emma sighed again, shielding her eyes from the light. "Yes, that's what I said. Shine that thing somewhere else."

Maggie swung the beam away from Emma. "Are you thinking of moving to Rosemont?" Maggie inquired.

Emma refrained from responding for a moment. "Not really."

"Why would that even come up then?"

"There's an assistant director position open at the museum there. Ollie encouraged me to apply. Said he'd put a good word in for me."

"But you're not taking it?"

"No. Like I said, that town's not big enough for both of us."

"I thought you were happy working here?" Maggie asked.

"The tomb's not going to need an archeologist on site forever. Look, let's just drop it, okay?"

"But…" Maggie began.

"Drop it! And turn that light off."

Maggie clicked off the flashlight. She sighed and sunk her chin into her hand. Silence consumed the space again. They sat without speaking as time crawled by.

Maggie checked her phone again. She groaned as she toggled her phone off.

"How long's it been?"

"Fifteen minutes," Maggie answered.

Emma moaned. "Seems like it's been an eternity."

"There's something we can agree on."

A shout interrupted their conversation. They scrambled to their feet and pressed against the room's roof. "Maggie!" Henry called.

"Yeah?"

"We can't budge the gem. It's no good. We'll have to find another way to open it. Is there anything on your side?"

"We'll check!" Maggie yelled. She toggled on her flashlight.

"We didn't find anything when we came down," Emma said.

"Well, let's check again, come on!"

Emma toggled on her flashlight and they searched the immediate area. They found nothing.

"HENRY!" Maggie hollered. "We can't find anything! We'll keep looking, but there's no trigger here!"

"Okay! We're talking through ideas here!"

"Come on," Maggie said to Emma, "let's keep searching. Hey! Maybe I should press that heart button again!"

"NO!" Emma shouted. "No, don't touch anything else!"

Maggie shrugged. "Fine. You take one side and I'll take the other. Yell if you find anything."

Emma rolled her eyes but stalked to one side of the room. Maggie ambled to the other. She swept her beam up and down the wall. She searched for any triggers, but found nothing. Maggie made it a quarter of the way down the wall when she heard a muffled voice.

Both Maggie and Emma raced up the steps. "Henry!" Maggie called.

"Maggie! We're working on a plan up here to try to move the pedestal or break through the floor. It'll take us some time. Sit tight."

"Okay! We'll keep searching on our end, too!"

Maggie and Emma returned to their search. Maggie finished her wall and began a search of the back wall. She ended with her flashlight beam aimed at the heart carving. Maggie's gaze lingered on it.

"Don't touch that," Emma warned.

Maggie spun to face her. "Did you find anything?"

"Nope." Emma placed her back against the wall and slid to sitting.

"Me either," Maggie replied, joining her on the floor.

Emma clicked off her flashlight. "Looks like we wait."

The chamber plunged into darkness as Maggie toggled her flashlight off. Within twenty minutes, the sound of work above reached their ears. Muffled scraping, banging and pounding filtered through the stone floor.

Maggie glanced upward. She hoped to see a glint of light peek through the ceiling at any moment. Blackness still surrounded them. The ruckus continued for over an hour. Maggie's head began to pound in unison with the racket.

As she massaged her temples, the noise ceased. Maggie breathed an internal sigh of relief. She continued to rub at her forehead.

"Wonder if they made any progress," Maggie said.

"Well, there's no light shining through from the room above and we're still down here, so they haven't made enough," Emma answered.

"Ugh," Maggie responded. "At least the pounding stopped. It's starting to give me a headache."

"You'll have a worse headache when our air starts to run out."

"Thank you, Emma. You're always a ray of sunshine."

"Why do you think they stopped?" Emma inquired.

Maggie shrugged as she considered it. She had pondered the same thing. "Maybe they're trying a new strategy."

"Or maybe they're stuck."

"Maybe they broke a tool and have to get another one."

"I don't know. It seems strange though," Emma said.

"They'll start up again soon," Maggie answered.

They sat for thirty minutes with silence filling the chamber. "I can't believe they haven't started up again," Maggie said.

"Perhaps they went to eat," Emma conjectured.

"Doubt it," Maggie answered.

"Doubt it? What time is it?"

Maggie checked her cell phone. "Five," she answered as she clicked off the display.

"Dinner time, just like I said."

"Henry would never leave me down here to go eat dinner," Maggie argued.

"Oh, right. I forgot. He worships the ground you walk on. He'd starve to death rather than eat BEFORE he rescues you."

Maggie rolled her eyes in the dark. "I'm just saying that he wouldn't stop working. If they are eating, I think they'd continue working. Do you really believe everyone up there would head off to dinner and leave us down here?"

Emma sighed. "No, I don't. But it's better than the alternative."

"What's the alternative?"

"They stopped working, period."

"Why would they do that?" Maggie inquired.

"That's the million-dollar question. But I haven't heard anything for a while up there."

"Neither have I."

"Which worries me."

Emma's statement settled on Maggie like a lead weight. Worry grew within her. Why had the work stopped? Had they hit a problem? Did a tool break? Did something happen to one of them? Maggie bit her lower lip as a crease deepened in her forehead.

Another few minutes passed. Maggie strained her ears for sounds of any activity above them. No sound penetrated through the ceiling.

Maggie climbed to her feet and clicked on her flashlight.

"Where are you going?" Emma questioned.

"To find out if I can hear anything from up there." Maggie climbed the steps and listened. No sound reached her ears.

"Anything?"

"No," Maggie said with a shake of her head. "HENRY!"

The sound of Maggie's voice echoed in the silent chamber. "HENRY!" Maggie called again.

No answer came. "HENRY! UNCLE OLLIE! ANYONE?"

No one responded. Emma joined her on the steps. "There's no one there." With her eyes wide, Maggie faced Emma.

"HELLO!" Emma hollered. She pounded against the ceiling.

"No one's there," Maggie repeated. She crumpled to the step below her.

Emma collapsed next to Maggie. "Dinner time?"

"This long? It's been over thirty minutes. Close to an hour!"

"Maybe they went to get help or more tools."

"Maybe, but…"

"But?" Emma questioned.

Maggie shook her head. "No, it's not that. Neither of those."

"How do you know?"

"They would have said something," Maggie contended. "They wouldn't have just left."

"What could have happened?"

Maggie rose from her spot on the step and descended to the floor. She paced the room. "I'm not sure but we may be on our own."

"Let's not panic just yet," Emma answered.

"I'm not panicked," Maggie said, ceasing her pacing and spinning to face Emma. "But we need to be realistic here. They aren't up there working! We may need a new plan."

"Let's just sit tight."

"Sit tight? You've been yammering on about running out

of air and you pick NOW to sit tight? How long can we survive down here?"

Emma glanced around the room and shrugged. "How big would you estimate this chamber is? About fifteen by twenty?"

"Yeah, that seems about right," Maggie said as she swung her flashlight beam from end to end. She pointed the beam upward. "About a ten-foot ceiling, maybe?"

Emma nodded in agreement. "So that's…"

"Three thousand cubic feet," Maggie finished for her.

"Right," Emma said. "So, that gives us…" Emma paused, her forehead scrunching in concentration. "Maybe eighteen hours."

"That's it? Then we suffocate?"

"No, but the carbon dioxide levels will be high enough that we'll start to feel drowsy. We'll only suffocate AFTER that."

Maggie flung her arms out. "Great. So, we've got eighteen hours before we fall asleep, never to wake up again. Minus what we've already used."

"We haven't been down here that long. We can wait a little longer," Emma responded.

"Okay," Maggie agreed. "Fine, we can wait a little longer. But we need a plan and a time to start it. We don't want to wait until we're almost out of air to try to find a way out of here."

Emma shrugged. "There may not be a way."

"Emma, there's a way," Maggie answered.

"You don't know that," Emma argued.

"Okay, given your knowledge of tombs, do you really believe this is a dead-end?"

"It could be." Emma hesitated. "But given my knowledge, I'd estimate the probability of that is low."

Maggie breathed a sigh of relief. "Good. Okay, so there's

probably a way out. We just need to find it. Now, how long do we wait before we make a move?" Maggie checked her phone's display. "It's quarter after five. We estimate they've been gone about forty-five minutes already. How long do we wait before we decide they aren't coming back?"

"I don't know," Emma said with a sigh.

"Come on, Emma, make a decision!"

"You make it! You're Miss Wonderful, oh-so-smart and beloved Maggie Edwards."

Maggie sighed. "Okay, let's just AGREE on a decision. We're in this together, whether you like it or not. How about we wait until seven? If they aren't back by then, we start to search for another way out."

Emma considered the statement, then responded, "Okay. Seven. If there's no movement by seven, we'll begin another search."

Maggie climbed back up the steps and sat down next to Emma. "I really hope they're just having a nice long dinner."

"Me too," Emma answered. "I wish I was having a nice long dinner."

"Me too," Maggie agreed. Maggie dug in her pocket. "I have a granola bar."

Emma glanced at it. "No, it's yours, you can have it."

Maggie opened the wrapper. She broke the bar in half. "Here," she said, handing half to Emma, "we'll split it."

Emma accepted the chocolate-covered bar. "Thanks." She clicked off her flashlight. "We should conserve batteries."

"Good idea." Maggie switched off her light.

They made short order of the small amount of food. Afterward, they sat in silence. Maggie strained to listen for any sounds. None came. With every passing moment, Maggie's hopes sunk lower.

At one point, Maggie thought she heard sounds of their return, but instead, it was Emma shifting on the step to find a more comfortable position. Maggie checked her phone multiple times.

"What time is it?" Emma finally asked.

"Six thirty-seven," Maggie answered. "Twenty-three minutes to our deadline."

Emma sunk her head into her hands as Maggie's cell phone back-light dimmed. They waited as their time ran out. After thirty minutes, Maggie announced, "It's after seven."

"Maybe we should wait longer," Emma suggested. "It's only been a few hours. We still have at least twelve hours to go."

"We can't wait until the last minute. We need to leave ourselves plenty of time to search and find a way out."

"It won't hurt to wait a little longer."

"Emma," Maggie stressed, "they are NOT coming back. They've been gone for hours. They never told us they were leaving. Something isn't right here."

"Unfortunately, I'm starting to agree with you. But I'd rather not face that."

"We have to face it," Maggie responded. "And the sooner, the better. Come on." Maggie rose and reached for Emma's hand. "Let's get started."

Emma sighed but grabbed Maggie's hand and stood. "We should use one flashlight and work together to conserve batteries."

"Okay," Maggie agreed. "We'll use mine and save yours."

Maggie toggled her light on. They rechecked the area near the steps but found nothing. They began a thorough inspection of the walls, ceiling and floor. As they searched, they went through any items on the floor. Most articles were pottery or tools.

After a two-hour search, they found nothing. Maggie sighed as Emma clicked off her flashlight, plunging them into darkness again. "That's it," Emma said. "There's nothing."

"Except the heart carving," Maggie reminded her.

"The thing that got us into this trouble."

"And maybe the thing that can get us out!" Maggie retorted.

"I'm not on board with trying that again."

"We may not have another choice."

Maggie toggled on her flashlight. "I'm pressing it."

"No!" Emma exclaimed.

"Yes! Emma! What choice do we have?"

"Perhaps we should wait a few more hours. Only press it when we have no other choice."

"No! I'm NOT waiting until the last minute. Let's just try it."

"Fine, go ahead. But if we end up worse off, you won't have to worry about suffocating. I'll kill you myself."

"If that pedestal slides open, I'll kill you for making us wait down here this long."

"Deal. If we're saved, you kill me. If we're doomed, I kill you. Okay, press it."

Maggie nodded. She crossed to the carving. Her light hovered over the etched heart. Maggie's pulse quickened, and she swallowed hard. As much as she wanted to press the stone, a pang of fear held her back. Maggie shut her eyes for a moment and steadied her nerves. She breathed out a long breath. "Here goes nothing." She reached a shaky hand out. Her fingers caressed the rough stone. She pressed the carving.

CHAPTER 19

A whirring noise filled the chamber. A whoosh of air gusted past Maggie. She spun to face the steps leading upward. No light filtered down from the chamber above. Maggie's brow furrowed. "What happened?" she inquired.

Emma toggled her flashlight on and swung the beam around. "There!" she shouted.

Maggie followed the direction of the light. Along the wall across from the steps, a new opening gaped.

"Well, it's not all I hoped for, but it's a start," Maggie admitted. She moved toward the doorway.

"Wait!" Emma said, racing ahead of Maggie. "There could be a booby trap."

"I'll help you check."

They swept their beams across the exit door. Maggie studied both sides of the doorway on the right side while Emma studied the left. "Find anything?" Maggie inquired.

"No," Emma admitted.

"Me either," Maggie answered. "Think it's safe?"

Emma shrugged. "I guess it's no worse than staying here."

Maggie began to step through the opening when Emma pulled her back. "Wait."

"Now what?"

"We move slow, check everything as we go."

"Okay," Maggie agreed. She stepped through the doorway. "So far so good."

Emma followed her. "Switch off your light. Let's conserve our batteries."

Maggie toggled her flashlight off. They relied on Emma's light beam. Together they inched down the corridor. The stone walls only allowed them to proceed shoulder to shoulder. They made it ten steps down the hall when Maggie ground to a halt.

"What was that?" she whispered.

"What?" Emma inquired.

"Shh, listen. I heard something growl."

Silence fell between them as they both listened. "Do you hear it anymore?" Emma breathed.

Maggie paused before answering, her ears straining. "Yes!" she exclaimed. "There! Did you hear it?"

Emma rolled her eyes. "That was my stomach."

"Oh," Maggie answered. "Sorry."

"Let's keep going."

They continued their slow creep down the hall. Maggie traced her fingers down the rough stone wall as they plodded forward. Emma kept her flashlight beam swinging from side to side in an effort to uncover any concealed traps or hidden triggers.

The floor seemed to shift, and Maggie sensed her feet sliding forward. "Are we going down?"

"Seems like it," Emma answered. "We've been in a gradual descent since a few feet into the corridor."

Ahead, Maggie detected a spot on the floor darker than

SECRET OF THE ANKHS

the ground surrounding it. She pointed toward it. "What's that?"

"I'm not sure," Emma responded. "Careful."

Maggie nodded and guarded her footing as she crept toward the dark spot. "Is that…" Maggie's voice dropped off.

Emma grimaced. "Yeah, yeah it is."

They approached the black spot, now realizing it represented a large pit. Emma shined her light into the hole. Maggie's eyes widened as she spied the bottom. Metal spikes poked from the bottom. Emma swung the beam across the crater. The floor continued uninterrupted on the other side.

Emma pointed the light in the direction from which they came. "Now what?" Maggie inquired.

"Go back?" Emma said, phrasing it as question.

"Shouldn't we try to get across? There's no way out back there."

"How?"

"Jump?"

"Jump," Emma said in an unimpressed voice. "Jump? Are you crazy? We'll be impaled if we don't make it."

"Or we'll die from carbon dioxide poisoning or suffocation or whatever."

"I'd rather fall asleep and die than be skewered!"

"Give me the flashlight," Maggie said. She wrested the flashlight from Emma. Maggie trained the beam on the cavity's edge. She followed the border, searching for anything they could use to assist them in crossing the crater.

Maggie raised the beam to the walls and ceiling. She found nothing that would help them to cross. Maggie stared at the gaping hole for another moment. "It doesn't LOOK that far," she conjectured aloud.

"Maggie, that's at least six-feet across!"

"Seems do-able." Maggie swung the flashlight's beam up

the corridor behind them. "We could get a running start. We could make it."

"You try first. If you get lanced, I'll know not to try."

Maggie gave Emma a wry glance. She rolled her eyes. "Fine." She shoved the flashlight back into Emma's hands. "I'll toss my flashlight over there first. Take yours and point it at the other end. I'll get a running start and jump first." Maggie reeled back and lobbed her flashlight over. It landed on the opposite side and skittered across the floor. "See. Nothing to it," Maggie said in a shaky voice.

"Wait. I'll shine it from the spot you start in so you can see the whole way down."

Emma followed Maggie a few feet up the chamber. She aimed the flashlight at the other side of the gap. Maggie squirmed. She shimmied her shoulders back and forth in an attempt to loosen up. Maggie rolled her neck around, then grabbed her ankle, pulling it toward her backside. She switched ankles. With a deep exhale, Maggie squatted a few times.

"Finished with your Olympic preparations?"

"Don't rush me," Maggie responded. She took another deep breath. "Okay," she said with a hard swallow. "I'm ready."

Emma squeezed Maggie's arm. "Good luck," she said.

"Thanks."

Emma pointed the flashlight's beam down the corridor toward the gap. Maggie bit her lower lip and squeezed her eyes shut as she offered a silent prayer. After another hard swallow, Maggie began her run.

She pumped her arms. Due to the gradual descent, she picked up speed easily as she ran the short distance to the hole. As the gap approached, Maggie leapt through the air. She landed just short of the other side. Her arms hit the edge, and she clutched at the stone floor to find purchase.

"Maggie!" Emma called. She raced toward the hole.

Maggie clung to the side. "I'm okay," Maggie answered in an unsteady voice. "I just need to climb up."

Maggie pushed with her feet. The stone did not provide any traction. Her feet slipped with each step. She slipped further down, her arms grabbing at anything to stay up.

Emma trained her beam on a stone protruding from the wall. "Can you reach that stone?" she questioned. "Maybe you can use it to pull yourself up."

Maggie glanced at it. "Yeah. Yeah, I think I can. I just need to shimmy over there." Maggie hefted herself up as high as she could on her forearms. She inched toward the stone jutting from the wall.

When it was within her grasp, Maggie reached out and clasped it. With a solid object to grip, she hauled herself up, scrambling out of the pit and onto the ledge. As she pulled, the stone shifted downward. A clanking mechanism sounded as the stone slipped.

"What was that?" Maggie asked as she stood.

"I'm not sure."

"Okay, your turn," Maggie encouraged.

"Uh…"

"Oh, come on, Emma. I made it. I'll pull you up if you land short. You should make it. You're about my height."

"Okay… just… give me a minute."

Maggie wrinkled her brow. A grinding noise sounded throughout the corridor. "What is that?" Maggie toggled her flashlight on and pointed it up the chamber. Her eyes grew wide.

"Emma! JUMP!" she screamed.

Emma glanced behind her. A large stone ball rolled down the corridor. It threatened to crush her in its path if she did not move quickly.

Emma blanched at the sight. She turned to Maggie, fear apparent on her face.

"JUMP!" Maggie shouted again. Emma dropped her flashlight and raced the final few steps to the gap. She leapt across the chasm headlong. She smacked into the wall. Maggie grasped at her forearms as Emma's fingers sought to cling to the stone floor.

Emma slipped through Maggie's fingers. She slid further down, her fingers clutching at the edge. Maggie dove toward the crater. She slid toward the edge, the front of her body hanging over. She reached for Emma as Emma's hand slipped from the edge. Maggie clasped Emma's hand in hers and pulled. She heaved Emma upward as Emma ran up the wall, using Maggie to steady herself.

Maggie pulled her over the edge. They collapsed in a heap as the stone ball smashed Emma's flashlight into a pancake before rolling in the pit behind them. Maggie rolled onto her back. Her chest heaved from the effort as she gasped for air. Emma lay next to her, still breathing hard from her scramble to safety.

Maggie glanced sideways at her as her breathing began to return to normal. "You okay?" she inquired.

Emma nodded, then answered. "Yeah. Yeah, I think so." She hesitated for a moment. "Thanks for the save," she said as she glanced at Maggie.

Maggie returned her gaze to the ceiling. "Sure." Maggie laid for another moment, staring at the ceiling. "I can't believe a giant ball nearly squashed you."

"Oh, please," Emma groaned. "I don't even want to think about it."

"Whatever you do," Maggie warned, "don't tell Piper."

"What?" Emma inquired, her brow scrunching.

"Don't tell Piper. I'll never hear the end of it if she finds out. I teased her about there NOT being a big rock that would roll down and kill everyone like in Indiana Jones."

"Ohhhh," Emma answered. "Wow, bad call there."

"Tell me about it," Maggie answered. She rolled onto her front and pushed herself up to sit on her haunches. "Well, should we keep moving?"

"Ugh," Emma groaned. "I guess so."

Maggie stood and reached down to pull Emma to standing. Emma climbed to her feet and brushed herself off. "Wow," she muttered. "I'm filthy."

"Well, we are in a tomb," Maggie joked.

"Funny."

"Ready?"

"Yeah. My legs are still a little wobbly, but we should keep going."

Maggie picked up her flashlight from the ground. "Down to one flashlight."

"I hope it holds out."

"Fingers crossed," Maggie said. She handed the flashlight to Emma. They began their slow creep up the passageway. "I hope there are no stone balls on this side."

"Don't tempt fate," Emma whispered.

"What are the chances…"

"Shh, I'm serious."

Emma swung the flashlight beam around the entire corridor as they crept along. They moved at a slow, cautious pace, both women afraid of another mishap. After a tedious twenty minutes, they reached the end of the passage.

"Whew," Maggie gasped out. "Made it."

"Yeah, but made it where?" Emma questioned. Her flashlight's beam rested on the end of the corridor. A large stone wall blocked them from moving further.

Maggie shut her eyes for a moment. "I'm really getting tired of this tomb," she grumbled.

Emma sighed.

"It can't be a dead-end, right?" Maggie inquired.

Emma shrugged. "I wouldn't think so."

"Guess we'd better search for the trigger that opens this wall," Maggie suggested.

"Yep," Emma agreed. "I'm almost afraid to find it."

Maggie chuckled at the comment. Emma pivoted the flashlight to face the left wall. She swung the beam up and down as they both searched.

"There!" Maggie exclaimed as they searched the right wall. "Another carved heart."

"Guess we'll push it," Emma said. Her fingers hovered over the carved stone for a moment before she pushed it. The wall blocking them slid to the side. Emma breathed a sigh of a relief. "Let's check for traps."

"Okay," Maggie nodded.

After finding no signs of a concealed trigger, they entered the room. Emma swung the flashlight around the chamber. It appeared devoid of anything beyond a large wooden rod in the room's center.

Maggie took a few steps into the room. She stumbled as her foot caught on the stone floor below her. "Whoa!" she exclaimed as she flailed her arms in an attempt to keep her balance. A boom reverberated throughout the chamber. A hiss sounded and a scraping noise began.

"What happened?" Emma asked.

"I almost tripped over this divot! Ugh, why is this dust falling on me?" Maggie held her hand out as dust trickled from the ceiling.

Emma raised the flashlight's beam to the ceiling. Her eyes widened. "Uh, Maggie?"

"Yeah?"

"We need to go."

Maggie's eyes raised to the ceiling. Her jaw went slack, and she gulped. The room's ceiling inched toward them.

"Ummm," Maggie began. She searched the room in the dim light. "Go where?"

"There's no exit!" Emma shouted. She swiveled the flashlight wildly around the space.

"Back the way we came?" Maggie suggested.

Emma pointed the light at the entry door. "It's closed!"

The ceiling continued its crawl toward them. "There must be another way out of here!"

"Where?!" Emma exclaimed.

Maggie grabbed the flashlight and scanned the room with it. "There!" she yelled, pointing across the room. "There's an outline of a doorway."

They rushed across the room toward it. "Where is the trigger to open it?" Emma squealed in a panicked voice.

They searched the immediate area. Maggie pressed on every inch of stone surrounding the door. It triggered nothing. "Nothing's happening!" Maggie cried.

The ceiling slid closer to them. Maggie could almost touch it when she reached up. "We have to figure something out!" she exclaimed, scanning the room again.

"The lever!" Emma called over the din.

Maggie nodded in understanding. "Let's try it!" She dropped the flashlight on the floor, pointing it toward the mechanism.

They hurried to the lever. It stood at a forty-five-degree angle with the floor. Maggie grasped it and tugged it up and away. It didn't budge. Emma also grabbed hold of the wooden pole. They struggled to move the ancient mechanism.

"Pull!" Maggie shouted.

"I am pulling!" Emma shot back.

Maggie glanced upward. "Well, pull harder!" she insisted.

The ceiling skimmed the top of their heads. Maggie and Emma leaned their weight back, both groaning with effort to shift the lever.

As the ceiling threatened to flatten them, the mechanism broke free. It swung toward them. "The door's open!" Emma shouted.

"Let's go!"

As they let go of the lever, it began a slow slide back to its original position. "The door's closing! Hurry!" Emma screamed.

Maggie and Emma rushed across the chamber, bent over as the ceiling continued crushing down on them. Emma dove through the closing doorway. Maggie followed behind her. As the ceiling approached the floor and the doorway slid closed, Maggie reached through the opening and snatched the flashlight before it was squashed.

She leaned her back against the door, her eyes closed as she breathed a sigh of relief. Maggie rested her head against the stone door.

"Oh my God!" Emma breathed.

"What is it now?" Maggie questioned, her eyes still closed. "Pit of poisonous asps? Viper den? Bed of scorpions? Flesh-eating scarabs?"

"No, look!" Emma scrambled to her feet.

Maggie popped her eyes open and glanced around the room. Her eyebrows raised at what surrounded them. Her jaw slackened, and she pushed herself to her feet.

"Oh, WOW!" Maggie exclaimed.

CHAPTER 20

Maggie's eyes scanned the new chamber. In complete contrast to the previous areas, this space enjoyed a level of opulence rivaled only by Cleopatra's chambers. Golden walls sparkled under the flashlight's beam. Intricate carvings and murals decorated each surface.

The contents of the room also sparkled. All manner of treasure filled the chamber: bejeweled chalices, golden staffs, jewelry with gemstones so large some were the size of eggs, gold and silver pieces and statues.

Maggie picked up a handful of coins, letting them slip through her fingers and back into their chest. They clinked against each other as they fell back into their places.

"This is amazing!" Maggie breathed.

"Incredible," Emma acknowledged.

"Do you think this is Marc Antony's burial chamber?"

Emma swung the beam around the space. "Not his burial chamber. His body isn't here." She paused. "But I'd bet this is the antechamber to his burial chamber."

Emma rested the flashlight's beam on a doorway across

from where they entered. "I bet that leads to his burial chamber," she said.

"We should check this room for the ankh," Maggie responded.

"Yes," Emma agreed.

"I hope we find it!" Maggie replied. "It'll make all this worth it."

Emma rested the flashlight's beam against an object mounted to the wall. "Torches," she murmured.

"Yeah," Maggie answered. "Got a lighter? We can save on flashlight batteries."

Emma dug a lighter from her pants' pocket. She flicked the spark wheel, igniting the lighter's small flame. Emma marched around the room's perimeter lighting the torches.

"That's better," Maggie said as the last one caught fire. "We'll be able to make at least a cursory search with the light from the torches."

As they approached the room's center, Maggie draped herself in some of the jewelry. "What do you think? Is it too much?" she asked as she shoved a large ring onto her finger after hanging a ruby necklace around her neck and donning several bracelets.

"For you? Nah," Emma responded.

"Can you imagine having this much wealth?"

"No," Emma admitted.

"Here, try some on," Maggie suggested.

"Pass. Let's just finish the work."

"Oh, come on, Emma. Have some fun. We've earned it! When are you ever going to have an opportunity to do this? Once we get out, they'll send in the catalog team and you'll never see this stuff up close again!"

Emma side-eyed her. After a moment, she gave in. "Okay, okay."

"Here," Maggie said, handing her several items. "Try the sapphires. It'll bring out the blue in your eyes!"

"Mmmm," Emma mumbled. "I'm not sure. Sapphires? Or diamonds?" Emma held up a sparkling bracelet.

"Both!" Maggie exclaimed.

She shimmied next to Emma and fastened the ostentatious sapphire necklace around Emma's neck. With Maggie's help, Emma fastened a sapphire bracelet and a diamond bracelet on each wrist.

"Not complete without a ring!" Maggie added.

Emma accepted the emerald ring and shoved it on her ring finger. "Well? How do I look?" Emma struck a pose.

"Fabulous, darling," Maggie answered in a posh voice.

Emma admired the jewelry. Maggie dug her cell phone from her pocket. She toggled on her camera app and leaned close to Emma.

"Selfie!" she announced.

Maggie held her bejeweled wrist and hand near the necklace as she posed for the camera. Emma gave the camera two thumbs up, flashing the emerald ring and both bracelets. Maggie snapped a few shots before pocketing her phone.

"Never show those to anyone," Emma warned. "Do you realize how much trouble I'd be in if anyone saw those?"

"Just between us girls!" Maggie promised. "I'm always getting you into trouble, aren't I?"

"You've been doing a good job of it recently," Emma answered. Maggie sat silently for a moment. "Never mind," Emma continued. "We should get back to checking for the ankh."

"You're probably right," Maggie admitted. "Goodbye, beautiful jewelry!" Maggie peeled the pieces off one by one and set them back where she found them. Emma did the same.

"Did you happen to notice the time when you had your phone out?" Emma inquired.

"Almost one," Maggie answered.

"Yikes," Emma responded with a yawn, "no wonder I'm so tired."

"Not as chipper at 1 a.m. as you were in college, huh?"

Emma yawned again. "Not even close."

The yawn proved contagious and spread to Maggie. "Oh, stop doing that. Perhaps we should take a quick nap. Who knows what is waiting for us after this? We may need the energy."

Emma glanced around the room. "We have a lot of ground to cover," she replied.

"We can press on," Maggie said.

"No, maybe you're right. We're safe at the moment. And after all the adrenaline rushes, I'm beat."

"You and me both," Maggie agreed. "It hit me like a ton of bricks while we were fooling around with the jewelry." Maggie pulled her phone from her pocket. "I'll set an alarm for an hour from now. We'll have a quick nap."

"Sounds good," Emma answered mid-yawn. They stretched out on the floor near the jewelry in the room's center.

Despite the eerie silence, Maggie nodded off within minutes. Her alarm chimed an hour later. Maggie jumped, startled, as she searched for her phone to snooze the alarm. She flung her hand next to her, expecting to find her phone on her night table.

After a moment, Maggie recalled their current predicament. She shot up to sitting. Maggie grabbed it and swiped the alarm off. She still felt tired, but there would be no sleeping now.

She took a minute to recover from her sleep-induced

stupor. The room remained quiet. Emma must have slept through the alarm, she surmised.

"Emma, wakey, wakey," Maggie said as she stretched. Maggie glanced to Emma then leapt to her feet. She backed a step away as she swallowed hard.

"Emma!" Maggie whispered. "Emma! Wake up!"

Emma began to rouse. "Huh?" she groaned. On her back, Emma rolled her head from one side to the other.

"Emma, don't move!"

"What?" Emma inquired as she opened her eyes.

"Don't move!" Maggie whispered again.

Emma glanced at Maggie. In the process, she realized the cause for Maggie's alarm. Emma's eyes widened as she stared at the scorpion on her chest. She swallowed hard and creased her brow.

Maggie's eyes darted around the room in a desperate search for a tool to help. She rushed to the corner of the room and retrieved an object. She crept toward Emma, holding it high.

"Whoa! Wha-what are you going to do with that?!" Emma shouted.

"Stab it!" Maggie announced. She lifted the ceremonial knife higher.

"NO!" Emma shouted.

"Why?"

"If you miss, you'll stab me! Even if you don't miss, you still might stab me!"

Maggie slumped her shoulders. She dropped the knife and searched for something else.

"Hurry!" Emma urged.

"I'm trying!" Maggie answered as she searched through items for anything useful. "How about this?" Maggie held up a chalice.

"How's that supposed to help?"

"I'll cover it with the chalice and then we'll knock it off you."

"It could still sting me. Besides, that looks way too small!"

Maggie tossed the chalice aside. She picked up a golden scepter. "Here! I'll knock it off with this!"

"No! If you miss, you'll make it angry!"

"Emma! We're running out of options here. I have to do something!"

"Not that!"

"What do you propose? That I ask it nicely to leave?"

"Do you imagine that would work?"

Maggie offered her a wry glance. "I won't miss." Maggie eased the scepter near the scorpion, lining up her shot.

"Ahhh!" Emma exclaimed as the scorpion recoiled to the close proximity of the object.

In a split second, Maggie reacted to the movement. She swung the scepter and knocked the scorpion across the room. It smacked onto the floor and scurried into a darkened corner. Maggie dropped the scepter, quivering from the experience.

Emma breathed a sigh of relief as she jumped to her feet. She brushed the spot on her shirt where the scorpion had sat.

"Oh, that was so gross!" Maggie exclaimed. "Are you okay?"

"Yeah," Emma answered. "Yeah, I'm okay. Thanks for the save."

"You're welcome."

Maggie allowed Emma a few moments to recover from her scare. "I guess we should keep searching for the ankh," Emma said after a few breaths.

"Yeah. Ugh," Maggie said with a shiver. "I hate the idea of searching with that thing in the room. You should have let me stab it."

"You smacked it into the part of the room we already checked, at least. We should be okay."

"Wait!" Maggie exclaimed.

"What now?"

"What if there are more?"

"Good point," Emma said. "We'll be careful. Don't pick anything up." Emma grabbed the scepter Maggie dropped. "We'll use this to poke around."

Maggie nodded. They continued exploring the chamber. With their new method of probing items, this half of the chamber's exploration took twice as long as the first half.

After a thorough inspection, they found nothing. "Ugh," Maggie groaned. "Not here either! You've got to be kidding?!"

"Maybe we missed it."

"I am NOT going back through ALL this, especially with that creature lurking around."

"It's hardly a creature. And the scorpion is probably just as afraid of us now as we are of it."

"You go through the stuff then," Maggie snapped.

Emma held up her hands in defeat. "Perhaps we'll find it in the burial chamber itself. Assuming the burial chamber is in the next room."

"I like that assumption. Let's hope it's in there. We'll only check here if we can't find it there."

"If we can return here. We're not having the best luck with getting out the way we came in."

"True," Maggie said with a sigh. "Well, let's hope our luck holds out, it's in the next chamber AND we can get out going forward instead of back."

"From your lips to God's ears," Emma replied.

She glanced across the glittering space toward the doorway leading out. Nothing obstructed their path into the next chamber.

They approached the doorway. Both women hesitated a few feet from the egress. Maggie crossed her arms and stared at the doorway. Emma pursed her lips as she peered at it.

"What are the chances we can just… walk through it and nothing happens?" Maggie inquired.

"With our luck lately? Slim to none."

"I didn't spot any triggers," Maggie answered.

"Me either, but perhaps we should have a closer look."

Emma used the flashlight's beam to scan the entire doorway. Maggie tapped her foot on the sill, retracting it quickly. She eyed the jamb for another moment before she leapt through.

Maggie landed on the other side. She spun to face Emma. "I made it!"

"Yeah. So far so good."

"Your turn," Maggie encouraged.

Emma took a deep breath and hopped over the sill into the room. Both breathed a sigh of relief. Emma swept the flashlight beam across the room. As opulent as the previous room, the centerpiece of the chamber contained a large pedestal topped with a sarcophagus.

Maggie pointed to it. "There! Is that him?! Is that Marc Antony?"

"Wow," Emma whispered. "I'd bet so. Let's find out."

"Okay," Maggie agreed. "Careful!"

Emma nodded. She aimed the flashlight at the floor and scanned it as they approached the body. They made it unscathed. Emma used a similar technique to approach the walls and light any torches along them. She rejoined Maggie at the room's center. Emma studied the pedestal and sarcophagus. She circled the funerary display, inspecting it.

"Well?" Maggie asked after a few moments.

"It's him," Emma confirmed. "See these markings here?"

She pointed to a few hieroglyphs on a painted cartouche decorating the sarcophagus. "This confirms his identity."

Maggie's eyes widened. "Wow! We found him! Emma, we did it!"

Emma smiled at Maggie. "We're the first people to be here in thousands of years! We're the first people to lay eyes on the body of Marc Antony!"

"Pretty thrilling, huh?" Maggie asked.

"My heart is hammering in my chest!"

"I bet the ankh is here!"

"One way to find out!" Emma exclaimed.

"Where should we start?"

They picked a corner to begin their search. After two hours, their quest proved fruitless. Maggie moved to the sarcophagus. She examined the surrounding items. Maggie crouched to inspect four jars at the foot of the pedestal. Placed in a neat line, the stone jars were decorated with lids in various shapes. An Anubis head adorned one, a cat topped the second. The third's lid was shaped into a snake's head and a falcon head capped the final stone jar.

"Could it be in one of these?" Maggie questioned.

"Ah, no," Emma answered with a chuckle.

"How can you be sure? Shouldn't we double check?"

"It's not in there," Emma assured Maggie.

"I think we should check," Maggie countered.

"Go ahead," Emma said. "If you like organs."

"Organs?"

"Those are canopic jars," Emma informed her. "They hold the organs of the body. One holds the stomach, another the intestines, another the lungs and another the liver."

"Ew!" Maggie said as she recoiled from the jars.

"I'm surprised to see them in a tomb from this dynasty, but it seems they were committed to following the ancient practices." Emma bent to study the jars. "It's interesting. They retained the practice of the canopic jar, but the lids don't follow the standard pattern."

"Let's leave that for the archaeologists to worry about," Maggie requested.

"I AM an archaeologist," Emma retorted.

"Then you can worry about it when you're deconstructing and cataloging all of this. Not now."

Emma continued to study the jars for a moment longer. Maggie glanced around the funerary chamber. She slapped her thighs with her hands. "No ankh so far. Where could it be?"

"Perhaps we missed it in the previous chamber."

"Where was Cleopatra's ankh?"

"I'm not certain, I didn't catalog that piece."

Maggie pulled her lips into a thin line, frustrated by their lack of progress. She spun in a slow circle as she eyed the room. After her inspection, she focused on the sarcophagus.

"You don't imagine it's in there, do you?"

"In where?" Emma inquired.

Maggie poked her finger toward the body. "In there," she mumbled. "With him."

"Wrapped with his body? I'd doubt it." Emma paused for a moment. "Although..."

"Oh, no," Maggie moaned. "Please don't tell me we have to unwrap him!"

"No," Emma corrected, "maybe not in with his body but near his body! I didn't catalog Cleopatra's ankh, but if I remember correctly, it was found near her. There was a big discussion in the mess tent about such an unglamorous object being found near her."

"That makes sense," Maggie stated. "But I didn't see it anywhere on the pedestal or the floor." She glanced around near the sarcophagus.

"Neither did I. Let's have another look."

SECRET OF THE ANKHS

Maggie and Emma knelt down near the sarcophagus. Together, they made a careful search of the surrounding area and the pedestal. They worked around the entire platform. As they approached the head, Emma snapped on the flashlight and aimed its beam under the base.

"Look!" she exclaimed. She pointed under the slab of the funerary base.

"A heart-shaped gemstone!" Maggie responded. Emma and Maggie exchanged a glance. "You don't imagine it opens a passage leading further down, do you?"

Emma grimaced at the stone. "I hope not."

"Should we press it?" Maggie inquired.

"I'm afraid to," Emma admitted.

"Do you expect it'll trigger a trap?"

"It may."

"There's only one way to find out," Maggie answered. She reached toward the ruby.

"Wait!" Emma said, batting her hand away. "Let's think this through."

"What is there to think through? So far, we've come up with nothing. We haven't found the ankh yet and we're stuck in the bowels of a tomb."

"We're not 'stuck' completely," Emma countered. She pointed toward an opening on the far wall. "There's an exit door."

"Okay," Maggie answered. "So, if we press this, we'll either find another chamber with the ankh or we won't, right?"

"Or we'll trigger some trap that ruins our chance of escaping this place."

Maggie nodded as she considered Emma's statement. "Okay, you make a good point. I don't want to be trapped in here but…"

"But?" Emma answered as Maggie's voice trailed off.

"But," Maggie continued, "it wasn't a trap the last time we pressed it."

"How do you figure that?" Emma argued. "We're stuck in the 'bowels of a tomb' as you put it because of the last time you pressed one of these."

"Technically, yes, but we found Marc Antony! We were only temporarily stuck. I say we push it. No risk, no reward." Maggie reached for the gemstone again.

"And I say we don't," Emma retorted as she blocked Maggie's hand. "Better safe than sorry."

Maggie shoved Emma's hand away and reached for the ruby heart again. "Nothing ventured, nothing gained."

"Look before you leap!" Emma cautioned.

Maggie dropped her hand to her side. "We can trade idioms all day, but eventually we have to make a decision."

"We've made a decision. We just can't agree on that decision."

Maggie ruminated for a moment. "Okay, let's compromise," she suggested.

"Push it halfway?" Emma inquired.

"No. You go through that exit door and then I'll press the heart and see what happens. If anything goes wrong, it'll be me who deals with the consequences."

Emma considered the idea. She shook her head. "No. No, I'm not going to leave you here."

"You're not leaving me. You're just waiting for me in the other room in case something goes wrong."

"I'm not a coward. If we press it, I'm going to stay and be part of it."

"So, should we press it?"

"No, wait!" Emma exclaimed as she climbed to her feet.

"Wait for what?"

"Let's check out the exit door first and see if there are any booby traps. In case we need to rush out, I don't want to trigger something."

"Good idea," Maggie agreed. She climbed to her feet and joined Emma. Together, they searched the door jamb.

While they inspected it, Maggie asked, "You keep calling this the exit. What are the chances this really leads us out of here?"

"They usually built an exit," Emma answered. "I'd guess this tomb was no exception, particularly given the unusual layout with the double burial."

Maggie nodded. "Good. Because going back may not be an option."

"I agree. Forward is our best hope."

They concluded their examination. They found nothing. "All clear," Emma said. "Well, I guess we can press that heart and see what happens."

"Okay," Maggie agreed. They returned to the funerary display. Emma shined the light on the gemstone. "Ready?" Maggie questioned with a deep breath.

"As I'll ever be."

"Together," Maggie said. Both women placed their hands on the gemstone. "On three. One, two…"

"Wait!" Emma said.

"Now what?"

"On three or after three?"

"After three. I'll say push. One, two, three, push. We push on push."

Emma nodded. "Okay." She exhaled a long breath. "Let's do this."

"One, two, three, push."

The gemstone retracted into the bottom of the slab. A swooshing sound echoed in the chamber. A panel slid open in the sarcophagus base.

"Emma!" Maggie exclaimed. She pointed under the gem. "Look!"

"We found it!" Emma said.

The blue-green ceramic ankh stood inside the small hidden chamber. "We did it!" Maggie cried.

Emma inspected the ankh and the surrounding chamber. With great care, she reached in and extracted the polished item. A smile crossed her face. "The last piece of the puzzle!"

"Yeah! Now to get out of here and use it to find the library!"

Maggie climbed to her feet, offering her hand to pull Emma to standing. Emma accepted. She stowed the ankh in the pocket of her cargo pants. They started toward the exit door.

"Oh, I wonder how much farther it is to get out?" Maggie questioned. "It doesn't matter. I'm so excited to tell everyone we found it!"

"Me too! There may be another chamber, two at most. I'd say no more than that before the back door."

"Lead the way!" Maggie responded.

Emma did another quick inspection of the doorway before they stepped through it. Maggie followed her after they ensured they would trigger no trap.

They found themselves in a small, nondescript chamber. Devoid of any markings, the bare stone walls pressed close to them in the tiny room. Directly across from where they entered, a doorway yawned into the area beyond.

Emma stepped toward it. She glanced around the doorway. Something seemed off to her. The doorway appeared odd. She swung the flashlight beam around it. "I don't see anything."

Maggie took another step toward the door when Emma grabbed her. "Wait!" Emma screamed. She pulled Maggie back.

"What is it?"

Emma leaned over and blew across the floor. Loose sand and dust scattered toward the corners of the small space. A miniscule contour showed on the floor, outlining a separate block. In the center of the stone piece, a pattern was carved.

Emma pointed at it. She pulled Maggie a step back before she tapped her foot on the brick. It descended into the floor. A large blade dropped from the ceiling of the doorway. It slammed into the door's sill with a thud. The sickening sound of metal scraping on stone reverberated.

The stone trigger began to rise from its depressed position. As it returned to its original state, the blade retracted into the ceiling, resetting itself for another deadly game.

"Whoa, close call! How did you see that?"

Emma pointed to the small black crevice. "Something didn't look right to me. I noticed that slit. And when I glanced at the floor, I saw the outline of that carving."

"Good thing you did. Do you think it's safe to go through as long as we don't step on that tile?"

"I assume so. Though I hate to take the chance."

"Me too, but we don't have any choice."

"Nope," Emma agreed. "I'll go first."

"We could play rock, paper, scissors for it," Maggie suggested.

Emma shook her head. "No, I'll go first. I have the flashlight and the best idea of what to search for on the other side to be sure there are no other triggers."

"But you're also the best one NOT to get caught in a trap because you stand the best chance of finding your way out."

"You can't talk me out of it, Maggie," Emma stated. Before Maggie could object, Emma leapt over the trigger tile and through the doorway.

CHAPTER 21

Maggie held her breath as she awaited an all clear from Emma. She saw the flashlight's beam bobble around beyond the doorway. Within a few moments, Emma shouted in. "Seems clear! I'll stand back so you can jump through."

"Okay!" Maggie called in. "Here I come." Maggie took a step back and leapt forward. She sailed through the doorway, grinding to a halt just before she bumped into Emma. "Made it!"

Emma investigated their new surroundings with the flashlight. It appeared they were in a narrow tunnel.

"Yikes," Maggie said with a shiver, "it's tight in here."

"Yes," Emma agreed. "I'd guess this is the tunnel leading out through the back entrance."

"Boy, I hope so!"

Emma scanned the surrounding area. "Okay, let's go, but slow. And keep your eyes peeled. We may run into another trap."

"Okay," Maggie answered with a nod.

Together, they crept down the corridor. The unadorned

SECRET OF THE ANKHS

walls pressed them close together. With each step, they scanned every inch of the space in front of them.

Twenty minutes into their traversal of the tomb's corridor, Maggie gasped as the light's beam panned over a dark spot on the wall. "There!" she exclaimed.

Emma approached it with caution. She studied it in the light before she ran her finger over it. "Just a pockmark in the stone."

Maggie breathed a sigh of relief. "Good."

"Good catch in case it wasn't though."

"Thanks. I hope this corridor comes to an exit soon. My eyes are starting to glaze over."

"Mine, too. Everything is starting to look the same."

"Yep."

"Want a break?"

Maggie shook her head. "No, I'd rather keep going and find the way out."

"Onward toward the exit then," Emma answered.

"Onward to breakfast and a nice nap on my cot."

"That too," Emma agreed.

They continued their slow crawl down the passageway. After another twenty minutes, Emma's flashlight beam struck a solid wall in front of them. Emma swung the beam around.

Maggie's brow creased in confusion and frustration. "Where do we go from here?"

Emma stared at the stone wall. She studied it, moving the flashlight back and forth to search every inch. "Umm," Emma began.

Maggie glanced at the sides of the passage. She pressed her hands against the walls on both sides. Nothing budged. They were solid.

"Did we miss a turn or something?"

"The way we scoured the walls, doubt it," Emma lamented. She spun and leaned against the dead end.

"Well…" Maggie hesitated, staring at the wall behind Emma. "This can't be a dead end!"

"Do you see a way through?" Emma snarked.

"No. But why is it here? They just put a corridor in for fun? They dug the passage and then decided not to finish it?"

"Or they used it as a back entrance to bring items in Antony's part of the tomb, then they sealed it when they were done."

"Sealed it?" Maggie said with a gulp.

Emma's shoulders slumped, and she stalked a few steps away. She nodded before speaking. "Yeah, sealed it."

"But you said…" Maggie began.

Emma interrupted her. "I said they built them with a back entrance. I didn't say they left them open."

"So… what? You told me that just to ease my nerves? You lied so I wouldn't panic? What, Emma?"

Emma shook her head. "No! No, I… I genuinely hoped it was a back entrance. An unsealed back entrance. I… I didn't realize they sealed it. I mean they did sometimes but… I hoped this one wasn't."

Emma stared wistfully at the dead end.

"Well, maybe we missed something," Maggie said.

"It's solid," Emma answered. She smacked her hand against the hard stone wall. "I don't even see a seam. I'm sorry, Maggie. We're stuck."

Emma stalked away and slid to sitting. She sunk her head into her hands. Maggie sat down across from her. Emma sniffled, wiping at her cheeks. Maggie opened her mouth to offer a consoling statement, but her mind found none.

"Emma…" Maggie began after a moment.

"Don't," Emma answered. Her voice cracked through her tears.

"Don't cry, Emma."

"Don't cry? What do you propose we do? Dance? We're stuck in here, Maggie. We're going to die in here."

Maggie considered her statements. Emma was right. They'd reached the end. "Maybe we could try to go back the way we came."

Emma made a face at Maggie. "Okay, you're right. It's probably not possible."

"I'm sorry, Maggie," Emma said, breaking down in sobs.

Maggie crawled to sit next to Emma. She pulled her into a tight embrace. "Don't be sorry, Emma. There's nothing to be sorry about!"

Emma pushed her away. "We're going to die, Maggie!"

"But it's not your fault. I was the one who pushed us to find a way out of that first chamber!"

"I'm the one with the knowledge of ancient tombs. I should have stopped us. I should have realized."

"That's silly," Maggie contended.

"I guess it doesn't matter," Emma responded. "You hated me before this anyway."

"I don't hate you," Maggie said.

"Could have fooled me," Emma retorted. "You detest me because of what I did giving away our location when we found this place."

Before Maggie could answer, the flashlight's beam flickered, then extinguished. Darkness enveloped them.

"Ugh," Emma moaned. "Par for the damn course." She tossed the flashlight down in disgust. It clattered across the stone floor, flickering twice before dying again.

Maggie heard the sound of more sniffling as darkness descended again. She reached to Emma and wrapped her arm around her. With her other hand, she stroked Emma's hair. She remained silent for a moment before she spoke again. "It's true I was angry before, but I don't hate you."

"You don't have to be nice to me just because we're going to die and I'm upset," Emma said.

"No," Maggie began, "I'm not, I'm…" Maggie's voice dropped off. Maggie creased her brow.

"You're what?" Emma questioned. "Lying? You're lying and you really hate me?"

"No," Maggie answered. "I can see you."

Maggie stared at the clear outline of Emma next to her.

"What?" Emma questioned; confusion apparent in her voice.

"I can see you!" Maggie exclaimed, her voice rising with excitement. "I can see you! I can see you!"

Emma turned toward Maggie. "I can see you, too!"

Maggie stood. "Which means there is light coming from somewhere!"

"Which means we may be able to get out!"

Maggie searched for the light source. "There!" she exclaimed, pointing toward the ceiling.

"I see it!" Emma answered.

Maggie reached for it, but it remained just outside her grasp. She hurried toward the discarded flashlight. After retrieving it, she shook it and smacked it a few times. "Come on!" Maggie groaned. "We just need a few more minutes to investigate this!"

"Try switching the batteries around," Emma suggested.

"Good idea," Maggie said. She popped open the battery compartment and swapped the batteries inside. Maggie flicked the switch and light streamed into the passageway.

Both women breathed a sigh of relief. Maggie clicked the flashlight off to conserve the batteries. "I can't reach the opening. Should we go back and find something we can climb on?"

Emma shook her head. "I'd rather not go back. One of us is going to have to boost the other up."

Maggie considered it. Emma squatted down. "Climb on my shoulders."

"Maybe it's better for you to climb on my shoulders."

Emma stood straighter. "How much do you weigh?"

Maggie frowned. "Never mind, let's just try your way."

Emma guffawed at her. "Oh, Maggie," she moaned.

Emma crouched and Maggie swung her legs over Emma's shoulders. Emma stood with a grunt. "You should have answered the weight question," Emma choked out.

"Quiet, you," Maggie answered as she flicked on the flashlight. She searched the area near the crevice.

"Anything?" Emma groaned. She wavered as she attempted to hold Maggie on her shoulders.

"No, hold still."

"Sorry! I'm having trouble staying upright period, let alone still."

Maggie swung the flashlight's beam to the corner. "Here!" she exclaimed.

"What is it?"

"A hole!"

"A hole?" Emma questioned as they were plunged into darkness.

"Uh-oh," Maggie said. She shook the flashlight and banged on it. The flashlight refused to offer any additional light. "No!"

"I need a break," Emma stated. She fell to her knees and Maggie toppled off her but managed to regain her balance.

Emma collapsed to the floor, gulping air. "You okay?" Maggie inquired.

"Yeah, I just needed a minute. Any luck with the flashlight?"

"No," Maggie lamented. She knocked it against the wall. "It's dead."

"Did you see anything in the hole while you were up there?"

"No," Maggie answered. "The light died before I could look in there."

"Use your phone."

Maggie dug in her pocket and toggled it on. "Can't," she answered. "It's dead, too."

"You wasted it earlier. You and your selfies! We're going to have to go by feel."

"You mean…" Maggie gulped. "Stick my hand in there and feel around?"

"Yeah," Emma answered as she climbed to her feet.

"Let's switch, you go up there and feel around the creepy hole and I'll be the base."

"No. I can lift you, we've proven that, so, come on, just get up there." Emma crouched again.

Maggie set her mouth in a thin line as she swung her legs over Emma's shoulders again. "Okay, ready."

Emma stood with a grumble. Maggie felt around in the corner, locating the hole.

"Did you find it?" Emma inquired.

"Yeah."

"Well? Is there anything in it?"

"I'm not sure. I haven't put my hand in yet."

"What are you waiting for? Come on, Maggie!"

"Ugh, all right." Maggie grimaced as she steeled her nerves. "Ugh," she moaned as she reached her fingers inside the crevice. Her fingers touched something cold, and she retracted her hand.

"What are you doing?" Emma shouted.

"Sorry, I touched something, and I didn't know what it was!"

"Maggie…"

"Shh, okay, I'm going to try again."

Maggie squared her shoulders and reached into the fissure. She located the cold item again. She let her fingers explore it. "I feel something. It's cold. Feels like a ring. Maybe metal."

"Anything else?"

"No. I'll try pulling this."

"No!" Emma shouted.

"What?"

"Don't pull it."

"Why not?"

"It may trigger something."

"Yeah, a way out, I hope."

"We have no idea what that could do. It could trigger a trap. Even if it opens a way out, we have no idea what is on the other side of the opening. It could be a mountain of sand!"

"If it's a mountain of sand, we wouldn't be seeing light! I'm pulling it!"

Maggie reached into the hole. Her fingers closed around the cool metal ring. She tugged at it. Nothing happened. Emma stumbled underneath her. Maggie held fast to the ring, but Emma's wobbling caused Maggie to twist it.

The ring spun at a ninety-degree angle. A loud clank boomed in the small space. Emma lost her footing as a door swung open above their heads. Sand poured through the opening along with sunshine. Maggie clutched at the ring, dangling in the air as Emma collapsed to the floor below her. Maggie heard a sickening smack as Emma hit the floor.

Sand continued to gush through the opening. It buried Emma as she laid unconscious. Maggie lost her grip on the door trigger. She fell onto the layer of sand with a thud.

"Oof," Maggie grunted as she hit. She wriggled for a moment as the air returned to her lungs. The moment she was able, Maggie pushed herself up to sitting. She spun onto her knees and began a desperate dig through the sand.

"Emma! Emma!" Maggie called in a frantic voice.

As quickly as Maggie dug, the grains filled in any hole she attempted to create. Maggie groaned as she struggled against the shifting sands. Maggie's digging turned frenzied as she failed to find her friend.

She tried multiple spots, clawing as deep as she could. On her fourth try, she touched warm skin. Her fingers closed around Emma's. "Emma!" Maggie choked out. She grabbed hold of her hand and tugged. Too much sand still covered Emma to free her.

Maggie worked at a feverish pace. She shoved sand to each side. Emma's form became visible as the sand fell away. Maggie cleared the grains from around her head. She pulled Emma's head up. Maggie found no traces of blood. She prayed Emma's head injury proved minor.

"Emma! Emma!" Maggie called as she tapped Emma's cheeks with her hand.

Emma's forehead pinched, and a moan escaped her lips. A choking cough followed before Emma's eyes fluttered open.

"Emma?!" Maggie questioned. "Are you okay?"

Emma squeezed her eyes shut for a moment before she popped them open. She groaned. "Uh, yeah," she mumbled. "Yeah, I think so."

"Do you feel any pain anywhere? I don't see any blood from your head."

Emma struggled to sit up. Maggie helped her, pushing more sand aside to free her abdomen. "Easy," Maggie cautioned. Emma glanced upward. "What is it? Do you feel faint?"

Emma shook her head. "No. The sky," she answered. A smile crept across her face. "It's the most beautiful thing I've ever seen! We did it!"

Maggie smiled at her, then glanced at the cloudless blue sky. "We did!" She hesitated for a moment. "There's only one problem. That exit hole is pretty high."

Emma frowned and glanced at her legs. "Help dig me out so we can figure a way out of here!"

Maggie dug the sand from around Emma's legs as Emma dusted sand from her hips. They freed her within minutes. Emma climbed to her feet with Maggie's cautious eye on her. "Do you feel faint at all?"

"No," Emma answered. "I'm okay. My head is a little sore, but I'm okay."

Emma gazed up at the cavity. She reached up with her arm, trying to gauge the distance. "Do you think you could get up there with a boost from me?"

"No, no way," Maggie argued. "I'll boost you up. You've been the base too many times."

"It's fine," Emma countered. "I just want to get out of here! And you're the best one of us to climb up there then pull me out." She cupped her hands. "Step in, I'll boost you up."

"Okay," Maggie answered.

She placed her foot in Emma's hands and leapt up. On the first try, Maggie failed to grasp the edge of the opening. With Emma's assistance, she made it on the second try. Maggie grasped the edge. Sand spilled into the chamber as she struggled to crawl out.

Emma grabbed Maggie's feet and pushed. With the extra assistance, she tumbled through the opening, rolling down the sand bank outside. Maggie breathed a deep sigh of relief as the morning sun beat down on her.

Maggie scrambled to her hands and knees and crawled to the edge. She peered inside, spotting Emma shielding her eyes as she stared out the hole.

"Come on!" Maggie shouted down. She shimmied to the edge, allowing her arms to dangle inside.

Emma reached up but could not grab hold of Maggie's hand. "Jump!" Maggie instructed.

Emma held her arm up as she leapt off the floor. After four jumps, she gave up. "It's no use. I can't make it," Emma said with a sigh. "Go for help. Just hurry."

"No way," Maggie argued. "I am NOT leaving you." Maggie inched further toward the opening, allowing more of her body to hang into the hole. "Try now." She dangled her arm into the hole, stretching it as far as she could.

Emma leapt up with her arm outstretched. On her third try, she connected with Maggie's hand. Maggie tightened her fingers around Emma's wrist. "Hang on!" Maggie shouted. "Give me your other hand!"

Maggie rolled onto her stomach, reaching her other hand down to Emma. Emma clung with both hands to Maggie's arm. She released one hand and swung it toward Maggie's other arm. Emma clasped her wrist, then worked to steady herself from swaying too much by bracing her feet against the wall.

Maggie tightened her grip on Emma and inched backward. After a few feet, Emma released her grip on Maggie's arm and grasped the edge of the opening. Maggie kept hold of her and continued to pull her over the edge.

Emma crawled up and out of the tomb. The two women sprawled on the hot sand, gasping for breath. "Ugh," Emma groaned. "Thank God!"

"Yeah," Maggie answered, still gulping air. "Told you I'd get you out!"

"You did!" Emma admitted.

They laid for another moment in silence as they recovered. Maggie poked her head up and scanned the area. "Where are we?"

Emma picked her head up and glanced around, her forehead wrinkling. "Couldn't have come up right in the middle of the encampment, could we?"

They pushed up to sitting and scoured the horizon in all directions. "There!" Emma exclaimed, pointing behind them.

Maggie followed the direction of her finger. A smile crept over her face. She climbed to her feet. "Race you to the camp!"

Emma rolled her eyes as she climbed to her feet. "Let's just walk it."

"Okay, fair. It's further than I thought. It didn't seem like we went that far!"

They began their trek across the sands toward the encampment.

"Whew!" Maggie exclaimed after only a few steps. "I'm glad you talked me out of running! It's HOT!"

"Yeah, no kidding. Welcome to summer in the desert."

"Ugh," Maggie groaned. "I can't wait to get back. I want some breakfast. Those horrible, powdered eggs even seem appealing."

"Yeah, that granola bar really didn't last as long as I hoped."

"And a big glass of water," Maggie continued.

"And a shower," Emma chimed in.

"And a nap," Maggie added.

"Yeah, a nap. And when we wake up, Ollie's found the library's location and we make a huge find!"

"Yes!" Maggie agreed with a laugh.

"Almost there."

"Thank heavens!"

Emma crinkled her brow as they approached. "They must have called for help to rescue us," she commented.

"Why do you say that?"

"There's a helicopter here," Emma said as she motioned to the chopper on the outskirts of the camp.

"Oh, yeah! Wonder if they made any progress. Boy, will they be surprised to see us come strolling in!"

"Yeah, I bet!"

They reached the edge of the encampment. Maggie lumbered past the first tent before she ground to a halt. Emma, trailing behind her, bumped into Maggie. "Hey, what…" Emma began.

Maggie's jaw went slack, and her eyes widened. Slowly, she raised her arms up in the air. Next to her, Emma swallowed hard and followed Maggie's lead.

Across from them, a bulky, bearded man held a large weapon pointed at them. He smirked at them. "That's far enough," he barked in a crisp British accent.

CHAPTER 22

The gunman continued to sneer at them. Another man dressed in khaki appeared, rounding the corner of the tent in front of them. His brow furrowed as he came across the scene.

"What have we here?" he questioned, his accent British, as well.

Seconds later, two more men came into view. They dragged a man between them. Maggie recognized two of the men immediately. James Michael Dean, with the help of his associate, strong-armed another man.

"Uncle Ollie!" she shouted.

"Maggie!" Ollie gasped.

"Came across these two on my way to the chopper," the first man stated. "Should I tie them up with the others?"

The man in khaki shook his head. "Load them onto the chopper with the professor," he instructed. "They may prove useful to us as we proceed."

The armed man nodded his head. He waved Maggie and Emma toward the chopper with his gun.

The other two men shoved Ollie into the helicopter

before they turned to grab Emma and Maggie. They bound both women's wrists with zip ties before they forced them onto the chopper.

"Uncle Ollie!" Maggie exclaimed as she collapsed onto a seat. "Are you okay?" Blood oozed from a cut above Ollie's left eye.

"I'm okay, Maggie. How are you? How did you get out?"

The men climbed aboard. The rotors began to spin overhead as the engine wound up. Their cabin mates coupled with the chopper's noise silenced any further conversation.

The helicopter began its bobbling climb into the air. Maggie, sandwiched between two of the armed thugs, peered out the window as they rose away from the camp. The helicopter spun in the air, circling to face a new direction.

Maggie glanced back wistfully as they sped away from the camp. She fought to keep the white tents in sight as they decreased to specks on the horizon behind them. As they threatened to fade from her vision, a loud explosion boomed. The force bobbled the small helicopter even at this distance.

Maggie leapt from her seat, lunging across the man seated next to her to stare out the window. "HENRY!" she screamed. Black smoke poured into the sky from the encampment.

"Sit down," one of the thugs yelled. He grabbed Maggie and roughly shoved her back into her seat.

Tears filled Maggie's eyes as her stomach turned over. Perhaps everyone else had evacuated the camp before their assailants arrived, she ruminated. Not likely, her mind corrected. Had she just lost her boyfriend and friends? She swallowed hard. Probably. Given her current predicament, Maggie could only hold on to the hope they somehow survived.

The group remained silent for the remainder of their ride. The helicopter approached a city Maggie did not recognize. They flew toward a tall building. The helicopter slowed and descended until they landed on the roof. The whir of the engine quieted as the blades slowed to a stop.

"Out," the man in khaki ordered. Emma climbed out first, followed by Maggie. James Michael Dean and his armed companion followed before Ollie and the man in khaki stepped out.

They led the group into the building and down a flight of stairs. Maggie, Ollie and Emma were marched to a door leading to a large penthouse apartment. Maggie scanned the space as they entered. The apartment was lavishly furnished.

Across the room, a large window overlooked the city. Bright light shined in silhouetting a man standing near it. The man turned as they entered. He raised his glass to them. "Ah, Mr. Bryson, I see you were more than successful. You've brought the professor and some unexpected guests." Another Brit, Maggie noted.

The man in khaki responded as he circled around the group. Two of the other three men took posts near the door, their guns at the ready. James Michael Dean glared at Maggie with a smirk on his face. "Yes, sir. My apologies for the professor's unforeseen companions. They appeared out of nowhere at the last minute. The professor told me they were not on site. Clearly, he was being untruthful."

"No matter," the man answered. "We still hold all the cards. What about the ankhs?"

"We only recovered two," Mr. Bryson answered. "The professor claims they do not have the third."

Bryson swung the strap of a small, padded bag over his head and plopped it on the table. He opened it, revealing two of the ankhs.

Maggie slid her eyes sideways toward Emma. Emma glanced at Maggie, swallowing hard.

"And what of the others?" the man inquired.

"Disposed of," Bryson answered.

"Good," the man answered. "Now, professor…"

Maggie interrupted. "Who are you?" she demanded.

"Maggie!" Ollie hissed. "Shh!"

"A wise suggestion, Ms. Edwards," the man answered. "You should listen to your uncle."

Maggie raised her eyebrows at him and squared her shoulders. "You just killed my friends and shoved me, Emma and my uncle into a helicopter at gunpoint. You clearly know us. I think it's only fair we know who you are!"

The man returned Maggie's expression, raising his eyebrows at her. He poured himself another drink before he spoke. "You're either very brave, Ms. Edwards, or very stupid."

"Well, I'm not stupid. Now, who are you and what do you want?"

"Ah, now the second question I will answer. I'd argue the first is immaterial."

"Agree to disagree," Maggie retorted. "But I'll take the answer to the second question. And I'd like to have these removed also!" Maggie waved her bound wrists in the air.

The man chuckled and smirked at Maggie. "Search them and remove their restraints."

"Hey!" Maggie objected as one of the man's goons patted her down. He pulled her phone from her pocket, tossing it on a nearby table. He moved on to Ollie and finished with Emma. As he patted her legs, his hand struck something in her pocket. He pulled open the flap and extracted the ankh.

"Well, well, well, what have we here?" Bryson questioned as he pulled the item from the man's hands. He delivered it to the other man.

The man accepted the item, and a smile crossed his face. "You've been holding out on us, professor," the man said.

"He hasn't," Maggie contended. "He had no idea we found that."

"Maggie!" Ollie warned again.

"Really? You mean to tell me the good professor didn't know his prized assistant and his niece were in possession of the third ankh?"

"No," Maggie retorted. "He didn't. We didn't exactly have time to catch up and share the good news with guns shoved in our faces."

"I'm sorry you haven't enjoyed your time with us so far, Ms. Edwards," the man answered. "But this is encouraging news, regardless of who was aware of it. Now we can move along to the next phase of our plan."

"Which is what?" Maggie demanded.

"None of your concern," Bryson countered.

"Au contrare, my dear Bryson," the older man corrected. "It is very much Ms. Edwards concern. You see, Ms. Edwards, her uncle and her secretive little friend are imperative to our next phase. In fact, it rests entirely on their shoulders."

"What do you mean?" Ollie interjected.

"I mean, you are going to tell us the location of the library."

"We don't know it," Maggie responded.

"She's right," Ollie added. "I haven't even seen the third ankh. And with the previous two I made no headway on identifying the location."

"No matter, we'll give you a few hours, professor," the man answered.

"A few hours?" Maggie inquired. "This may take years of research."

"Then you had better work fast," the man suggested.

James Michael Dean approached them and herded them toward another doorway across the room. Maggie glanced at

Emma and Ollie. Ollie gave her a quick nod, signaling her to follow their instructions.

"Now, if you wouldn't mind stepping into your new work area. I think you'll find all the materials you need to complete your work."

Maggie allowed herself to be shown into the next room. She glanced around as she entered. A round table with a stack of paper and pencils sat in the middle of the sparsely furnished room. A few armchairs were placed around the room's edges. A large whiteboard on a stand stood near the table. A bulletin board with a map of Egypt hung on the opposite wall.

Mr. Bryson followed them in. He set the ankh retrieved from Emma's pocket on the table. He opened the bag he carried earlier and laid out the other two.

"There you are, professor. As my employer proposed, I suggest you work fast. He'd like an answer by 6 p.m. this evening. Which gives you about," he said as he checked his watch, "eight hours to solve this."

"Or what?" Maggie questioned.

He set his gaze on Maggie, narrowing his eyes. "Or we shall take action designed to speed your work," he growled.

"What exactly does that mean?" Maggie pushed further.

"Use your imagination, Ms. Edwards."

"So, in other words, it means nothing. Idle threats," Maggie retorted.

Mr. Bryson smirked at her. "I assure you it's anything but idle."

"Really?" Maggie countered. "Then what action will you take. Surely you can answer that."

"Oh, I can, Ms. Edwards. If you don't provide an answer by 6 p.m., only two of you will continue to work on the project. The other will join your unfortunate colleagues in leaving this world sooner than they expected."

Maggie set her jaw. The mention of her friends' demise coupled with the threat made her blood boil.

"Eight hours?!" Ollie exclaimed. "This may not be solvable in a mere eight hours."

Mr. Bryson shrugged his shoulders. "As I've already stated, I recommend you work feverishly, professor." He strode to the door. Before stepping through, he spun to face them. "Oh, and if you are considering lying about its location, I'd reconsider. Late or wrong answers pay the same price."

Mr. Bryson pulled the door shut with a slam behind him.

Maggie whirled around to face Emma and Ollie. "What are we going to do?" she whispered.

"I'm not sure there's anything we can do," Ollie responded.

Maggie scanned the room. She raced to the large sliding glass door leading to the balcony beyond the room. Maggie grabbed the handle and tugged. She fiddled with the lock and tried again. The door didn't budge.

"It's stuck," Maggie grunted.

"I'm sure they didn't leave an exit open," Emma answered. "Besides, it doesn't help us. Are we going to parachute from the top floor?"

"I don't know," Maggie said with a sigh. "Climb to the balcony below? We'll figure something out! We can't stay here!" Maggie pointed to the table. "What about the pencils? Are they sharpened?"

"Yes, why?" Emma inquired.

"We can wait for them to come back and stab them with the pencils and escape."

"Did you see them?" Emma asked. "I don't think that's going to work. We'll likely end up with a broken hand, wrist, arm or worse."

Maggie's shoulders sagged. "What if we don't solve this in eight hours?"

"I don't want to think about that," Emma answered. She sunk into a chair near the table.

"We can't think about it," Ollie answered. He approached the table and studied the ankhs. "We must focus all our energy on solving this puzzle."

Maggie crossed her arms, her lips forming a pout. After a few moments, she stalked to the table. "Fine," she answered. "Any ideas?"

Ollie stared at them. "Afraid not," he answered.

"Emma?" Maggie inquired.

Emma shook her head. "This is the first I'm seeing these," Emma responded. "I've got nothing."

Maggie sighed. She grabbed a marker from the whiteboard's tray. "Okay, we need to brainstorm. Any ideas, shout them out, I'll write them here and then we'll work on each one."

Silence filled the room. Ollie sunk into the chair next to Emma.

Maggie held her arms out to her sides, her eyes wide. "Well? Come on! Ideas! Quick!"

Emma shook her head. "I've got nothing. I'm exhausted, hungry, my head is splitting. I can't think."

"None of my ideas seem to work," Ollie responded.

Maggie sunk into the chair across from Emma. She capped the marker and slammed it on the table. "So, we've got nothing."

Emma slumped across the table with a moan.

Maggie sunk her head into her hands. "I can't believe we survived all that in the tomb to die at the hands of those thugs because we can't figure this out."

"What happened down there?" Ollie inquired.

"What didn't?" Emma groaned.

The comment elicited a chuckle from Maggie. "Truth," Maggie answered. "We waited in that first room for a long time. But after a while, we didn't hear anything from above."

Ollie nodded and interjected, "Those goons surprised us. They disabled the guards. We were so intent on freeing you two, we never saw them coming."

"How terrifying," Maggie said, grabbing and squeezing Ollie's hand. "Are you all right? In all the commotion, I completely forgot to ask what happened to you. And now…" Tears formed in Maggie's eyes. She swallowed hard.

Ollie clutched Maggie's hand with both of his. "Maggie, don't cry. It wasn't that bad. They roughed us up a bit, tried to find out where you were and if we had all the ankhs. In the end, they decided to take me and the two we had and return here."

"And…" Tears spilled down Maggie's cheeks.

"Oh, Maggie," Ollie said. "Don't cry."

Maggie sniffled, attempting to hold back her tears. "Henry always used to say that." Sobs choked her as she uttered the statement.

"Shh," Ollie consoled her. "It'll be all right. We don't know they're gone."

"Did you see the explosion?" Maggie cried.

"Henry's smart. He knew they were setting those charges. I wouldn't be surprised if he got away before they went off."

Maggie bit her lower lip and wiped her cheeks. She took a few deep, steadying breaths. "Okay," she said, breathing out a long breath. "Okay, think positive, you're right."

Emma gave Maggie a consoling smile and reached across to squeeze her hand.

Maggie sniffled again. "It would be easier to think positive with some food. Emma's right, we haven't really slept or eaten since we split a granola bar last night. I'm guessing you haven't eaten either," Maggie said to Ollie.

"Do you really think they'll order in for us?" Emma inquired sarcastically.

"Doesn't hurt to ask! Plus, it's not like we're making much progress."

Maggie strode to the door and tried the knob. The door didn't budge. Maggie pounded on it. "Hey! Hello!"

A clink sounded as the lock unlatched. The door opened into the room and Bryson stuck his head in. "Solved it already? See what the proper motivation can do?"

"No," Maggie announced. "We did not solve it. We need something."

"Oh?"

"Food. None of us have eaten anything in a good while. We can't make any progress without some food."

"Food?" Bryson questioned. "We aren't short-order cooks, Ms. Edwards."

Maggie gave him an annoyed glance. "I'm sure an enterprising man such as yourself can scrounge up some takeout. Maybe you could even make something homemade."

"I'd watch that quick-witted tongue of yours, Ms. Edwards. You wouldn't want to find yourself without it one day."

"What is the issue, Bryson?" a voice called.

"They are requesting food, sir."

The man approached the door. Maggie peered around Bryson to make eye contact with him. "We're starving! We need something to eat! We're not stalling, we're hungry!" Maggie entreated.

"I'm sure we can provide you with something to quell your hunger, can't we, Bryson?"

Bryson scowled at Maggie but acquiesced. "Fine. I assume you are not picky?"

"Not really. Do you have any takeout menus?"

"No," he said flatly. "I will do my best."

He slammed the door shut. Maggie wandered back to the table. "Well, at least we'll get something to eat. Maybe that will spur something."

"In the meantime, tell me about your adventure trapped in the tomb. And finding the third ankh," Ollie encouraged. "It will pass the time at least and may provide a clue!"

Maggie grinned at Ollie. "You won't believe half of this story."

"Try me."

Maggie recounted the tale of their escape from the depths of Cleopatra's tomb. Emma interjected with a variety of archaeological details as Maggie related their experiences.

"Amazing!" Ollie answered as Maggie concluded her story.

"Nothing was more amazing than finding Antony," Emma said, a dreamy expression on her face. "It was… incredible. I feel so privileged to have experienced that, despite all the havoc!"

Ollie nodded in agreement with her statements. "Too bad that goon took my phone," Maggie lamented. "I've got a fabulous picture of us draped in some of that jewelry!"

Ollie chuckled at Maggie's statements as the door burst open across the room. "Food, as requested," Bryson announced. He dumped several takeout bags on the table. "Now get to work."

He stalked across the room, glaring at them as he pulled the door shut.

"Nice guy," Maggie said with an eye roll as she dug into the bags. She doled out the food and everyone dug in. They made quick work of their meal. Maggie shoved the empty takeout container away from her as she wiped the corners of her mouth.

"Whew, now I'm stuffed," Emma confessed. "And tired. I could use a nap."

"Maybe you should curl up in that nice armchair," Maggie suggested.

Emma yawned but shook her head. "No, we need to work on this."

"We can spare an hour for you to get some sleep," Maggie replied.

"We've got six hours left," Emma responded. "We don't have time for a nap."

"Fine, fine. But we've got no ideas either," Maggie answered. "We're spinning our wheels here."

"Ollie," Emma said, "you've been researching this the most. Is there ANYTHING you can suggest?"

Ollie shook his head. "Nothing definitive. I conjectured once we had the pieces, they'd somehow fit together to form a message."

Maggie stared at the pieces. "Do you mean they'd spell something out if we saw them all together?"

"More or less," Ollie answered. "With these protrusions, I assumed we'd spot something, coordinates or hieroglyphs once we joined these."

Maggie placed the ankhs in a line and stood over the table. She stared at them, moving her head to different angles and distances. "I see nothing," she admitted.

She rearranged them, sliding the last piece to the first spot and moving the other two down. They all checked the configuration. No patterns emerged. They tried every configuration of the ankhs but found nothing.

"Maybe if we turn one upside down and place them together like this," Emma suggested. She flipped one ankh to point between the other two.

"Nope," Maggie answered, "I don't see anything, do you?"

"No," Emma admitted.

Ollie rearranged the ankhs, swapping the two ends. "Still nothing," he said with a sigh.

SECRET OF THE ANKHS

Again, after trying every configuration, they found nothing.

Maggie glanced at the clock on the wall as she slumped into her seat. Time ticked away on their deadline and they were no closer to a solution.

Maggie slouched down in the chair, resting her head on the back. Ollie picked up two of the ankhs. "I even wondered if these somehow fit together because of the strange ridges on them. However, the back sides are flat on each of these. So, they cannot interlock."

Ollie demonstrated by placing two ankhs together.

"Perhaps they fit top to top," Maggie suggested.

She grabbed the two ankhs from Ollie's hands and pushed them together. She slid them around, trying to lock them together. They didn't fit. She tried another combination of ankhs. After several tries, she gave up.

Maggie discarded them on the table and sunk her head into her hands. "Ugh, this is useless. Maybe I'm doing it wrong."

Emma shook her head. "I don't think that idea makes sense. Fitting them face to face doesn't leave any place to fit the third."

"You're right," Ollie answered. "And fitting them together doesn't suggest any location, anyway."

Maggie leapt from her seat and paced around the floor. She settled in front of the window, gazing out over the city. The door popped open, drawing her attention back to the room.

"Progress report," Bryson demanded.

Maggie ignored him, her lips forming a pout. She returned her attention to the horizon.

"We haven't made much progress," Ollie admitted.

"Well, that's a terrible shame for one of you if this trend continues," Bryson answered.

"We have nothing to go on. This type of research could take weeks, months, years, not hours!" Ollie countered.

"No one cares, professor. I suggest you tear yourself from the horizon, Ms. Edwards, and the three of you put your heads together and find a solution."

"We may not be able to," Ollie argued. "That's the point. Please... I... I'll stay with you and continue to work on this for as long as it takes. I can find a solution. It will just take time. But please, let the girls go."

"I'm sorry, professor, that is not an option."

"Please," Ollie tried again. He leapt from his seat and approached Bryson. "They can't help."

"They managed to find the third ankh, so I'd disagree with your assessment, professor. In either case, it's not an alternative. They stay. Unless you fail to find a solution. Then one of them will go, albeit not in the way you'd prefer."

CHAPTER 23

Ollie sighed as Bryson stalked away. He slammed the door behind him, leaving them alone again.

Ollie dropped into his chair. "I'm sorry, Maggie and Emma."

"Don't be," Maggie said, joining them at the table and wrapping her arm around Ollie's shoulders. "And thanks for trying. But even if you succeeded, I'm not about to go anywhere and leave you with these thugs."

"Me either," Emma agreed. "We've got four hours left. Maybe if we can make slight progress, that will be enough to appease them."

"But how?" Maggie inquired. "We're getting nowhere! They don't spell anything, they don't fit together, they don't form a pattern."

"Okay, so, we've ruled all that out. What's left?"

Maggie shrugged. Ollie spun in his chair, staring at the ankhs. "What is it?" Maggie questioned. "Do you have an idea?"

"Perhaps..." He paused, his brow furrowing as he grabbed one. "Perhaps there is something we've missed on these.

We've not inspected them carefully. Perhaps there's writing on here or a way to open a compartment in them that will provide some information."

"Oh!" Maggie exclaimed. She grabbed one of ankhs. "Maybe! I'll check this one."

Emma grabbed the remaining ankh. Maggie brought the object close to her face and studied it. She turned it over and over, inspecting each part closely. Maggie rubbed her finger along the bottom of the ankh, searching for any etchings. She found nothing. She scanned the edges of the ankh. Maggie searched the ridges on the top for any hidden engravings. As she scoured the object, she spotted something inside the circular region.

Maggie's pulse quickened. "Here! Here!" she exclaimed. "Is this something?"

"Where?" Ollie inquired; his voice filled with hope.

Maggie pointed to the small imperfection in the interior of the circle. Ollie adjusted his glasses and examined the area Maggie pointed out. Emma leaned over Ollie's shoulder, studying the spot.

"Well?" Maggie inquired.

"I see what you're meaning," Ollie answered. "But I'm not certain it's anything." Ollie picked up the ankh he was studying and compared the areas. "This one has nothing in that area."

"Is there anything else in the circle? Perhaps at a different location?" Maggie asked.

Emma grabbed the ankh from Ollie and rotated it to examine the interior of the circle. "I don't see anything like what Maggie found." She repeated the action with her ankh. "Nothing on mine either."

Ollie squinted at the ankh. "I'm sorry to say this may just be an imperfection."

Maggie's shoulders slumped. "Give it back, I'll keep searching."

Ollie handed the ankh back and returned to studying his ankh. Emma returned to her seat and continued her probe. After another fifteen minutes of careful study, Maggie dumped her ankh on the table. She heaved a long sigh. "It's no use. I can't find anything on it. No carvings or clues or locations. Nothing!"

Maggie slumped backward in her chair. Emma continued her search but gave up soon after Maggie. "I can't find anything either," she admitted. Emma set the ankh on the table and leapt from her seat. She stretched a bit before stalking to the window. "I'm starting to consider your plan about jumping."

Ollie abandoned his inspection of the ankh as well. "I'm trying not to become discouraged, but…" Ollie paused and sighed. "With such little time left on our deadline, I cannot help but feel pessimistic."

Maggie rubbed Ollie's arm. "I wish I could say something encouraging, but I'm fresh out of inspiration," Maggie said, defeated.

Ollie clutched her hand. "Maggie…" he said, his voice hoarse with dismay. He searched for more words but found none. Instead, he squeezed her hand before returning his gaze to the ankhs. He shook his head.

"Short of coming up with a miracle idea, it looks like one of us is about to draw the short straw," Emma lamented.

Maggie rested her chin on the table. Her fingers explored the ankh she had just inspected. She traced the patterns created on the ankh's surface. Ollie crossed his arms and leaned back in his chair. He shook his head. "I really believed those peaks and valleys were the key," he murmured.

Maggie's brow creased. She cocked her head and eyed the ankh. "Peaks and valleys?" she repeated.

"Yes, I believed the ridges were the key."

Maggie grabbed the ankh and studied it again. She picked up the other two, examining them as well.

"What is it, Maggie?"

Maggie raced to the bulletin board and pulled the map down. She spread it across the table. "You said peaks and valleys," Maggie gushed. "It made me think these protrusions aren't carvings. They aren't hieroglyphs designed to be read by placing the ankhs together. They're actual peaks and valleys!"

Emma joined them at the table, curious about Maggie's new idea. "What do you mean 'actual peaks and valleys?'" she questioned.

Maggie glanced at the map and the ankhs. "See this depression?" She pointed out a curved shape running through one of the ankhs.

"Yeah?"

Maggie picked up the ankh and rotated it to a new orientation. "Doesn't this curve match this curve?" Maggie pointed on the map to a curve in the Nile.

Emma glanced between the two. She positioned the ankh over the curve, her eyes flitting between the map and the item. "Yeah," she admitted. "It does."

Ollie leapt to his feet and studied the map. "You may be on to something there. So, your idea is the peaks and valleys on the ankhs are peaks and valleys in the topography!"

"Bingo!" Maggie exclaimed.

"We must try to fit these onto the map and match them to the features," Ollie stated.

"It would be easier if we had a topographical map. And it looks like this map's scale is a little too small," Emma noted.

"I'll ask for another map with a different scale," Maggie said with a grin. She raced across the room and pounded on the door. Maggie bobbed on her toes with excitement as she waited.

The door popped open. "Yes?" Mr. Bryson inquired. "Do you have news for us?"

"Maybe," Maggie responded. "We need a topographic map of the area in a larger scale than that map." Maggie motioned to the map laying on the table.

"A topographic map?"

"Yes," Maggie confirmed. "With a larger scale than that map's."

Mr. Bryson clasped his hands behind his back. He set his jaw and offered an unimpressed glance at Maggie. "This had better not be a stall tactic, Ms. Edwards."

"Do you want answers or not?"

Bryson did not respond. Instead, he strode from the room with a huff, pulling the door shut behind him. Maggie wandered back to the table. "I hope this works," she said.

"It's the best shot we've got at the moment," Ollie answered.

Maggie grabbed a breadstick from the takeout bag and munched on it. After a few moments, she leapt from the chair and paced the floor. "How long does it take to get a map?"

They waited for a nerve-wracking twenty minutes before the door swung open again. "Here are a variety of topographical maps of Egypt and the surrounding areas." He shoved the bag of maps toward Maggie.

"I don't need a variety," Maggie retorted as she snatched the bag. "Just the right one."

"I suggest you make it work, for your sakes!" Bryson spun on his heel and departed.

Emma peered into the bag and pulled a few maps. "Are they going to work?" Maggie inquired as Emma opened them up.

Ollie pulled a few others open. "Let's see what we've got."

"This one's too small of a scale," Emma said as she shoved one map to the side.

"Same here," Ollie added, discarding his map.

Emma pulled open another map. "No good," she said with a sigh.

"Are you kidding?" Maggie said in an exasperated tone as Emma pulled another map open.

She paused a moment. "This could work. What do you think?" She turned the map toward Ollie.

"It's not perfect," he said as he leaned in to take a closer glance, "but it may do. Spread it out on the table."

Maggie cleared everything from the table and Emma spread the map out. She smoothed the chart with her hand. Maggie handed her the first ankh. "Okay," Emma said, "this one went here." Emma placed the ankh on top of the corresponding curve in the Nile River.

"What's the next one look like?" Ollie inquired.

Maggie held one out. They scanned the topography, trying to match the terrain.

"Here?" Emma asked, pointing to a region in the northeast corner of the map.

"No, those peaks are shaped differently. The ones on the map are triangular, but on the ankh, they are more square."

"Ah, yeah, you're right," Emma conceded.

"Down here!" Ollie exclaimed, pointing to a region in the southeast.

"Yes, yes, I think you're right!" Emma burst out. They laid the ankh on the corresponding section of the map.

"One more to go!" Maggie exclaimed. She held it out. "I bet it goes here." Maggie hovered it over an area on the map. "This would make all the circles touch."

"You're right, Maggie," Ollie answered. "The terrain matches."

Maggie set it down on the map. "We did it!"

"Now, what does it mean?" Emma questioned.

As Emma posed the question, the door burst open. "Progress report," Bryson demanded.

Ollie pushed in front of the two women. "We used the topographical map you provided to match the shapes on the top of each ankh. They match with features on the map. We believe this is the way the ankhs were supposed to be used to locate the library."

"So, where is the location?"

A satisfied smile crossed Maggie's face. "Right here!" She jabbed at the portion of the map enclosed by the three ankhs.

"How certain are you?"

"Well..." Emma began.

"Certain," Maggie assured him, interrupting Emma. "Nothing else makes sense. It has to be here."

Bryson scanned the group, searching for any indication of disingenuousness. He snatched a pencil from Maggie's hand and marked the area on the map. "You'd better be correct. It's your lives if you're not."

"The location makes sense," Ollie chimed in.

"How so, professor?" Bryson questioned.

Emma nodded in agreement. "It's near the Valley of the Kings," she stated.

Bryson nodded and opened the padded bag that held the ankhs when they arrived. As he began to load them into the compartment, a commotion sounded from the other room.

"We've got trouble!" a voice shouted in.

Bryson snapped his head toward the room. "That's our cue." He swung the bag's strap over his arm. Two other men rushed into the room. "What's going on out there?"

"Couple of uninvited guests on their way up," one said. "Looks like Taylor."

"Henry?!" Maggie gasped.

"That man is like a cat, he never runs out of lives," Bryson growled. "Where is Mr. Richards?"

"Already evac-ed to the chopper and waiting."

Bryson nodded. "Grab the professor and the blonde and let's get out of here." Bryson balled up the map and shoved it into his pocket before he seized Maggie's arm. "Let's go, Ms. Edwards."

"Ow!" Maggie protested as he shoved her from the room behind Ollie and Emma. The two men forced Ollie and Emma through the penthouse and into the hall. Maggie and Bryson lagged behind as he secured the zipper to close the padded carrying bag.

When they entered the hall, Maggie caught sight of the second of the two men shoving Emma into the stairwell leading to the roof. A shout from behind her caught her attention. She spun to face the opposite direction, searching for the source.

Bryson tightened his grip on her arm, dragging her back a step. He pointed a weapon grabbed from his waistband and fired multiple times. A figure darted into the stairwell. Maggie spotted the barrel of a handgun peak around the wall.

"Wouldn't try it, Taylor. I'm using your precious girlfriend as a shield!" Bryson shouted. He shoved Maggie in front of him.

"Henry!" Maggie called.

Bryson clamped his hand over her mouth, garbling any other message she attempted to shout. "Come out, Taylor. Show yourself."

Maggie tried to warn Henry, but she couldn't get anything out. Henry stepped from the stairway; his arms raised. "Let her go, Bryson," he bargained.

"Sorry, Taylor, she's good insurance. You hardly are in the

position to make any demands. Now, if you don't mind, Ms. Edwards and I have a rather important date."

Bryson began to drag Maggie backward toward the stairs leading to the roof. As they started to move, Maggie grasped the hand clasped over her mouth. Instead of pushing it away, she held it to her face, opening her mouth and biting down hard on Bryson's fingers.

"Ow!" he screamed. "You little bitch!"

He pulled his hand away as Maggie stomped on his instep. He cried out in pain as he lifted his hurt foot. Maggie swung her elbow into his gut, doubling him over. Henry used the diversion to close the distance between them. With one upper cut, he sent Bryson sprawling onto the floor. Bryson's head snapped back as he fell backward. His arms and legs flailed as he struggled to maintain his balance. The bag he carried flew from his body, smacking into the wall.

Stunned, Bryson rolled on the floor struggling to regain his composure. Henry pressed his ear. "Right, copy, we're evac-ing now." Henry grabbed Maggie's hand and pulled her toward the stairwell. "Let's go, Maggie."

"Wait!" Maggie exclaimed, tugging her arm back. "Emma and Uncle Ollie are still with them!"

"We can't go after them, Maggie," Henry argued. "Tarik said the chopper's about to take off. We'll never make it past the stairwell."

Maggie bit her lower lip. She glanced between Henry and the stairway leading to the roof. After a second, she nodded. "Promise we'll get them back," she said as she darted toward the wall.

"I promise, princess, now let's go."

Maggie scooped up the bag from the floor and flung it over her head and across her body. "Okay," Maggie answered.

They raced to the stairway as Bryson began to recover.

He raised his head, staring after them before he lifted his weapon and blindly fired three shots. Bullets buzzed by them, ricocheting off the walls near them.

Henry placed himself between Maggie and Bryson and returned fire as he shoved Maggie into the stairway. "Go!" he shouted.

Maggie barreled down the stairs with Henry behind her. They hit the second landing, rounding to the next set of stairs as Bryson burst into the stairway above them. He leaned over the railing, glaring at them.

"Keep going, Maggie," Henry urged as she glanced up at him. He pointed his weapon at them and fired. The bullet clanged against the metal railing next to her. Maggie recoiled, shrinking to the other side of the stairs. She leaned against the wall as she scrambled down.

Her ears rang as Henry fired back before following. Maggie rounded to the last set of steps. She sprinted down them two at a time, hitting the landing hard and pushing through the door into the building's lobby.

"Car's to the left, silver BMW." Maggie nodded as she rushed to the door. She exited into the hot evening air. Maggie spotted the car and dashed to it. She dove inside, pulling her door shut and locking it as Henry slid behind the wheel. He fired the engine as Maggie belted in.

Bryson emerged from the building and scanned the area. His eyes narrowed as he spotted them in the nearby car. He leveled his gun. Henry threw the car into drive. "Hold on, princess." He gunned the engine.

CHAPTER 24

Maggie's grip on her seat stiffened, every muscle tense. She braced herself against the roof of the car. "I hate it when you say that," she breathed.

They shot down the street and past Bryson, who fired twice more. The bullets peppered the car. Maggie glanced backward as they continued driving. Bryson jumped on a sport motorcycle. He shoved the helmet from the handlebars onto his head. Within seconds, he lifted the kickstand and sped after them.

"He's following us," Maggie stated.

Henry glanced in the rearview mirror. He made a quick turn onto a side street. Bryson had no trouble following, gaining on them easily. "We're out. Got a bit of trouble here. Bryson's following us," Henry announced. There was a momentary pause before he answered, "Right, I'll try to get there."

Maggie kept her eyes on the motorcycle as it approached them. "Uh, if you're all finished chitchatting, he's gaining on us and fast," Maggie informed Henry.

"I'm trying to lose him, princess," Henry promised. He

swerved onto another side street. Bryson's motorcycle took the bend with ease.

"Still on us," Maggie warned. Henry tromped on the accelerator, urging more power and speed from the engine.

Henry swung left onto a larger street with more traffic. He merged with the other cars to a cacophony of horns as other drivers slammed on their brakes or swerved to avoid them. Bryson's motorcycle shot from the side street and wove through the snarled traffic.

Henry approached the traffic in front of them. He zigzagged past cars. Bryson followed with ease. As they approached two side-by-side cars, Henry swerved into oncoming traffic. Headlights blinded Maggie as they sped toward the approaching traffic.

"Oh, I really hate driving with you," Maggie lamented as she slid down in the seat, squeezing her eyes shut.

"We haven't even done anything dangerous yet, princess," Henry quipped.

Maggie felt the car veer back into the proper lane. She popped her eyes open. "Where's he at?" Henry questioned.

Maggie scanned behind them. "I don't see him. Maybe we lost him!"

"Doubt it," Henry replied.

"I don't…"

"Maggie, look out!" Henry shouted.

Maggie spun in her seat. She glanced out her window, shocked to find Bryson's motorcycle next to them. He pulled his weapon from his waistband as he kept pace with them.

Maggie witnessed his actions. She unlocked her door and flung it open. It smacked him square in the leg closest to her. Maggie pulled the door shut as Bryson wobbled on the motorcycle, falling back a few feet behind them.

"Good job, princess," Henry said.

"Not good enough," Maggie answered. "He's still on us, coming up fast again."

They zoomed through a red light. Cars screeched to a halt, trying to miss them as they rocketed through. The sound of metal on metal reached Maggie's ears. She glanced behind them to find two cars with crumpled hoods. Bryson looped around the entanglement and continued toward them.

"Oh, great!" Maggie lamented.

"What is it?"

"Cops!" Maggie announced. Blue lights flashed behind them, joining the chase. Within seconds, a second car raced toward them from the opposite direction. As they passed it, it swung around to follow them. "Maybe this will get Bryson off our tail."

"Doubt it."

"Will you stop saying that?"

"We're trying, mate," Henry said. "Got cops on our tail." He paused. "Will do."

"Will do what?" Maggie questioned.

"Don't ask," Henry responded.

"Ugh," Maggie groaned.

Henry continued down the road. Cars scattered as their high-speed chase caravan approached. Ahead, a red traffic signal stopped traffic. Brake lights lit the now darkening skies. Henry swung into the opposite lane. He flew past the stopped cars and into the intersection. Bryson followed. The police cars slowed but still pursued them.

As Henry entered the intersection, he turned the wheel and pulled the emergency brake. The car skidded sideways, rotating to face the direction they came. Maggie braced herself against the roof, squeezing her eyes shut as they spun. Her stomach turned as they completed their half-loop. When they ceased their spin, they faced the single headlight of

Bryson's approaching motorcycle, followed by two sets of flashing blue lights.

Henry slammed the accelerator, speeding toward Bryson. He deftly swung around them and skidded into a half-circle, his knee scraping against the pavement. Within seconds, he was vertical again and pursuing them.

The two police vehicles attempted to block their way. Henry did not flinch. He plowed through the space between them. The car jolted as they smacked into one car, clipping its front bumper and spinning it sideways.

Bryson wove through the space between the cars and continued on toward them. "One problem solved," Maggie answered as she watched the two police cars fall behind as they attempted to reorient their cars to follow.

"Good," Henry replied. "And now for problem number two."

Maggie ducked as a bullet cracked their back window. Henry swore under his breath. He swung the car off the main road. After two quick turns, they found themselves on a side street with the single headlight still trailing them. "Come on, come on, you bastard," Henry urged.

"We want to lose him, Henry, not have him catch up!" Maggie said.

"Nearly there, mate, ten seconds," Henry said. "Maggie, how far back is he?"

Maggie used the mirror to spot him. "Fifty feet."

"Five seconds, he's fifty feet behind me and closing."

They streaked down the road, rocketing toward the next street ahead. As they passed another side street, headlights glared into Maggie's window. Another car barreled toward them. The sound of squealing tires reached Maggie's ears as the car skidded sideways. It fishtailed onto the road they drove.

The other car emerged just as Bryson's motorcycle passed

the street. As they swung onto the road, the rear end of the car struck Bryson. Maggie spotted his flailing form fly from the bike. The motorcycle teetered and collapsed, skittering across the pavement before coming to a rest. Bryson's body hit the pavement hard and rolled to a stop yards away from the scrapped bike.

Maggie sucked in air as she witnessed the accident occur. The car responsible raced toward them, pulling next to them. From behind the wheel, Tarik saluted to Henry, who returned the gesture. Tarik sped ahead, pulling in front of them.

They wound through the city streets, led by Tarik. After twenty minutes, Tarik eased his car next to the curb. Henry did the same. Tarik jumped from the car and approached them. Maggie and Henry climbed from their bullet-ridden vehicle.

"You've ruined the paint job, my friend," Tarik teased.

"Sorry about that, mate, couldn't be helped."

"Maggie, it's good to see you," Tarik said as he embraced her. "I'm sorry we weren't able to get Ollie and Emma."

Maggie offered a tight-lipped smile. "Yeah," she answered. "Yeah, I'm sorry, too."

"And I'm sorry you had to drive with this maniac again," Tarik said with a grin, lightening the mood.

The statement elicited a chuckle from Maggie. "Hey, at least this maniac got her here without a scratch," Henry responded.

"Too bad the same can't be said for the car."

Maggie glanced around, running her fingers through her hair. "Where are Charlie and Piper? Please tell me they are safe."

"They're completely fine, princess," Henry assured her.

"Yes, staying with Sefu," Tarik mentioned. "Come, let's get to his place. I'm sure you are exhausted."

"Yes," Maggie admitted. "Though I'm more interested in finding Uncle Ollie and Emma."

They navigated the streets on foot to Sefu's safe house. Tarik led them through the apartment building's front door and up two flights of stairs. They wound through the halls before Tarik pushed through a door. Inside, a group of men leapt from their seats at a large round table. Tarik waved his hands, a wide grin on his face. He spoke in a language unfamiliar to Maggie. Whatever he said immediately relaxed the others in the room. They burst into laughter and one clapped him on the back. Henry shook hands with a few of them. Maggie recognized Sefu, the man who provided their camels when they traveled into the desert in search of Cleopatra's tomb.

Piper vaulted from her seat in the corner and raced to Maggie. "Maggie!" she exclaimed. "Thank God you're okay!" She flung her arms around Maggie's neck. Charlie approached them from his seat near Piper.

"Piper!" Maggie answered. "Oh, I feel the same way." Maggie stepped back and reached for Henry's hand. She wrapped her arm around Charlie in a half hug. "When I saw that explosion at the camp, I…" Maggie's voice trailed off as she recalled the moment she believed her friends had been killed. A tear rolled down her cheek, and she sniffled.

"We were far enough away that it only caused some minor injuries," Henry assured her as he squeezed her hand.

Maggie sighed and nodded. Charlie squeezed her shoulders. "Yeah, chicky," Charlie added, "I'm far too wily to get blown to bits by some two-bit Brit poser."

Maggie smiled through her tears. "I know that," she answered. "I was worried for Henry."

"Don't worry, chicky. I took good care of lover boy for you."

Maggie burst into a giggle. She wiped her tears away. "I'm

sure you did. Now we just need to get Emma and Uncle Ollie back."

"That'd be easier if we knew where they were going," Henry said.

Tarik joined them, leaving Sefu and his friends at the table. "Do we have any idea where they are going?"

"Probably to the library location," Maggie replied.

"Library location? How did they figure it out?" Henry inquired.

"We found the third ankh," Maggie explained. "Emma and I, when we were stuck in the tomb."

"Yeah, speaking of, what happened there? How d'you get out? How d'you end up with those thugs?" Piper rapid fired questions. She sank into the armchair she'd occupied when Maggie entered the room.

Maggie and Henry dropped onto the couch across from her. "Well, after a while, we didn't hear you guys working anymore. We agreed that if we didn't hear anything by seven, we'd search for our own way out.

"Obviously, we heard nothing, so we searched the entire room and ended up pressing the heart carving again. It opened another passage. We followed it through, searching for another way out. Along the way, we found the third ankh! We found Marc Antony's burial chamber. It was really amazing.

"Anyway," Maggie continued, "after we found the ankh, we found a back door. It took some work, but we climbed out. And then after all that, some thug shoved a rifle in our faces and loaded us onto a helicopter with Uncle Ollie."

"The nerve!" Piper quipped. "If you think that's bad, try being zip tied to a chair while they beat some answers out of us."

For the first time, Maggie noticed the bruises on each of them. Even Piper's wrists were purple with bruises from the restraints. She shook her head. "I didn't notice this before." Maggie caressed a blue-black bruise on Henry's cheek.

"I'm fine, princess." He grabbed her hand and kissed it. "Now, what did you say about finding the library? How did they work it out?"

"They didn't," Maggie responded. "They shoved us in a room and gave us a few hours to work out the location. We almost didn't make it! But finally, we figured out how the ankhs work."

"Do you remember the location, Maggie?" Henry inquired.

Maggie nodded. "More or less, yes. It's near the Valley of the Kings. But we can find the exact coordinates!"

"How?" Tarik questioned, his brow furrowing.

Maggie swung the bag across her chest around. She unzipped it and revealed the contents. "I have the ankhs!"

Henry's eyes grew wide. "Maggie!"

Maggie bit her lower lip and smiled. "We can figure out the exact location again, and I'm sure these were just not for locating the library. I'd bet they're also needed to open the library."

"Which means we have a bargaining chip if we need it," Henry added.

"How do the ankhs give the location?" Tarik asked.

Maggie pulled one from the bag. "These contours match topography of the area. You place these on the map on the location they match, and they form a ring. The center of the ring is where we proposed the library is located. We were on the way to check it out when you arrived."

Henry nodded. "Let's grab a map."

Tarik shouted across the room to Sefu in his native tongue. "I requested a topographical map from them."

"Oh, it has to be a certain scale," Maggie said. She passed

along the information and one of the men, who Tarik identified as Sefu's brother, departed to retrieve the map.

"We need to arrange transport there," Henry said. "I'll speak with Sefu about it."

Maggie's eyes grew wide, and she creased her brow as Henry stood. "We're... we're not going to... will there be camels involved?"

Henry chuckled and kissed the top of Maggie's head.

"This time we can drive," Tarik answered with a laugh.

"With those special sand tires, huh?" Maggie answered with a wry glance.

"You got it," Tarik answered.

With that information, Maggie leapt from her seat on the couch and paced the room. "Calm down, princess," Henry called from across the room. "There're no camels."

"It's not that," Maggie answered. "But... I hate this waiting. Anything could happen to Uncle Ollie and Emma."

"They'll keep them alive, especially when they discover they don't have the ankhs," Henry assured Maggie.

"I agree, Maggie," Tarik added.

"But what if they're already at the library and they don't need them?"

"It's likely they do," Henry answered. "Plus, they aren't there yet."

"They were leaving for the site when you showed up on your rescue mission!"

Henry shook his head. "No, I doubt it."

"He's right, Maggie," Tarik said. "They wouldn't head into the desert with the sun setting soon."

"They gave us a deadline of 6 p.m., that had to be for a reason!"

"Likely to give them time to make arrangements to travel to the location," Henry conjectured. "Maggie, it's fine. No one is going to that site before morning. Especially with Bryson's detour."

Maggie sighed and nodded. She collapsed to the couch, gnawing on her lower lip.

"So, while we wait, what else happened down in that tomb?" Piper asked. "Anything else?"

Maggie glanced at Piper. Piper raised her eyebrows at her. "Well? Did you two just waltz through the corridors admiring the hieroglyphics before you strutted out into the desert in your designer duds?"

"Not quite," Maggie answered.

"So, let's hear it!"

"Well, we had a few mishaps along the way, including a scorpion attack, a collapsing ceiling, a pit full of spears that we had to jump over and…" Maggie hesitated. "Some other stuff."

"Other stuff, chicky?" Charlie questioned.

"Yeah. A few other odds and ends."

"Such as?" Piper prodded.

Maggie shrugged. "What we thought was a dead end that turned out to be an exit that we had to climb out of. And," Maggie's voice lowered to a mumble, "a big stone ball that almost killed us."

"And you found Antony's tomb?" Tarik inquired.

"Wait, wait, wait, wait, wait," Piper interrupted. She leaned forward in her chair, her jaw slack. She cocked her head to the side. "Did you say… big stone ball?"

Maggie glanced sideways and licked her lips. She shrugged. "There might have been."

"I KNEW it!" Piper said, slapping her thigh. "I TOLD you there would be an Indiana Jones rolling ball ready to kill someone in that tomb!"

Maggie pursed her lips and shook her head at Piper. "And

to answer your question, Tarik, yes. We found Antony. Emma was beyond excited."

"Was his tomb grand?" Tarik queried.

"Very!" Maggie said with a nod. "The jewelry was AMAZING! The statues, the items they left him for the afterlife, wow!"

Henry rejoined them. "All set?" Tarik asked.

"Yes. We leave at daybreak." Henry wrapped his arm around Maggie, pulling her close to him. Maggie squeezed his hand and smiled up at him. "We'll get them back, princess."

"I know," Maggie answered. "You promised."

"Ah…" Piper hesitated. "When you say 'we…'" Her voice trailed off again.

"I mean Tarik, Maggie, Charlie and I," Henry answered. "You don't have to go. Sefu and his family will make sure you're safe."

Maggie checked Henry's watch. "How much longer do you think Sefu's brother will be?" she questioned.

"Got a hot date, princess?"

"I'd like to have a date with a shower and a bed," Maggie admitted.

"Why don't you hit the shower now. By the time you're done, he should be back. We'll mark the location, and you can get some rest," Henry suggested.

"Should be back?" Piper repeated. "He could have driven to Cairo and bought a map in the time it takes Maggie to shower."

"Very funny, Piper," Maggie answered. "Okay, I'm heading for the shower."

Maggie disappeared through the doorway Sefu pointed out. She spun the handles on the faucet and removed her clothes while she waited for the water to warm. Maggie tested the water with her wrist as she stared blankly at the wall.

After adjusting the water, Maggie stepped into the steamy shower. The events of the past twenty-four hours exhausted her. Maggie struggled to stay upright as exhaustion overcame her. Worry for her Uncle Ollie and Emma plagued her. She sniffled as a few tears ran down her face.

Maggie bit her lower lip as she wiped the tears away. She recalled her conversation with Henry. They would find them, she assured herself.

Maggie finished her shower and toweled off. The simple act of washing the dirt and grime helped improve her outlook. She dusted her clothes off as best she could before slipping back into them.

Maggie emerged into the living room. "Feel better, princess?" Henry queried.

"Phenomenally," Maggie answered. "Is the map here?"

"Right here," Sefu answered her. He referenced the open map on the table. "Just what you wanted."

"Perfect!" Maggie answered.

Henry already had the ankhs placed on the table near it. "Now, what are we matching here?" he asked.

Maggie picked up one of the ankhs. "See these peaks and valleys? They correspond to topography on this map. Here," Maggie said, pointing out a curved depression. "This matches the river here." Maggie pointed to an area on the map. She set the ankh on top.

"Ah, I see!" Tarik responded. "Yes, it matches the terrain. It makes a three-dimensional copy of it."

"Right," Maggie said, nodding her head.

Piper picked up the second ankh. "So, this one would go here." She plopped it down on the map.

"Yep!" Maggie confirmed.

Piper swung the last one into place. "And this one fits here."

"You're good at this!" Maggie said.

Piper shrugged. "I'm good at spatial reasoning. So, is the area outlined by the three of these where the library is located?"

"Yes, that's what we concluded."

Henry marked the map before replacing the ankhs in the carrying bag. "Okay, we have our location. We leave at dawn. Now, you, princess, should try to get some rest."

Maggie stifled a yawn and nodded.

"There is a bedroom just through that door," Sefu informed her.

Maggie glanced at the doorway, then turned back. "Thanks, though if anyone else wants the bed, I'm good on the couch."

"On the couch? You've been up for over twenty-four hours! You should go to bed!" Piper argued.

Maggie poked Henry's side. "I'll just use this big lug as a pillow. It'll be fine."

"Big lug, huh? We'll see who lets you lay on him later," Henry quipped as he wrapped his arm around Maggie. He kissed the top of her head. "Go get comfy, I'll be over in a minute."

Maggie nodded. She yawned a second time. "Okay. I think no matter where I sleep, I am going to be out the minute my head hits a cushion of any kind."

Maggie settled on the couch, pulling her feet up and curling into a ball. Tarik offered her a blanket, and she draped it over herself. Despite her statement moments before, Maggie laid awake until Henry joined her on the couch. Piper opted to take the bed for the night. Charlie and Tarik settled into armchairs near them.

Maggie lifted her head as Henry plopped onto the couch

next to her. He wrapped his arm around her and she laid her head on his shoulder. "I'm really glad I got you back, princess," Henry whispered.

"I'm really glad you came for me. I can't wait to get Uncle Ollie and Emma back, too."

"Tomorrow, princess. Tonight, you rest." He kissed the top of her head again.

Maggie shut her eyes and within seconds, drifted to a dreamless sleep.

CHAPTER 25

Maggie shot up to sitting in the darkened space. A shrill ringing echoed in her ears. She blinked several times as she tried to get her bearings. It took an extra moment for her to realize where she was. Sefu's safe house, she reminded herself, as she felt Henry stir next to her. He grabbed his ringing phone from the coffee table.

"Taylor," he said into the phone after swiping it open.

He leapt from the couch a moment later and stalked across the room. He disappeared into the hall. Maggie followed him. "Who is it?" she whispered, squinting against the corridor's lights.

"I want to speak to both of them," Henry snapped.

"Who is it?" Maggie breathed again.

Henry pulled the phone from his ear and toggled the speakerphone on.

"… no position to make demands, Taylor," Bryson's voice answered on the other side.

Maggie's heart stopped at the sound. She stared wide-eyed at Henry. Her pulse quickened and her mouth parched as Henry answered.

"You called me, remind me again how I'm in no position to make demands," Henry answered.

"Oh, how terribly imprecise of me. Let me qualify. You're in no position to make demands if you want to see your friends alive again."

Maggie bit her lower lip at the statement. Henry held up his hand, signaling for her to dismiss it. "See, I think you're lying, Bryson. If you wanted to kill them, you wouldn't have called me. They'd be dead."

"We can continue to trade threats back and forth, Taylor, or we can get down to business. Rest assured I possess the conviction to end your friends' lives if I must."

"I'm not discussing anything with you until I've heard from Ollie and Emma," Henry answered.

A sigh sounded on the opposite end of the line. Maggie heard a scuffle and then Ollie's hoarse voice came through the phone's speaker. "Henry!" Ollie called.

"Ollie!" Henry answered. "Are you okay?"

"More or less. Emma and I are okay. How is Maggie?"

"She's fine," Henry assured him. "She's with me now."

"That's quite enough, professor," Bryson barked. "Now, Taylor…"

"Uh-uh," Henry interrupted. "I want to speak to Emma."

"The professor just told you she's fine."

"I want to hear that for myself," Henry countered.

Another tussle sounded on the other end before Emma's voice came across the airwaves. "Henry?"

Poor Emma, Maggie lamented to herself. She sounded exhausted and frightened. "Emma, are you okay?"

"I've been better, but I'm unharmed for the most part," Emma answered.

"There," Bryson's voice said immediately after, "you've heard for yourself. Now, let's stop playing games. My employer wants the ankhs back. Your troublesome little girlfriend stole them from me during our last encounter."

"Stole them from you? You stole them from us, you jerk!" Maggie shouted at the phone. Henry held up his hand again to shush her.

"Ah, the illustrious Ms. Edwards. I'm sorry I didn't manage to eliminate you from this equation earlier."

"Believe me, buddy, the feeling is mutual," Maggie snarked.

"Unless you'd like me to eliminate your friends, let's discuss returning the ankhs to my employer's possession."

"We do nothing until we see our friends in person and can verify they are unharmed. After that we'll exchange the ankhs for Ollie and Emma," Henry answered.

"That's not going to work, Taylor. We'll return your friends after we have the ankhs."

"No dice, Bryson. Even exchange in person."

"I'm afraid that's impossible. My employer requires the professor's assistance in finishing the search for the library. Without him, the ankhs may be useless to us."

"Not my problem. Emma and Ollie for the ankhs, final offer."

"No deal, Taylor. I suppose we'll simply have to take them by force from you. Consider the offer for a peaceful end to this situation rescinded. The next time I see you, I shoot first and pry the ankhs from your cold dead hands."

The line went dead. Maggie threw her hands in the air as Henry toggled off his cell phone. "Ugh!" she exclaimed. "Now what?"

"Now we continue with our plan. They'll be searching for the library tomorrow, too. We'll get Emma and Ollie back then."

Maggie grimaced and shook her head. "I should have bit that guy harder."

"It'll be all right, princess," Henry reassured her. Maggie didn't answer. "I promise." Maggie offered him a half-smile. "And you know…"

"How you are about your promises," Maggie finished for him.

Henry grinned at her and smiled. "So, we've got no worries! By this time tomorrow, princess, we'll be right as rain."

Maggie wrapped her arms around him. "I'm holding you to that," she whispered before she gave him a peck on the lips.

Henry winced. "That was a little scary, princess."

"Good," Maggie said with a wink. "Call it motivation."

They returned to the apartment and Maggie sprawled on the couch next to Henry. "Can you sleep? We can get a few more hours before we leave."

Maggie considered it for a moment. "I hope so," she began. "I think so. I'm worried about Emma and Ollie, but I'm also exhausted. Adrenaline only goes so far."

"Close your eyes, princess. Get some sleep. Tomorrow we get our friends back."

Maggie nodded as she closed her eyes and snuggled closer to Henry. Her mind wandered to Ollie and Emma. Guilt coursed through her as she imagined them stuck with those horrible men. Soon they'd be home, Maggie assured herself. They would find them, and they would get them back. With that thought, Maggie drifted off to sleep again.

* * *

MAGGIE AWOKE to the smell of coffee and eggs. She climbed from the couch and glanced out the window. Darkness still hung over the city. A large white moon brightened the night sky. Maggie meandered to the kitchen. Henry handed her a cup of coffee before she even requested one.

"Thank you," she murmured before taking a sip.

Henry set a plate of eggs in front of her. "Scrambled, your favorite."

"Mmm, thank you," Maggie murmured as she picked up her fork and dug in.

"I have been meaning to thank you, Maggie," Tarik said as he piled eggs onto his fork.

"What for?" Maggie queried.

"I've never gotten breakfast from this guy before. But since you've arrived, Henry makes me breakfast all the time."

Maggie chuckled. "I'm glad this is working out for you."

"Oh, it is. He's so much more pleasant these days."

"Watch it, mate," Henry warned. "You're about to get yourself into trouble."

"I'd agree with that, mate," Charlie chimed in from the living room. "Since you've been dating chicky there, you've become quite a charming chap. Some may even say friendly. Soon you'll be running tours and making balloon animals for children."

Henry rolled his eyes and Maggie smiled at him. "Well, I think you're quite a charming chap," she said with a grin.

Piper stumbled in from the bedroom with a yawn. "Good morning," she mumbled.

"Good morning," Maggie answered. "Coffee?"

"Please," Piper grumbled as she slumped into a chair next to Maggie.

Maggie retrieved a cup for her and refilled her own. She plated some eggs from the skillet and set them down in front of Piper.

"Thanks," Piper answered. "What time do we leave? Do I have time for a shower to wake up?"

"Aren't you staying here?" Tarik questioned.

Piper took a few bites of her breakfast and a sip of her coffee. She shook her head. "I decided against it," she answered.

"You'll be perfectly safe here. Sefu will let nothing happen to you," Tarik assured her.

"It's not that," Piper countered. "What kind of friend am I to let everyone go into the wilds of the desert without my help? Where they'll have to face the elements, nature, crazy men with guns. Dr. Keene and his assistant need our help. I can't abandon my friends now! Not when they need me the most!"

"That was quite a speech!" Henry said.

"And quite a brave decision, fair maiden," Charlie said, approaching the table.

"Thank you, kind sir," Piper answered.

"Well, eat up and get showered, we leave in thirty," Henry announced.

"Good thing I'm faster in the shower than you, boss lady," Piper said as she ate a few more bites. "We'd be late for sure if she had to shower."

Maggie gave her a wry glance. "I'm glad to see you back to your normal self, Piper. Last night's hug really had me worried for you."

Piper shoved down her last few bites and stuck her tongue out at Maggie. She leapt from her chair with a chuckle and dashed to the bathroom.

They cleared the breakfast dishes and Henry prepared several items in the remaining time. Piper emerged from the bathroom with ten minutes to spare.

As the sun rose over the horizon, they exited the apartment building. Sefu arranged for two vehicles to transport them to the Valley of the Kings to begin their search. Sefu, Tarik, Charlie and Piper piled into one van, leaving Henry, Maggie and Sefu's brother, Seth, in the second. Henry carried the ankhs in their cushioned case across his body along with several hidden weapons.

Maggie breathed a shaky sigh as she stared out the window. The buildings sped past her as the sun crept further over the horizon behind them. They left the city behind, traveling into the desert.

In forty-five minutes, they arrived at the Valley of the Kings location. Tourists already milled about near the visitor's center, even at the early hour. The hot desert sun, now fully above the horizon, lit the magnificent location.

"Wow," Maggie murmured as she stared at the entrance to the tourist attraction. "It's really something!"

"Too bad we don't have time to take the tour," Henry lamented.

"I will take you next time," Seth promised.

"You're on," Maggie agreed. "I'd love to visit here. You know, sometime when we're not being chased by men with guns and my uncle and friend aren't being held captive."

Seth swung the car into a parking space next to Sefu's and they climbed from the van.

"The fastest way to this location is to cut through the west valley. We'll continue into the desert once we get there."

Maggie nodded, and they proceeded to the visitor's center to purchase their tickets for the site. The group set off on their trek, climbing the hilly route from the parking lot to the West Valley. This path included far fewer tourists than the crowded East Valley.

"Most of the tombs open to the public are in the East Valley," Sefu explained. "It's quite a trek to this one, so we'll have a far quieter journey there."

"That's good," Henry answered. His eyes scanned the horizon, searching for any sign of trouble.

"Spot anything?" Maggie asked as they climbed the hill.

"Nothing," Henry said with a shake of his head.

"Should be easy to spot," Tarik offered. "We've left most of the tourists behind."

Maggie glanced around. No one accompanied them on the path. "How long until we get to the location?" Maggie inquired.

"Perhaps an hour's walk," Tarik said as he checked their handheld GPS system.

They veered off the marked path before reaching the sign for the Tomb of Ay, the only tomb open to the public in the West Valley. They left all traces of civilization behind, entering a time long forgotten. Other tombs dotted the landscape of the West Valley.

"What are these?" Maggie inquired as they passed the sites.

"Unknown tombs, mostly," Sefu informed her. "One is for Amenhotep III, but the others are unidentified. None of them are open for touring."

Within a few more moments, they left even these slight traces of civilization behind. They continued through the hills surrounding the West Valley into the desert. Maggie searched the sands for any traces of the other group. She found none.

Despite the early morning hour, the sun already heated the air to uncomfortable levels. Maggie fanned herself as they ambled through the sand.

"Whew!" Piper exclaimed after twenty minutes of their expedition. "It's way hotter than I bargained for."

"As Emma would say, 'Welcome to the desert,'" Maggie said.

"Not too much further," Tarik promised. "Should be just over this dune."

"But..." Piper said, giving a side-ways glance to the group. "The dune's huge."

They continued on their journey. As they reached the

peak of the dune, Henry slowed. He scanned the area in every direction.

Maggie began down the sand bank, heading toward the location on the GPS. "You coming?" she asked when Henry didn't follow.

He shook his head. Maggie stopped short.

"What's up, my friend?" Tarik inquired.

Henry's eyes scoured the sands. "Something's wrong."

"What?" Maggie asked, climbing a few steps to rejoin him.

"Nobody's here," Henry answered. "Could be a trap."

Maggie searched the area. "I don't see anyone or anything. Not even a footprint in the sand."

"That's what worries me. Do you imagine Bryson's crew had a leisurely sleep in rather than try to beat us to the site?"

"Knowing that jerk, he'd want us to do the work for him. And his employer didn't seem too keen on hard work either, so perhaps we did beat them."

"I don't like it," Henry said, his hands on his hips.

"What do you propose?" Sefu inquired.

"Why not continue to the site, mate? Piper and I can stay here as lookouts. If we see anyone coming, we'll give you a shout," Charlie suggested.

"I agree," Maggie said. "We should continue to the site. I can't spot anything from here, but it appears as though we've got our work cut out for us. Unfortunately, I don't see a giant library anywhere."

Henry considered the idea for a moment before he responded. "All right. Keep your eyes peeled," he said to Charlie and Piper.

"Will do, mate. Oh, here," Charlie said as he pulled earpieces from his pocket. "We can keep in touch with these."

Charlie placed one in his ear. Henry accepted the earpiece and placed it, giving it a test. Satisfied, he motioned down the sand dune. "All right, I guess we're ready."

They proceeded down toward the spot identified on their GPS. Henry's head remained on a swivel as they traveled away from Piper and Charlie.

Maggie glanced backward. Piper waved from the top of the dune. Maggie returned the wave. "So far so good up there," she informed Henry.

It did little to ease his nerves. "I don't like this."

"You mentioned that," Maggie said as they continued their journey.

"This is the worst place to be for defense. We're surrounded and on the low ground."

"We'll search for the library in rounds. Two at a time, the others stay alert," Tarik suggested.

"Good plan," Henry agreed. "Maggie, you do the searching and one of us will help you, the others keep watch."

"As usual, I always have to do the hard work," Maggie joked.

"I have every faith in your investigative skills, princess," Henry said, cracking a smile for the first time since they arrived.

"There's that charming chap," Maggie answered with a grin.

Henry rolled his eyes. "Remind me to speak with Charlie about that comment later."

"Charlie may be joining you as a charming chap by the looks of it," Maggie said, motioning to the couple they left behind. Piper clasped Charlie's hand as he pointed out several things in the West Valley behind them.

"Hey," Henry shouted into the radio, "stop showing off to Piper and pay attention up there."

Maggie overheard Charlie's response through the earpiece. "Don't get your knickers in a twist, mate. We can see the whole valley from here. No one's getting past us."

"Happy now?"

SECRET OF THE ANKHS

"Not in the slightest. The faster we find this place, the better."

"We're here," Tarik announced as the GPS beeped, indicating their arrival.

Maggie spun in a circle, searching the area. "Well," she began, "I don't see anything."

"Let's have a look around before we talk about next steps," Henry suggested.

With Piper and Charlie covering the east, Sefu and Seth spread out to watch the south and west directions. Tarik jogged a few steps away, keeping his eyes on the northern horizon.

Maggie and Henry combed through the area, scouring the sands for any sign of a structure. After fifteen minutes of searching, Maggie threw her hands in the air. "There's nothing here. At least not on the surface."

"I don't see anything either," Henry admitted.

"It could be buried," Maggie postulated.

"When I programmed the GPS, I programmed for the center of the area shown by the ankhs. The area cordoned off by the ankhs was much larger," Tarik hollered.

"Good point, about how large?" Henry called back.

"About a five square mile radius," Tarik shouted.

"So, it could be anywhere," Maggie said.

Henry spun as he studied the area. "What would Ollie do?"

Maggie considered it, her mind flitting to Uncle Ollie's situation. She pushed it from her thoughts and forced herself to concentrate on the situation at hand. "He'd say..." Maggie hesitated, her brow wrinkling as she summoned her inner Ollie. An idea occurred to her. "He'd say it's likely contained in this valley somewhere. Probably not right in the center, but around some landmark."

"Where'd that come from, princess?"

"Listening to Uncle Ollie talk about archeology for decades. Let's check the edges of the valley, near the rock face."

"All right, princess, let's try it. You good to keep watch?" Henry shouted to Tarik.

"All good, my friend."

"Charlie," Henry said, "we still all good?"

"All good, mate," Charlie confirmed.

"Let's have a look," Henry said to Maggie.

They approached the edge of the valley. Maggie stared up at the rock face in front of her. The sheer cliff shaded them from the sun. "At least it's cooler here," Maggie noted.

"Any idea what might signal something significant?" Henry asked Maggie.

Maggie shrugged. "Ankh carving? Scroll? Tablet? Library sign?"

"Very funny, princess."

"Let's just have a brief glance over the cliffs marking the perimeter and see if anything stands out."

"All right, professor."

Maggie scanned the rock face in front of her, her eyes panning up and down. "You know," she said as she stepped to the north to continue the search, "if this whole government agent thing doesn't work you, you could try comedy, babe."

Henry rolled his eyes at her. He scanned the horizon in all directions again. "Will you pay attention to what we're doing and stop gaping around?"

"You're looking, I trust you."

"I might miss something!"

"I'm not gaping around. I'm scanning for the enemy."

"Everyone else is scanning for the enemy," Maggie pointed out.

"I don't like this. No one's here yet? They're not searching for the library or us?"

"Perhaps they're searching for us back in Luxor," Maggie responded. "You said Sefu's safe house was secure. They should have no idea we're here yet."

"But why didn't they come here?"

"Because they think they need the ankhs, and they don't have them. So, they are searching for us to steal them back."

"Why not find the library at the same time?" Henry questioned.

"Don't have the manpower to split the team?" Maggie suggested in a questioning manner.

"I don't buy it. Bryson wouldn't be this sloppy."

"Well, he is a bit under the weather," Maggie said.

"It wouldn't stop a guy like Bryson."

"Do you have a history with him?" Maggie inquired, stopping short from her search.

"Yeah," Henry admitted. "A long and unfortunate history." Maggie raised her eyebrows. "Remind me to tell you sometime." Henry pulled his collar to the side and pointed out a circular scar under his collar bone. "He gave me this."

"Is that a bullet wound?" Maggie asked. Her jaw went slack.

"That it is, princess."

Uneasiness grew in the pit of Maggie's stomach. She swallowed hard. "Let's keep searching." Maggie bit her lower lip, glancing warily to the clifftops in all directions.

They approached the northern most area of the enclosed valley. The rock squeezed together on each side, but a small passage still existed between them.

"Let's check in here," Maggie suggested.

They passed through the thin opening and into a circular space. Maggie approached the rock wall across from the opening. A small outcropping stuck into the sand on the right. She bent down to study it. "Henry!" Maggie exclaimed as she glanced at it.

"What is it?"

"I'm not sure, but it looks like a carving in the stone here." Maggie blew on it. Sand flew into the air. She brushed more away with her hand. Her pulse quickened as her fingers felt the outline of a carving. "This is definitely something!" Maggie's voice rose with excitement as she continued to uncover the remaining portion of the engraving.

"We may have something here," Henry informed Charlie. "Keep an eye out while we work."

Maggie did not hear a response through Henry's earpiece.

"Do you have a brush or something?" Maggie inquired.

"No, sorry."

Maggie groaned. She dug in her pocket and pulled out a small compact. "The government owes me a new powder brush," Maggie commented. She popped open her compact and removed a small brush.

Maggie swept the soft bristles over the stone. She followed the line of the etching, brushing sand from the crevice of the carving. Maggie sucked in a breath as the shape became obvious. She raised her eyebrows, her heart thudding in her chest. "It's the shape of an ankh!" she exclaimed.

CHAPTER 26

Henry peered over Maggie's shoulder at the carved shape. "It is! But it's upside down."

"It has to mean something!"

"I'd be inclined to think so," Henry agreed. "But why is it upside down? Does it point toward where the location is?"

Henry turned and stared behind him. Maggie continued her work. "No," she said, shaking her head. "There's another here." Maggie worked on brushing the sand from another carving below the first. She uncovered it section by section. "And I'd guess," she said as she worked, "there's a third one, right about... here." Maggie began to brush sand away in a third area, revealing another shape.

A smile formed on Henry's face. "Fantastic work, princess!" He kissed the top of her head as she finished her work.

"The library's got to be around here somewhere," Maggie surmised.

"Do we need to use the ankhs, perhaps?"

"Uncle Ollie seems to think we do, or the bad guys

wouldn't be after them," Maggie responded. "But not here. These are too small."

Henry removed an ankh from the bag and compared it. "You're right."

"Which means we're close, but not there yet." Henry replaced the ankh as Maggie examined the stone carving. "I'm not spotting any clues that give us any more information. Though, I'm not as good at this as Uncle Ollie."

"All right, let's have a thorough search around this area. This must be the spot."

"I agree. Should we get help?"

"I prefer to leave them on watch," Henry countered.

"Okay," Maggie agreed. She stood from the stone and surveyed the area. Her eyes narrowed as she spotted a flat area in the stone face. Maggie wandered to it. She touched the flat stone, letting her fingers explore the area.

Henry joined her and investigated the cliff. Maggie kicked the sand around on the ground near them after she searched the flat rock.

"Got something!" Henry shouted, drawing Maggie's attention.

"What is it?"

Henry's fingers pried caked sand from an inset in the stone. "Give me your brush."

Maggie handed him the makeup brush. He used it to clear more sand from the depression. A smile crept across Maggie's face as he worked, and she bounced on her toes. The shape of an ankh began to form as Henry labored to remove the sand.

Henry blew more sand away and swept the last grains from the cavity.

"That's it!" Maggie exclaimed. "We found it!"

"Excellent work, Ms. Edwards," a new voice responded.

Maggie's eyes went wide, and she gulped. Her muscles tensed and her posture stiffened. Both Maggie and Henry swiveled slowly to face the new arrival. When she turned, Maggie raised her arms as she spotted the gun leveled at them.

"You're so clever, I knew you could find it and save us the trouble," Bryson snarked.

He stood inside the opening to the circular space. Behind him five other men, including James Michael Dean, stood with guns leveled at the other members of their group, all of whom had their wrists zip tied. Maggie cursed whatever method the group had used to circumvent their sentinel system, though the sight of Ollie and Emma with the rest of her friends added a measure of solace. At least they were reunited. Now, they needed a plan to get away.

"I'm so glad we could help you. I knew your feeble mind couldn't work it out," Maggie retorted.

"Maggie…" Henry warned under his breath.

"What?" Maggie questioned. "He's not that smart."

"Mmm," Bryson murmured. "I did manage to capture the vast majority of your dim-witted friends, so I wouldn't be too sure about that. Now, toss the ankhs over."

"Let our friends go first!" Maggie shouted back.

Mr. Richards approached from the rear of the group. "Now, now, children," he chimed in, "I'm sure we can come to some amicable agreement regarding our situation."

"The only agreement that would appease me is you letting our friends go and leaving," Maggie argued.

"Now, Ms. Edwards, let's not be hasty," Mr. Richards countered. "No one has harmed you or your friends."

"Yet," Maggie interrupted him.

"We can all share in this together," he continued. "In fact, I believe that's best. You keep the ankhs for now."

"Why?" Henry questioned.

"Because we haven't found the library yet," Mr. Richards answered.

"I'm sure we can," Bryson added.

"But wouldn't it be more prudent to let them do it," Mr. Richards countered.

Understanding dawned on Bryson's face and he smirked. "Why, yes, sir, I believe you may be correct."

"So, in other words, you mean to use us as guinea pigs to disable any traps," Maggie surmised.

"Given how clever you are versus how stupid I am, that seems to be the wisest solution," Bryson replied. "I'm sure we can make it to the inner sanctum of the library before we run out of you."

Maggie set her jaw, disgusted by the turn of events but resigned to their situation. "Okay, fine, cut everyone loose and we'll get to work."

Bryson chuckled. "No, Ms. Edwards, you may find me stupid. But I'm not that stupid. Garrity, tie up Taylor and give his girlfriend the ankhs to get started."

"What? No!" Maggie exclaimed.

"Maggie, just go along with it for now until we have an opening," Henry whispered.

"I need a helper. I can't do this alone!" Maggie argued.

"Well, it's not going to be Taylor."

"My Uncle Ollie then," Maggie requested. "And Emma."

"No. One, not both."

"Take Emma," Ollie instructed. "I can offer advice with my hands tied."

"Fair enough, professor," Bryson answered. "Cut Ms. Fielding's restraints and send her over with Ms. Edwards."

One of the men flipped opened a pocketknife while the man named Garrity approached Henry. "Give her the bag," he instructed, waving the tip of his gun toward Maggie. Henry pulled the strap over his head and handed the bag off to Maggie. With a grunt from Henry, the man secured his wrists together in front of him. "Let's go, Taylor, back with the rest of them." He prodded him with the nose of his gun, marching him back toward the rest of the group.

After Emma's bonds were cut, the man led her toward Maggie.

"We've really got to stop meeting like this," Emma said.

"Tell me about it," Maggie answered. She slung the bag with the ankhs over her head and around her body.

"Enough chit-chat, get to work, ladies!" Bryson snapped.

"Okay, okay!" Maggie exclaimed.

"What do we have so far?" Emma questioned.

"We found a carving over here," Maggie said, stepping toward the outcropping.

"Whoa! Hold it right there," their guardian shouted, leveling his weapon at them.

"Really?" Maggie questioned, holding her arms up. She glanced at Bryson and shouted, "I can't work like this. I can't even move without Mr. Itchy Trigger Finger pointing his weapon at me."

"Ease off a bit, Reynolds," Bryson advised. "Let the illustrious Ms. Edwards have room to work."

Reynolds rested the gun against his shoulder, a disapproving but resigned expression on his face. Maggie crossed to the stone. "It shows the three ankhs."

"I see," Emma said, stooping to study it.

"So, we figured we must be close. Just before you joined us, Henry found this." Maggie stepped back toward the flat portion of the rock face. She pointed out the depression in the stone they had uncovered moments before.

"This must be a marker for the library," Emma commented.

"I agree," Maggie said.

"Well, that's a first," Emma answered. Maggie gave her a wry glance.

"This one is a lot bigger. Roughly the size of the ankhs. Do you suppose we use them here?"

"But which one?" Emma queried. "And why is there only one? Which one do we use? Ollie's probably the better one for this, he should have elected to do this instead of me."

"We need Uncle Ollie!" Maggie shouted back to the group.

Bryson rolled his eyes, but Mr. Richards offered an approving glance and Bryson acquiesced. "Get moving, professor."

Ollie hastened across the opening. Maggie informed him of the developments, earning a warning from Bryson. "Stop stalling, Ms. Edwards," he called across the space, his voice echoing off the rocks.

"I'm not stalling. You're hampering me at every turn. It's your fault this is taking so long!"

Bryson offered an unimpressed stare at Maggie, who shrugged her shoulders in response. Henry offered a chuckle. "What's so funny, Taylor?" Bryson snapped.

"You're not going to win, mate. Believe me, she's stubborn. It's best to just let her go."

"I'd second that," Charlie chimed in. "She's really obstinate. I've never seen her lose an argument."

"Yep," Piper added. "She's my boss and…"

"ENOUGH!" Bryson shouted. "I do not care to hear the opinions from the peanut gallery. The promise of a bullet should cure any hardheadedness on her part."

Henry set his jaw. He approached Bryson. The man named Garrity shoved him back. "Touch her and…"

"And what, Taylor?" Bryson spat.

"Stop arguing!" Maggie shouted. "I can't hear myself think!"

SECRET OF THE ANKHS

"You're stalling!" Bryson countered.

"I'm not!" Maggie argued.

"Give them some time, Bryson. No need to be hot under the collar just yet," Mr. Richards interjected.

"Yeah, listen to your boss and calm down," Maggie added.

Bryson shut his eyes for a moment, his mouth drawn into a grimace.

"Now, back to what we're doing," Maggie said with a sigh to Ollie and Emma. "Is this a trigger of some kind? But which ankh do we use to engage it?"

"I'd bet it is," Ollie said after examining it. "Though I do not see any indication of which ankh is appropriate."

"Caesar's?" Emma conjectured. "He's the oldest."

"Perhaps it's the opposite order?" Maggie suggested.

"There's only one way to find out," Ollie answered.

"Okay," Maggie agreed. She reached into the bag and found Caesar's ankh. Maggie pulled it from the pouch and held it in front of the carved depression. She hesitated a moment before pulling it back. "Wait! What if we're wrong?"

"Then we're wrong," Emma answered.

"What if it causes some cataclysmic thing to happen? Like the earth opens and swallows us all up?"

Emma eyed the militant group behind them. "Does it matter?"

"Good point," Maggie agreed. She lined up the ankh with the cavity and inserted it. Nothing happened. "Did I do it wrong?" Maggie pressed on the ceramic item a few times.

"Try another one," Ollie suggested.

Maggie nodded. "All right." She dug in the bag for another ankh. Within the course of five minutes, Maggie had tried all three. None produced any noticeable result. She pulled the final one from the carving. "Ugh, now what?"

With a furrowed brow and pursed lips, Ollie stared at the outline in the stone. "Hmm," he murmured, "perhaps we haven't cleared enough sand away to trigger any mechanisms. Each ankh you tried remained raised from the stone face when inserted."

"Oh, maybe!" Maggie exclaimed. "All I had was a little makeup brush."

"The makeup…" Emma groaned.

"Well, it got us this far," Maggie retorted.

"It did some of the work, though a precise set of tools would be far better for us to remove the sand without damaging anything," Ollie responded.

"We need some tools!" Maggie shouted over to the group. Bryson sighed. "Like archeology stuff. Brushes."

"Yes," Mr. Richards called, "we have a set of excavation brushes with us." He motioned for one of the men to deliver them from the duffel bag he carried around his chest.

The man pulled a pack of various sized brushes from his bag as he crossed to them. He handed them to Emma. She pulled two from the kit, handing one to Maggie.

Maggie began on the left side of the carving as Emma began on the right. They carefully swept away sand from the cavity. "Wow, this is tedious," Maggie lamented after a few minutes.

"Welcome to archeology one-oh-one," Emma said.

"Every time I think I've got it, there's just more sand. It's endless!"

They continued their work for a few more moments before Maggie smacked her lips. "That's it, I quit." She threw her hands in the air.

"What is it, Maggie?" Ollie inquired.

"I can't get this sand out of here. I got one part down pretty far, but this is like solid rock! It won't move!"

"Let me see," Ollie offered.

"Right here," Maggie pointed out. "This part goes in further and this…" Maggie's voice stopped mid-sentence.

Her brows knit together, and she cocked her head at the outline. "Wait a minute!"

"What?" Emma asked, ceasing her work.

"This IS solid rock. This isn't going to be a flat depression in the stone. It's a contoured one! We were using the ankhs wrong! They go in face first with the contours against the stone!"

Ollie adjusted his glasses and squinted at the carving. "I think you may be right, Maggie."

"So, we still have some clearing to do," Emma conjectured.

"Yes, and then we should be able to match the contours of the carving to the contours on the ankh," Ollie said.

Maggie and Emma spent over forty-five minutes clearing grains of sand from the impression in the stone. "That's it... I think," Maggie stated as she shook her arm, trying to revive her sore muscles.

"Let's see which shape it matches," Emma said.

Maggie pulled two ankhs from the bag and Emma retrieved the third. They compared each shape to the carved curves in the stone. "This one?" Maggie questioned, holding up the ankh in her right hand.

Emma studied it. "Yes, that looks like a match. The curve here matches the curve there." She pointed to an area inside the recess.

"Should we try it?" Maggie asked.

Emma nodded. "Yes, let's keep our fingers crossed it works," Ollie commented.

Maggie fitted the piece into the outline. "Here goes nothing," Maggie said, glancing at Emma and Ollie before pressing it into the cavity. She took a deep breath and held it before her shaky hand pushed the ankh into the stone's face.

Maggie nudged the ankh further and further until it fit flush with the stone. As it slid into place, a boom reverberated in the enclosed area. The ground shook, knocking down everyone close to the flat rock face. The sight Maggie spied as she lifted her head and recovered her senses left her awestruck.

A gaping hole yawned where the flat rock face had stood a moment ago. Maggie climbed to her feet.

"Wow, incredible!" Emma exclaimed.

Maggie reached to pull Ollie to standing as he struggled to gain his footing with his hands bound. Emma assisted her in getting Ollie to his feet. "Could you cut these off him?" Maggie requested. "He's at a real disadvantage and could get hurt."

"Not my problem," Reynolds barked at them as he climbed to his feet.

"I'm not going another step until we're not being put in harm's way because of these restraints!" Maggie contested. She crossed her arms and refused to budge.

"Get in there!" Reynolds shouted at her, waving his gun toward the new entrance.

"What's the problem?" Bryson shouted.

"She's refusing to go in unless I cut Dr. Keene's wrist ties."

"You don't have a say in this, Ms. Edwards. Now get moving!" Bryson answered.

"I'm not going anywhere while he's bound up like that. We're risking our lives and that's making it more dangerous."

Bryson stormed toward them. "I've had enough of your demands. Get moving and check out the next area now!"

"You do it!" Maggie countered. She stood firm, her face set in stone.

Bryson grabbed her by the arm and dragged her toward the entrance. "I said get in there."

The rest of the group approached them, driven forward by Garrity and his compatriots.

"Fascinating," Mr. Richards said as he stared at the gaping entrance.

"I agree," Ollie answered.

"Tell your goon to get his hands off me," Maggie snapped.

"There's really no need for violence, Bryson," Mr. Richards advised. "I'm sure Ms. Edwards will accommodate our requests."

"I want my uncle cut loose," Maggie demanded. "That wasn't even a trap and he could have been seriously hurt! He needs his hands if he's going to continue to help us."

"I don't see the harm in it," Mr. Richards said. "Go ahead, Bryson."

Bryson flinched, betraying his irritation, but followed orders. Ollie rubbed his wrists after his bonds were cut.

"We'll need flashlights at least before we proceed any further," Maggie said.

Garrity was already pulling several flashlights from one of the duffel bags. Ollie accepted two of them and handed one off to Emma. Maggie grabbed the last one from Garrity. She flicked it on and pointed it toward the entrance.

"Just a moment," Bryson said before she went any further. "There's a new set of rules moving forward. You three will enter each new area and search it for traps. Reynolds will follow. Once it's cleared, we'll all join you. We'll be keeping a close eye on you, Ms. Edwards."

"Whatever," Maggie grumbled. She spun back to the entrance and approached. She waved the flashlight around the space as she peered inside.

"Careful, princess," Henry called to her.

She turned to smile at him. "I will be," she promised.

Ollie and Emma joined her outside the cavernous entryway. "Simply incredible," Ollie said in a hushed tone as they trained their flashlight beams inside.

A large stone floor greeted them. In the center, a massive

bas-relief depicting several scrolls protruded from the floor. Across the mammoth space, two colossal pillars held the mantel of a roof at bay. Large stone steps led upward past the pillars.

"Wow," Maggie whispered.

"Yeah," Emma agreed.

"We must inspect the area for any booby traps," Ollie stated.

"Do you imagine they built this like a tomb? Full of traps?" Maggie inquired.

"I'm not certain, but better safe than sorry."

"I agree," Emma said. "If they went through the trouble to hide the ankhs, its likely they safeguarded the library entrance in other ways."

"Astute analysis, Emma," Ollie said.

They scrutinized the area leading inside the chamber. Maggie swept her flashlight beam along the ground. A faint line of sand marked where the stone face had stood moments ago. Maggie blew the sand away.

"I don't see anything on my side," Maggie reported after searching the floor and wall.

"Nothing on mine either," Emma said.

"I haven't seen any noticeable triggers above us," Ollie noted.

"Should we try for it?" Maggie inquired.

Ollie nodded. "Yes, let's try."

Maggie lifted her foot. She hesitated, her foot floating in the air as she took a deep breath. With a glance at Ollie and Emma, Maggie crossed the threshold. After her second foot stepped onto the floor inside, Maggie whirled to face them. "Made it!"

Emma and Ollie followed while Reynolds remained outside. "Stay there while we investigate the space," Ollie advised.

"No," Bryson countered. "He goes."

"He should stay. We don't know what may trigger a deadly trap inside this chamber!" Ollie argued.

"I don't trust you, professor!"

"Where are we going to go?" Maggie snapped at him.

"If it's all the same, I'd rather wait here, boss," Reynolds chimed in.

"Fine, but don't linger too long," Bryson warned. "And you keep your eye on them," he said to Reynolds.

Maggie studied the chamber in a slow pivot. Light spilled into the chamber from the desert sun, illuminating the space. Her flashlight splayed across the undecorated walls. Maggie took a few steps further inside. Ollie grasped her arm, stopping her.

"Wait!" he warned.

"What is it?" Maggie asked, glancing around as she searched for some trap.

Ollie pointed to the bas relief. "Careful not to step there," Ollie cautioned. "It may trigger something."

"Oh," Maggie answered. She trained her flashlight beam on it. "Really? I don't see anything."

"It's a good location for a hidden trigger," Emma explained. "An unsuspecting person would tread right across it because of its location."

They circled around the structure, careful not to step on it. Maggie continued to search the walls, floors and ceiling as they moved toward the stairs. They finished their ring around the bas-relief and approached the steps. Three stone stairs led to a platform and a recessed stone wall.

The stone columns at the top of the stairs dwarfed the group. "What do you think?" Maggie asked. "Safe or not?"

Ollie raised his eyebrows as he stared at the steps. His eyes traversed the length of each tread from end to end. He wandered to one side, exploring the stringer. He narrowed his eyes at it before crossing to the other side. With a shrug, he returned to the center. "I don't see anything," he admitted.

Without another word, Ollie stepped onto the first tread. Emma gasped. "So far, so good," he said. He climbed the next two steps. He stood at the top and spun to face Maggie and Emma. "Well, seems safe."

"Gee, Ollie, that was a risk," Emma said.

"Can't let Maggie take all the risks first, figured it was my turn!" Ollie grinned from the top. "You girls stay there a minute while I inspect the area."

"But..." Maggie began.

"Just give me a few minutes for a quick inspection!" Ollie swept his flashlight beam around the space above them. After a brief search, he called down, "Okay! Come on up. One at a time!"

"Go ahead," Emma said.

Maggie proceeded up the stone steps. She reached the top landing with no mishaps. Emma followed. As she stepped onto the landing, Bryson's voice echoed in the chamber. "What's going on in there?"

"We're inspecting the area," Ollie responded.

The answer must have satisfied Bryson since he did not respond. Maggie returned to investigating the landing. In front of them, an ornately decorated panel faced them. Maggie inched toward it, careful with her footfalls not to trigger anything. Emma and Ollie crept toward it, too.

As they closed the distance to the ornate panel, a crash reverberated through the chamber. It almost drowned out the scream accompanying it.

Maggie, Ollie and Emma spun to face the entrance. The bas-relief stood at a forty-five-degree angle. It settled back to the floor with a resounding clang.

CHAPTER 27

Bryson raced into the chamber. He gaped around. "Where's Reynolds?"

"Reynolds?" Maggie questioned.

Ollie's eyes grew wide. Maggie's mouth opened as realization dawned on her. Bryson took a few more steps into the chamber. "STOP!" Ollie shouted, holding his hand in front of him. "Don't move!"

Bryson froze. "What's going on here, professor?"

"Whatever you do, do not step onto that panel!" Ollie cautioned.

Bryson shifted his gaze from the group to the bas-relief on the floor. He inched backward, away from the edge. When he stood a safe distance away, Bryson reached out and tapped the bas-relief with his foot. It swung open, revealing a gaping hole in the floor before settling back to its position with a resounding clang.

"Oh!" Maggie exclaimed as it crashed to the floor.

"Guess we know what happened to Reynolds," Emma muttered.

"This is your fault, professor!" Bryson exclaimed as he circled the bas-relief at a safe distance.

"It is not!" Maggie retorted. "We had no idea he came in here until he was gone!"

"She's correct," Ollie confirmed. "Had I known he was coming, I would have prevented him from any danger, just as I did with you."

Bryson glared at them but did not push the matter further. "What have you found?"

"We were just about to discover that when Mr. Reynolds met with his unfortunate accident," Ollie answered.

"Fine. Don't do anything else until I've moved everyone inside."

"All right," Ollie agreed with a nod.

Bryson followed the outline of the bas-relief as he approached the door.

"Well, that's one of them down," Maggie muttered under her breath to Ollie and Emma when Bryson stood out of earshot.

"And four to go," Emma murmured back.

Bryson waved his arms, signaling for his colleagues to force the others inside. Ollie shouted as they entered, warning them to be careful of the trap in the floor.

With everyone gathered inside the chamber, Bryson signaled for Ollie to proceed with his investigation of the back wall. They approached the ornate carving and searched it for any hidden triggers. To the right of the decorative panel, Emma discovered another ankh outline.

"Here," she called to Maggie and Ollie. "Another spot for an ankh."

"Which one matches?" Maggie inquired. She pulled both from the bag. They studied the contours in the ankh-shaped cavity, comparing them to the two ankhs Maggie held in her hand.

"This one," Emma said. She grabbed it from Maggie and fitted it to the outline. "Here goes nothing," she said, repeating Maggie's earlier statement.

Emma pushed the ankh in until it was flush with the stone. The moment it fit fully into the space, another boom shook the chamber. The decorated stone wall snapped in two and swung away from them. Maggie craned her neck to peer into the new opening.

"One more left," Emma said.

"Careful entering," Ollie cautioned.

Maggie nodded. "Let's check the entire door first."

Maggie stood aside to let Ollie's trained eye scrutinize the opening. He found nothing to suggest any danger. The trio proceeded through the door into the dark room beyond. Little light filtered from the preceding chamber into this one, making it difficult to discern any features.

Maggie slid her flashlight up and down the nearest wall. As she swung it toward the room's center, the light did little to pierce the blackness. It fell short of reaching the far wall.

"This will prove difficult," Ollie admitted.

"Yes," Emma agreed, "it's so dark in here, it'll be hard to spot anything dangerous."

Bryson appeared behind them. "What's going on?"

"We're inspecting the chamber," Ollie answered. "This will be slow-going. There's very little light. Working with the little light our flashlights provide will be tedious. But better safe than sorry!"

"Don't drag your feet, professor."

"We could just be cavalier about it and if another one of your guys is harmed, oh well," Maggie threatened.

"Spare me your threats, Ms. Edwards. If we lose another man, you lose one, too."

"Then let us do our job!" Maggie argued.

"Do it as quickly as possible, Ms. Edwards. My employer isn't keen on delays."

"Then stop talking and let us work," Maggie said with a sigh and a roll of her eyes.

Bryson remained stationed near the entrance as they worked their way into the room. They swept their flashlight beams across the floor and up the walls, searching for any hidden danger. The chamber appeared circular. Six massive pillars, inset from the exterior wall, held the ceiling at bay. At regular intervals along the walls, decorative stanchions climbed from floor to ceiling. Unlit torches extended from each.

Emma trained her beam on the ceiling several times. "What is it, Emma?" Ollie questioned.

"Nothing," Emma answered. "Just making sure the ceiling isn't inching down on us. I keep feeling dust falling on me."

"I feel it, too!" Maggie admitted. "I thought it was cobwebs or something."

Ollie swung his beam to the ceiling. The high roof stood at least ten feet over their heads. Maggie positioned her flashlight to enhance Emma's and Ollie's light. Ollie adjusted his glasses and squinted at the ceiling.

"What are those black marks?" Maggie questioned.

"That's what I was curious about," Ollie answered. "It's impossible to tell from this distance."

"Switch off the lights," Emma said.

Everyone followed her instructions. "What are we looking for in the dark?" Maggie questioned.

Emma toggled her light on. "I wanted to see if any light came from them."

"I didn't see any," Ollie responded.

"Me either. So, what are they?"

"I'm not certain," Ollie answered, "but we should exercise extreme caution."

The girls nodded in agreement. They proceeded a single step further into the chamber. Maggie's muscles tensed with every movement. She swallowed hard as she scrutinized every inch of the stone floor and walls.

As they crept further into the room, Maggie's brow crinkled. She stooped down, training her flashlight beam on the stone floor.

"What is it, Maggie?" Ollie questioned.

"Thought I saw a dark spot."

Ollie crouched down to study the spot Maggie concentrated her beam on. Emma bent over his shoulder. "This dark line, you mean?"

"Yes," Maggie answered.

Ollie blew on it to clear away any loose sand. It became apparent that it outlined a small square block, about two inches in length. Ollie stood, splaying his arms to the sides and pushing the girls back away from the small square.

"I'm relatively certain that triggers something," Ollie said.

"Something bad," Maggie surmised.

"Probably," Emma agreed.

"Do you think it's the only one?" Maggie inquired.

Ollie glanced around the room. "I'm not certain, though I would be surprised if it was."

"Given its size, it's likely never to be triggered," Emma added. "If this truly triggers a trap, there would be multiple triggers to assure it discharges to protect the library."

"They're tiny! How will we find them all?" Maggie questioned.

"Let's see if we can spot another one. Perhaps there is a pattern," Ollie suggested.

From the block near them, they wove their flashlight beams back and forth in a grid pattern, searching for any other similar squares.

"Here's one!" Emma called.

"And another over there," Maggie shouted, her beam trained on another square outline.

Ollie swung his beam, locating a fourth.

"They're everywhere!" Maggie exclaimed as they found a fifth and sixth.

"We'll have to map a path through them to the opposite wall."

"What can we use to mark the safe path?" Maggie questioned.

"Sand is the most readily available asset here," Emma proposed. "We could leave a trail of sand."

"It's not great, but it's the only option we have," Ollie agreed.

They backed their way to the entry. "We've found what we believe is a trap trigger," Ollie explained to Bryson. "There are several. We must map a pathway that is safe to traverse, so no one is harmed."

"So, get going," Bryson barked.

"These things are everywhere! We need to mark the path with sand."

Bryson stared at her, a blank expression on his face. "Could some of your guys fill one of the duffels you have with sand and bring it in?" Maggie asked, annoyance in her voice over having to make the request.

"Perhaps one of you could do it."

"We're busy canvassing every inch of that floor for trigger tiles. Do you think you could do SOMETHING?"

"I could do it, just untie me, mate," Henry offered, overhearing the conversation.

"Nice try, Taylor," Bryson snapped. "Garrity! Empty that duffel you have and fill it with sand and bring it to the professor. Carry on, professor. You'll have your sand soon."

"Thank you," Ollie answered. "It would help to have a

lighter as well. As we reach these pillars, I can light the torches to provide additional light."

Bryson pulled a lighter from his pocket and tossed it to Ollie without a word.

"Okay, let's continue, girls," Ollie said as he caught the lighter.

Ollie, Maggie and Emma retreated into the chamber. "How are you so patient with them?" Maggie whispered.

Ollie shrugged. "I try to focus on the incredible find," Ollie said.

"I'm with you," Emma breathed.

"We need a plan," Maggie answered as they continued searching the floor.

"Yep," Emma agreed.

Bryson's appearance cut their conversation short. "Garrity nearly has your sand," he informed them.

"Stay there," Ollie advised. "We haven't found all the tiles nor marked a path. I don't want you treading on one of these triggers mistakenly."

"What exactly do these things trigger?" Bryson inquired.

"We're not sure," Ollie answered.

"And we DON'T want to find out," Maggie followed up, shooting Bryson an irked glance.

Bryson rubbed his chin and stared at the floor suspiciously. Garrity stepped through the door a moment later. "Here's the sand, boss," he said, dropping a filled bag on the floor in front of him.

"Good, good," Ollie said.

"Emma and I will start shuttling sand to create the path. You keep searching for a safe way through," Maggie suggested.

"Okay," Ollie agreed.

Maggie and Emma picked their way through the tiles and returned to the entry. "Okay, where's the shovel?"

"Why?" Bryson snapped.

"To carry the sand," Maggie retorted. "How else do you propose we carry it? With our hands?"

"Fine," Bryson answered. "Give each of them a shovel, but stay here after." Garrity returned to the first chamber to retrieve shovels.

Maggie raised her eyebrow at Bryson and smirked. "Scared?" she teased.

He ignored her as Garrity returned and handed the shovels to Emma and Maggie. Each of them scooped a shovelful of sand from the bag and started across the room, dumping the sand to outline a path among the tiles.

They made it halfway through the room before Maggie collapsed to the floor near the entrance. "Whew!" she said, wiping a bead of sweat from her forehead. "I need a breather!"

"Keep going," Bryson ordered.

"Give her a minute," Emma snarked.

Bryson opened his mouth to reply, but Maggie climbed to her feet. "It's fine. I'm fine." She scooped more sand, lumbering across the room with it and dumping it in a line. After another hour of work, they identified a clear pathway across the room. Maggie and Emma finished spreading the last of the sand to mark the path. Ollie stared at the wall across the room.

"The third and final ankh," he said.

"What's over there?" Bryson yelled.

"A spot for the last ankh!" Maggie shouted back.

"Stay there while we put it in!" Ollie hollered.

Maggie withdrew the final ankh from the bag she carried around her chest. "You should do the honors," she said, handing it to Ollie.

He smiled at her, accepting the ankh. With a slow breath, he turned it over and fitted it into the outline. He glanced at

Maggie, then Emma, then back to the ankh. He pushed it into the cavity. A click sounded, but nothing happened.

Maggie frowned, cocking her head to the side. "What gives?!" she exclaimed. Ollie pushed on it again. "Is it broken?"

Maggie spun to search the room. Her flashlight beam struck the pillar behind her. "Look!" she exclaimed. "Another ankh shape!"

"I've got one, too," Emma announced, her beam trained on the pillar across from Maggie's.

"Maybe we need all three ankhs to open the last door."

"But removing them might leave us trapped," Emma conjectured.

"I wonder if any of the other pillars have these?" Ollie questioned.

"We can check," Maggie said.

"Careful," Ollie warned. "We must pick our way through the tiles to each. We don't have a marked path."

Ollie removed the ankh from the cavity in the wall and slipped it back into Maggie's bag. "Okay, here we go," Maggie said with a deep breath.

"If there is a fourth, we're in trouble," Emma said.

"Yeah, we don't have four ankhs."

"If there is a fourth, there's most likely six. One on each pillar," Ollie explained. "If that's the case, probably only one of them opens the final door."

"What do the others do?"

"I'm not sure we want to find out," Emma replied.

They followed Ollie single file as he inched toward the next pillar. They made it and circled around to the side facing the outer wall. "Aha!" Ollie exclaimed. "There is another here!"

"What are you three doing?" Bryson yelled.

"Trying to find the way into the next chamber," Ollie

answered. "We've made an incorrect assumption about how to proceed."

"On to the next pillar," Emma said.

The group made their way through the tiles to the fourth pillar. After circling around it, they found another spot for an ankh.

Maggie sighed, slapping her thigh with her hand. "Well, that's great! Another one!"

Within thirty minutes, they verified that each pillar contained a cavity shaped like the final ankh. "Now what?" Maggie inquired.

"They are all identical. Each of them matches the contours of our last piece," Ollie said.

"So, how do we know which one to use?" Maggie questioned.

Ollie shrugged. "I'm not certain. There is no indication anywhere of which may be correct."

"We'd better inform our friends," Maggie said.

They crept through the minefield of tiles and returned to the entrance where Bryson and Garrity stood sentinel. "Well?" he demanded.

"We have a slight problem."

"Not what we want to hear," Bryson responded.

"There are seven spots for the ankh to be placed. One of them does not work. We tried it. We have no idea which of the remaining six is correct," Ollie explained.

"So, try them all," Bryson suggested.

"Well," Ollie responded, "I am not opposed to that method, though we may trigger something with an incorrect choice."

"What if we station someone at each pillar? Then if we try one and it triggers something bad, we can toss it to the next and hope we find the right one before... we're... well, you know," Maggie said.

"I don't like this plan," Bryson argued.

"Why?" Maggie questioned.

"It puts my men in harm's way. We'd need three of them to cover the remaining pillars. That's more than half of my remaining crew."

"You could untie Henry, Tarik and Sefu," Maggie suggested.

"Fat chance, Ms. Edwards," Bryson said. He glanced into the first chamber, then back to Maggie, Ollie and Emma a few times. "We'll give you the punk rocker and her boyfriend."

"That's only five, we need six," Maggie countered.

"Not my problem," Bryson snapped.

"It sort of is," Maggie argued.

"Fine," Bryson acquiesced. "Garrity, you'll do it."

"But sir!" Garrity began.

"I said you'll do it. Now follow the instructions the professor gives you."

"Okay," he grumbled.

Maggie rolled her eyes. "Cut Piper and Charlie loose and we'll get everyone in position."

Ollie led Garrity to the pillar to the left of the entrance. Bryson shouted the order to one of his men, who cut the wrist restraints on Piper and Charlie. He led them to the second chamber and shoved them through the opening. Ollie quickly explained the plan to them.

"Once we get everyone in position, Maggie will begin with the pillar to the right here," he said as he motioned to the pillar. "If it unlocks the next chamber, stay where you are until we can safely move you to the next chamber. If not, Maggie will slip the ankh into the padded bag and toss it to you, Piper.

"You'll try the ankh, if it works, don't move, if it doesn't remove it as quickly as possible, place it in the bag and toss it to Charlie. We'll continue around the room until either the next chamber is unlocked or we trigger something else. If anything goes wrong, don't panic. We'll need to keep the ankh moving despite any danger."

"What kind of danger?" Piper questioned, a perturbed expression on her face.

"We don't really know," Ollie admitted.

Piper glanced around with an uncomfortable countenance. "You don't have to do this if you don't want to, Piper," Maggie said.

"Yes, she does," Bryson challenged.

"No, she doesn't," Maggie argued. "We could get someone else."

"No," he retorted.

"One of us could try to move between columns," Maggie assured Piper.

Piper swallowed hard. "No," she said with a shake of her head. "No, I'm good. I won't let you down."

"Okay," Ollie said with a nod. "Let's get you all in place." Ollie led each person to their column, pointing out the trigger tiles on the floor to avoid. When he finished, Ollie positioned himself at the fifth pillar near the back wall. Emma stood to his right and Garrity on his left.

Maggie stood at the first pillar. "Ready?" she asked, scanning the room for everyone's response. Flames flickered overhead, casting everyone in shadows. Tiny nods answered her question. Maggie took a deep breath as she eyed the ankh outline.

After a deep inhale, she blew the breath out through her mouth. Maggie swallowed hard and raised the ankh into position. Her hand trembled as she placed it in the outline. With a final glance around the room and a nod from Ollie, Maggie pushed the ankh into the hole. A click sounded again. Everyone glanced around the chamber, finding nothing else had changed.

Maggie shrugged. "Guess that didn't work," she said. She dug the ankh from the depression and placed it in the bag. "Ready?" she asked Piper.

Piper nodded and readied her hands to catch the bag. Maggie zipped the bag shut and tossed it underhanded to Piper. She caught it mid-air and unzipped it.

"Okay, here goes," Piper announced. She lined up the ankh and pressed. A click sounded, then a screeching noise.

"Uh-oh, that's not good," she groaned. A shout arose from the outer chamber as the stone door to the first chamber slid shut, cutting them off from the rest of the group. From the decorative colonnades on the walls, spears now poked out. The poles and the walls they were attached to crept inward. They were trapped and about to be impaled like an onion slice on a kebab.

"We'll be skewered!" Piper shouted.

"Calm down, Piper," Ollie advised. "Remove the ankh, place it in the bag and toss it to Charlie."

With a grimace on her face, Piper pulled the ankh from the column and placed it in the bag. She struggled with the bag, tugging on it with a groan. "I can't get it zipped!" she cried.

"Don't worry about that," Ollie said, his voice calm and measured. "Just toss it."

Piper nodded and turned to Charlie. She tossed it toward him. He snatched the bag, clutching it tightly, so the ankh did not fall.

Charlie pulled the ankh from the bag and inserted it into the outline in the column. Maggie scanned the room; nothing had changed. The walls continued their slow creep toward them. Maggie pressed her lips together, fidgeting in place as she watched the slow progression of the spears. With a frustrated growl, Charlie yanked the ankh from the cavity and placed it in the bag. He pulled the zipper. It didn't budge.

"Zipper's stuck, going to toss it with the bag open."

Charlie flung the bag to Emma. It shifted mid-air. Emma lunged forward to grab it before it hit the floor. She clutched the edge of the bag, closing her fingers awkwardly around a chunk of fabric. "Got it!" she exclaimed as she bobbled the bag in a desperate attempt to hang on to it. As she pulled the bag toward her, the ankh toppled from the unzipped top. It slid across the floor, skittering to a halt in the center of the room.

Emma stared after it with wide eyes. Maggie's jaw dropped and a hushed silence fell over the room's stunned occupants. Without thinking, Maggie darted toward the ankh.

"Maggie, watch!" Ollie shouted.

Maggie leapt over groups of tiles in a hurried attempt to reach the ankh. She made it unscathed and scooped the ankh from the floor. She set her gaze on Emma. "Ready?" she questioned, breathless.

Emma nodded.

"Don't drop it this time," Garrity hollered.

Maggie lobbed it to her, and Emma caught it without trouble.

"Stay there, Maggie," Ollie advised as Emma placed the ankh into her column. She shoved it into the space. With a disgusted groan, Emma removed the ankh. She stuffed it into the bag as the spears inched closer.

She tossed the bag to Ollie. As he removed the ankh, Garrity shook his head, shouting, "I can't. No way, I have to get out of here."

"Garrity, calm down," Ollie tried.

Garrity hyperventilated, sucking in short, quick breaths

as he eyed the approaching walls. "Come on, mate, just relax, we're nearly there," Charlie counseled

"We don't know if this is going to stop us from being killed!" he shouted. "I have to get out of here."

Garrity fled from his column toward the sealed entrance to the initial chamber. "NO, STOP!" Ollie cautioned. Garrity did not heed the warning. He ran headlong toward the stone door. In his frantic scramble to escape, he tread on several trigger tiles.

Maggie tensed, covering her head with her hands as she shrunk away from Garrity's path. With each tile Garrity depressed, a metal arrow shot from the ceiling. The black dots they spotted earlier launched the barrage. The first arrow missed its mark, glancing off the floor and clattering across the room.

The second arrow struck, plunging into Garrity's back foot. He yelped as he stumbled forward. Blinded by pain, he stepped on several other tiles. Multiple arrows shot from the ceiling. One plunged into Garrity's shoulder. He howled again as another plunged into his forearm. Garrity collapsed to his knees as another pelted him. He crawled forward on his hands and knees as another arrow struck him in the back.

A tear rolled down Maggie's cheek as Garrity gurgled his final breath.

"Ohmigod, ohmigod, ohmigod," Piper exclaimed.

Ollie rammed the ankh into his column. "Maggie, I need someone at the last column," he stated as he pulled the ankh from the pillar when it failed to stop the deadly trap's progression.

Maggie nodded, recovering from her shock and snapping into action. She picked her way through the tiles, climbing over Garrity's dead body. She reached the final column and signaled for Ollie to toss the ankh.

Ollie slung the ankh over inside the bag. Maggie caught it and removed the ankh. She lined it up.

"Hurry," Emma cried, distress in her voice. Maggie realized the reason. The ever-approaching spears were now inches from them. Maggie swallowed hard as she jammed the ankh into the hole.

CHAPTER 28

A grinding noise filled the chamber, followed by a hissing. Maggie spun to face the exterior wall. The spears receded into the decorative columns. The walls retreated to their former position. Two holes gaped at them now. Both the original entrance glided open along with the wall across from it with the ankh outline.

Maggie slumped against the pillar in relief. "We did it!" she exclaimed. She slid to the floor as a voice called her name.

"Maggie! Maggie!" Henry shouted. He rushed through the doorway, stopping short when he entered the room. His eyes widened as he spotted the dead body in the room's center.

"I'm here," she called, pulling herself up to standing. "I'm fine. We're all fine."

Bryson pushed past Henry into the room. He stared at his colleague's body. "What the hell happened?" he demanded.

"He panicked," Ollie informed Bryson.

"That's bull! I don't believe you!"

"It's true," Maggie answered. "We hit a snag, and he just lost it. We tried to stop him, but he ran from the column to try to escape. Arrows shot from the ceiling and killed him. It wasn't our fault."

Bryson grimaced at them. "We did the best we could do, dude. We nearly died in here because of your greed," Piper railed against him. "Don't stand there and get ticked off at us for risking our lives because your guy couldn't hold his stuff together."

Bryson's jaw tightened as he continued to frown. He took a deep breath before he addressed them. "Fine," he growled. "I suppose there is nothing to be done about it now. We proceed. But I warn you, professor, another slip up and I will even the score."

"It wasn't a slip up," Maggie retorted.

"Actually, it was," Emma countered, "on your guy's part. Quit blaming us."

"Let's move on," Ollie suggested. "We've made a pathway using the sand that everyone should follow. Be careful not to step on any of the small square tiles. They can prove deadly."

Mr. Richards ambled into the room, followed by Tarik, Sefu and Seth who walked at the end of the rifles pointed at them by Bryson's remaining two team members. Ollie moved the others to the room's center.

"Oh, no," Mr. Richards lamented, "what happened to Garrity?"

"The professor claims he panicked and triggered one of the traps. It resulted in his death."

Mr. Richards frowned. "Terrible shame. Everyone, please be more careful and listen to the professor going forward."

The group gathered on the fringes of the room as Maggie, Ollie and Emma made their way to the new doorway. Bryson picked his way carefully across the room to zip tie Charlie and Piper's wrists.

Ollie peered into the next chamber with his flashlight.

"What do you see, professor?" Bryson inquired after finishing his tasks.

"It appears to be a long, sloping corridor. Your group should remain here while we inspect it."

"No," Bryson argued. "From here, we move forward together."

"That could prove dangerous," Ollie countered. "We have no idea what traps may lay on the opposite side of that doorway. We want to prevent any further mishaps."

Bryson narrowed his eyes at Ollie. "As do I, which is why I propose we move forward together. I will not tolerate another 'accident.' What better way than to watch your every move."

"I cannot be responsible for anything that happens if you proceed into that corridor with us when we have no idea what dangers may be present."

"We'll take our chances," Bryson snapped.

Bryson motioned for his associates to push the group forward. Ollie entered the long hallway. It extended beyond the reach of the flashlight's beam. Maggie inched forward next to Ollie. Emma crept on Ollie's other side.

"I feel like Dorothy going to see the wizard," Maggie said as she swung her beam over the ceiling, wall and floor.

"We need to get rid of the wizard," Emma whispered in a hushed tone.

"Yep, we need a plan. We're running out of time," Maggie agreed.

"Let's concentrate on making it through this corridor alive," Ollie said, refocusing their attention.

"What are you three discussing?" Bryson inquired.

"Making it through this passage alive," Ollie answered.

Finally, Maggie's light bounced off a wall at the end. "Looks like the end's up ahead."

"Careful," Ollie cautioned.

They crept to the corridor's end. Maggie, Ollie and Emma swung their flashlights around searching the walls, floor and ceiling near the wall.

"Is this a dead-end?" Bryson queried.

"I doubt it is," Ollie answered. "We need to find the way to open it."

"Here!" Emma exclaimed. She pointed her flashlight toward a pulley wheel.

"Should we try it?" Maggie inquired.

"Hmm," Ollie mumbled. He followed the pulley system into the ceiling. He rubbed his chin as he pondered the question.

"What's the hold-up, professor?" Bryson asked.

"We have discovered this device, but we don't know what it does. It could be a trap."

"Or it could lead to the library, correct?" Bryson asked.

"Yes," Ollie confirmed. "It could."

"Then use it," Bryson said.

"Just a moment," Ollie objected. "I'd prefer to have a better idea of what this does before we plunge headlong into it."

Bryson leveled his gun at Maggie's head. "I said use it."

Maggie swallowed hard, a lump forming in her throat.

"All right, all right," Ollie acquiesced. He reached toward the pulley wheel. Ollie grasped the handle on the wheel. He pulled it. It didn't budge. Ollie grabbed it with both hands and tugged. With a groan, the wheel started to turn. He twisted it clockwise, spinning it around several times.

As the wheel spun, a clanking sounded, and a trigger engaged. The stone wall at the end of the corridor lifted little by little. Ollie continued to spin the pulley until the door raised into the ceiling. As Ollie let go of the wheel, it untwisted, and the stone began to fall.

"We need to wedge it," Ollie shouted, grabbing hold of it

SECRET OF THE ANKHS

to stop its spin. One of their guards passed a file to Ollie. He shoved it into the wheel to hold it from moving.

After a careful check of the doorway, Ollie led the group into the next chamber. Their flashlights did little to light the room. A stairway led down to another level.

Ollie studied a channel running down the stairway. He removed the lighter from his pocket and lit the fuel in the channel. Flames raced down the side of the stairs and around the room. The chamber lit up in a dazzling display of light, revealing its contents.

Ceiling-high shelves lined the room filled with tablets and scrolls. Various other items were stuffed into the space. Statues, jewelry, golden coins and other valuable ancient items.

Maggie's eyes lit up as the room did. "Wow!" she exclaimed.

"Indeed," Mr. Richards agreed. "Amazing!" He proceeded to the top of the stairs.

"Careful!" Ollie cautioned.

"Get going, then, professor," Bryson prodded.

Ollie, Maggie and Emma proceeded down the stairs, ensuring the safety of the structure before the remaining group members were forced to the lower floor.

"We've found it, sir," Bryson said, congratulating Mr. Richards.

"Yes, our buyers will be quite pleased."

"The take looks promising," Bryson agreed.

"Yes," Mr. Richards agreed. "I have a few calls to make. I suggest you finish your business while I do so."

Mr. Richards climbed the stairs and disappeared through the doorway into the corridor beyond. Maggie swallowed hard as she realized they were out of time. Mr. Richards removed himself from the chamber while Bryson dealt with the more unpleasant details, specifically, their demise.

She glanced at Henry, who raised his eyebrows at her. She understood the gesture. If she found an opportunity, whether it be to escape or even to delay the inevitable, take it. Maggie offered a subtle nod.

"Well," Bryson began, twirling to eye everyone in the group, "it appears we have reached the end of our time together."

Charlie stepped in front of Piper, shielding her with his body.

"Now, Bryson," Henry said, "let's not be hasty. Most of these people are innocent. Don't take whatever grudge you have with me out on them."

"Oh, shut up, Taylor. You're not going to talk your way out of this one."

Bryson took stock of the group as he clicked the safety off his weapon. "It is rather a shame about you, Ms. Edwards. Such a pretty girl. We would have made a lovely couple under different circumstances."

Emma stood behind Bryson, staring at Maggie. She winked before she rolled her eyes. "Oh, you can't even be serious! Of course, of course!" she exclaimed, flinging her hands in the air. "The beautiful, beguiling Maggie Edwards can charm her way out of a death sentence by batting her eyelashes. What else would I expect?"

Bryson spun to face Emma. Maggie raised her eyebrows at her. "Are you kidding? Seriously? You are so jealous. It's incredible. Even in this moment, you can't stand it that men find me attractive!"

"I guess it's easy," Emma stated, "you're always throwing yourself at them, so of course they do."

"Oh, well, I guess it's better than being a sell out like you!"

"Now, ladies," Bryson began before Emma interrupted him.

"I didn't sell out! I couldn't bat my eyelashes and get out

of the situation you stuck me in the last time. And here we are again! My life hangs in the balance thanks to Maggie Edwards!"

"That's enough!" Bryson shouted over them. His pleas did little to stop their bickering.

Maggie drew her mouth into a thin line. She balled her fists and tensed her muscles. "That's it, Emma! That is the last straw!"

"Oh, yeah?" Emma said, matching Maggie's stance. "What are you going to do about it?"

"I'm going to kill you before he does!" Maggie screeched. She dove toward Emma and knocked her onto the ground. They rolled around in a tangle, knocking into Bryson. They clipped him at the knees, and he toppled backward. With the wind knocked out of his lungs, it took him a moment to recover. Ollie swooped in and snatched the gun from his hand as his arms flailed. He trained it on Bryson before he recovered.

Tarik and Henry used the distraction to elbow the remaining guards closest to them. Charlie elbowed the guard Tarik attacked in the back and Tarik knocked him out with a head butt. His gun clattered to the floor where Tarik retrieved it.

Piper raced to Henry's side. She kicked the guard hard in the shin as Henry used his clasped wrists to swing upward, stunning the man with an uppercut to the jaw. The man stumbled backward two steps. Henry pursued him, swinging his arms again, his clasped fists smacking into the side of the man's jaw. The second blow knocked the man unconscious. He collapsed to the floor. Henry scooped his gun into his bound hands, training it on the man.

"Man, did that feel good," Piper exclaimed. "Ever since he nearly killed me in that fire, I've wanted my revenge!"

Bryson groaned on the floor, still conscious. "Wouldn't

try it if I were you, mate," Henry warned, swinging the gun toward Bryson.

Bryson narrowed his eyes at him. "Planning to shoot me with the safety on?" he snapped. Bryson rolled to his side and began to climb to his feet. With Henry's bound hands, he remained unable to release the weapon's safety.

Maggie snatched the gun from Henry's hands and clicked off the safety. "I'm not," she answered.

"I wouldn't push her, mate," Henry said with a grin. "Like I told you, she's real stubborn."

* * *

MAGGIE STARED AT THE HORIZON. The sun already sunk low in the sky, painting it red, orange and yellow. She clasped her arms across her chest. Activity buzzed around her. After turning the tables on their captors, Henry had called in the cavalry. Helicopters shuttled additional men to the site. They carted Mr. Richards, Bryson and the remaining two members of his team off. Now, they worked to secure the site before cataloging of the site's assets. Ollie bustled around; his enthusiasm for the find obvious.

Maggie smiled at him, delighted to witness his excitement. She scanned the horizon. Her eyes fell on Emma, who sat at the end of a dune a few feet away. Emma stared at the horizon, lost in thought.

Maggie sauntered over to her and plopped down in the sand. "Mind if I sit?" she questioned.

Emma glanced sideways at her. "You already did," Emma answered.

"Yeah," Maggie said with a chuckle. They sat in silence for a few moments. "Nice move in there," Maggie said after a while. "You set that fight up well, Bryson never saw it coming."

"He led himself right into that one," Emma said with a shake of her head. "I have to admit, it felt good knocking him over after that remark."

Maggie chuckled. She paused a moment then said, "You know I didn't mean anything that I said in there."

Emma glanced at Maggie again before returning her gaze to the horizon. "Really? I'm not a sell out?"

"No," Maggie admitted. "It was wrong of me to be mad about that. It really was unfair."

"So, I'm forgiven? Not that I think I needed it, but..." Emma's voice trailed off.

Maggie gave her a closed-mouth smile. "Yeah, forgiven."

Maggie's forehead wrinkled, and she peered sideways at Emma. "You... didn't mean what you said, did you? All that about me throwing myself at men and whatever."

Emma shrugged. "No, I guess not."

"You GUESS not?" Maggie giggled. "Don't hate me because I'm beautiful," she said. She struck a pose.

Emma chuckled. "Funny. I don't hate you because you're beautiful. Though it is frustrating how you always get your way."

"I don't ALWAYS get my way," Maggie countered.

Emma glanced sideways at her with an unconvinced expression. She glanced at the library entrance as she sifted sand through her hand. She pursed her lips. "Well, the great Maggie Edwards does it again! Another fantastic discovery under your belt."

"You were a big part of that, too," Maggie reminded her.

"Plenty to catalog, at least. It should keep me busy for a while. There's a whole new set of things to work on back at the tomb site and this library..."

Maggie interrupted her, blurting out, "You should take the job in Rosemont."

Emma furrowed her brows and stared at Maggie. "Really?"

"Yeah," Maggie said with a nod, "yeah, definitely."

"You sure Rosemont's big enough for the two of us?"

Maggie grinned at Emma. "I'm sure," she said. "Plus, there's a great guy I can introduce you to. I think you'd get along."

Emma eyed Maggie for a moment before she returned her gaze to the horizon with a nod. "I just might."

"Good," Maggie said. She gave Emma's shoulder a squeeze before she climbed to her feet.

Henry approached the girls from the makeshift headquarters being set up near the entrance of the library. He stopped a few feet from them. Maggie approached him, slipping her arms around his waist.

"Well," he said, gazing at the library entrance, "the great Maggie Edwards does it again."

Maggie rested her chin on his chest and gazed up at him. "Well, the team did."

"You're right, the team."

"Led by the great Maggie Edwards," Maggie said with a grin.

"Of course, princess, of course," Henry said, matching her expression.

"So, what's next for the great Maggie Edwards and her illustrious team?"

Henry raised his eyebrows as he pondered the question. "I'm not sure. Perhaps a nice long break. I could use a vacation."

Maggie pulled back and looked at him. "How do you feel about Scotland?"

Made in the USA
Monee, IL
01 July 2021